Svera Jang

Seema Gill

Indigo Dreams Publishing

Indigo Dreams Publishing

First published in Great Britain 2010 by:
Indigo Dreams Publishing
132, Hinckley Road
Stoney Stanton
Leicestershire
LE9 4LN

www.indigodreams.co.uk

ISBN 978-1-907401-14-5

British Library Cataloguing in Publication Data. A CIP record for this book can be obtained from the British Library.

Designed and typeset in Goudy Old Style by Indigo Dreams Publishing.

Printed and bound in Great Britain by Imprint Academic, Exeter.

Cover artwork by Seema Gill.

To

Joginder Kaur, Richard, Mona,
Maya, Guldeep and Jyoti.

Foreword

After the death of my father, the death of my marriage, a big lump of grief grew within me like an ulcer. I shouted 'Help' and looked around in the emptiness. Who's there? Anybody? Friends? Family? I realised every one of them was going through their own pains, their own struggle, the 'jang'. My daughters needed me, a mother, to soothe the pain of being let down by their father. My doctor would have easily prescribed me more tranquillisers. I didn't want them. I had taken so many. This was my pain, my struggle. I had to deal with it myself. I then remembered the words of my mother: "The very first thing before you rise, is to let your palms gently caress your face and only then you should open your eyes. Watch your palms. They tell you a story. Each line depicts your struggle as a woman. They are the hands of a creator!"

I then decided to put my pain on the palm of my hand to have a good look at it. "Operate it, damn it. Bite your tongue. Cut it to pieces. Clean the blood. Wipe your tear." My inner voices spoke. But how? What tools have I got? Where do I find the surgeons blade to get rid of the ulcer? I looked at my hands again. They were the hands of a grieving child, a shock stricken wife, a humiliated woman, a disappointed human being, a vulnerable mother. Of course, my mother was right. A woman is the creator of life. She is the one who soothes, the one who gives. She lets the seeds grow, tends and reaps. She is the mother earth. She witnesses everything on her own body. Harsh winds, soothing breezes, typhoons, lightening, thunder storms, Tsunami, earthquakes. And yet she keeps on producing. She gives strength against weakness, hope against despair, optimism against depression, light against dark, even life against death!

It struck me like lightening. My hands....can draw, knit, paint, write! I write. Words! Images! Words...images...words...words...words. My mind was so full of images and words that they were screaming to come out. First, everything was muddled up, entangled, knotted, bewildered, confused. But there were memories, stuck on my mind like beads. In the many files of my brain, they were stacked, stored, safe, hidden. Not all of them were ugly. Some of them were beautiful images, beautiful words. I made a thermos full of tea and sat down on a comfortable chair in front of my lighted screen. I sat for a long time. It was past midnight. Children were sleeping. The dog, Simba, was snoring. The chipmunk was quiet. The lamp post was drizzling light outside. No cars, no people, no birds, just me with my faithful companion, the night.

My fingers were itching. The first word punched on the computer was Mother.....It was a soft whisper, a soft cry...a soft flicker, a glowing ember. The tapping began. The process started. Images came tumbling down like a train. Words poured down like a waterfall.........sometimes loud screams....violence...soothing....crying...but oh, they were alive and kicking.....

I, dear reader, don't want to tell you more. I don't want to show you more. I don't want to expose the secret yet. You have to read the whole book. I am sure, when you start, you won't stop until you are through!

Good luck! Good luck Nina, Minna, Gulu, Jonny....Mum? Where are you now? I do see you sometimes. You speak to me through the starling on the Grand Union canals where I was walking with Jonny. I stopped to watch her. She didn't fly away. She started to speak her strange language and I was struck with awe. I knew it was you. Sometimes you are that rainbow over my cottage, a butterfly in my garden, a fox prowling through my solitude. And Dad? You used to sit by the window of my House on the Cliffe each morning, a beautiful ring dove, muttering a few things. Rest in peace, both of you.

Mina, Nina, I am always within you. Take my strength for your struggle, your journey. Whatever you are going through, never give up the struggle. The struggle keeps us alive!

Can't speak now. Have a lump in my throat from thinking about everyone of you who have helped me, touched me, taught me, supported me through this journey!

Thank you for your much needed help Richard. Thank you for your editing, Dawn and special thanks to Ronnie for his faith and support!

Seema - August 2010

CONTENTS

THE DREAM

Lingam. Snake. Giver and taker of life. Curled like a womb in comfort and protection. The only escape through the tunnel. She is at a point of no return. Alone, breathless, silent except for the sound of her lungs crying out for air in a dark crevasse. Attached only by umbilical cord, a hangman's rope dangling, half conscious, half confused, swept into the corner like a discarded piece of flesh. Numb. The space is bubbling with hot vapours, lava curling up against something creeping. Two blue marbles pierce the darkness and with a blink of the eye disappear into her fear. She seems an easy prey. The slimy creature hisses in excitement, advancing towards her. It's gaze is fixed upon her destiny. White fangs ready to spit venom into her body and entrance her with its seductive poison. Birth and death. The game starts. To hypnotise her into a trance is the first objective, then strike, bite and administer the venom. Thereafter she will act according to the rules. Steadily her senses will be tranquilised, blinded, speechless, immobilised with no sense of direction. Then the monster will wrap itself around her like a hangman lovingly preparing the noose, like lava around Pompeii, like maggots around the tea table, wrapped up like a cocoon, womb becomes tomb, lingam squeezing the life out of mother giving birth. Her lungs cry out
"I am breathless. For God's sake inhale me."

Stricken by the deep, cruel intention lurking behind those blue eyes, she is helpless, crumbling, yet drawn to lay down paralysed in awe, at the feet of the footless. Fatal attraction kills rationality. Her frivolousness incites the creature to more action. It starts to release threatening sounds whilst advancing closer and closer. Death's door opens waiting to swallow and she begins to shake like a chankana. Rattle baby's rattle snake. At the back of her mind she knows that she must escape her paralysis; gather up the fragments of her 'self' to fight back. Now. Take the first step. For God's sake take the first step. The reptile can smell her determination. This is a battle of wills. Send more hypnotic shrills. Send more hypnotic shrills. Send more hypnotic shrills. Waves of vibrations, snake rattle and roll with her intention and she can feel herself weakening. Stumbling, vision blurred, she falls into the gutter. She has been lying there for years, numbed by the systematic denigration inflicted upon her by an abusive man.

Who is she? Where is she? How did she get here? The beast is waiting for her to regain some consciousness, so it can continue the game, like a cat would a mouse and a snake would a pussy.

In her paralysed state, strange thoughts cross her mind. What is darkness she asks herself, but one side of a coin on which the other face is light. Toss the coin, perchance that it might fall lightface up and in the light, she can see the serpent. All her self-created foe is exposed, frozen in fear. Now that she sees the other side of herself, the light takes away some of the fear from her. She slowly lifts her head to face him. Dizzy and baffled with a new strength she gets up, folds her hands towards the light as in worship, listens to the beat of her heart and her feet start to move. She doesn't know where she gets this rhythm. She was never a dancer before, sweating heavily with the effort, tearing off her clothes like layers of misconceptions, dressing the wound of miscarriage and continuing the ritual. Twisting and twirling, she steps upon the body of the creature, chopping the air with her arms, trampling it with her vigorous feet until the snake starts to bleed, choking, dying. It is a Tandava Dance - the dance of Shiva, the God of strength, Kali squeezing all life from the penis and collapsing exhausted.

A four-wheeled wooden vehicle with two white horses, a Rath, driven by a vague shape appears through the huge river of light. Silver shining hair floats behind the round head. An old woman stands, aloof, on the Rath, holding the horse reins in one hand and a huge piece of cloth in the other. The cloth strikes the air like a magic pennant making waves in the tranquillity from which the figure emerges slowly and the round head turns into the features of an old nanny that she knew from her childhood. The old woman steps out of the Rath to push the woman away from the dead body of the python. Then she gently covers the naked woman with the cloth. Feeling the soft silky touch on her body, she sighs in relief. The nanny carries the woman in her arms, watching her face. The woman stares back into the shrewd eyes but is too exhausted to speak. Finding refuge in the cradle of old arms, she starts sobbing with tiredness. The wrinkled face draws near to whisper.

"There, there, hush now. Your children are alone. Go back to them. They need you. You have been fighting for too many years, the battle of a human being, a woman, a battle against evil. Everyone has to fight that battle, at least once in their lifetime. You have survived. You had my blessing. I knew you would win in the end. I have always been with you. I am your strength. I am your mother. I am your friend. I am your soul mate. I am... I am..."

The words are wavering. The woman can hear them no more but the echo enchants her ears. She is fast asleep now.

CHAPTER 1
The Grey Zone

"Wake up, wake up from your dream. You can't sleep now. You have to continue. The battle is not over yet. The storm is just beginning to gather. Wake up."

Someone is shaking the woman. Slowly opening her eyes, stretching her arms, looking at the crumpled sheet drenched in a sticky substance, she shouts.

"Who was shaking me up?" Her gaze travels around, but there's nobody else in the room. Scared silence pours all over. Light shining through the window falls on her face like suffocating illumination. Perhaps dreams are dead memories being reborn. Maybe my life is a jigsaw piled high and waiting to reassemble, like troops, blown apart by circumstance, longing to regain a collective cohesion. She remembers the old woman with long grey hair, small shrewd eyes, strong features, and soft smile reminder of mother.

"Who am I?" She asks the mirror.
"You are the sum total of your struggle," replies the face in the mirror.
'What is my name?"
"In your awakening you will come to know yourself as Svera."
"Why am I here?"
"To wrestle with your own struggle, your Jang. When the jigsaw is fully assembled you will face yourself as Svera Jang."

If I face myself, who is talking and who is listening?

"Are you hearing me?" said the mirror, "because if you are, you've just named yourself."
So my mirror came to name itself Svera, meaning the dawn - an awakening and Jang, meaning the battle. Svera Jang. I am not her now, but she was once me. I have described Svera in such detail that sometimes it feels that I cannot be that woman. How could I? How could I let myself be abused by a man? How could I let myself be

defeated by Pain, Humiliation, and Honour? All these devils joined hands to pester me.

Every time I touched them, they jumped all over me, choked me. The Devil of Honour prodded my soul with coughing, whooping laughter of disgust. It wanted to be victorious. I had to fight all those devils until they became weaker and weaker and weaker, meek at last. Eventually, I found the strength to write about this woman Svera Jang. Writing about her, I had to be objective. Do you think I could? Oh, yes, it has been very painful. Some ghosts of memories came to haunt, some came to remind me of my cause.

The more I wrote, the more I realised Svera was constantly fighting and searching for something. Hope? Longing? Desire? Or was it the freedom from all these illusions? Hang on hope is not an illusion. Or is it? I know I was searching for a place, a land where the freedom prevails in its real sense. One thing was sure, it was a universal search. It started. It ended. It started and ended. It started over and over again. And again. A never-ending story of life, mapped out on the face of every breathing soul. The search for that total freedom of mind was her dream and the dream was her search.

Her search started more than a quarter of a century ago, about the time Svera Jang fled the strangulating norms and traditions of her land. A land of five rivers – the Punjab, once the land of glories. By the time she left it was a rainbow bleeding with racial tensions. She had hoped to pursue the search in the foreign lands of golden democracies.

Did you know, mother? You also waged your struggle. Your search. The search is forever reborn with each new generation. Yours. Svera's. My daughter's. Everybody's.

CHAPTER 2
The Wheel Of Journey

Dear Mother, I touch your feet to bless my journey, a colourful piece of glass in a kaleidoscope; my life is in the spiral of ever changing movement. Luminously drunk with its speed and energy, I'm a daydreaming traveller wandering through life's spectacular landscape. The lemon moon through the windscreen is dancing like a panchromatic firefly, reminding me of freedom, flickering briefly, and then vanishing into the changes. The disappearing shades of sunset in the sky, glimpsed through the window of a flashing train, confirm the faith that tomorrow will arise. My headlights shine on an oil slick on the road ahead, creating a rainbow arch shimmering. Rainbow is beautiful, as I would wish my love to be. Rainbow hopes for pot of gold, if only I could find the end. Rainbow disappears, yet we have faith that it will return. Hope, Faith, Love, the witches of the east. Symbols of freedom, yet I find myself caught in a traffic jam on the highway to nowhere, as if all my mental blocks were stacked in a queue in front of me.

But then again, raindrops falling on my windscreen remind me everything changes constantly and take me back to the storm before the monsoon when the dust, deviously settled over everywhere like choking norms and traditions. I write with my fingers in the dust, "I am strong." But as a child I was frail, delicate and shy, yet it was my duty to take care of my younger brother, Jake. Walking on the crowded dusty road between my school and home, Uncle Karl's newly opened bicycle shop was a midway stop of rest for us. I used to tightly clutch Jake's soft plump palm in one hand while holding my own shoulder bag full of books and his small bag with the other. The route from school to home was along our city's busiest grand trunk road, which was a trading post for all the merchants from nearby villages. It was a tough job to navigate through this human and mechanical jungle, towing a small boy and two bags of heavy books. Early morning oxen carts loaded with wheat corn, maize, rice, peanuts and lentils delivered to the shops of dhoti clad Banias (merchants). Blaring trucks, scooter rickshaws, fast taxis brought to a screeching halt by cows standing in the middle of the road, India's own make of Ambassador cars, animals, hustlers and chickens all had a place and part to play, interwoven like spaghetti junction. The road further down towards the medical centre was ornamented with orange, yellow, white, brown sweets, meat stores, cloth shops and was crowded with hungry visitors, wives, servants and men buying their lunch. Half way between home and school could be found a haven from this chaos - Uncle Karl's bicycle shop!

Uncle Karl was a tough, retired military captain who enjoyed sitting on his chair behind a desk, like a lord surveying his domain, noticing every minute detail and keeping the shop working with military efficiency. Although his workers were well organised, he didn't treat them differently from his own two sons who would give a helping hand to his business after their college hours. He kept a tight budget and maintained a strict watch over his business and yet on occasions he was very generous with his sister's children.

Soaked in the smell, dust and heat of tramping along five kilometres of bustling market place on our way back home from school, Jake and I would make a daily stop for a rest in his shop. He kept cold drinks in a box filled with ice cubes. Limca for us, Coke for the boys and Fanta for himself. In my innocent, small child way I always thought that Limca was the drink of heaven, a very wonderful lemonade. With his blue shorts, white shirt, red tie, white socks and brown sandals, Jake would manage to settle himself on a big chair dangling his legs half way down to the floor, enjoying his drink with a sort of look in his eyes that said he didn't give a damn about the world of business around him. Looking at my beloved little brother watching the workers patch, repair and sell bicycles, I would get lost in my own world of fantasies. The routine of visiting the shop suited us children perfectly well. We got delicious drinks, rest and Uncle Karl got the satisfaction of looking after his sister's children. I was nearing my eleventh birthday and hadn't yet reached the physical height and strength of a teenage girl. I was the youngest and shortest amongst other girls in my class. Every morning, each class of the Henderson school had to make a queue according to the height. The shortest girl, I stood in front. My best friend Asha was right at the back of the queue. Raani next, Shammi and all the other girls. Raani was jealous of my friendship with Asha. So much so that she used to pull my long hair, sometimes very hard. She was one of the tallest and strongest. I never dared to fight her.

Being a Christian school we had to sing the morning prayer in praise of Jesus. Henderson was an old missionary school probably built by the British in the 1940's and was situated on a beautiful broad road with posh bungalows on both sides. The school offered competitive education up to tenth standards. First and second standard was co-education. Jake who was now seven and having completed two years, was to be transferred to a boys school. It was his last day. We arrived at Uncle Karl's shop, and found him sitting on his leather chair twirling his moustache, glint in the eyes. I was a bit intimidated by his smile, which made me nervous.

After a short exchange of the usual greetings and small chat about how our study was going on, Jake and I settled down quietly watching the road, waiting for our drinks. The workers peeped at us with mysterious looks on their faces. Then Uncle Karl pointed his finger at his worker who quietly disappeared into the back of the showroom. We waited and waited until he came with a beautiful shining bicycle of my size to place just in front of my chair.

"I had it ordered especially for you Svera. You won't have to rely upon anybody else but you and your bike for transportation," Uncle Karl announced, proudly looking at me still twirling his moustache.

Jake looked at the flash brand new bicycle and he looked at me and he looked at Uncle Karl with his open lips and was totally gobsmacked. I sat glued to my chair staring at the cycle in disbelief.

"Svera, Svera, look what you got." Jake suddenly shouted. I didn't know what to say, as if I had become speechless, but I felt a lump stuck in my throat. Then a huge sigh of gratitude came out and I stood and went over to hug my uncle. I clung to him like excited chick to mother hen.

"Ok. OK. It's O.K little Guddi", he said shyly, pushing me away from him. "Go on and try it, girl." Shivering with delight I touched the magnificent machine that didn't need petrol, fuel or any mechanical device other than my hands and itching feet to mount and ride on it where ever and whenever I wanted. I was going to fly on the wheels of my bicycle towards freedom.

For the next fifteen years, the bicycle became the symbol of emancipation for a young, shy, curious girl, growing up to be a strong, independent, self-propelled woman. The bicycle was free. It did not need expensive fuel. It was environmentally friendly, provided healthy exercise and didn't get stuck in traffic jams. The spinning wheel of the bike gave me the wings, the speed, the imagination and the dreams. On weekend mornings, I would sling a bag on my shoulders, get my bike out and ride eight miles on a semi-tarmac roads to visit my uncle's family in the village. Peddling smoothly on my bike, inhaling the fresh country air with images of a rural life spread on the canvas of golden yellow wheat fields like splashes of colour in a surreal painting.

Clink, tinkle, chun! I heard the chinking glass bangles of a newlywed village girl as she walked with pride on the luke-warm soil of her dreams. A basket full of food on her head, one hand holding a can of lassi, she was going to spend some moments of bliss with her lover.

Under the shade of a large pipal tree they would nibble the food of love while listening to the grasshopper's chirping. On a day when the dark clouds pregnant with rain, appeared from nowhere, its water would break and suddenly give birth to twins. I would start to move my feet vigorously on the pedals. Sometimes, in the monsoon it felt as if the clouds have taken the fertility drug and given birth to a nation. Heavy rain pour was more strong then the mighty force of the Victoria Falls. Drenched, I'd start to imagine myself dancing with handsome Vinod Khana, the film actor. If I were lucky, I would witness a fantastic rainbow before I got home to my uncle.

The wheels of my bicycle spun faster and faster, so did my teen years. I was soon thirteen, fourteen, fifteen and was becoming an expert in manoeuvring the rough patches of my journey between blaring truck drivers, rickshaw pullers, vegetable hawkers, cows and your concerned voice of warnings, mother. Potholes in the highway were so big that a buffalo might fall into them. Potholes were so big that a shepherd could drive a herd of sheep into them and they would come out as brand new woolly jumpers on a production line, complete with labels and expensive price tags. So big that a man could lose himself in the abyss of his own dreams and sooner or later emerge on the other side of madness. An insanity which sees men enslaved to their machine, constantly in debt to pay for it, chained to working for its upkeep, willingly donating their meagre wages to the bank balances of some already super rich oil barons, feudal rulers and presidents elected by petro dollars, pouring pollutants into the atmosphere which poison children, yes, you've guessed, I'm in a traffic jam on the M1 motorway coming from the South into a cold Northern city of West Yorkshire.

It's a long way from India to Bradford. Restlessly tapping my fingertips against the windshield, I'm thinking, I have become an addicted consumer of machines and commodities and my desires are running headless horses. I'm searching for something to distract me from the stiffness of a jam of illusions. I was once addicted to love so much that it overpowered me with its deceitful nature, killing my rationality with its dagger. When I was unaware, it caught me, turned me into a lifeless entity, a walking skeleton. I'm frightened. I close my eyes, slide down a blind on the window of my mind, handcuff myself to the sky to prevent me from falling into another trap. My senses open up to reason with me. The wind is playing games with my impudent hair. I'm dreaming, thinking, dreaming, fantasy, reason, logic. Faith. Hope. Love.

Crucified morals.
God.
Jesus.

"If I speak in human and angelic tongues but do not have love, I am a resounding gong or a clashing cymbal. And if I have the gift of prophecy and comprehend all mysteries and all knowledge; if I have all faith so as to move mountains but do not have love, I am nothing." *Corinthians, Chapter 13.*

If I do not have love, I am nothing? How many times love has been crushed by the mighty wheels of honour? I've witnessed people abusing others in the name of honour. Save the honour and become a martyr and God will compensate you in heaven, they say. What about you, mother? You were told to keep your head covered with a dupatta, symbol of modesty, subservience, and a fine silky web woven to trap your honour.

"Keep your hair covered with dupatta. You are the izzat, the honour of this family until you get married. Then you will belong to your husband, his family. You can do whatever you want then." A young woman like you would be reminded time and again. You were merely a four-month-old baby when your mother died, leaving you at the mercy of fighting with honour and norms. For the fear that your stepmother would treat you badly, your dad vowed not to get married again. For the fear that you might take advantage of his love, he became over protective and over strict. When you grew up to be a healthy girl of thirteen, you had finished eight years in the village school, you wanted to become a teacher. For the fear of losing his honour, he refused to let you study further in a nearby town. He was scared of you becoming independent, choosing a husband for yourself, be allured by vices, men, freedom. Once when you were working in the house your dupatta slid down from your head. Your father was very upset with you. He warned you not to let that happen again. When you were sixteen, he arranged for you to get married. The irony is that if grandfather hadn't arranged that marriage then I would never have been born into this universe. Grandfather saved his honour. But you carried the scars of his prejudices into your life and passed some on to your daughters. The sins of the fathers, grandfathers, passed down the generations. Well, I am the generation of daughters that says "this oppression of women by men who let fear rule their lives, stops here! I do not want to carry fear." Land is another symbol of honour. Disputes are created, brothers are divided to own a piece of land as inheritance. Factions, hatred, even wars are waged in the name of honour.

Honour can so becomes powerful that it can make things disappear, even life, wiping all the traces of existence. Drive the metal vehicle of savagery; crush a life to save the family honour. Najma was only twenty when a Mercedes ruthlessly crushed her.

This seems like an event of the present, but it has happened before, many places, time, space and culture do not hold back the notion of revenge, hatred for the sake of love. "I killed her, for the love of Kayan". Kilgour, a jealous lover from Trinidad in the 50's had told the jury. Like the story of Sohni Mahiwal from a village in the Punjab.
Sohni a young beautiful girl fell in love with Mahiwal from another village, another cast. Every night she would climb into a clay pot that she kept secretly on the riverbank then she would paddle across the water to meet her lover. One day, her brother found out and instructed his wife to swop Sohni's glazed pot with a pot that was unglazed. Without knowing Sohni set out in her clay pot as usual to cross the river, but the pot soon became waterlogged and sank. The beautiful Sohni drowned. I was thinking about Najma with my eyes tight shut, I was denying, as if it couldn't have happened.

Oh yes, thinking loudly and watching silently behind my closed eyes, a truly mad nightmare, only that it had happened in reality on a hot sunny July day in Bradford. It happened to Najma. It could easily be Sohni, Sita, Julie, Svera, and Firdaus. A girl like Sara with deep cuts, bleeding arms, lost babies, abused honour, circumcisions. What's in a name? Najma was wearing a pale silk shalwar and black velvet kurta with a golden chiffon dupatta, the one she wore for Id festival every year. She had sneaked out of her in-law's house to meet her lover. Head covered, silent steps, she darted across the street like a scared gazelle.

"Hey, where to, darling, all dressed to kill?" asked her childhood friend Jan, with a gentle kiss on her cheek. "Well, I haven't got time to hear your answer, I am just rushing to the shops before my kids come home for lunch, but seriously Najma, that's a look to die for." Jan hurried off leaving Najma blushing. As Najma turned and stepped onto the road, in a fraction of a second, a black Mercedes hit her. She fell down lifeless and the car reversed to deliberately crush her body several times. The cold-blooded murderer sped off towards the M606. She was flat on her back, big brown eyes wide open, staring towards the vast blue sky in disbelief, one finger pointing up, asking Allah if she had committed a crime of passion that merited such a death.

This town of cultural taboos is so cool that it's frozen in a time zone. The wheel of time keeps on changing, why doesn't our stagnant culture change? There are Najmas who refuse to be tamed into meekness. But Najmas and Sitas will be reborn again and again to wage their struggle.

A silent explosion of revolt is about to burst inside me, so I'm opening my eyes to forget the scene. The trouble is, that when I am awake, I am still in my trance, my mind still working, and I can't stop thinking about Najma. I take a large sip of water hoping to quench my thirst for answers, I'm getting thirstier. Hundreds of other engines spitting black fumes, in anger pawing the ground, snorting, ready to scatter off into all consequences, reminding me that I have to set off too. Hands steady on the wheel, one foot on the accelerator, in the fear that other vehicles will catch up, overtake me, because I'm the winner, head of the queue, addicted consumer, and competitor. The broken down car that had caused the jam is being towed away. Clear vision, straight ahead, impatient to get going because speed and the thrill of the road keep me alive, but then my eyes spot him under the lamp post. Desolate, stuck in a small SOS booth, one hand holding the phone and the other dialling desperately. The most striking feature I see, even in the dim light is his dark charcoal hair, foliage of small curls climb gently from the chest towards the line of his neck. He lifts his head and I gasp for breath. I pinch my cheeks, rub my eyes and look at the road. No! It couldn't be the ghost of Jaz?

The moon in the sky is still glowing like a firefly, only there's no Sukhna Lake and no Jaz, but this is Ahren. He seemed to be spontaneously planted there on the road in front of me, by fate, to interrupt my journey. His blackberry eyes move in desperation, searching for someone, suddenly recognising, he walks towards my car as I find myself helplessly nervous, other drivers hoot at me, pushing my car to drive away from the cue. I put on my hazard lights because something inside tells me he's danger. His sensual lips open and close as if to whisper incantations of love. I'm interrupted by a Yorkshire accent.

"You wouldn't mind giving me a lift to work, would you, my bloody car broke down?" he says smiling, in a strangely hypnotic voice as he opens the door to enter.

His dimples, two deep pools resting on the majestic topography of his cheekbones, inviting me to take a dip. His right shoulder pressed against my left, yin and yang, we seemed to fit together like nut and bolt, lovers, as he adjusted himself into my passenger seat. Turning towards me with dazzling look and strange warmth in his eyes, he makes himself comfortable.

I could have immersed myself in the sea of his majestic disposition and drowned in the confusion of his hidden intention. I was not prepared to confront him like this in a collision on the road, keeping my thoughts quietly tucked inside myself, I bit my lower lip.

"Was it Karma that was pulling me towards him?" I had asked a palmist, who suggested it would be so.

He kept on smiling and here was the paradox. Behind that angelic warrior visage, he was a soft pale daffodil, a fragile entity in many ways, wounded by the lack of love from his parents. This was an early spring evening in Bradford and the city was wrapped in flirtatious mood. Heavy clothing wasn't necessary for once. Lovers and friends strolled in the streets, clothed in their own little comforts. People in vehicles moved with the rhythms, lost in their lazy conversations. Humbly, the trees bowed down, making long shadows on the road, covering the footprints of travellers. Galaxy 105 radio station was playing George Michael *Spinning The Wheel*. My desire swirled like incense smoke in a draft that can only be felt in those moments when love renders one incapable. Lost in the moment, I was watching the wheel of time spin faster and faster. I was travelling along with him helplessly, towards an unknown zone. He was as ambivalent and carefree as a Mediterranean breeze, playing games with my aspirations as he always did. Bastard!

The red traffic lights turned orange, then green, to my relief. We entered the large car park in front of a nightclub on the city's outskirts. The city was resting under the spell of a lukewarm spring like this when Ahren had first hit my life like a comet. Mark introduced him to me, at a book launch held at Waterston's. As Peter Paulin ended the launch with The Last Symphony, I saw him standing tall surrounded by a group of women. In the midst of their excited conversation, he was looking handsome with cream trousers, blue jacket flashing like a commodity available to be picked up.

"Jesus. One thing I can't figure out is how people can pursue such monotonous life style, striving only for something as demeaning as sex. They think they will attain their happiness, through the devil's..."

"But lust is life, my friend. The lust for life, I mean." The red haired woman interrupted his pocket book philosophy, chuckling in amusement. She was exhaling clouds of cigarette smoke along with her red, pouting self-assurance. This tall, dark handsome man was a perfect image of Jaz. Oh, to be allured by this living illusion. Wouldn't it be just like living in the paradise of bliss...I thought, but only a thought, I swear mother.

"What are you doing Svera? What are you thinking, girl! Svera?...Stop...You are mad." A commanding voice came from somewhere. I could hear it so clearly. I even saw your body with wings floating in the air, like the angels do. Uncle Karl's pointing finger!
"Leave me alone, guys!"
I wanted to shout at the ghosts of my past, but frantically, I bustled into the crowd of intellectuals who were busy sticking their fingers into all sorts of free dips, snacks, drinks and each other's gossip, like hungry wolves desperate for food for thought. I reluctantly picked a few of my favourite bites as I heard Ahren telling intimate details of his Jamaican mermaid, Alisha.

I saw Mark listened intensely and blushing, his eyes rotating to see whether someone was listening to their conversation. He spotted me and I raised my hand to say hello and the chinking of glass bangles on my arm formed the word "lust" in my mind. Ahren continued speaking of his girl friend. I could see in his eyes that he was besotted by her, nearly mad. Living together for six years in a heaven of lust that tore them apart at times. I wondered how they could make it last so long without being able to communicate.

Communication with him was smooth and slinky like his suit, a silver key to the door of our first introduction. When he opened his mouth, the prostrate defences of my sensibility melted right there in front of the crowd. I was dumb founded as his slim muscular body swayed with elegance as he spread his arm to shake my hand.

"So what do you think of Mr. Paulin's poetry?"

"I enjoyed it." I said and felt that he was inevitably soon to become a staccato symphony in my own poetry. I had already gathered enough knowledge from overhearing his conversation with Mark, to realise that he was on the brink of making or breaking up with Alisha. But I could not envisage him as a vulnerable man who would seek the company of a mature woman like me. His love for Alisha had probably caused him much more pain then I would have anticipated. He was like a wounded tiger when it ended.
"Oh, Svera, she has broken my heart again. I am doomed," he would moan softly in his husky voice, filling my lap with his slithering words. I hated and loved those moments when he was hurt. He was drawn towards my abundance and comfort. He needed to heal, to nurture and to overcome. He regularly started to visit the poetry group I was member of. When everyone had finished reciting their poetry, some of us would stay behind to catch up on gossip.

"Svera, I love your company. Please come and sit near me. I want to listen to your magic words. They soothe my heart. Let the verses filter through the silky steam."

Sitting opposite on the table, slowly inhaling the Silk Cut, he would shut one of his snake eyes, the other one piercing deep through my skin. Together we would light the embers of our past for a couple of hours.

He was adopted by his granny at the age of four when his father, a Muslim man, left the family for another woman. In his youth he used the nose-corrupting white powder to counterbalance the bitterness he felt about his parents. At first I wasn't aware how much and for how long he would influence my life, but I started taking refuge in the Riviera of his futile youthfulness. Maybe it wasn't merely fate that brought us together. We had met for a reason, at this specific time, in this peculiar city of extreme contradictions between cultures. We met to negate the stereotypical images of Asians. It's not common that a Sikh woman has friendship with a mixed race guy whose father was Muslim and Mum White. Peter had left me. Nina left home. My dad had died. I was going through my journey of pain, death, doubts, delusions, forgiveness, truthfulness, and self- control, fear. I was trying to find the meaning of love, of its unrequited, one- sided wound, sharp like a razor cut with the hurt of losing someone you have loved and thinking that it was everlasting. I had to free myself from all the morals I had held and let a new power of fearlessness develop in my spirit. Everything subject to arising is also subject to cessation. If time is not a line, then love that is generated between people never disappears. It's absorbed into the eternal ocean. I had to learn to let Peter go. In his midlife crisis he wanted change. Infidelity was his notion of change. I found myself deep in the extreme state of panic, self pity and hurt. I realised meeting Ahren at that vulnerable time of my life was going to be tough. However, after the book launch, a strange liking grew between us, as we started to see each other more often than once a week at the poetry sessions. Sometimes we met in a cafe, other times, at my house. He would phone.
"Svera, could I come for a cup of coffee with you?"
He admired and loved the exquisite style of my Victorian house.

Drinking tea and smoking, we would sit for hours to discuss anything from poems, films, music, and my past to my dating of men. He didn't seem to approve of the way I dated men.

"You go to a singles club Svera? A woman like you doesn't need to go to a place like that," he would say.

"Where else am I supposed to meet a man, Ahren"?

"Well, go to Sainsbury's. What about the bookshops? The atmosphere is intellectual. If you linger at the mind and body section you'll surely meet a decent guy. No Svera, singles bars, nightclubs, dating agencies. You should keep well away from all that."

"Ahren," looking at him mischievously I said, "I'm a member of one."

He was shocked to see the huge list on the table in my kitchen marked with an orange highlighter with all the men on offer.

"This is appalling. Looks like a computerised cattle market. Why have you outlined this: *Young male 35 no strings, fun?* You realise what he means?"

"Of course I do. Wouldn't it be fun to explore this young, tall, handsome guy your age who is making himself available?"

I teased him. I could see he was jealous.

"I think you should find a rich guy. You wouldn't need to work and worry about paying your bills."

"I don't know, Ahren. But why do you suddenly talk about money?"

"Svera, money is important. Daulat Raja Hai. Why not? Daulat. Money. Money is everything. It's a shrine and I want to worship Daulat like an opportunist pundit falling to his knees on the marble footsteps of its divinity," he said. I looked at this handsome man in his mid thirties with strange feeling of maternity. A son I never had? A spiritual brother? The ghost of my lost lover, Jaz?

"I am concerned about you Svera Jang. As if.. as if...I am sure we have met before. Do you believe in reincarnation?" he said, as if reading my thoughts.

Ahren worked as an interpreter and also as a part time stripper in the nightclub where I had just left him. I knew he gyrated his firm buttocks in front of those available middle-aged women. However this dubious work was fulfilling his desire to become rich. I was slowly heading towards home on the Drighlington By-pass, having a sudden encounter with Ahren on the road. I was finally beginning to relax. The image of his face shimmered clearly in my mind. It looked so familiar. I was so sure I had met him somewhere before. At a different place, in a different setting. But where? Ahren, a child of mixed marriage was a mixture of confusion and determination. Aimless, fighting to achieve some vague identity.

Strangely enough Ahren was also devoted to spirituality and development. He so much lusted after the truth. That's what attracted us spiritually. Who was this man? Why was he here, with me? Where was he heading? Was I being distracted from my destination by his entry? These questions obsessed me.

Exhausted by my long journey on the road, I sat to relax in my lounge, in front of this glowing fireplace. I poured a brandy, soon becoming overwhelmed by the warmth of my own solitude, eyes shut. The fragrance of his body hesitated on the doorstep of my memory, very close to me, I felt my fingertips travelling over his face, my lips tasting the juices of the pain from his eyes, those deep black eyes drew me towards him, madly. I imagined Svera to be as tiny as a Genie who would float around and touch his troubled face when he sought after Alisha. Alas, I had to open my eyes to reality. I peeped down at the bottom of the crystal glass. Another face appeared. It was Jaz surfacing again, this time from the magic liquid of Brandy. A Genie in the goblet. Passionate, fragile and dangerous. So unique a resemblance with Ahren that I was frightened. Diving up to the surface, he firmly demanded my attention. Looking straight through the eyes of my memories, from the present back to the past, where I am going to take you. Are you ready?

CHAPTER 3
Thorns and Crystal Of Memories

It is old, yellow and stained with memories; this small photograph that has travelled the world with me, always finding a place on my bedroom walls. Men in green uniform, tall, sturdy, smiling, tired, proud, standing on barren land in some unproductive, forgotten corner of Borneo. They worked hard to turn that soil into fertile territory. Some of them were of peasant background. They could grow anything, from factory farm produced commodities to the seeds of freedom. One of the men in the photograph was my father, then in his mid thirties, upright, head held high, nearly touching the unlimited boundary of the sky. Sardar Heera Singh Such. The protector of his country. A soldier, traveller, giver. An honest, happy-hearted individual, who was rarely home. He had to be out there on the borders of his great land, to defend her from enemies and intruders. That had always been the image of him that I held dear to my heart throughout the years. That was your fate, to wait for him. You, the woman who married him, a man of the earth who planted the seed perchance to become my father.

"I shall call you 'Amrit', the holy water. You are as pure as nectar and as innocent as a little baby dove." Holding me in his arms with a kiss on my tiny forehead, he placed a grand necklace of twenty-four carat gold in your hand. "This is for giving me a beautiful girl, and for all the pain, you suffered in the long wait. Even the Koh-I-Noor cannot compare with this. You will have my love and respect all my life, until the day I die."

You were still living in the family house Uncle Karl had inherited from your father, my granddad. You had spent five long years there when your husband was away in the war. You did not even know if he was alive. I was considered a lucky phenomenon in my family, a child who had kept her father alive, even before she was born, you told me so.

I was conceived when he came home after five years of fighting and surviving the Second World War, as if it was all pre-planned by the Gods in heaven. I was bound to be born to you and him. As if I came to demand a debt you both owed me from my previous life. That's what the belief said, in mythology. I did not have faith in beliefs then; I do now.

Scrolling up and down this lighted box of icons and symbols has helped me set right the pieces of my life puzzle. I can delete a part, cut it, and paste it in a different space, between lines. I can correct it, spell check, punch a button and print it out. Unlike old days when the communication was conveyed by drum beating, smoke sending and word of mouth. You used to tell me tales about his survival, when I grew old enough to understand them. Now, I tell you my story mother.

Stories and myths are silver and gold, trapped beneath the soil of countries, cities, in houses, behind walls, wanting to come out of the closet to brighten life's dim grey scars. People hold them like treasures as my father held me in his arms. I hold your hand; take you to a country, a village, and a room, on a bed where you see a woman with a baby girl by her side looking at a shining yellow necklace bestowed upon her for giving birth to me. Can you remember your own story? And you mother? It must have been quite a weight to carry around your neck in those days when girls were considered to be a burden. Some people had been known to kill unwanted daughters, as soon as they were born. A boy will grow up to work and bring dowry. A girl just costs you money. You had to raise and protect her yet she wouldn't bring any income and when she got married, you had to give dowry. If you didn't count your daughter as a blessing, then she was a burden. With a heart of pure gold, my father stood tall in the dark room, looking at his baby girl reflecting his rays onto the woman he loved and respected. You had been living in fear. To expect a girl is to anticipate rejection. You were totally drenched under the heavy reign of love and generosity from your husband. With a necklace made of solid gold and a solid man with a heart of gold, you shivered even in the midday of a warm June 1947. You could not find the words to thank him. How could you? How could any woman?

"I shall call you Amrit," he spoke softly to baby Svera, who slept peacefully in his strong cradling arms. I can still hear the echo of his voice like a sweet melody penetrating each corner of my soul as I try to create words to describe him, visualising the face of a war veteran, a handsome man who had returned home after five years of absence from his family. Against the raw memories of Japanese cruelty, the man must have experienced joy and pride to hold a tiny baby in his arms. My father Heera Singh was a very peculiar and rare heera (diamond) indeed. He disowned the family property, giving everything to his brothers. He did not want to wage a war against his own blood. Not after fighting so many battles already. Not for a mere piece of land. Brothers and sons fought and were so often killed for land. Land was a value. Much more worth than gold.

The women did not own land. They inherited gold as their property for security. Being the youngest of her four sons and two daughters, his mother pampered him with all her affection, gifts and riches. He was even kept tied to the healthy breast-feeding ritual until the age of eight. No wonder he had survived all those lashings in the Japanese POW camp in Borneo for five years. Having the most fertile land in their village, Heera Singh's brothers strove hard to tend it, took control of it, while he chose to cultivate himself to become the only village intellectual.

Recently, I discovered a ten-page diary with his name which was sent to me by my brother Amar, after my dad had died. Kept in a plastic folder, it had been lying amongst other odds and sods with some of my father's drawings of flowers, leaves and houses. I particularly like one of a horse; it has faded over the years, but serves as a vivid reminder of my six foot four inch father riding, with his upright military dignity, good sense and ability to talk to all living things including animals. The diary is a sketch of life in the village and dramatic incidents in the war, all written in good English on an Indian typewriter.

"I was born in a small village in Ferozepur district and went to school when I was seven. I was the youngest amongst three elder brothers and two sisters. It was a primary school before the partition with only two teachers who were Muslims. They were very strict and sometimes beating of the pupils was served as punishment. The school was five miles away from our village. Sometimes on the way home we would fight. The other boys were from banian (merchant class) families and were considered to be physically weak, so I could easily beat them. I was the strongest amongst my classmates. I finished four years in this school. At that time amongst the two of the brightest students, I was chosen for the scholarship to continue my higher education. High school was in another town, six miles away from my village. We had to be in the school by seven, so I had to get up five in the morning every day. My mother had to get up at four to prepare my breakfast and lunch.

When I left from home it would still be dark. My father accompanied me for a while. One mile away from my home there was a pipal tree. People used to say that there were ghosts in the tree. I had to pass that tree every day. I was scared. It was not fun. Our house was in the middle of the village. We had a large yard and in that yard we had a platform built with mud where we would sit and talk in the evenings. Those days everyone respected each other and celebrated festivals together. People used to help each other at the time of crisis. In my village, I was the only one who could read Urdu and English.

So, when people got letters from outside, they came to me. In 1931, I passed my matriculation examination. By then I had bought a bicycle for only 50 rupees. The college education was very expensive. A friend of mine urged me to travel to Malaya with him but at that time my family was arranging my marriage. My father in law was a big landlord in one of the villages in Ambala district. My wife was a kind hearted young woman of sixteen. She was only educated up to eighth grade but she was very intelligent. She got along with my family very well. My mother admired her a lot. Her name was Joshili, which means she was hot tempered and brave. She kept my family in good order. But soon after my marriage I had to seek employment.

Since I didn't particularly like doing farming, I left my share of the land to my brothers. I never demanded any share in the crops ever. I knew, if I demanded, it would create tension. I decided to go to Sialkot to get one year's military training. After completing that, I did two years to specialise in the educational field. I wanted to become Laisnaik (Corporal). The Punjabi people in the military had some communal groups and I didn't want to belong to any. They did not like me, so when the time came for promotions, they promoted another man. That night I could not sleep. After thinking what to do for two days, I decided to have a meeting with my British Major. When the major asked me what the matter was I did not answer but gave him the letter I had prepared for this purpose explaining when they did not promote me I did not want to stay in this company. This Major called for the junior officer and the head clerk and ordered them to promote me at that very moment. Soon afterwards I was selected to go on a course to become Educational Inspector (engineer). After the training I was posted in Poona. In 1939 our company became mobilised because now the Second World War had started.

Our company moved to Malaya. We went to a town called Epu. We were given the task to demolish a bridge in Thailand. The work of the engineer in the war is to blow up the bridge and block the road. After blowing up the bridge we started slowly retreating as the bridge was burning. I was in charge of my head quarters. Two months passed, we started to have many difficulties. Once in Perith in Malaya, we were in charge of blowing up another bridge too. But that morning when we were about to blow the bridge, twenty Japanese aeroplanes came to bombard us. They bombed our camp all day. Everybody were scattered and had to leave the bridge. I was laying down in one rubber plantation together with two others. The Japanese aeroplanes were coming and going. It became dark and our men gathered. We were JCO, we had to go back and to report to our company. The Japanese had destroyed all the vehicles. I had to report to one Captain Porter. He gave me one group of men and asked me to go to the major. In the Sikh Platoon there was one truck with Guru Granth Sahib (Sikh's holy book). It was the 'field temple'. I was given that truck and twenty men. I started moving towards the bridge to report. Suddenly Japanese aeroplane came. We stopped and took our positions to let the aeroplane pass. The boys were very afraid from the whole days bombing so they ran away. Only three of them stayed with me. We went together with these three to report to the major. He ordered me to blow up the bridge that night. I checked everything and blew up the bridge at four o'clock early morning..."

There were other details of the war. My father was kept in a small and narrow cell for three weeks. He could not stand, only kneel. Every day, the Japanese would take him out for interrogation, beat him severely and lock him up in the cell without food and water. After the war, when he returned home, he constantly suffered knee problems.

Soon after the world war ended, the British government clearly stated its intention of granting independence to Indian subcontinent. In July 1947 one month after my birth, the British parliament passed the Indian Independence Bill, creating two independent States: India made up of provinces with a Hindu majority and Pakistan, with those having Muslim majority. The new border cutting Punjab in two left 5 million Sikhs and Hindus on the Pakistani side and 5 million Muslims on the Indian side causing violent outbreaks. On both sides of the border the majority of population slaughtered their minority neighbours. Millions of terrified people fled in trainloads, in wagons or on foot. The refugee convoys suffered attacks. Tens of thousands of young girls, women and children were abducted. Hundreds of thousands perished. My father was called to guard trains filled with Muslim refugees fleeing India. He was later posted to the Border security Forces to deal with India-Pakistan Wars and series of conflicts between the two countries. Before he left to take up his posting at the Jammu and Kashmir borders, he wanted to celebrated my birth in style. Sweets were distributed in the village, clothes were given to the poor. Clay lamps were lit and fireworks set off. It must have been like celebrating Diwali in your house. In the middle of your postnatal duties to take care of baby Svera and brother Amar who was seven, my aunt had taken for granted the authority to baptise me with a name in a Gurdwara! I used to despised that name, when I was a kid. I thought that I could never forgive you for letting her do that and for not giving me the name my father had chosen.

The lilac petals of remorse spread a stale odour constantly around my teen years. I was unable to cleanse the scent with the soap of my maturity when I grew older. In India girls are not supposed to make decisions without consulting their elders. So you and your sister decided my future, my actions, mother. You wanted to decide. You always did.

I have never been very close to my brother Amar and my contact to him has lapsed to an occasional post card and a brief telephone conversation over the years. From being a university lecturer, revolutionary intellectual he has changed to being a disillusioned 'communist' in Canada. In his last days, my father used to say to me, "You are my third son. These two have become coward souls." He meant I was a daring woman who had gone through much in life and was still a strong personality. I am fascinated by my father's honesty while he served and his later determination to develop his writing and creative skills which hadn't had much opportunity to flourish when he was young.

Because of my father's job, our family was forced to travel. Chandigarh was the only city where we had a house, which we proudly called our family home. It was in Chandigarh we did our college and university education. Amar taking a masters degree in physical education and was engaged in the landless peasants movement, the Naxalbari. I was a young woman of eighteen. With Jake and Gulu being too young, I was put in charge of the household affairs including paying the bills and keeping accounts. We had subscribed to three newspapers: The Tribune, Nia Zamana in Punjabi for you, mother, and occasionally The Guardian. The paperboy distributed newspapers very early each morning. Sometimes Jake and I argued over who should read The Tribune first. I always managed to save some money from the budget and spend it on buying Illustrated Weekly of India, Film Fare, Punjabi magazines like Nagmani and Aarsi.

Being the two mature children, Amar and I learnt to live with our father's impeccably weird qualities that led his life to remain uncomplicated, honest and dignified. His principles left him in the same rank until the time of his retirement. He refused to lick the arse of his superior. He refused to take bribes. He refused to let his soldiers loot the Pakistani villagers. All his soldiers respected him and used to call him, Bapuji. We shamelessly nagged him for not having his share of the rich land. How could he not partake of the loot when his soldiers went to settle the many border disputes?

"You wouldn't have become what you are today if I had ever allowed myself or my soldiers to plunder shops and steal from people on the other side. I have witnessed corrupt officers; their greedy minds and their children who gamble, cheat, and become drug addicts. I am satisfied with my small wealth. But I have been blessed with riches - my family, you my children, and your mother, my good old woman, who looks after you."

He would say this twirling his colonial handlebar moustache, one of the two defiant remnants of the British Empire which remained in our home. My brothers and sister would watch the prism of light across his face from the veranda and were spellbound.

He looked at me as I sat absorbed in the other remnant of Empire, Dr Jekyll and Mr Hyde, a classic of the 19th century by Robert Louis Stevenson. Colonel Brandon William Court had given it to my father during the war as a token of friendship. I read this book over and over and came to know it inside out. I would have no argument against the light he shed on our lives. In his eyes a gentle heavenly smile sparkled when he said, "You are a book worm, Guddi."

In May 1964, when Indian Prime Minister Jawaharlal Nehru died, Lal Bahadur Shastri took over as the new Prime Minister. Lal Bahadur initiated a meeting held in Tashkent in the USSR to create permanent settlement between India and Pakistan. The day after the meeting, Lal Bahadur Shastri suddenly died of heart attack. Indira Gandhi served as Prime Minister until India held the next elections. She won the election in 1967 and became the first woman ever elected to lead a democracy. My father had a few more years to serve in the BSF before his retirement.

JUNE 67. I could hear the shutters of the iron gate of our house sliding to one side, the footsteps approaching up the stairs, whispering sounds, like winds in a desert, followed by laughter. Then the key turned in the door leading to the small lounge on the first floor. The lights were switched on and the whispers turned into talking. Oh, yes I could recognise those voices anywhere, particularly, in that city where I spend some of my youthful years. Our three-story house was the only one in the street that had a balcony on both sides and a rooftop where we could sleep at night in the summer time.

Cuddled up in between the piles of magazines, books, papers and crayons, I sat counting minutes, waiting for you to come down from the roof top, holding my breath in fear that, again, you would find me here by myself writing poetry, doing sketches and dreaming. That wasn't allowed.

The whole scenario ran in front of my wide-open eyes. You standing there with your frowning brow, raised finger and thundering words. I always took risks of disobeying your norms and orders. I preferred to face your anger and loved the confrontation. The energy of two women, one domineering, the other one trying to be free of that dominance. You must have heard them coming upstairs too, mother.

I could imagine you lying in your bed, awake, waiting for Amar to return home safe from one of his late night outings. Soon there would be the clattering of pots and pans, the irresistible smell of stuffed Parathas, soaked with pure ghee, filling the night with their delicious aroma. I could smell the cardamom from strong brewed tea as it entered my nostrils.

"And what are you doing at this hour of the night, Miss Mariam?"
Amar peeped through the door to the large lounge, intruding upon my tranquillity. Now that was not my real name, but knowing how much I hated my own name, Amar would tease me with this one he had invented. His words used to force me to bite my tongue. Closing my eyes, shutting my ears, I could hear an angry voice from within my heart, saying, "Look I am not Mariam, a weak, delicate girl at your services, but a grown up woman of twenty". A 'midnight firecracker' triggered off at the time of Independence. Born in the middle of racial, religious and communal wars, having the antidote to resist them was not a disadvantage. You had your particular reason to hate wars, Mother. You hated the long wait. You hated your husband departing from you time after time.

I had my reasons for detesting old traditions. You know I used to make fun of all the old values and religious hypocrisy. Amar knew that and yet he chose to name me Mariam. Only in your imagination, darling brother, I wanted to tell him.

They were always together, Amar and his friends: Ash, Deep and Jay. Jeans, sporty T-shirts, fashionable trainers and thick steel bracelets. They would all look alike. Ash was taller than both Deep and Jay and was clean-shaven with short hair. He did not have a girl friend and oh how I fancied him, but it was Deep who I came to admire and yearn for. Medium height Deep had a nicely trimmed beard and a thin moustache. He wore a turban, which suited him handsomely. Jay was short, stout and his big muscles made him look like a wrestler. According to Amar, Jay was in love with a girl from his village but she was from another caste and he was not allowed to marry her. They always met when she came to visit her brother who lived in our town.

I used to go through Amar's diary in order to find any trace of his secret girl friend. In my teenage innocence I believed he did not have one, and it was not until later that I discovered he had a girl friend in Simla where he used to teach. I must have been a very naughty girl of eighteen to invade his privacy. According to my own belief, I just wanted to help him. I wouldn't mind him getting married to a girl of his choosing. I was even ready to defend him, mother, if the occasion ever arose. But things never came to light. It was just one of those secrets buried deep down under the thick proud layers of Amar's chest and mine of course.

I wonder if he ever knew how I dared to snoop into his privacy. I worshipped him for everything he did. He was not only my brother, but also my idol. He replaced my father who was always away from home. He was very brave. Being the eldest son of a father serving in the army, he was not in the least afraid of getting involved in the Naxalbari, the landless peasant's movement of Punjab. I could not discuss everything with him. I just admired him for his courage. What I hated most about our relationship was that all he ever wanted from me was trivial favours, like mending and hand washing his delicate sportswear. He would never talk openly to me, as I was his 'little' sister. The age gap stretched between us like a river. If I dared cross it on the clay boat of my courage, I could drown. There was this gender, a rotten egg of taboos poisoning my rebellious spirit. I was left with no other choice but to obey and respect.

I would much rather have argued, demonstrated and discussed with him. I used those energies to fight with you whenever you raised your voice in protest against him, mother. The more this age gap between Amar and I deepened, the closer the tie between my brother Jake and I grew. He was five years my junior and I got closer to him as well as deeper into the world of words and the fantasy of travel to unknown destinations.

Unlike the other girls of my age who would wear the traditional shalwar, kurta, silk saris, bindis, painting their nails, I chose to wear jeans, tops or any clothes I felt comfortable in. I sometimes bought cloth of my choice to design and stitch my own shalwar and kurta. I remember your treasure, a shining black trunk, where you kept, amongst other things, the clothes from your dowry. A long black velvet shalwar I picked up to be made into a jacket with collars and a long zip by a tailor in town. Jake had his eyes on the stuff for a long time. But it wouldn't fit his tall muscular body. I would wear it with my jeans and go to town on my bicycle to show off. I would have those broad collars standing up in a true Elvis style.

Now when I come to think of Jake, I have fond memories of this sophisticated young man who wanted to be the Bruce Lee of Punjab. When he was as young as two, the sight of his own running nose would make him shriek with disgust. He hated flies, cockroaches, dust and bird droppings. Later he went to weight training, karate and swimming. He succeeded in developing a well-toned body and was considered very handsome. All the young girls in the neighbourhood would stand in front of their porches in the evenings as he walked out of our house in his tight fitted T-shirt and designer jeans to go to his karate classes. He used to buy the 'Phantom' magazine in English for us to read and was much more liberal in his views of how the girls should behave than Amar.

"You should be wearing more suitable clothes, Svera?" Amar would often complain. Giving half an ear, I would silently listen, thinking about how many notions of suitability would be imposed upon me in the future. Suitable manners. Suitable talking. Suitable husband? The list would be never ending and although I didn't say a word to oppose him, as soon as he was out of my territory I would do just as I pleased. Sitting in our first lounge, face to face with Amar, I could hear Ash, Deep and Jay talk in very low voices. Their words rustled against the silence of the night like the soft waves on Sukhna Lake. At times, a fist would fall on the table like the tail of a dolphin slapping the water. I was curious to know about that rage they displayed. But I was not allowed to explore their mutinous domain. I decided to pack up my stuff, when I heard Deep, entering the room.

"Don't you think we are taking a risk, to wait so long? Our comrades are in jails. We have to strike now, or else..." Deep spoke to Amar as he entered the room. He stopped when he saw me in the room and changed his conversation.

"Oh, Ms. Artist is still awake. Let's see what you have been up to?" he said.

And, without my consent, he took some of the papers from the pile. They were portraits of Lenin, Ho Chi Minh, LuMumba and the famous freedom fighter, Udham Singh, who came to England on a heroic mission to seek vengeance on the murderer General Dyer. I watched his face with my pulsating heart as he looked at me with his big oval eyes. Actually the colour of his eyes were slightly blue. They reminded me of the clear glossy surface of Sukhna Lake. I was attracted to Deep and his blue eyes imagining myself to be the Madhu Bala singing this track in the film called Mr. and Mrs 55, one of the romantic movies of the 70's. "Nile aasmani, bujho to yeh naina babu kis ke liye hein. Nile asmani." Your sky blue eyes, take a guess who they belong to, lover. I purposely denied the age gap between us. I was a wading bird in the shallow water of this romance.

He was as handsome as the tenth Sikh Guru Gobind Singh, who fought against the Moguls from the North. Deep was fighting against the landlords who oppressed the peasants of the Punjab. I also compared him with Bhagat Singh the young revolutionary, who fought against British Imperialism and was hanged together with his two comrades. That night when he looked at my drawings, I saw his expression change like a chameleon.

"This girl surely has some talent. Why don't you let her enter the Art College," he suggested to Amar who was standing near the window with his arms folded on his broad chest.

I knew his thoughts were wandering over the vast fields of our village where he had spent most of his childhood and youth. Carrying the rest of my paintings and writing under my arm, I left the room to go and help you in the kitchen. You had already prepared the meal for your 'boys'.
"May I also have a cup, Mum?" I pleaded, while you got started with your usual lecture of not to drink tea in the night and not to spend too much time downstairs and not to use all that electricity.

A fine silky web hung around me for ages, choking, demoralising and suffocating. What I was allowed was merely to carry out my duty to bring the big wooden tray stacked with cups, plates, tea flask, parathas, salad and mango chutney to serve them and then come back to you for cleaning up. After performing the boring rituals, I returned to the kitchen with a pinch of sour taste, which stayed, beneath my clenched teeth like a silent protest for some years. You had already gone to sit beside them. You had the privilege, to listen to their secrets, to nurture their needs. I perfectly accepted your right to do so.

Maybe you didn't even notice that I loved and admired those boys as much as you did? Why didn't you, Mum? It was your affection they needed when they came home to you, hungry, tired and sometimes disillusioned. I was just a teenage girl, to serve, to listen and to obey. Excluded from discussion and actions, I sought escape into my imaginative world of words. Amar's friends finally went home and you and Amar had gone upstairs to sleep after giving me instructions not to stay up too long. Wrapped up on the sofa within a shawl of thoughts, a note pad in my lap like a holy book, I listened to the soft melody of Krishna's flute in the silence of the night.

I was Radha, a yogin yearning for my lover, forming verses. This was my holy temple, a space, only I owned, my solitude. Chanting my poetry, I was going to stay there and say anything I wanted, through my words.

Fireflies fluttering amongst the broad leaves of the pipal tree in the courtyard made perpetual moving shadows through the curtains. There were millions of stars, weighing down from above the sky like white Jasmine bushes. I could almost smell, touch them. I was carried away together with the summer breeze, on a soft, gentle yet strong journey of words, which sounded like magical chimes blowing the sirens of freedom in my heart.

I fancied myself being close to Deep, but this fancy never turned into reality. I imagined myself sitting beside him, looking into his blue eyes reciting my long poem about Laila Khalid, the Palestinian female freedom fighter.

But that was just a dream, an entranced, young Radha yearning to be wooed by a handsome young noble warrior, like Krishna, fighting for truth, justice and equality. I sat in my room for a long time listening to the sounds of my heart. Envisaging the clear, soft Sukhna Lake lapping over us like poetry, like dancing fireflies. Shining brightly for him, but ultimately destined to disappear into the night.

CHAPTER 4
March, The Month Of Love

A Bulbul is resting in the mirage of a pipal tree singing a sonnet, the call for her mate. Holi, the festival of colours has started today. Everywhere, people are drenched with splashes of colours and the ritual dance of lovers to mark the immortal love of Krishna for Radha is igniting the streets of the Punjab.

Another popular legend behind Holi festival is that long ago there was the King of Asuras (demons) named, Hiranyakasipu. His brother was slain by Vishnu, the preserver and protector of the universe for terrorising gods and goddesses. Hiranyakasipu wanted to destroy Vishnu and keep other gods in heaven subdued. He began to perform severe penances and meditation. He had wished his death be not caused by man or beast, with a weapon or without a weapon, during day or night, indoors or outdoors, on earth or in the sky. He wished to be granted the undisputable lordship over the material world. While he was occupied, the Gods destroyed his palace. Hiranyakasipu's queen who was pregnant was sent by the gods to Sage Nara's hermitage to learn about religion and the glory of Vishnu. The child within her Prahlad, too absorbed all knowledge. Hiranyakasipu brought his wife back to his city where Prahlad was born. He declared, "there is none stronger than I. I shall be worshipped as the lord of three worlds." Prahlad meanwhile was growing up. His father asked Prahlad, "Son tell me what you think is the best thing in life'? Prahlad replied: "To renounce the world and seek refuge in Vishnu". Hiranyakasipu laughed. Then he called his son's teacher, saying: "Guard him closely. Don't let him out of your sight. The followers of Vishnu are secretly influencing him." After some months, Prahlad's teacher sent Prahlad to meet his father. His father asked him: "What have you learnt?" Prahlad said: "I have learnt that the most worthwhile occupation for anyone is to worship Lord Vishnu." Hiranyakasipu was very angry. The wicked king ordered his soldiers to kill Prahlad. The soldiers started to attack Prahlad when he was meditating. Their weapons could not touch him. Mighty elephants could not trample him. He was pushed off a cliff and was unharmed. The demon Holika, the wicked aunt of Prahlad, was immune to fire, captured prince Prahlad and entered a fire furnace. Prince Prahlad was safe and was not burnt at all. Prahlad was sent to his teacher to try again. This time, the teacher tried to get Prahlad interested in means for acquiring wealth and physical pleasures. But Prahlad said, "How can the pursuit of physical pleasure and wealth bring happiness? It will only lead to envy and anger?"

The teacher eventually gave up, when Prahlad told his father that Vishnu is the soul of all created beings and is present everywhere. Hiranyakasipu roared, "Where is Vishnu? If he is everywhere why is he not in this Pillar? If he is not there then I shall cut off your head with my sword. Let Vishnu protect you." As the demon god was striking the pillar with his sword, Lord Vishnu, in the form of Nara-simha (nara, means man, simha, means lion) emerged from the Pillar. His look was neither beast nor man. Narasimha caught Hiranyakasipu and it was the twilight hour, carried him to the threshold of the courtroom which was neither indoors nor outdoors and while holding him on his lap, killed him. Prahlad was installed on the throne and he rules wisely and well for many years. The legend goes that before Holika was burnt to ashes, she begged for Prahlad's forgiveness and the prince forgave her and announced that her name would be remembered once a year. The significance of the festival is to mark the burning of self-conceit, selfishness, greed, hatred, infect all the undesirable demonic tendencies, thoughts and behaviour. The victory of righteous forces over demonic forces. To start off the festival, preparations are made on the eve of Holi to burn huge bonfires to ward off evil spirits.

People and children are singing on the streets, smearing each other with Gulab- the bright coloured powder and splashing coloured water. After playing Holi with my family, I am soaked with coloured water. Stung by a yearning of love, I take my bike and go for a long lonely ride, feeling the colours of joy thrust into each pore of my impulses.

Here I was, a young Svera, drawing aspirations from the superstars of the Indian movies. There was Madhubala, with her wine dripping eyes, sensual lips, bursting with desire, strolling on the banks of a river, singing, for her lover. Mala Sinha, dreaming, yielding, crying, laughing. Nutan, the dramatic Kathleen Hepburn of the Indian movies who would silently listen to the melodious voice of Sunil Dutt, "Jalte hein jis ke liye, teri aankhon ke diye..." The words I have found for you my love make the flicker in your eyes glow. Nutan would be tempted by such sentiments and still rebel against the norms. Just like Svera did.

In retrospect, the majestic building of the Art College, where I had enrolled myself acting on Deep's advice to my brother, represented independence to a certain extent. I was not merely sitting, tied to a chair, as a helpless victim and waiting for somebody to come and set me free. I was trying to break the strings of boundaries, limits and norms. Something was turning me inside out. I felt the pain. It was the longing for a Jaddoo, a miracle. That's what I needed, a Jadoo.

I was impatient. I was sentimental. I expressed these impulses through writing. I was not sure that what I wrote was publishable. I did not care. Sometimes I wrote for hours, and threw it all in the bin. I felt alone both in my writing and in my heart.

The sun as sharp as Holi colours representing energy, life and joy, smoothly fell down onto the still waters of Sukhna Lake, touching his muscular, bare legs as he sat on the sand. His feet soaked in the lukewarm water. His dark penetrating eyes with long lashes were huge and translucent, reflected purple in his drowsy eyes. A crinkled white shirt hung on his body, half-buttoned, showing his delicate brown hairy chest. An open notebook waiting to be explored, poised patiently on his lap. One hand, holding a pen, resting on the chin, the other one holding a half-burnt cigarette. Looking across the clear blue waters over to the other side of the lake, he was lost within himself.

The flawless summer breeze ruffled his shoulder-length hair. For an instant he looked like the ghost of Shakespeare, about to create Romeo and Juliet in the solitary atmosphere of an eastern lake. I hadn't in fact seen a portrait of the famous poet in his twenties, but in the young, vulnerable, imagination of Svera, he was a tall, dark, romantic and handsome man. To be so close to imagination turning into reality was quite a shock. My eyes lingered on him as I stepped down from my bike to settle on the bench behind him to wait and watch. A leaf slid slowly down on the surface of Sukhna Lake and a flock of restless grey sparrows swirled. Stirred by these soft sounds, he turned his face to look at the sky. He noticed me and was baffled.

"I'm sorry, I did not see you. Have you been sitting here watching me?" he asked, frowning.

"Oh, no, not for long. I suppose you were in the middle of your creative meditation. I thought my presence might disrupt it."

I was looking directly in his big eyes but I wasn't intimidated by him.

"You won't believe it if I told you what I came here for. I came to spend some time with my sweetheart," he said, avoiding my stare, smiling shyly.

He took a small pouch from his pocket and crumpled some brown resin on the palm of his hand.

"This is what I call true bliss. The total freedom from all the other illusions. Freedom of mind, yaar (sweetheart)."

He started rolling the substance into thin white paper.

"Freedom? Where? I wouldn't mind having some of it." I said.

"It's here in my pocket. Meet my sweetheart, darling. This is Ms Freedom. Marijuana. I won't share her with anybody, but you can try her."

"Freedom in your pocket?"

I looked into his poppy eyes. The large lids falling to caress his cheekbones, lazily as the flower hanging about on a windless sultry day. I had only heard about the stuff and I knew that it was some kind of dangerous drug, but I didn't really understand how it could make people see or feel freedom. One thing I knew was that it was bad stuff. I did not know what to say to him, since I did not know him well enough. Seeing me reluctant he tried to spice up the conversation.

"My name is Jaz. I write poetry when I inhale this magic stuff into my soul and get high. And your name is...?"

He tried to keep his eyelids open, staring at me nervously. Of course I remembered his name. I had read some of his poems in a monthly magazine. Amar had once mentioned that Ash had a brother who was a well-known poet. I did not know the writer of very strong political themes was so young, handsome and smoked marijuana.

"I'm Svera. Svera Jang."

"Hmmm. Jang. Whose Jang are you fighting then, Sve...ra. Very inspiring name indeed for such a girl like you. Svera... the dawn? Awakening..." He inhaled the stuff slowly and stretched himself like a lazy cat.

"My body could use some of that awakening Svera. But not just now. Can I ask you to join me in my venture into the struggling world of political prisoners? First it was my brother. And now they have taken my best friend. Just because he wrote words they couldn't digest. Bastards. Huh, how I hate the cops. I have spent hours sitting here by myself. Thinking why? Why him? You, Ms. Svera, arrived just in time. I could do some awakening with your dawn."

He nearly seduced me with his angelic eyes and offering of this marijuana.

I wanted to taste the sweet wine of his black berry eyes., but refused to take up his offer.

I managed to say, "Actually, why don't we take a walk. I have to get back to my college soon."

There were very few people on the lake and the sky was already turning crimson. Soon the sun would bid farewell to its earthly pleasures. Soon the fireflies would come out, creating Jadoo over Sukhna Lake, perhaps to bring the miracle in my life. He slipped his hand into mine and was ready to follow me on the road.

"It's O.K with me. What do you say about going to Soho's for a cup of coffee?"

We started walking towards the town centre, him holding my hand, my bike and my attention. The road looked deserted, only the fractured rays of sunshine scattered like broken mirages of light and shadow. We walked past the government administration office, an ant hill skyscraper with a constant flow of well dressed men and women, proud but poorly paid worker ants, administrative slaves of the nine to five routine engulfed in the vastness of the ant hill. The broad tarmac road was glazed with a faded gleam as the late evening sun soaked our feet.

The face of the young man beside me stretched beyond horizons, mysterious, sad, agitated with the system. Lost again in his own secretive world, he looked very slender and elegant. A touch of glow seeped through my skin, as he looked at me with desirous eyes. I wanted to get to know him. I wanted to cross his frontiers.

"I know where I have seen you before. It was the Russian book exhibition at the university. You were there with your brother, Amar. Ash once introduced me to him in one of their meetings. But I didn't know he was hiding a young pretty sister in his house."
I ruminated on this suggestive compliment.

"You are being kind. I had heard about this handsome, talented Shakespeare who was Ash's 'little' brother, but I did not know he would be at my disposal so soon. It is my pleasure to meet you, Jaz."
I took his long thin hand into mine in gratitude and to feel his warmth. I felt his humid fingers melting and was wondering why Amar hadn't introduced me to him. I realised Amar could see the danger.

"So, you are an artist, Svera, studying in the famous Art College of our honourable city? I assume you draw handsome models. Dressed or undressed? You can tell me all your secrets, girl!"
He laughed, with a flicker of devilish nature in his eyes. We were now sitting in a fashionable air-conditioned cafe of our beautiful town. Chandigarh, the capital of the Punjab where I spent my precious volatile teen years.

"What's wrong sweetheart? Don't be cross, I am only joking," he moaned, softly caressing my face with his eyes. They were shining, piercing and mocking. I felt the urge to hurt him. I knew he had an affair with Ash's wife while Ash was in jail. My mother had told me of this.

"You sleep with your sister-in-law, don't you?"
I lashed at him with these words. His light brown face twitched in pain and turned paler than a crescent moon. He let my hand go and rolled another cigarette. I found myself remorseful for teasing him so harshly.

I never believed those rumours anyway. It wasn't me. It was the devil inside me speaking. I wanted to retreat and say something soothing, even romantic. Something to make him forget the pain. But I was too proud. He was silently smoking.

"Do you always smoke that much?" I tried to break the ice between us.
"In an encounter such as this, I do. I think I will have to see you again. It seems I am doomed forever. Very soon, Svera..." he whispered wearily, and left. I sat and slowly finished my coffee.

The familiar sensation of longing for a miracle kept tingling my mind like the rays of the July sun, playing with my toes, waking me up from my dreams of Jaz on the roof top of your house, mother. It was a while before our liaison was going to start. Finally he arrived, bringing with him his usual mysterious look and a couple of published poems.

"Go and make some tea, Svera. The poor man must be starved."
You commanded as he entered our house. You did not give us enough time to exchange our glances. You were more thrilled to have his visit than I was. Just the way you were with Amar's friends. You liked to be the centre of attention, the queen of their hearts, the Goddess queen mother. I was so jealous. Sitting there, majestically on the big armchair beside him, you started your enquiries. Was his brother soon going to be released? How was his sister-in-law doing? While sulking in discontent, I was preparing the tea steamed with cinnamon, cardamom adding the pinch of my passion.

At last Jaz asked me if I also wrote poetry. Now, this was something frightening to answer. How could I know that what I wrote was poetry? I did not know what to say, but you did, mother.

"Oh, yes. You can always find her sitting with her papers and pens, scribbling at midnight. Go and get your stuff, Svera."
Another command, but how grateful I was that you helped me out of that situation. I wanted to kiss your feet. I never thanked you for that. Can I do it now?

Slowly, the night is dispersing
the crimson light is sculpting itself through the fog
to become the svera – the dawn
Drenched in the aftermath
of her own awakening
The light will soon break through
the fragile tormented earth.

He was reading it. He was holding my written words under his beautiful gaze. A well-known poet, Jazwin Rathaur, giving a touch of scrutiny to my poetry if that's what he thought it was. Breathing and palpitating for his approval, I was set aglow by sensational thoughts.

"This is the problem with our Indian girls. Modesty. 'The crimson light sculptures itself through the fog...' Wow. Why? I mean why are you reluctant? This is indeed quite good what you've got here, Svera. I think it is terrifically good. I could send it straight to Aarsi magazine. I could do it, if I may," he said looking through the black shalwar kameez that I was wearing specifically for the occasion.

"I don't know. It's not that I write a lot. But I have this urge inside me. I want to be a writer," I was embarrassed to find my voice trembling.

"Don't worry too much, just keep writing. You will be a poet one day Svera Jang, you will. I promise you that."
I didn't know why he was so certain about me. But it felt good, to be acknowledged and appreciated and what's more by a writer.

"A motherless kid, this Jaz. Listen Svera, I know you like him a lot. But remember his sister-in-law. She is a smart woman, a flying witch, with her feet on the ground. You'd better watch out. She won't let any other woman come between them. The poor orphan lad."

You tried to wrap a sheet of muslin warning around my young careless spirit. Was it strong enough to protect me? Jaz and I had other plans. Kulu my cousin, a teacher, eighteen years older than me, had warned me as well. She was experienced in love and was nurturing a broken heart, I should have listened to her. But the encounter was inevitable. My desire ruled my heart. Logic was an ugly creature, annoying me with its growling tone.

One day, I found myself knocking at the door of a flat in the student accommodation, sector 14, south of the city. The ghost of Shakespeare once more stood alive in front of my bewildered eyes. Now it was the ravishing smile splashing out of his large oval eyes giving off dangerous signals as I shyly entered into the room.

"Sorry about this mess. I stay here sometimes, when I need solitude for writing," he said, spreading his long delicate arm in a gesture of welcome to the sofa. He was wearing a light blue shirt this time, unbuttoned, exposing his body. He must have done it purposely in order to display muscularity in front of his vulnerable guest.

Does he do that to other women? Does he have many female admirers or maybe even lovers? I sat glued to my seat, a bit puzzled at my own courage, visiting a young man alone on my own. I wasn't so sure who I trusted in the game. Myself, or the guy who happened to be Ash's young brother. You are not allowed to have a relationship with your brother's friend's brother, say the norms. I had packed some of them together with other traditions in a basket and thrown them away in the clear waters of Sukhna Lake, where I first met him. They were already at the bottom, drowned, as revolt is too heavy a stone to float on the surface.

While Jaz was busy preparing a cup of tea for me in the kitchen, my eyes travelled through the small room; a large bookcase, piled with books, magazines and papers, a writing desk with an armchair.

A cassette player playing my favourite song, "Mujhse pehli se muhabbat mere mahboob na maang..." The song written by famous poet Faiz Ahmed faiz, "Do not ask me for that past love." Faiz was awarded Lenin Peace Prize in 1963. Posters, photographs and even an outdated calendar with Madhu Bala, the Marilyn Monroe of the then Indian movies, an extraordinary, ravishing beauty and a damn fine actress on top of that. Then I saw the half empty bottle of Johnny Walker, the Scotch standing on the table, telling me of his other vice. Before I uttered a word, he started, "I couldn't get you out of my thoughts, for a while, Svera. So I have been drinking heavily."

I did not know what to say.

"After reading your poem, I have developed a kind of addiction for you. All this time, while you were absent from my vision, I had to get help from my other sweetheart. I know you are going to be my first."

He was now rolling his notorious stuff, talking in his silky voice. He was pacing across the room, restlessly. To me he was an Indian Romeo and not the youngest tiger of the Naxalbari movement. He did not fight with his claws, but with words. If you saw him on the street with his slender body and flamboyant moods, you wouldn't be able to detect his strong political convictions. Any young girl would die to get close to him. I felt dazed by the dream that was becoming reality.

I sat there, sipping the tea made with his own tender hands. I was digesting the wooing words, like pieces of coconut burfee as they extended from his voluptuous mouth, seductively sweet words, which drew me closer and closer so that every minute seemed like hours of, elicit encounter.

He poured himself a small glass of whisky and sat down close beside me. We did not speak, he just took my hand into his. He was stroking it with his long fingers. He wanted to look deep into my eyes. I was trying to avoid him. He turned my face towards him, holding it with both his hands. For a while he held me there, without saying a word, demanding that I meet his gaze. My eyes were shut trying to resist the truth that I knew I would have to confront at some point, if not now. I wanted to open them but felt too weak. He gently parted a kiss on my closed lids and I felt a trance taking a grip on my mind. The hold was strong and my weakness melted into an everlasting convergence...

I am sitting near the furnace with my eyes shut. It's March the 20th 1999. The muscles of my face twitch while I try to visualise the scene. A vague light flickers and disappears into the darkness and a familiar smell penetrates my senses. It feels so close.

"Jaz?" I say loudly and try to return to reality. Looking at me with their striking blackness are a pair of intense eyes. A bag on his shoulder, crinkled cream shirt, half buttoned, he stands at the door.

"No, it's only me, Ahren. I've just come in. Are you lost again? Oh, it's so unbecoming of you, Miss Jang," he says with a devilish smile.
"This time it was Jaz," I reply, waking up from my trance, hiding my memories in my lap, together with my notebook. I begin to climb the stairs to continue my search...through words.

The hot summer of 1971 departed when the Monsoon breeze abruptly appeared in the horizon, bringing storms where dust would penetrate deviously into each object of life. After the storms, heaving clouds would gather like the expectant desires of a lover, only to burst into thunder and lightning followed by relentless rain which lasted for minutes, hours, days, months. Those were the lazy days when we all stayed in, eating pancakes, sucking delicious ripe mangoes, drinking hot milky tea, looking into the pouring rain, sitting on the veranda, daydreaming.

Then winter appeared on the scene bringing its offering of a mild sunshine, spreading fragrance everywhere. I would wake up in the morning, take a walk on the curling grass, and bathe my thirsty soul in the early dewdrops soon turning into transparent vapours, just like my desires. For hours, I wandered amongst the rose bushes in the courtyard, letting my feet suck the moisture from the grass, playing with the pebbles of Jaz's poetry in my mind. Your stern voice would take me out of the spell mother.

"You have to go to your college, Svera, but please help me in the kitchen first." I would be reminded to attend my chores, shopping, budgeting, mending Amar's clothes, writing letters, etc., etc., etc.

I would rush through my worldly plights to give myself just enough time for reading, writing, forming words for my poetry. The best of all was doing my yoga asnas. Svera Jang was beginning to ripen up beyond the layers of fantasy and reality.

Your nagging was like sweet sour lassi that Uncle Karl sent from the village that I would love and hate to drink. "Here this is good for your health Svera". You would give me a large glass filled with this thick colourless liquid, which I would gulp down my throat standing on the balcony dreaming about a rainbow that appeared now and then in the sky after the rains.

CHAPTER 5
Simla – The Malabar Hill - 1972

The rainbow always appears when the sky drizzles flakes of rain and pieces of sun at the same time. This one is from the past, in another city with a vast blue sky.

"You can't seduce a rainbow Svera. It won't fall into your trap so easily, girl, Seduce me instead" One hand in his pocket, the other one pointing at the sky holding a fat thick brush in his slender fingers, Jabbar, a second year student, who boasts of being 'sickly' in love with me, desperately sought my attention. Whenever there was an occasion, or we happened to be alone, he would try to whistle a romantic tune imitating Vinod Khanna, the hot filmy duniya hunk of the seventies. I must admit I felt the tingle of a sweet pain in my heart for him, but at that time, my eyes were lost in the majestic splendour of nature. I was gazing at a huge dinosaur shaped cloud bursting out showers and light from the orange fireball, creating the prismatic arc over the hill.

"She thinks she can." said Nitu, my class mate.
"Svera is always lost in herself. If you ever listen to her strange stuff about freedom this and freedom that, you'll find yourselves drowned in a lake of boredom."

She continued whispering to the other girls who were busy, giggling, discussing how many golden bangles they owned and how much dowry their parent have been collecting for their wedding. To some, the concept of freedom was having their mother's permission to wear make-up, nail polish, go to the mela with their relatives, attend the temples each Sunday and see Hindi movies. I wasn't particularly nice to Nitu either. I found it horrendously amusing to make fun of her long, red painted nails. "Have you been digging up dead bodies to carve some flesh for your hungry teeth Nitu?" I would tease her in the morning when she entered the class room flashing her newly bought sari with a matching black beaded purse, walking on pointed high heels.

We were sort of friends but we also fought over our favourite things: teachers, boys, clothes, and all of the petty rivalries that make adolescence such a vulnerable time. I remember once we were given an assignment to produce something totally different, creative. Not a painting but a piece of creative art. I drew a tall, delicate Chinese lady feeding chickens. I had seen her in a magazine. She had a long silk dress, a fine hat, with a basket in her hand throwing corn to the mother hen and her chick. I painted her face with watercolours. I made her dress with mustard colour silk cloth and glued it to the corners of the paper so that it ruffled and fell nicely.

Her sleeves were made of black lace. The hat was made of fine straws and black velvet. After painting her hands and placed a tiny straw basket in one of them, real corn glued on, some of which fell down on the beak of a paper hen and her chick. We were marked. I got an A. Neetu stole that piece of art from me and never returned it. Later on I found out she had been flirting with Jabbar who persistently tried to woe me. Sometimes he would ride on his bike all the way from the hostel of the Art College to stand in front of my house looking like a heartbroken Ranjha. Finally when I did not commit myself to his wooing, he gave up on me. I wasn't meant to be with Jabbar. I came to know that Nitu and Jabbar had a short-term relationship, but lost in love to me, he didn't commit himself to Nitu either and became someone else's sweetheart. Writing about Nitu, I came to realise how warm my friendship had been with her, despite the small grievances we had over 'things' and people. Nitu will always remain one of the most treasured items in the box of my memories, but I never forgave her for stealing the gracious Chinese lady I had produced.

It has become a ritual for me to sometimes look in my boxes of files, old newspapers and drawings. Stacked in a brown box, I found a press cutting from 1989 that I was going to use as facts for the bank robbery in Copenhagen. Other interesting newspapers from India popped up from the bunch. One of them carried an article describing Nitu's death. In chapter 11, I was in India with Peter in February 1975, visiting you, mother. You told me that Nitu had graduated and gone to work in Jullundur. I couldn't meet her. After staying in India for three months, I went back to Copenhagen. After some months, you had sent me this newspaper about her death.

Writing about Nitu has taken me back to the many seasons of my growing up in India: the summer, the Monsoon, the autumn, the winter, the spring and the autumn again of my life. In India, in Denmark, in Africa, Bradford, London. I have been living in many cities. Sometimes, it was not of my free will or choice, but by force. When I was a child, it was my dad's job which forced the whole family to move away to another city. Later on, when I got married, it was Peter's wish to pursue his career. Looking at the press cutting, a cold chill ran through my body. "Killed For Love" was the headline of the article in one of the prestigious weekly of India, July 1975.

Nitu was an attractive and independent young woman of 25 when she was offered a job as an Arts & Crafts Teacher in a school in Jullundur. She was sad to leave her family but happy for the offer of a job she had so desperately wanted. Her lodging was arranged in the house of Mr. Suri, a friend of her father. In the beginning she felt happy, but soon Mr. Suri's ways began to irritate her. She left his house to stay at Mr. Chaudry's house where a female colleague with whom Nitu had developed a friendship had lodging. Mr. Suri then sent a telegram to her parents stating:

Your daughter has run away.

Nitu's father, Mr. Sharma left for Jullundur immediately and went straight to Mr. Suri's house. Mr. Suri informed Nitu's father that his daughter was living with a woman of bad reputation. Mr. Sharma asked

Mr. Suri to fetch his daughter. A few minutes later, Mr. Suri returned and said that some 'goondas' were in the woman's house.

"You had better come along to sort things out," he pleaded.

They both arrived at Mr. Chaudry's house. Mr. Suri went inside and came out looking wild and angry. He went back with a stick he had brought with him. Mr. Sharma watched helplessly as he had only one arm, he had lost the other in childhood. A small crowd gathered outside and two policemen brought a quick close to the scene. Mr. Chaudry revealed the bitter truth to Nitu's father that Nitu had developed an intimate relationship with Suri.

On the way back to Chandigarh, Mr. Sharma and his daughter sat side by side in the bus silently. The parents decided that Nitu shouldn't return to Jullundur. Suri was arrested. As soon he was granted bail, he rushed to Chandigarh to tell Mr. Sharma that the police had extracted false information from Nitu that she had been raped. He asked his friend to protect him from the police, Mr. Sharma declined. Both Nitu and her father started getting threatening letters from an apparent stranger. The Inspector General of Police in Chandigarh called Suri for interrogation. Suri denied writing threatening letters. The Sharma family went about their normal lives. Nitu's recent 'sins' had created a rift between herself and her mother, sister and brothers, but the youngest brother stayed loyal to Nitu. One evening, Nitu was playing with her brother in the backyard of their house. All the others were out. About five in the evening, Suri arrived at the house carrying a bag, which contained an album with nude photos of Nitu, some with himself, three contraceptives and a sharp dagger in its sheath. He entered the house from the front and went upstairs.

Nitu who had stayed outside playing with her brother for a long-time felt tired and went inside the house to go upstairs into her room only to find herself in the hands of a madman.

She rushed to the window and tried to jump out but Suri caught her by the hair and pulled back. She screamed. Her brother looked up and saw a leg pulled back over the ledge of the window. He rushed in, grabbed an axe and went up. Suri held her by the hair with his left hand and the dagger in his right. Brother shouted at him to let his sister go. Suri picked up a toy pistol pointing at the frightened brother to warn him.

The action of the drama was incredibly fast. Suri picked up his dagger again threatening to kill her. Nitu struggled free and ran to jump out of the window for a second time, screaming. Suri staggered after her and dragged her again by the hair. Two neighbours came in and asked Suri to let her go. Suri threatened them. They went out, leaving Nitu and her brother to face the situation. Suri pulled her down on the landing and killed her with repeated thrusts of the dagger on her neck and throat. She fell over the edge of the landing, legs down and there she laid on her back, her eyes wide open staring at the roof. Suri rushed back to the room, bolted himself in and shouted "I am going to kill myself."
He went on like this for sometimes, mustering courage. Outside a large crowd had gathered. In the emergency ward, the doctor gave Suri treatment and found his four grievous injuries were self-inflicted. Suri was tried by the Sessions Court and condemned to death. On appeal, the sentence was reduced to life imprisonment...

As I stood in the vague twilight dreaming state on the top of Malabar hill, finding Nitu's rowdy statement to be rude, I had no idea that one day my classmate would meet a horrible death. The noisy remark was a boisterous cloud in contrast to the apple-bloomed Simla city ready to disappear softly in the lap of the silhouetted valley. All the first and second year students were having a break. We had arrived in Simla to find inspiration for our landscape sketching. Absorbed in the heavenly blunder taking place in the sky I just wanted to ignore her existence. "Yes, Nitu, if you are talking about me, I can even lure a moon to fall into my lap at any time if I want to," I said, hurrying away from her and Jabbar.
I took my small mirror to adjust my hair and saw this majestic phenomenon of colours still holding up half the sky.

This one is from my present in a totally changed setting. It could be the same rainbow. A rainbow can travel like a free agent of nature, wherever it finds the sunshine drizzling through the rain. This is a photograph, but the scene would appear to you like a slide from a holiday collection. The binocular lens of the nature created this: silver grey-haired women your age with multi-coloured clothes, laying abreast the thick lush green plantation spread over the caramel coloured soil. Their wrinkled fingers crawl like worker ants on the succulent red fruits snapping them off to fill yellow cane baskets. With my lazy queen ant hands, I am trying hard to catch up, only able to fill my bag with a few big red berries.

It was on one of those rare occasions when the late July afternoon sun humbled down golden threads of its splendorous light, just like Robin Hood from Sherwood Forest would do for the poor earthly creatures. Yes, it was here on the outskirts of this peculiar city, Bradford, England. In this vast field of Strawberries where I had brought twenty five women your age to re-live their pasts, Mum. The year is 1999.
"Hai ni Pammi - I feel one with this golden brown soil. When I was your age back in Roorki, I used to bring a basket full of chapattis for my love who would toil on our land from dawn to dusk."

Gulabo, the old woman with a stick looked up towards the sky as if talking to herself. I wondered whether it was the mild sun, or the memories of bliss from the fields of her village which created flimsy lakes in her eyes. These older women had the 'freedom' to come to a community centre twice a week and I had arranged this trip for them to enjoy picking strawberries, fresh from the fields. Looking through my sunglasses, the reflection in Gulabo's eyes, the myriad coloured dresses, red strawberry in green fields against the blue sky and her grey head wrapped in the pink dupatta anxiously ruffled against the wind. I felt a flamingo craving deep inside my lower belly. I wanted to pluck the rainbow and use it as a rope to skip one step towards the line of telephone masts ornamenting the horizon through which I imagined myself skipping one step backward to where I once saw the rainbow on the Malabar hill at Simla, 1972, with Jabar. Nostalgic memories. I could even hear the sound of Svera skipping in Karl's courtyard singing ek, do, teen, char. I was lost in my past, when Pammi my friend who had come to this trip said in a brisk voice.
"Let's skip, a step forward, one, two, three, four, five."

"No. It's che-six for me," I said.
Let's jump, skipping on the ropes of our own little rainbows.

CHAPTER 6
Through The Looking Glass

Listen Mum, I have a confession to make, but let me catch my breath, and all this skipping backwards and forwards is becoming a bit nostalgic. I want to put my arms around you to feel the glow of your wisdom on my skin, to get close, like real pals, only then I can tell you more about Svera. Who was that girl? What did she do? How? When? Where and Why? Maybe even you didn't know her very well. But you know that she is not the I of now. That young girl, who now seems a stranger to me, was once me. She is trying to whisper a story in my ears. She tries to haunt me, like a ghost. Sometimes, like now, I can hear and even see her walking on a foreign land, a place I might not be able to fit into. She is using me as a tool to project her own voice. We shall let her.

During her rocky transformation into womanhood, Svera was a strong girl. She was filled with contradictions. That's the way she has always been. Changing, inspiring, questioning. She was like a rose with thorns, soft yet solid, caring and firm, strong and vulnerable at the same time. That's why zigzagging her way through these curves in her life she has learnt to survive. On one of those memorable days, I see Svera with a basket full of washing, thud, thud, thud, ek, do, teen, char, climbing the nineteen stairs to the rooftop of your house in Chandigarh. Purple bedding, white towels, peach, blue, turquoise green, pink clothing.

The sun was a orange ball of fire, in the fine blue sky, drizzling hot breeze, spinning in the atmosphere like a huge dryer. There were no shadow, just light and heat. That young man purposely hanging about on the balcony of his house was on the lookout for any vulnerable target for his hot intentions, smiling at our Svera. You with your hawk eyes watched every movement from the balcony downstairs. Thud,

thud, thud, your angry feet climbing the stairs. Svera's ears burning red as your footsteps approaching closer, closer and closer. Oh boy what a spectacular drizzling heat fell from your words, stronger than the sun. The red hot iron bars of your words grilling Svera's palpitating pink piece of flesh in her chest with the sound, dhak, dhak, dhak, dhak.

"Svera, what took you so long, girl? Have you been throwing furtive glances at that munda (young fellow)? I warned you, Svera. Svera...Svera..." Svera angrily wrung the big towel in her hands and then shook it hard with a vigorous movement to take the rest of the water out.

The puddle from the damp clothes lay like a pool of freshly extracted words wrung from a reluctant consciousness.

Words building the barriers of feudal norms, rules that society had created and her Mother, Amar and all the other conformists had imposed upon her. Svera did not want the constraint put upon her by anybody. She just wanted to revel in the sunny spell of her teen years. She wanted to be left on her own, without you, with girls her age. To go out, to flirt with boys. To have the freedom of choices. This realisation of Svera has struck me. It fell into my lap, not like a flash of lightning, but like a rainbow, enlightening me, frightening me too. Aren't you dying to know how it happened? O.K, if you persist so strongly. Here it comes.

It seemed like yesterday, September the 19th. 1999, I drove my nineteen year old daughter to the midland town of Nottingham. "I have to go, Mum. I need to learn to be on my own. I'm fed up with you always being here for me. I want to be with others of my age. I want to have fun. I promise I'll work hard for the next three years. I'll be all right. Think about yourself. You deserve your freedom, as much as I do mine. Remember, I love you very much." A mischievous twinkle appeared in her eyes as she spoke. I didn't want to face the decisive finality of the words she spoke. I kept a brave face, parting from her, hiding my pain.

Driving back, following the curves and bends of the M1 North, I looked at the misty evening, just like my state - foggy and confused. The orange headlights with fast running tracks represented the past. The ceaseless rhythm of the engine reminded me of the present and to concentrate. I was forced to listen to the erratic beat of my heart against the roaring sound of the engine. It was in this ambiguous, strangely hypnotic state that I became aware of a presence on the seat next to me.

"Whoa, you scared me............" I gasped.

I saw a slim girl in jeans and a white cotton top, her hair braided in two plaits, hands folded. She appeared very self-assured. She gazed at me in a lost, vacant way, an other-worldliness written on her face. Wondering how she got into my car I was about to interrogate her when she opened her cute little mouth.

"Hello there. Respect! It's me. I came to see how you are," she whispered softly.
"Who are you," I demanded.
"Don't worry about that. You have turned into such a worrying agony aunt, about this and that, what is important is that I am here to soothe you."
"To soothe me? What do you mean? Who asked you to?" I was annoyed.
"You did, in your dreams and in your heart. But listen, I'm dying to ask you this. How does it feel now, when your own daughter has left you, just the way you left your mother twenty-four years ago. Can I call you Mum?"
She spoke boldly like a clarion call from another time. That bitch is still haunting me. I suddenly realised who I was up against. I was furious.
"How dare you enter into my life like this. Get the hell out of here, girl. Go and play your games elsewhere."
My steering became unsteady as my anger reverberated through the car. She put her hand slightly on the wheel to straighten it up.
"This is going to be fun. But before I go, let's put the record straight. I asked you a question. You don't have to answer. I have come to

demand my freedom. You always drag me out from the past. Let go of me. You have to. For your sake and for mine. Please."

She was whispering, pleading, hissing like wind. I was surprised by her vulnerability. I saw a side to her that I had never experienced before.

"You? Demanding freedom from me? You? Preaching to me about freedom? Can't you see I'm moving forward? You dare pointing fingers at me?" I shouted.

"Calm down, woman. At a time like this, you have to listen to me. I'm doing you a favour. I'm telling you my story. It is because of me that you write. You owe that to me. If I didn't exist, you wouldn't write. Be nice to me," she insisted.

This was the final straw.

"Get out," I shouted, pushing her out through the window with one hand, trying to steady the wheel with the other. Her presence had begun to disturb me. It was a hard push that I gave her, yet she did not fall onto the road, but laughed, floating away like an ethereal being. I could hear an echo in the wind. "I want my freedom, I want my freedom, I want, I wan.. aan... aa... ha, ha, ha".

To tell you the truth, I was shaken by her visit. In my youthful tantrum I realised I had rejected a conciliatory overture from the main composer of my past. But why had she come? For what reason had she chosen this moment? I thought about my daughter. How she would be arranging her new room, meeting new friends. Perhaps meeting a man like Jaz? A searing pain stabbed through my ankle. Yesterday, I had an accident. I tripped over something, fell down, bruising my knees, but it was my ankle that hurt most of all. They say we choose when we have accidents. But who would choose to inflict pain upon themselves like that? The pain that I was feeling at my daughter's departure and my mother's intrusion was worse than any bruise or broken bone that I had suffered before. I turned on the tape to escape this encounter with my past.

"Yesterday, all my troubles seemed so far away... Why, she had to go I don't know she wouldn't say. Oh, yesterday..."

This song used to bug me, this Beatles song. I love it now. Yes, yesterday, it seems so far away. I don't long for yesterday. I turned the tape off, pulled the car over and wept profusely. A deep wail, a long cry came from the very centre, of my belly, waking the serpent – the Kundalini force. All of the players on the stage of my life entering and exiting at the same time. Jaz, you mother, my daughter, my brother, my father, my husband, my lovers..... and Svera. It had all come like a thunderbolt. I barely noticed the tapping on the window and the questioning face of a policeman demanding to know if I required some form of assistance.

Later when I had the time to reflect, I thought about this encounter. This was about three generations: Svera, you the mother and my daughter. I was looking through the binoculars from a distance. It was all about changes. The longing to step out from the shadows of her father, her brothers and you, mother, was not a mere fantasy, not for Svera. She yearned to change her life. Small strategies began to take shape in her mind, strategies which were going to help her to make that change. She knew it was inevitable. Her dream was to cross the borders. The grass on the other side always seemed greener in comparison to the stultifying atmosphere in which she lived. To leave would not be easy, but she had to do it.

CHAPTER 7
The Demon Of Honour

Here, I am, the narrator, sketching out Svera's story in front of you. I trust that you will slowly begin to understand who she is. How fortunate I am to be able to nurture this bond between us as the story unfolds.

The decade of 70's was misty and cold. Cold as a shark in the polar sea. Death was in the air. Not only could you smell it, you could see it on the crossroads of dreams, ideals and revolts for freedom. Meanwhile the Communist party of India aimed to carry on the class struggle and free the land from the clutches of feudal landlords. Indira Gandhi who was the hope of the poor, re-elected herself by campaigning with the slogan "Abolish Poverty." However in 1975, she was found guilty of violating election laws. Later, the Supreme Court of India overturned the conviction. Also, she implemented a voluntary sterilization program to control population growth and her opponents criticized her administration. To secure her power and because of escalating riots, later, she had declared a state of emergency. The rulers 'used' emergency as a shield to exterminate their opponents. Many journalists and political personalities were put behind bars. Blood was streaming from the freedom rainbow to soil the purity of democracy. To stem the Naxalbari movement, hundreds were killed in 'fake' encounters with the police. Deep, whom I had secretly vowed to marry, was killed in a so-called police "confrontation". They killed him in the fields of wheat corn, like a dog. Not that such conflicts have been expunged from the face of this earth. They still lurk, in disguise, anywhere, everywhere, the killing of the innocents, wars, turmoil, disasters. They all take place side by side with the dominance and the brutality of the rulers. Sometimes even wars are 'created'. How else can they create a market for their killer weapons? The gruesome thing is that sometimes in this vicious game they happen to kill their own people, by mistake. A warplane can drop bombs on the wrong side of the front line, just by mistake - friendly fire.

We were living on the edge of manipulation, injustice, disharmony, in a society that was supposed to be democratic. The foundations of our beliefs were shaken. Amar was the one who led the way, to cross the barriers, when he went to settle in Europe, leaving us in the middle of racial tensions and conflicts. Amar had the freedom, I didn't. My town in the province of Punjab, notorious for guarding the frontiers from the North where I spent most of my teen years was not merely the breadbasket of the country but a peculiar anomaly, garnished with spicy contradictions. The place that helped me thrive intellectually was the university. The famous Sukhana Lake, where I met Jaz, my love. You plucked the thorns of my youth, Mum. Every year on my birthday, you gave me a red rose to nurture. You reminded me that you cared. I was becoming a disillusioned traveller in the city of my dreams. A handful of schools, colleges and spectacular architectural buildings represented light. I saw in this city blooming with science, technology and advancement there was a curious division of upper and middle classes, travelling gypsies, workers from the Himalayan Mountains and rickshaw drivers. In this jungle of anarchism, Holy cows were the most respectable guests. The low caste people were considered worse than cow shit by our honourable Hindus.

Do you think I am talking in metaphors? Me, the narrator? No way. I, your eldest son's little sister, Svera, the so-called Mariam, was about to take off on a journey in an everlasting search for her life. But it was only in the summer of 1973 when my dreams materialised. Before they did, Karma had to play its own little game of light and shadow with my innocent heart. The bitch of a sister-in-law dropped a poisonous bomb of her jealousy in our house.
"Your daughter should stop meeting Jaz. I won't allow any such nonsense from her."
It was a dangerous concoction. Jaz was sitting there with me, his eyes glued to the floor as he held his poetry book in his hand, spellbound helplessly by the iron chains of his duty. He had to protect her honour. He had to protect his brother's woman while he was imprisoned. A mere paper tiger, so he seemed to me at that time. I saw the pain of insult in your shrewd eyes. You were speechless. You watched them leave your house. I watched my love go.

"She has degraded my honour. I warned you, Svera," you said.
Honour, honour, honour. What is this, Honour? A ruthless creature? A cannibal? Or a word with its cruel intention ready to tame people into slavery? What about my love, my heart? That night I couldn't sleep. The demon of honour turned into a whirlwind in the sky making me toss and turn, hissing by my bed. That night I entered the bushes of broken emeralds, bled my inquisitive feet on those translucent shards. I had to let my love go, unwillingly. I wanted to own nothing Mama. You knew that. You taught me that I only needed this magical weapon, courage. When I woke up, I was running a fever. Your pride, your honour had been stepped upon. I felt the dard, the ache, I felt the hurt in my heart. Only a miracle could save me from falling apart. I longed for a miracle, anything. They say if you hope for something intensely enough, it will arrive at your doorstep.

Do you remember, Ma? Maybe you have forgotten. I'll remind you.

The Danes had landed like aliens, into the boisterous lap of a modern city, Chandigarh in the Northern province of Punjab. They had come from their hometown Copenhagen, the capital of Denmark. An adventurous place of goblins, Vikings, the little mermaid in the freezing North Sea, the writer H.C. Anderson with his ugly duckling tales. You must be wondering who these Danes were. How did I happen to meet them? Why me? As if I was supposed to? As if the fate led me to them. Not totally on its own, perhaps. At that time, we are talking about those authentic late 60's golden years - the years of the Beatles with John Lennon's heart-swinging "She loves you yeh yeh yeh!", Mick Jagger rocking the groovy air with a libidinous voice and then Bowie, the cutest of the Nancy boys. In India it was Hare Rama Hare Krishna, Zeenat Aman's first movie and she was the young Indian hippie chick singing on the soul shake down bliss of marijuana, "Dum maro dum, mit jaye gham", let's get stoned to forget our troubles. I had posters on my bookcase of sexy Marlin Brando, Kirk Douglas and Dean Martin.

It was also at a time when street theatre threw its spotlight on the darkest corners of racial conflict and slum dwellings. Performance art had its highest peak. My cousin brother, Rakka, was a performance artist in his free time and a fine actor, who used to act in plays in a theatre company touring the Punjab. He used to work on the famous Bhakra-Nangal dam as a skilled welder. His elder brother was a Senior Engineer. Once he even acted in a play with the famous film actor and peace activist Balraj Sahani. Rakka married a woman his family had chosen for him. He was never happy, but had a beautiful daughter. He at last rebelled against this arranged marriage and left his young bride behind for Denmark.

When Mr. Sahni died, according to his wish, he was wrapped in the flag of the Indian communist party. Millions of workers, peasants, revolutionaries and all the film folks attended his funeral. Well in Denmark, this Rakka used to own a pub right in the centre of Copenhagen where left wing students and activists met for drinks, Bhang and debate. He met Neils, Claus and Rosa, the three Danes who wanted to visit India. Rakka told them about this sister of his, a girl who spoke her mind through poetry, Svera. How could I ever forget the day when they sat on the veranda, absorbing the mild vapours of sunshine, sipping the sweet Darjeeling tea. Svera, the young girl was wearing her favourite jeans with a flannel shirt that her father had given to her at the time of his retirement.

It was a large khaki shirt he wore when he was fighting for his country in Borneo and in Malaysia, fighting for freedom. As she had washed it with the lukewarm water of her desires, It had shrunk to fit her, but the threads of freedom stretched from his soul to hers. Her first encounter with the Europeans was an outlet, a metaphor to achieve her search.

Here I will remind you how you and your brother, the retired military captain Uncle Karl had schemed to take me to a posh photo studio in my town, Chandigarh in the Punjab, the year 1973. Uncle Karl was a very dominant figure in his family of four grown up sons, three daughters in law, wife, and several farm workers who tended to his four mango groves and ten acres of fertile wheat fields. He also owned a large bicycle shop in a small town near his village.

When I now think about this 6 feet tall, sturdy, stubborn man in his seventies, still trying to provoke fear in his own family members as well the other relative and villagers, I am not able to describe how much I, Svera, the young woman despised her uncle whom the whole family admired and respected for helping the Mum, his sister when her husband was away in a camp in Borneo in the second world war. In his eyes, Svera was just a young, disobedient girl who on her occasional visits to the village refused to help her aunt in the kitchen. Instead Svera would silently sneak into his magnificent restricted lounge. In the eyes of the family she would be 'missing' for hours reading unaccountable books, admiring his treasures of paintings, travel documents, carved statues and pieces of armoury from his military service. After his retirement, he had rarely travelled further than two miles from his village to attend to his bicycle business. One spring morning he took the trouble to travel eight miles in a bus to attend to this important business of arranging her niece's wedding to a proper businessman in England. He was dressed in chocolate-brown trousers, a creamed ironed shirt, grey turban with a matching tie and black leather polished shoes. Waving his wooden cane with ivory handle, he stood outside the iron gate of your house announcing his arrival.

All this was happening at a time when you had made up your mind to nail me down to an arranged marriage, mother. Like a papadam with mango chutney before the main course, Uncle Karl had already planned a photograph to be sent to him of a tall, dark and handsome suitable boy who lived in London. It was supposed to be presented to me on the silver platter of expectations. The main dish was a yellow fish curry, too much haldi flashing the Gold Card of his financial status. When he had finished a heavy breakfast cooked by his beloved sister in pure Desi ghee, he announced, with a tinkle of mischief in his eyes, "Well, little girl, you, me and your Mum are going to make this special visit to a photo studio."

No matter how much Svera's rebellious self would have bluntly refused his command, she found no reason to argue and decided to see what happened next. At the same time this peculiar custom of exchanging photographs and consents between two families, of arranging two grown-up people's lives, began to get on her nerves.

Svera, this beautiful, 24 year old woman, sat on a leather sofa, dressed in a pink Shalwar and Kurta made from beautiful shining material, embroidered with black and red silk threads. She anxiously bit her lip in anticipation, staring at an old style camera, perched on top of a tripod. Uncle Karl watched her each movement talking in whisper to his sister, waiting for the photographer to start the shooting.

"I think she would look particularly good if the lighting is pointed from her right. I'm not sure this young photographer knows his trade very well", Uncle Karl suddenly said loudly, twirling his stiff moustaches.

"Stop fussing Karl, he is the same photographer who did your cousins wedding. He took some great photos". Mum said.

"Any man would be so proud to marry this woman", Karl murmured as to himself, producing a photo out of his pocket to Svera.

He then lowered himself in front of his niece and said mysteriously, "Look at this and imagine you are going to marry a Sheherazade from the Vilayat, Svera. You will live like a queen. Aren't you pleased my chicken?"

Shuffling uncomfortably, Svera took an investigative look at the face of a handsome young man in his late twenties who had a nicely trimmed beard, John Travolta hairstyle and was in fact looking like a prince of an Eastern estate, somewhere in the golden Vilayat. She imagined within years her slender and delicate body turning into a plump Indian housewife's depressed portrait with five or six spoiled kids, cooking chapattis every night, living somewhere in the East End of London, driving with her family in a black Mercedes Benz for occasional outings. What about her poetry? Would she ever have those peaceful, serene nights where she could sit alone, lost in her world of words? She looked at the photograph solemnly and sighed while she heard her Mum and Uncle Karl still fussing, talking about her.

"I remember my wedding. I was so proud, Svera. It was a magnificent ceremony, traditional, more traditional than they have now, Karl."

"I will arrange this one properly, you will see. I have already ordered the necklace. It is beautiful - and the cards, they are traditional, braided with real silver. Only the best for my little Svera."

"Were they expensive?"

"Don't talk to me about money, sister, I have also ordered seven crates of Johnny Walker Whiskey."

"I have arranged for all the dhals."

"On my farm, I have already 200 chickens, ready and waiting to be slaughtered. I have been feeding them like the bankers in New Delhi. And the yoghurt - gallons of it."

"Oh, Svera, my little chicken, my daughter, you are so lucky."

"The photographer will soon be here. Quickly, we must arrange her hair."

"Come on Svera. Move your head."

"I have the comb."

"Svera do as you are told."

Oh my God! Svera suddenly realised what she was up against. If she didn't refuse now, she would be doomed forever, like a chipmunk in a golden cage. How could she choose? Just like that from a 6 by 7 inch coloured photo, or shall we call it an advert? What sort of a choice was it that they had put her through? How could she let a stranger suddenly own her life as if she was a piece of land, an ornament, or a sweet dish like the notorious Ras-malai yaar, sitting amongst other sweeties in a halwai's glass cabinet, ready to be snatched by greedy customers. They must be having pretty sweet teeth, rotten ones. She didn't even want to know. She was so frightened by the thought of being possessed. Oh no, she was not that type of a sweet, readily available to be eaten, inch-by-inch, by her hungry owner. Not her, the Svera who was searching for an escape from all that. Svera who liked to fight her own Jang even if it meant she had to bleed, even if she had to chose between refusing her parents or being controlled by some stranger.

She took another good look at the handsome prince in the photograph and sighed, not this Svera, mate, you have to find a nice obedient wife for yourself.
"Stop it you two. Uncle Karl, Mum, I don't want to marry a man from a photograph. I don't want to spend the rest of my life with a man from a list!"
She stormed out of the studio, without looking back at the shocked faces of her Mum and Uncle Karl.

So, the arrival of the Danes into my life was just the little miracle, the Jaddo that I had wished for. The notorious Danes, came and a plan to fly away from that messy affair started to materialise. Denmark it was going to be. My next destination and destiny for many years to come.

By saying this, with all due respect to you, I do not mean that I wanted to revolt against you. But it was a small coup d'état against traditions. Nobody else would have changed them for me. I was overwhelmed at the prospect of leaving. I wanted change. I wanted light - to be able to see for myself, in the light of reality. Everything else was changing within me. Movement, that's what I wanted, constant displacement, not inertia. I wanted to choose for myself, and not something that my family, you, Mother or Uncle Karl wanted me to chose.

The danger of being static was lurking near my restless feet. Once in my childhood, I had this nightmare or more like a vision. It was the ghost of a huge monkey who would sit at the far end of my bed, trying to scratch my feet. It was so vivid almost real. I was haunted by that vision for years. I can still remember it. I wanted to be able to walk on my own two feet. I wanted to travel. You wouldn't let me, not alone to far away countries. I understood that, but I needed to leave. In order to achieve my goal and to win my battle, I had to join forces with my younger brother, Jake, to get your approval.

As I write about him once again, a transparent film unfolds in my memories. Let me project it for you. It was 1962. Jake was about ten. I was fifteen. We are getting ready for school. He is wearing navy blue shorts and a milk white shirt with a blue tie. I am wearing a white shalwar, blue shirt and a milk white long scarf. We are getting our school bags ready. We need to sharpen our pencils. There were no sharpeners those days so we steel Amar's shaving blade. We started to argue over who should use it first. Jake wants to snatch it from my right hand. I don't want to let go and hold it tight. My index and middle finger and his left finger get a very deep cut in the struggle. We are both bleeding heavily. We stand there facing each other in horror. The two red streams, gushing down on the floor to make one little puddle, start amusing us. We look at each other, sit down and draw funny shapes in the thick liquid. Suddenly, you appear and seeing the blood you let out a scream. Only then do we feel the hurt and start crying simultaneously with fear. We are both taken to see the family doctor for stitches.

After sharing our blood we kept on sharing our secrets, our schools, bikes, toys and sometimes our clothes. In our teens, even years later when we were grown up, we even shared our lies like when we wanted to buy criminal and thriller fiction from the pawnshops. We had fights over newspapers, sitting on the balcony very early in the morning, waiting for the delivery boy to arrive. We took three newspapers every day, one in English, one in Hindi and the other one in Punjabi. Both wanted to get hold of the English one first. Battles over newspapers did not give us scars but insight into events happening around us. When Amar left for Europe, Jake and I shared responsibilities for looking after you and our little sister. My baby brother, whom I used to protect when we were kids, had grown up to be my pal and my soul mate.

So Jake gave his assurance.
"She's not a fragile doll, you know, but a young woman now. She's responsible for her own life. Let go, Mother, let her go. She deserves to be given a chance. She'll survive."

An orange light was caged behind the iron bars of the stone coal furnace as the stars and the shadows of the blue night flickered away freely on the horizon. Your expression was ensconced in the past and my future was opening up in front of me as you began to cede your consent.

"Oh Jake, I know she'll survive. But she's only a young girl, travelling to far, unknown destinations. I wish...I just wish for her to succeed."
And your voice ebbed away into tears. You walked slowly out of the room retiring to your bedroom, a glow of a moonlight dispersing behind the clouds. I sat there thinking. Maybe you did want me to fulfil my dreams, knowing in your heart, the one that you couldn't fulfil. Your feudal father never gave you consent. He didn't want you to become a schoolteacher. He wanted you to stay home. Obey his domain. Get entangled in the arranged life that he had set out for you. You were not given the choice. You had always resented that. By the time you might have had a secret wish in your heart to let me pursue my dream. Yet you were sad to part with me.

My sister buried her face in my lap, crying.
"Why do you have to leave? You're leaving me alone to fight for myself. You are my support. Because of you I have the freedom. We both have the freedom. You're giving up so much, Svera."
She lifted her head to look into my eyes. Those eyes, filled with pleading and with doubts. Questioning me, searching me. And I suddenly got scared. Somewhere deep inside me, a fear of losing so much crackled like a dangerous fire.

It was for the sake of freedom. Something had to be sacrificed. I was sacrificing the bonds with my family. I was possessed by the illusion of freedom. It was all there, oozing like red-hot lava through my veins. I already enjoyed it in small doses. Love of my family, the freedom of movement, of expression, of travel, the mild equality of genders that you practised, unlike other mothers who ill-treated their daughters. You let me have parties. My friends and even boyfriends, visited me frequently. There was this smart guy I use to bring home for tea - a look-a-like Indian Tom Hanks. We met at evening French classes. We did not like our teacher, who boasted of having gone to Paris to learn French.

"Comment ça va, Mademoiselle? Shall we go for a coffee?" he would ask after the lessons and we would drive down to sector 17 for a chat. All suited and smelling of Old Spice, he was quite a cracker - a defused cracker! He was from a very well off family. We kept our reservations and traditions intact. Not that I tended to lean towards them, but we were both shy. I remained determined not to cross any barriers. It was Kismet that I was destined to leave, although I felt the hurt of parting from you, mother. You were a good mother and a damn good woman. Another mother in your situation would not have allowed her young daughter to travel alone to faraway lands. I went to get my passport.

You cried and placed your hand on my head.
"Take the bracelet of my strength, pearls of wisdom and honesty from your father, rings of love and sincerity from your brothers and sister. On your departure, these are the only jewels I can bestow upon you my daughter. But most of all have faith in yourself."
Holding these riches close to my heart, I left you all. It was June, 1973. Hot, hot, hot.

CHAPTER 8
This Casual Tenderness

"One should cease to care, Svera."

May 19th, 1999 - my kitchen, this house, this benevolent city, this city of cultural extremes where I had met Ahren. He was so self-assured. As he sat there in my kitchen, telling me not to care, the breeze and the light from the window spawned words like showers of illusory rain falling against his silhouette.

Last night I was lying in my bed listening to the sound of the silence, trying to reason with myself. I was confused and was asking myself who I was. The confusion was getting dense and the clarity was withering away, getting messed up in the debris of the past. As the ghosts of memories started to play with my insecurity, I felt at ease. After giving me a dose of comfort, the night slowly eloped, leaving behind her one Cinderella shoe. The shoe of magic. I had to find another one. I was searching in the wilderness, getting tired of my thinking, I was about to sleep when there came a bleak knocking at my door. It was gone midnight. A ghost?

"Are you a...s...leep Miss Jang?" It was Ahren, whispering my name softly. When he needed something or when he was confused, he called me Miss Jang, pretending to be a little boy.

"Nearly, but please come in." I covered my bare body with the naked truth of reasoning, reaching for the heavy quilt.

"I woke up from this dream. You were there with me. I can't really describe it. It was so intense. I was making love to you. I remember. It's weird, don't you think? I might be running a fever. May I?" he asked, and came to sit by my bedside. I placed my hand on his back. I touched his forehead, which was lukewarm, and I felt like a mother who wanted to comfort him. Looking bewildered he sat there for a while and then he bent down to kiss my cheek.

"Here, I have something for you. A present," he said and dropped a folded sheet of soft white paper. It was a poem. He left the room silently, before the musk incenses could spread through words:

This Casual Tenderness

This fragile dangerous man I know
Slides into your arms as wide as the sea
Falls into the ocean of your face
And hides within your desert smile
This fragile dangerous man I know
Loves inside your legs of summer rain
Slips into your heart like a thief
To count the fragments of its love
And steal its contents

Startled, I kept the fragrance close to my heart and slept in the embrace of a peaceful night. What am I searching for? I asked myself. A dim light had slowly begun to peel off layers of shadows and I awoke.

It was an evening when I was exhausted with memories. I rested, dozing, the arms of Morpheus stretched, leading me onto a deep crimson quilt, Ahren lying next to me, resting with his cigarettes, a mere brass ashtray separating us. "Aa ke dard jawan hai", "Come lover, my pain is young", Sunrise Radio pierced the air. The hurt, the dard, was in the singers voice and the dancer Bindu was writhing to relieve her dard, performing the Tandwa in a Hindi film from the 70's. As Ahren looks at me with his half-closed eyes, I can see myself flying away on the wings of fantasies, away to Punjab, to Jaz. I feel the denial in my heart for Ahren. We only abuse each other with this casual tenderness. We impose upon each other our lust and the quest for truth, the love for the quest. He thinks he can undress my soul with his snake eyes. I dress his wounds with my healing. Slowly, he is recovering. He is basking in the sunshine.

"Set me free, Svera. I'm a free spirit. I just came to you for comfort, for compassion. You're a natural healer Miss Jang. Let me lie down in the warmth of your passion, to relax. I want to shut my eyes. I can still see your beautiful face. It reminds me of my own. You are breaking through my darkness. You are a silver lining around my dard. Go and write, woman, write like no one has done before. You have to finish your story. You have this strong weapon, a passion for writing. I'm not your passion. So I won't stay forever. I am a free spirit, remember? Maybe I am a ghost who will soon disperse like mist."

"Who am I to set you free? If you are enslaved in your own illusion, only you can set yourself free".

He looked at me and slowly walked out of the room, leaving an echo behind him. The sound of his voice crashed against the wall like radio waves penetrating layers. Echoes and voices get recorded within walls forming themselves into spirits and ghosts. We give our energy and light to them, so they become alive. We don't share a bed, only the roof over our heads, would you believe, because nobody else does. I don't care if they don't. Ahren has shaken me from a slumber, as I shake him from his, a dream of falling in love again, the pain of facing denial. Should I cease to care, I often ask myself, or should I remind myself not to care. The silence fell upon the room, only to be interrupted by my live thoughts. Now I thank Ahren, for shaking me out of my dream, for dragging me back to reality. Why is this devout reality, called 'truth', so crude, Ahren? Just like the demon of honour. Just like the illusion of love. Yes, love, the illusory rainbow entices me. I am gripped by my dard. You ask me to cease to care. What for Ahren? Jaz? Father? Uncle Karl? Tell me, please. Won't you, please! Oh, please! Mother? You had taught me to care. I couldn't possibly stop. Not now. I kept meditating on the soft rug of your gifted roses. I kept walking on thorns that you tried to take away from my turbulent teen years. Now I keep on nurturing the red roses that you gave me on each of my 24 birthdays.

"Surely, Ahren, a man was never the answer to my search, not even you. I left Jaz, remember? You are so full of yourself, Ahren."

An amusing thought danced around in my room on its tiptoes. I looked outside the window. The crackling orange sky is bending to kiss the windows of enlightenment I sense part of some realisation. In my thoughtfulness, the truth is here somewhere. Roses, thorns and blisters, are shimmering through the light nurturing my soul. I thought of Jaz, a cadaverous rose who left memorable thorns of pain in my palms. I started to gather the blisters to let the healing begin.

I have paddled through another twenty-five years of my life since I left you, Mother, and I still care. You never gave me a clue, mother. Now when the blisters of memories engulf my heart, it hurts. Oh, yes it does. You only told me now that, after I left India, Jaz took to more and more drinking. He came to your house asking for me. But by then I had already married Peter. You kept quiet all those years. You only told me the secret one month before your death. How could you Mum? I am thinking that you've succeeded in protecting your bloody murderous honour. You muted his grief to save my honour.

Where are you now mother? Are you still wandering in the jungle of your honour, keeping the pearl of your culture safe. I keep my hurt, which is turning into soft rose petals - your roses. Sometimes it's my rainbow. Like a traveller it stretches from one continent to another. Wherever I travel, it travels with me. It is the same rainbow. The story of my search heaves with roses, thorns and crystals. The drizzling rain outside and a mirage of the light formed a rainbow when I left that morning to take my dog for a walk in the cemetery. Sometimes, memories are shimmering like a rainbow, like the one with Ahren.

The walk was my daily ritual. I particularly liked taking the dog into the grand private section. It had a Victorian eloquence and domineering garish walls. In this section the wealthy German immigrants had created their own tombs with pillars, Romanesque gates and plinths over 4 metres high. But there was one tomb that I was drawn to every day. Behind its metallic chain barrier and imposing Italian entrance various pots were arranged containing the ashes of the Strauss family. Their names were listed on the impressive tablet in front. Weilham Strauss had lived to be over 90. His wife Alma had lived well into her eighties. Then the children were listed, five in all: Helger, Dora, Heidi, Edith and one son Josef Strauss. I noticed he had died at the age of 35, (1856-1892). I came to Bradford in 1992. One hundred years later.

Returning home, I entered my Victorian house, daydreaming. Jaz, Peter, Ahren. I think about Jaz. Is he alive? Is he still searching for something. Is this all just Maya Jal? Illusion? Did he find what he was searching for? The sound of a song from my stereo interrupted my thoughts of Josef. An echo rose in my mind like a fog. Who is Josef?

Sau baar janam lenge, saa baar fanaa honge
Ai jaane wafaa phir bhi, ham tum naa judaa honge
 (We will be reborn a hundred times. We will die a hundred times
Still we will never part from each other, my love)

My house welcomes me with open arms.

CHAPTER 9
A Temptation

Hi there. It's me seeking your attention. Don't look down upon me. It's my turn to tell you a story. From my vivacious heights, framed in Victorian splendour I confront and withstand all the wicked moods of this city. I see the flickering lights roam like barbarians in a battlefield. Rising up to the sky, perpetually forming demarcations, bouncing back and forth, touching, energising everything, even things like me. You seem not to take any notice of me. You ignore my identity. Let me tell you that I have a soul too. The people who inhabit me give me that vital ingredient of life. Svera did that to me.

"How lovely and inviting it is."
"It's so comfortable in here."
"I could write verses on these walls."
"Simple, elegant, tasteful yet glamorous. I don't believe it's that old."
"Mysterious, sensual, caring."

How often have I heard people making such comments when I play the host. I thrive on such compliments. Svera and I would stand rubbing our hands in gratitude. With twinkles in our eyes we politely welcome our guests. The combination of my pale, vinyl emulsion and her ivory smile did wonders. She wasn't like that some years ago. Neither was I.

I have witnessed many things with my wide-open eyes. Whenever she was going through turmoil, I would get drawn through the transparent walls into her agony. I couldn't bear to keep myself apart. As if I stepped out of my everyday reality, of merely being a house made of stones, plaster and windows, to soothe her. I almost became a human being. I already had ears. Arms were now beginning to form in the shape of plants hanging over the several shelves, Svera had made. I even grew a third eye, the eye of Shiva. I was able to see through and beyond. The only thing I didn't have was a mouth to speak. I felt so helpless. Despite that disability, I learnt to communicate with Svera. You know well that everything in this universe is alive. Trees, stones, forests, animals, water, walls, words, pictures, books, they all have energy of their own. Some people communicate with those things by talking or whispering to them. They might seem lifeless to you. Oh, no Sir, everything is alive. Things decaying become life to other energies. It's the cycle of life. Svera cares about everything. She took good care of me. I started responding. I had to give her something in return. She chucked away everything old. She sort of refurbished me. Old images, mind you, not old songs. I can still hear her favourite track of "Saa baar janaam lenge...." She believes in birth, decay, death, rebirth, Karma and this moment, now.

She keeps on changing all the time. So she replaced the old concepts and values of images and paintings were replaced with the new ones. I especially like the one that is hung on one of my front walls as you enter, on the landing. The black Buddha engulfed by a white female body in an embrace. It is called Enlightenment. A very sensual picture indeed. What a dirty old rogue you must be thinking I am. Don't you ever forget that I have a soul too (winking my right eye). I have seen Svera becoming more alive, full of vigour, sensual even. Over the years, she has blossomed. I know it as well as the others who have known her for many years that her energy was trapped somewhere for many years. One of her admirers came to see her after ten years. He was surprised.

"My God, Svera how you've changed. You look so different, so smart now. More beautiful than ever."

That tall guy was rich, wealthy, conventional and old. He even proposed to her. If she had taken the offer, she would have become a kind of queen. She would have had owned three houses, great wealth and a status. He was a big shot from South Africa and yet he died a peculiar death. Having lovers in so many countries on his travels, he died alone in his mansion. She was very sad to hear of his death. He often visited Svera's family when she lived in Africa. Svera refused his proposal. Later, she became restless. I provided the peace, the harmony and the strength she needed for her struggle. It was the least I could do in return for the care she has shown me. Yes sir, that's what I gave her in return. Now, let me be your tour guide, an usher in the twilight zone of memories.

I'm sure Svera is getting attached to me, though she so often talks about deserting me. Maybe I'm holding her back. Don't think that I can survive without her. One day, a strong man will come to take her away. I will give my permission. I have to let her go. Let's go to the large Gothic cemetery that stands poised on the top of a hill gazing in my direction. I get the vibes of its atrocities, of its towering past. In between the fragments of these, shrouded in patchy fog, Svera often walks.

"Only one of your kind dares to walk in such a doomed place. What are you made of?" Kate, a friend of Svera's who is going through her own painful struggle, commented.
"You are not an average Indian woman. If you can walk in that cemetery, and bring up that devil of a dog, and resist a man like Ahren, you can only be a species from space or an ethereal being," Kate had added.
"Hey, you, what's wrong with you? If Svera finds peace in that majestic cemetery, let her." If I had two lips I would tell that woman off.

I have seen Svera walk on and on, maybe to find herself. She was travelling, as she always does, to somewhere. This woman will never stop. The mist is slowly stepping aside to give way. Ghosts of the past walk with her at times. They have no intention of harming her. They have a duty towards Svera. They are there to tell tales. At first they turned everything upside down and inside out, smashing, destroying, upsetting, tearing things apart in every direction. She was afraid of them. She has slowly learnt to confront her fears and fight them, defeat them. It took a long time for her to learn to do that. Only I know how many times she had faced these devils. Now she only sees them through the fish eye lens of her mind. They walk on tiptoes, as if they are afraid of her. She can hear them rustling, can even touch them. Sometimes they sit beside her bed, in consolation. She is not alone in her grief. They come to tell her stories from the past, then they depart. Everyone and everything is transitory. If things were static they would start to rot. Svera is trying to come to terms with that, to move on for change.

You've already met this guy, Ahren. I must tell you how he came to live with us. After breaking up with Alisha, he was restless. Living with his mother who had a lover annoyed him. Having only one possession in his life, the lust for his girlfriend, he felt loveless. One fine morning the phone rang. My ears itched for gossip. I took great interest in all of Svera's men. Wouldn't you? With your permission, I will step aside, withdraw myself within my secure walls. Still watching. I now hand over to Svera once more. She will tell you the story. Shhh! Listen!

This was a Sunday morning.
"Hey, Svera, what are you doing this afternoon?"
His voice rang like church bells in my ears. After a walk with my dog, I was in the kitchen preparing dough and kneading my thoughts, a cup of Kiwi Passion tea on the table. How should I respond to his call? Should I play the game of "Oh, I'm so busy today, I have to write. I have to visit a friend, do shopping, go to the gym, etc, etc..."
"Nothing special. Just baking rolls with walnuts," I said.
"Ah, I love walnuts. Can I come for a cup of tea?"
Transatlantic words swam across through this cable of communication.
"Yes, go on, why not."

My house was a mess. I hadn't been taking care of this soothing creature for a good week. It was aching for my touch. I usually tended it as if it was a living human being. It was one of those lazy afternoons.

Ahren came at two. I pottered around making sure everything was in its place, cleaning up the kitchen. I fed my dog and filled the thermos with boiling water. The doorbell rang. He stood there with his bicycle.
"I decided to ride. It's such a fine day, isn't it?" He brought his bike inside.

It was his first visit to my house. There was something about him that made me wonder. I can't say it was attraction. Something drew me towards him. I felt myself sliding down the slippery path of dubious attraction. I led him to my lounge. He was clearly impressed.
"Ooh. Such a big comfy room. My Mum's boyfriend, John is hanging around in the house, watching the bloody T.V all the time. I feel suffocated in his company. There's no peace there. But this place is lovely. So you live in this huge house with your daughter... Svera...?"
The pause mingled with the aroma of freshly baked bread rising like an apprehension in my chest. There was an indefinable distance between us as we sat together on the small two-seater sofa.

I was aware of body odour and his distinctive masculinity. Yin and Yang were swirling through the living room like dangerous rivers in a mountainous land.

I was surprised how rapidly I was tempted. I got up and sat on a separate chair. A mixture of disappointment and surprise swept across Ahren's face. I could see he felt rejected. But I sensed he didn't understand the female psyche enough to realise that my physical movement did not mean that it was a physical rejection. Impressed with the house, it was clear he wanted to move in immediately. When I showed him the available room, perched romantically high above the cemetery, he made up his mind. He made brief financial enquiries - how much was the rent, was the price of gas and electricity included, would I cook his favourite curry for him? I knew that he liked my cooking. After the book launch where we had met, he had loudly complimented my special chicken curry with coconut milk, demanding to know who the chef was. I stepped out of the shadows and promised him a recipe that would never fail to satisfy his palette. I digress. The fact is that he moved into my house the very next day. We embarked upon a roller coaster of emotion in which Ahren was an errant child and I the mistress taking him for his first ride with just a toffee in his mouth and his bus fare home. Some memories are like crystals. Transparent, flickering, shedding the dust of light to heal. Others are broken pieces of glass, casting shadows from the past that tries to encircle you in its trap and leaves you with bleeding feet after you've walked through it. Monsoon in India brought storm. Autumn in the West brings storm. The sunlight is short lived but it does occur. There is no consistency in the weather, not in this land.

In the summer of 1995, a storm entered this house like an uninvited guest. The inhabitant of this very city created another one -The Manningham storm. Watch out reader. Storms do not keep track of time, but you could try. Time is nobody's friend.

CHAPTER 10
The Storm In A Tub

"Leave me alone, Svera. I'm trying to relax. I have to gather my energy. It's important to me. Don't try and pull me into your depression, for God's sake woman. Go and write to your mother instead. I can't be bothered with your pettiness."

Sitting in the bubble bath with a newspaper in his hand a glass of whiskey in the other, this was not the first time that Peter had refused to communicate with me. He had done it often. I never got used to it. I wanted a dialogue, to patch up things, to bridge the gap between us. It was widening.

"Peter, I have a right to know. You promised only to stay for a year in Africa. Why won't you come home now?"

He looked up from the soapsuds. His moustache whitened by the foam. Ten years ago our lovemaking was spontaneous and wild. I would have stripped naked and jumped in with him. But now, looking at his portly frame, the very thought repulsed me.

"I'm working in Africa with a meaningful purpose and not for fun, Svera," he said.
"Your problems are nothing, compared to what people go through in Eritrea."
He threw the paper onto the floor and pointed threateningly at me. He sipped his Scotch and slid down in the white foam gulping the noxious liquid. I thought of the stagnant water down in our cellar where both the rooms were flooded. It would need a major act of will to empty it and to dry out the floor to make it habitable again.
"You wanted to be out there," I riposted, "where the real challenge is. We both agreed that you will stay away only for a year. It's been two years now, Peter."
He looked at me with those cow eyes.
"I had no choice..." he wailed.
Something pathetic about the way he spoke provoked a protest. I became furious.
"You said you'd had enough of travelling in Africa."
He seemed taken aback by my vehemence, but he rallied quickly and counter attacked.
"Your manner hasn't changed. Why do you nag me like this? It's upsetting me. Thank God I've got a substitute. I could go mad."
Hatred flashed through his eyes, making me think of the character of Mr. Hyde. He became silent as I stood motionless, staring at him. The word 'substitute' rattled through my brain. It conjured up the image of replacement, rejection...a substitute, a bit on the side? Did Peter really have a bit on the side ... or was it something even more serious?

"So that's why you are so anxious to stay out there," I said in a measured tone.
He raised his body slightly above the now diminishing foam. I glanced at the body I once adored but again I felt revulsion. He went on to another attack.

"Oh, stop feeling sorry for yourself. I haven't got time for such nonsense. Go see your counsellor or your doctor. Fa helvede."

I could see a disturbing sadistic look on his face. A look I had grown to dread. He had become a Jekyll and Hyde in the later years of our marriage, a hidden side of his character, that he had successfully submerged, floated to the surface like a tuna struggling, clumsily harpooned.

"Yes, I have a woman. She is the best fuck in Africa. Do you know anything about African women? Oh, they compare so favourably with Indian women. They will do anything to satisfy a man. I was bored of the same garam masala recipes of yours. Indians are so predictable in their cooking... and their lovemaking... Svera."

At this point he raised a suggestive eyebrow, which was shrouded by the smugness of his face. He pulled the plug out and stood naked in front of me. His penis looked like a shrivelled acorn. How could any African woman be satisfied with that, I thought? But Peter in his Nordic arrogance strolled to the can of deodorant on the shelf and sprayed his armpits, his manhood displayed for a non-existent audience.

"Yes Svera," he reiterated, "Now it's out in the open, yes, the African women are damn good."

He left the bathroom, a trail of soapsuds in his wake.

Oh, Ma! The sight of his contorted face frightened me. The revelation came to me like a poltergeist, moving everything upside down within me. The only thing I could think to do was to die. Then I thought of you. I thought of communicating with you by scribbling down words. I had to write. To you. I had found a shopping list in the dirty trousers that he had left to be washed. Baby bottle, baby oil, wallpaper for the baby room, a breast pump, milk powder, a cot. What baby? It was clearly Peter's hand writing. At first I didn't believe it. I sat down on the floor with a sharp pain in my belly, my heart palpitating. The naked, brutal truth was a razor blade. I felt it pierced through my womb. I was bleeding. I felt like falling into a pit, slowly dying. I felt a sticky substance clinging to my clothes. Red, thick and clotted. Ek, do, teen, char, panch, che, saat dead embryos. Ek- the first time, I remembered, it was Copenhagen. We were leaving for Tanzania. I was pregnant.

"No, we can't have another baby, not in Africa. Go and have an abortion. How would we manage?" he reasoned.

The old nurse at the hospital looked at me in disbelief.

"I can't believe you do this to yourself. This can destroy your womb," she warned.

My husband doesn't want it, I thought silently, frightened a bit at the thought of destroying the life within me. I prayed in silence to be forgiven. Later he wanted more children. So I tried. Seven times. Copenhagen, Tanzania, Copenhagen, Bradford, I tried anywhere, everywhere, many times. He blamed me. How could he? As I sat there remembering, I started to shake. The walls, the whole universe around me started to move, the roof over my head was spinning. I was drunk with pain, holding my stomach tight to shut out the hurtfulness. I wanted to hold onto something living. Your face sailed across the darkened space, Mother. You were touching my sweating forehead, trying to soothe me, as you always did. I remembered, you came to visit me in Tanzania. You had your hand on my head saying, "I told you, beti (daughter), not to try this nonsense. Miscarriages destroy your body. Is it worth it? You have two beautiful daughters. What else do you want woman?"

There were tears in your eyes. The fifteen-centimetre-thick mattress was slowly soaking in a thick fluid from my body. As red as the roses you use to give me. After keeping the embryo for four months in my womb, I was bleeding. Death of a soft petal. Oh God, why this? Why this punishment? Now? It's the summer of 1995. I am sitting on the floor. Holding my belly. The hurt is like a flashback. I look at my hands. Why can't they soothe my pains? What is the outlet from human hurt? Should I slash my arms and let my soul bleed out of my body? My hands? Oh no, how can I? They have held birth, they have held death - a tiny little piece of strong, mighty death. Oh, yes, I shut my eyes tight.

A tiny little dead embryo was taken out from my womb by the African doctor. He just placed it on my open palms like a little rose petal, a little doll, so cold my palms, so warm the flesh.

I had to be flown by helicopter to Kenya. The Tanzanian hospitals had insufficient equipment. The Danish nurse sent with me sat with the pilot, while I bled through this journey amongst the clouds. There was so much light around me. For an instant, I thought, I was in heaven. With a swift hard landing in Kenya, I realised I wasn't. It was the hospital, the little secluded waiting room.
"Before we take you to the operating theatre, I will have to check you and clean you a bit," the tall thin young man with a white coat told me in a cold icy voice.
"But... but I feel so weak doctor," I tried to resist as I saw him wash his hands and come to my side, bend over me to put his naked black shining hand inside my womb. I must have been numb, there was no pain. I stared blankly into the white walls, hearing the laughter of the nurse outside talking to another Danish nurse on duty.

"Det var jo en fantastik tur op i mellem skyeren. Det var so meget lyst," she was laughing and talking about the fantastic trip in the clouds, where there was so much light. My eyes became clouded as I stretched my palms to clear the vision. The doctor was standing near me with something in his hands. He placed it on my stretched palm.

"This is how developed it was. I think it was a boy. It looks almost human, like a doll with flesh, but dead now."
I felt as if I was holding death on my palm. I was beyond pain. I touched the foetus with my other hand to caress, to say good-bye. To let it go. I always do mother, I always do...
"He wants a son, Ma. I am trying. I will stop now, I can't, anymore, I can't."
I wept in your lap when I came back to Tanzania the same evening flown in by the helicopter.

It was still the summer of 1995, as I sat glued to the floor, I could still picture the dead foetus, thinking was he having a child, a son, the one thing that had been denied to me in my union with him. I knew then that he had claimed he had had a brief affair two years earlier. It was the longest brief affair I had ever heard of. I forced myself up again - on my feet, and back to face him. I could not utter a word, but managed to flash the crushed, rectangular piece of paper that hung between my trembling fingers in front of his eyes. A million anguished screams of dead embryos were pasted upon my face, of course invisible to him, as he lifted his cold hard eyes towards me. Under his gaze, I froze. I always had. Whatever Peter did, he still held that power over me. Those hard eyes were once sparkling corals in the shallow Pacific Ocean but now they were immovable rocks in a cold murky lake. He shouted at me; accusing me of snooping into his privacy. And then in his contrary way he denied everything. He said the baby food, baby oil were for a friend. Suddenly the hard veneer melted into childlike vulnerability. Was this Mr. Jekyll or was this Mr. Hyde? I never knew and I never would. I felt there was nothing more I could say. The die had been cast.

We had crossed our own personal Rubicon. The raging torrent between us could never again be traversed. Who had burnt the bridges? Me? Peter? The African woman? Or was it this Kismet, the Karma and the endless procession of a thousand lives born, reborn, dead and dying. Dark clouds gathered, in that late summer afternoon like horses trampling the sky, creating tremors of a storm. The horizon spread wide in front of me as I drove defiantly against the strong wind. I had to recite the mantra for not losing control of my senses. Predictions made in dreams usually come true. Disturbed by the mighty sound of the thunder, I couldn't remember the words from the mantra, you had taught me. Tati wa na lagai.....I tried to form words. My lips were trembling. My hands were shaking. Let me take a deep breath, a very deep one, I told myself. On the rug, poised in Sukhasana, the lotus pose, I gently closed my lids to perform in that yogic asna, to shut off from anger. It was soothing. The signals were sent thrusting into the universe, in the hope of getting the energy, the light back into my soul. We are all made of light and energy, sometimes causing shadows as we move around, living, breathing, waging our own struggles, leaving the traces of our energies, positive and negative onto other living and solid things, even walls of houses where we live.

Shadows are part of light. I was hoping to step out of the shadows into the light again. I was preparing myself to face a new battle, maybe the last one before the dawn, in order to live memories. I have done that many times in my life, letting go to continue. I will do it again and again and again.

As the summer slides into the open arms of the golden autumn chariot, leaves of memories fall on the surface of my Sukhna Lake. I hand-over to the spirit of my house and let 'it' revive the memories. 'It' helps me to do the balancing act. Together we play the game of hopscotch. I remember it so well from my childhood, in Uncle Karl's courtyard. I drew the squares on the floor with a piece of chalk. I had once found a round stone from Uncle's mango grove and kept it in my school bag, jumping on one foot, taking the stone, stepping back and forth, singing ek, do, teen. I would shut out all the other voices, noises, words of predictions and norms, concentrating on my game, balancing on one foot. In this way, I move back and forth from shadows to light. In shadows, I ruminate, think and step forward to light, to move. In this way we can continue the story step by step, picking up the pieces, gathering, demonstrating, showing - the personal becoming impersonal.

The house, the 'it' takes over now.

CHAPTER 11
Ride Down Memory Lane

Carl Peter Jorgensen landed on my doorstep, home for his holidays. It was the summer of 94. He had gone to work in Africa, leaving Svera behind with her two growing daughters.

This is your host, the house, who is going to take you on a ride down memory lane, while Svera performs her Asna. Only I, amongst the two of us, might be able to feel the real pain Svera has gone through. The ectopic pangs against his philanthropic, the Phi, Beta, Kappa. I just came across this word in a dictionary. It fits well here - Beta in Hindi meaning the son. He was so used to breathing that air, the philosophy that guided his life, saving the poor, the wretched of the earth. Something had to fall apart. It happened to be Svera's world. The dead fragments of seven embryos still feed the heart of these painful memories. Svera wanted to give him a Beta, a son. In his late -forties, the philosophical ball he seemingly always had so successfully managed to juggle, had fallen apart on the floor, like a piece of glass.

The Moon. She thought of him whenever she was lit by his beams. He would be shining for her forever, because she believed the planets had promised her a son. This use of metaphors sounds very mysterious, but please do not judge her. It is a philosophy of life. I have witnessed this story. It could apply to anybody else for that matter. So for God's sake, deep down in your heart of hearts, you and I know that it is the story of life - yours, Svera's, her daughter's and everybody's. Daughters are Chandnis, lights, born of the moon and the earth, and they will blossom into maturity to continue the cycle. Svera never believed in the planetary actions and reactions before, only when Ahren touched her life with his philosophical glow, shaking up all her beliefs. It could be the Karma. He was the transient moon that fell into her orbit admitting his fatal attraction. The search is not about another moon, maybe or maybe not, it is about, it is of that.. it is...

Well this is really not up to me to tell you. Svera might be able to explain. Do you think she might? Was her mother able to? Can anyone? What is the meaning of this four-letter word called love in today's world of subjective mechanism. Some forces are trying to play with it in the pretext of democracy or freedom. They temper and dismantle this word, make a show of it, in print and in vision. Only the honest human being could try and find the real meaning. Control your anxiety, at least for a while. Bear with me as well, as with Svera. Please.

I do not believe Svera is waiting for that particular moon. A man, I mean. She is an earth rotating in action, at speed.
The vitality is animation, her life and soul. Svera is one earth, there are others. Like the earth she withstands all changes, the autumn, the winter, the summer, the rain, the storms, the hails. It is the story of her

life. One begins and ends, another one starts, anywhere, anytime, now, tomorrow, the day after.

You might be thinking, what? A house talking in metaphors? You are damn right. You should know that, somehow Svera and I think alike. Sometimes, I step in to help Svera in her search. I am under this obligation. I repeat, do not ask me what Svera is searching for. I know she will continue and one day find what she is looking for. Or maybe she won't. She will still keep on moving. It is not a needle in the haystack of circumstances. It could be as pulsating as a nerve in the heart. The search keeps one moving and changing. Svera is going through changes. Trying hard to shed the old beliefs, to form new ones, to give birth to changes which have always brought her forward in life, like the seasons, they come and go, roll into each other. Change is a pretty damn good phenomenon. Alive and kicking. Kicking by no mean as in violence. I do not like any type of violence. I am the house, so you can close the door on my philosophical jabber and open the other one, your third eye, to peep into this scene.

One day Peter sat watching T.V in his usual old pyjamas. Suddenly he looked at Svera and announced,
"Svera you are fat. I am used to thin people."
He then proceeded to leave the room, his half-eaten meal on the plate.
Of course Svera would have to clean up. Why had he said it - compared to whom? His outburst possessed her mind for weeks. Inwardly she knew whom he was talking about. But she dared not admit it to herself. Now try and imagine this: she is lying beside him in bed silent for a while, puzzled, trying to reason things, questioning, making meanings out of meaningless logic. After a while she hears him say,
"I am living in two different worlds."
After this he continued to snore. His other world was slowly becoming a mystery poised in the travelling encampments of the native tribes of North Africa. It was a world far removed from the grim but paradoxically exotic streets of Bradford. Svera is so naïve. At time I can't stop thinking, the way she puts up with things. Maybe she knows. Maybe she is humble and not meek. This scene is the morning after. As slow and tranquil as a Sunday morning is expected to be, the cemetery

bathing in its own somnolent bliss. The sound of the traffic kept at bay by its decrepit walls.

A flock of magpies circled around to ambush their prey. Children kicked a football on the crescent path. Their impatient laughter and even the milk man ringing my door bell couldn't arouse Peter from his deep sleep, which he worshipped like a Nordic God. "We will all go for an afternoon walk in the forest," he announced as he came down to listen to the short wave radio in the kitchen.

He always listened to the Danish radio. It was another series of pointless news events that irritated Svera. A corrupt politician in Aarhus. A cyclist injured in Jyteborg. The evening lights in Tivoli in Copenhagen. The price increase in tax free Tuborg on the ferry from Malmo. Man steps in a puddle.

The banality of these news items drove Svera to distraction. But Peter clung on to them like a drowning man sinking in a dried up sea of culture lapping the shores of nowhere. He sipped black coffee while Svera cleaned up the detritus of the morning's hearty breakfast. Splatters of sunshine broke through the afternoon gloom. He must be in a pretty good mood, she thought, at least one of us was able to sleep late. So she went outside to clean her car. Then she heard him open the door.
"What the fuck do you think you are up to, woman? Don't you ever understand a fucking thing I tell you?" he bellowed loudly from the doorstep in his shoddy pyjamas and unkempt hair. Out of nowhere the thundering cloud of his voice had interrupted the tranquillity. Bewildered, she looked up at Peter and saw the angst-ridden wrinkles around his eyes spread deep to the brow of his forehead. When he was angry his face resembled the map of a hostile territory. A territory you'd dread to explore. The sky above him was clear blue. Svera felt nervous and looked through the patio fence. The neighbours were on their tiptoes. The net curtains characteristically chinked in such a typical English way.

For an instant, she was anxious about what the neighbours might be thinking. He continued, "Don't you ever stop cleaning that fucking car? Perhaps you would like to sleep with that instead of me. You might derive more sexual pleasure." It was a gratuitously infantile outburst. And yet again he had managed to toss the ball of blame into her court. The children stopped kicking their balls and looked blankly. The magpies disappeared into the gloom of the gathering clouds. A passer by scuttled away self-consciously as if anticipating the scene from the pitched voices behind that wooden fence.

The English never did like washing their dirty linen in public. But Peter was a Dane. He paraded his temper as he paraded his pallid body. That was one thing about Peter. He never really cared what people thought of him. The hatred on Svera's face for that insult was visible. She was one of those people who never wanted others to know what goes on behind closed doors. But I know that she did not like arguments and fights. She would be ashamed and cared about saving her so-called honour. He had dishonoured her before within the sacred union of marriage. Oh, yes, even outside the house, my territory, he had tried to disfigure that honour many times. This time she told him to shut up and not raise his voice. It wasn't dignified.

Wow! She had courage, I thought. Could I think? Me, a mere house? You never know. Strange thing do occur these days. The UFOs, the ghosts, the goblins, the shadows and even the trance. This woman, Svera, was in a constant illusion about shame, honour, dignity. But I also knew that she was waking up slowly. I might be right here. Let's see what happens next.

Peter returned to the house, sulking when Svera told him off. She just caught a glimpse of his now rapidly greying hair. She followed him in. and found him sitting in the lounge watching a football match. He was munching his favourite chocolate chip cookies, the major reason for his rapidly developing paunch. How he moaned about the fact he was now a 36 waist when only a few years ago he was 32. He would spend hours in front of the mirror holding his belly in, throwing his chest out in a forlorn attempt to produce a washboard stomach, playing the role of the young Nordic gigolo he always imagined he was. The trouble is, Peter, you never did realise what a fool you now look and the women never gave you a second glance except for some subservient African peasant women who saw you as a meal ticket to the European life style they read about in magazines that the expatriates brought into their encampments.

"Let's go then. I am through. I'll be ready in five minutes," she told him. The youngest of the daughters, Minna, was upstairs getting ready.

"I knew you would spoil this outing. No wonder you kept cleaning that fucking car!"

He tossed down the biscuit and continued the attack. Again Dr. Jekyll had overwhelmed Mr. Hyde. Svera was merely an innocent laboratory assistant in his experimental nightmares. It was 3.00 in the afternoon. He was furious because he couldn't handle Svera telling him off like that. She settled down on the sofa next to him. She did not plead for forgiveness, as she used to do.

She hoped he would calm down after watching the football match, but she miscalculated the calm before the storm. Before she realised, he suddenly got up and charged towards her like a bull, as if she was a red rag. He gripped her arms violently, shouting in her face, repeating that she always spoiled things. Trying to get him off, she pleaded with him to stop. But he was like a man possessed. He pushed her back as far down on the sofa as possible, sat on her and spat on her face. Again and again and again like a cornered alley cat - wild, furious savage. She pleaded repeatedly for him to let go of her, to release her from his suffocating grip. Eventually he did.

She could contain herself no more.

"You claim to be so radical, Peter. It turns out you were a fascist all along. Marx was just a front. By the time you are sixty, you will be an old fascist, racist, voting for N.D.P. It's a full circle Peter. Young radicals always betray their cause. It's only the strong that stick to the end. It turns out, Peter, you were just too weak. Real men don't hit women." She felt a searing pain across her face. Crouching down on the floor looking for her glasses she tasted blood in her mouth.

She caught a glimpse of Peter's greying hair against the creeping shadows of the late evening. The commentator continued to build up to a crescendo in the match on the T.V. Tears streamed from her eyes as she sat in a chair in the kitchen. I could hear her weeping and calling out for her mother.

You might find it hard to believe, but this is true. I witnessed the whole scenario and my poor self was moody for days. My walls can heave with sullenness.

For the next few weeks no words were exchanged between them. Svera and Peter became like ghosts haunting the same dwelling but from different eras, different times - now. The taste of blood in Svera's mouth could last as long as a memory. The bruising on her face stayed even longer. She told no one. She was tempted to phone her mother, but after a few tries, she gave up. She collected thoughts like she collected bruises, dark thoughts, moulded into words, these words, for mother, and for you. Words, words, words, words. Hurt, pain, damage, psyche, anger, unjust. Why? The bitterness incubated like a deadly virus. I, the house, became like a test tube of emotions in which the virus had every chance to breed. I could not breathe. All sorts of shadows were creeping like hyenas, ready to gulp Svera and me, alive.

Peter was totally unconcerned. It never ceased to amaze her how he could block off emotions and separate himself fully from his own actions. He strolled around the house as if nothing had happened, chewing his biscuits and listening to the non events on the Danish Radio, watching mindless TV in between half hearted jogging in the cemetery. It was as if he had let go not only his marriage but of his entire appearance. Jog, belly wobble, jog, jog, belly wobble.

Svera went to her work, came back, buried herself between my walls and became a static figure without a soul. I wanted her to socialise with the world outside, but being only a house, I felt myself physically handicapped. At that point I was unaware that I had started to possess a soul. I saw a change in Svera. It was the summer of 1994. I wasn't so sure whether she was beginning to break away from the doldrums or it was just a momentary reflection of her stepping out into the light. There is a long way to go girl, I wanted to tell her.

Svera thought of her mother who she had never told anything. She was afraid to tell her of the violence that took place within the four walls of her home. Shame and honour were demons following her everywhere she went. She was afraid of the reaction from her Mum.
"Leave the bastard now. Have you lost your self respect, daughter?"
How right that woman was - nagging maybe, but a wise old witch, my mother.

CHAPTER 12
The Slide Of Time Rolls

It's already the autumn of 1995. I have been awake all this time. I lay awake under the quilt of moonlit nights over my head. I lay awake when the pale sunlight gently peels my outer shell, watching over this city, as I watch over Svera. I have been on my guard all this time. I have to be awake, to watch. I am a house who has a spirit.

The residues of a storm rattled the neon signs of cultural harmony in Bradford. Svera stood in front of this broad window. In the distance, smoke rose from the trouble torn area of Manningham. Her neighbour, Jane, had just parked her silver Porsche on the roadside. She waved at Svera who is lost in her thoughts. They carry her on their wingless shadows back to the distinct day in July when she found the list in Peter's pocket. A storm in the bath had shattered Svera's belief in love. Peace became a rare commodity, both inside my walls and in this city. I could see with my own 'stony' eyes, Sir, that the peace between people had grown thinner and flat like a tire without air, like the layer of ashes, sooty and difficult to shake off. Social workers and defenders of 'culture' and of course the politicians who win votes on the promise of racial harmony had already started to play the game on the debris of these riots. Racism was a word people used and abused in order to achieve his or her own goals. This demon exists in every society, class and hierarchy in the world. On the name of racism, more resources were poured into projects to create equal opportunities, to mobilise these rowdy youths, to "bridge the gap" and bla, bla, bla. Without getting emotional about the issue, we all know who makes the best out of these type of incidents. Let's glaze over some snippets of the 'riots' from the local daily, Telegraph & Argus:

"Bradford, June 9th, 1995, Garfield Avenue. 9.30pm. Two police officers arrive, to sort out trouble. Officers are accused of roughly handling a mother and baby while chasing the youth causing disturbance. Angry crowd gathers, officers draw batons and two more youths are arrested. As scuffles break out police reinforcements arrive. It's 10.30pm and 60 people march on towards the Toller lane police station, demanding release of the youths. Fighting breaks out and another six youths are arrested. Mob of 300 gather on Oak Lane causing full scale rioting, angry youths are on the rampage windows smashed, cars torched at the BMW showroom. Community leaders try to quell the situation without any success. 4am, Saturday Police restore order. Evening, 6.30pm, 100 youths gather, knock down a wall and hurl bricks at the police station. 8pm, mob of 300 congregates in Oak Lane. Police block the street at both ends. Violence erupts. Officers in full riot gear, try to quell the disturbance. 9.15am. Youths move off down Oak Lane towards Manningham Lane and the city centre.

Windows at the Polar Ford dealership, Fleet Car Sales and Bradford Motorcycles, all in Manningham Lane are smashed. 10pm, crowds gather again in Oak Lane. Groups start moving towards city centre smashing windows of several pubs. Midnight, 200 youths gather on White Abbey Road, attacking a Citroen garage and several cars are destroyed. Gangs move on to smash other pubs, shopping centres and a bank The rioters lit tyres and mattresses to make a makeshift barricade against police. Petrol bombs are lobbed, properties destroyed, bricks and stones and milk bottles thrown on passing cars, people arrested, injured. The rampage which started at about 10pm in the evening carries on until 2am the next morning."

Months after the riots in Manningham, you could see evidence on the shop fronts. The city was gripped in the fever of riots. The air inside my boundaries was pregnant with humid. It might give birth to hunch - backed fears, even my walls could feel the threat. I felt choked.

Thank God we live in Undercliffe and not in Manningham. Somehow the dead of the cemetery guard the living in their beds at night. Perhaps if there was a huge cemetery in Manningham, there wouldn't be rioting. She moves away from the window thinking how much she wants to be with Joshili her mother, but she was not with Joshili now. She restlessly returns to the window, as if looking out is breaking out.

Svera's children are sleeping upstairs, safe and tucked in their soft beds. She had cooked parathas for them that evening. They loved to eat them with Danish Lurpak. I could read Svera's thoughts. She was restless, because she was not able to run away. The sky through the broad window made her reflect on the city. Even the magnificent blue magpies seemed like flesh-carrying creatures, moving at a vindictive speed, as the urban night slowly crept in, ready to expose yet more relentlessness. A young man walked his funny little poodle across the street. Svera looked up. Pieces of pale light gathered themselves to make a bow over the crescent as the red candle on the sill flickered to make obscure shadows taking her away in a different time zone. Beyond walls, boundaries and restrictions, insomniac, strolling somewhere else; her mother sitting on the veranda cracking walnuts; the clear milky sky of the Punjab. Svera sits on the floor, tasting the nuts, waiting for the sweet dish of Kheer her mother is going to cook. Her dream-catchers with their beads hung heavily, brushing against her neckline to touch the upper crust of her breasts produce a sweet sour tingle of pain, reminding her of the present, now. Strange how these earrings were a gift from Peter. She remembered the time he presented them to her. He kissed her gently and told her that only death would separate them. He was right in his way. The death of his personality had proved to be the death of their marriage. Huh, she shakes her head and the tinkle from earrings mingles with echoes. For a moment her absent body becomes aware, the soul trying to connect, somewhere with that part of her life, the past, stepping back into shadows, coming out instantaneously, into the light. She had to learn to do it. Finally, she withdrew herself from the window. She longed for a night of hot passion and romance with an anonymous lover. Perhaps George who lived opposite. On lonely evenings she had often imagined meeting him in the corner shop. Their hands clashing as they both went for the same bottle of milk. Then the stumbled apologies, the prolonged eye contact and the casual invitation to her bed. The next day nothing would be seen or known. It would be their secret, protected from the preying eyes of the claustrophobic crescent. Do you think it really happened?

Whenever she had seen George in the street there was an embarrassed nod of the head. The most words they had ever exchanged was when a fire engine was accidentally called. They both remarked how stupid it was that the resources were wasted and the young people today were irresponsible. In reality there was no spark between them, just two transient souls, living in the same neighbourhood, in the same age and time span.

I almost forgot to mention that Peter was leaving for Eritrea that very night. He was obstinate to the end. On his last night in the house he was struggling to finish a series of small reportage called "Letters from Africa". His only ever-published work was in a small left wing newspaper back home in Denmark. He wrote lengthy reports on his development work and was very proud of being published. He dreamt about being the famous author of political reports on development work in Africa. He drew his inspiration from Walter Rodney, Steve Biko. He wanted Svera to fall in love with Mao's red book. Oh, when Peter had something like that going on, everything had to stop. He became a martyr to his own intellectual exertion as if he was the only man who ever had to work to a dead line. Oh Peter, you were so boring, so serious. Did Svera ever see you smile in the last ten years of your marriage, even once?

That night they were going to share the same bed for the final time. She lay down in the huge bed while Peter got prepared for the night, his report finished and his own selfish chores completed.

A poem was flying like a butterfly over the surface of her heart's Sukhna Lake. It was one Svera had written for the old idealistic Peter:

I came to you
From the void of my Eastern
Poetic mysteries
Driven by
The magnetic forces
To give myself up
To gather flowers
In silence from another vacuum
I am wrapped
Around this moment like
A quiver of a wing
As strong as the skin
Of a dream, I shall stay here
To the sparkling music
Baring the mirror dimension
Of its bare banality, to survive
The new is death
Of our old values
And the old
Withers away behind
Obituary lines of this new

You expected of me
To give some of the old values up
Like a Cobra sheds its skin
To gives birth to
A spitting image of
Your reality
I tried.
I am the
Eastern culture
With my Eastern
Poetic mysteries
Drifted away

From the chapel
Of the Old East
Thriving on the pangs
Of my rebellious quest
Ready to give birth
To devilish
New East-West Enthusiasm

Svera is counting. Seconds, minutes, hours, one, two, three. Ek, do, teen, char. Tick tock, tick tock, tick tock. The beat of time is forceful. It stops for nobody, it goes round and round, like a carousel. The wait coiled in the air like a Cobra, the serpent goddess, the symbol of Kundalini force, ready to ignite, any time, this time. She had always waited for Peter. She knew he would be leaving in seven hours, six, five, four, three two, one...She remembers how her mother used to wait for her husband. I wonder if Svera's daughters have seen that yearning in Svera's eyes. They buy flowers, cards and shower her with kisses. They must know she is alone. She now expects Joshili to understand the agony. How can Joshili know? Maybe when Joshili reads these words. Svera wants to communicate with Joshili. To reveal, how her honour was disfigured. So it is a good time for me to retire, to withdraw within my own four walls, into my own void after filling these pages, while Svera is waiting.

Waiting, waiting, waiting...dozing off. Hush babe. Sleep tight. The night is a howling hyena, ready to pounce on its prey, the moon is enticing the earthly creatures, to perform their rituals, Svera shudders for a moment. If I was the man in love with Svera, I would take her in my arms and say sweet something. Sweet nothing, she loves to hear. Good night guys.

Hello. Who's there? It's only me, who is, was, will be. I am the narrator, the creator, as well as the one who jumps into the heads of all the other characters and become them. I. Me. I am yours sincerely, Svera of the present, playing the roles of figures in the cabinet of time and composing the pages to continue the story of the other Svera, in the hope of filling your void. You might imagine things, try to understand them, yourself. Me. Try to put yourself into my shoes or even laugh at me. I want you to. You might be wondering. Huh, what the hell is she talking about? Confusing me? Did I really startle you with my entry like this? I am so sorry. Get used to my style folks. If you can consume Bruce Willis mysterious stuff in "Sixth Sense" and Johnny Depp's monkey business in 'Sleepy Hollow', you can easily digest anything. You are able to. I am enabling you to see through these small black and white words. I am taking control here. This time, I am not in my favourite bedroom, sitting in front of my lighted screen, but while this other Svera is waiting in my bed, I, the narrator, will paddle back on the boat of memories to another time where Svera was the one I am writing about. The month is June, the year, 1973. Let me take you back on this beautiful sailing trip, so you can see when Svera met Peter.

Look here. This is when Svera travelled away from her mother, Joshili., remember? She wore her favourite 70's jeans, plaited hair, beady bracelets with a confident smile. Do you think she was a pretty woman? "You can bet she was, my Mum. Julia Roberts is nothing compared to her."
Minna was saying to her friend, when she showed the family album. I sometimes realise, maybe I haven't changed much and yet I always go on about changes. Maybe I am returning home to my youthful tantrum, wearing my favourite 70's flares with a self assured, mysterious smile, arms full of beaded bracelets have plaited hair. I suppose I am letting the change take place as it wants to submerge into my simple, ordinary, humble life. Now. Here.

Take a look at this scene. This is a photograph. Over there, can you see through my words? A beautiful forest on a lazy Danish summer day. On the beach, in the city, on the pavement, in the pub. Sometimes the summer is a small girl with two pigtails eating an ice cream, smudged all over her face. Other times, it is a middle aged, silly woman, with her mini skirt and high heels, walking as if on the moon, sucking a red lollipop in her cute red lips, attracting the hungry glances of inexperienced males. Can you see Svera through that broad window with the thin pale café curtains?

She is standing in the kitchen humming her favourite tune, "Aaa ke darad jawan hai"; darad, the pain. Why was she always talking about the pain? Was it the parting from you, mother? She is frying Indian parathas for Rosa and Niels.

"I am sorry. I totally forgot to mention it to you Svera. We have invited a very good friend of ours Peter for tea. He is here and would like to say hello to you."

Rosa enters with a thin guy with fluffy black hair, a big nose and deep blue eyes. He wears light blue corduroy trousers with a hole in one of the knees, and has big black wooden shoes on his large feet, extending his warm hand towards me.

"I love exotic food," he says and Svera places her trembling soaked hand into his. His deep blue cavernous eyes hungrily slide over her face and then linger on the steaming pan. Svera can see his comment is genuine. She offers him a chair.

Kia Muskurahat hai, Svera whispers to herself softly in Hindi meaning what a smile. "Kurie mat mari hai," she can hear your hot angry breath on her neck as an erotic tingle vibrates through her body at the sight of this Danish man. Silly girl, are you mad?

"Would you like to taste some parathas?" Svera asks wiping her hands, ready to cast the net over this prized Danish herring.

Who was the prey, may I ask you girl? Svera hears your nagging voice. It's a question she cannot answer mother, so shut up now and use your imagination. Watch and be silent.

"Yes of course, why not"? His smile broadens even more.

He slowly cradles the parathas into his Nordic mouth while stealing a knowing glance in her direction. She cannot refuse to return his glance with its promises, hopes and expectations. He eats one, two, three, four, five six, seven small cute baby parathas, fleshy, stuffed with round potatoes, sizzling, live, steaming. Vapours from Indian tea fill the kitchen with their hot spicy aroma.

"So, is this your first trip to a European country?" he asks.

His gaze is fully concentrated on her eyes.

"Yes, the only thing I knew about Denmark was a little land that produced great dairy products."

"Oh yes, we have plenty of cows here - butter, bacon, milk. I hope it doesn't affect my belly too much!"

He lifts his shirt, challenging her to look at his well-formed midriff. The skin-tight jeans enveloped perfectly. He has well-toned buttocks and washboard stomach. She can't resist.

"I think you have a wonderful figure," Svera says spontaneously.

There is a long meaningful pause and at that moment Svera knows she will embark upon a tremendous adventure from which there would be no turning back. Peter rallies quickly, hiding any vulnerable side.

"Tell me how to say thanks in Punjabi."

"Shukaria. It is the same in Arabic, Shukran," Svera says.

Peter looks at her, slightly perplexed with her knowledge of another language. We weren't all peasant girls in Punjab, Peter, she tells herself.

"So, I had heard, young people here live alone on their own and not with their parents, like they do in India. Do you have family?" She continues.

"Yes. I have a Mum, a brother and two sisters. They don't live in Copenhagen. What about you? Are you single?"

She doesn't answer instantly but simply gives him an enigmatic smile.

"My friends are going on a month's holiday to West Germany. They want to visit the shipyards. I am invited along. Rosa and Niels are going. Would you like to join us?" Peter asks.

"A shipyard, Peter?" The ghost of your voices flapping their wings on my shoulders, raising their eyebrows. Mother? Uncle Karl? Yes you heard it right, a shipyard. Svera wanted to raise the question whether there was more freedom in Germany. The utter banality of the invitation somehow makes him even more intriguing to her. She wore a red top with Lenin's picture printed on it in black and joined the party of people visiting the shipyard.

She could feel Peter's glistening eyes touch her skin, her thighs, her hands, her lips, as they visited one ship after another. On their way to hotel as they walked through the park, Peter made it clear that he wanted to spend some time with her alone. The party of people had booked their rooms and Peter had somehow contrived the situation so that they had a double bed. They saw very few ships that week. Oh Peter paid lip service to his dockyard comrades but his interest was in her. The revolution that was occurring between the sheets in a hotel room proved to be a quick coup and in no time at all it was going to develop into a marriage ceremony.

July 20th, 1973. One month after Svera's arrival. The time is 10 am. Svera is wearing a red dress, borrowed from Rosa. Would you believe there was no time to buy the wedding ring or a decent dress for Svera? The rings were bought later on of course. At that time Peter had no time as he was busy preparing for his trip to Sweden but of course Svera did not know that but found out only later. She eagerly stands in the middle of the city centre in Copenhagen, the Town Hall square, waiting. All of Peter's comrades are there waiting with her. The big clock on the tower strikes 11 am. There is a mad crowd of people, the huge town hall square, crackling voices in the street make thrashing sounds like waves in a sea. Svera is dizzy, drowning. She feels alone amongst strangers. She doesn't seem to recognise anybody. You, her mother, her sister, her brothers, her Daddy - where are they? She wonders where she belongs in this sea of Caucasian faces. She is breathless. For a tiny fraction of a second, she thinks about her lost love Jaz.

Then he emerges from the crowd. Blue suit, slicked back hair, blue shining eyes, he sweeps across the crowd, dashing towards Svera. A bouquet of roses, yellow and red, the symbol of the Vietnamese flags in his hands. She is blinded by thirty-six flashes form Niels's camera, everybody singing, throwing rice on Svera and Peter. The anxiety suddenly draws out of Svera and she feels an incredible tranquillity exude through her entire body. The whole film of thirty six shots is sent to a one-hour print shop. The photos all came out blank, full of transparent nothingness. You, mother, you told Svera that it was a very bad omen. But Svera didn't care.

Please, mother, listen to Svera's story. Can't you see it from her view for once? Were you never in love, yourself? Did you never experience the spontaneous meeting of minds, unsupervised, free, daring? That is what love should be, mother. Not a photograph of some distant man in a foreign city somewhere, faraway.

Now, the slide of life rolls, the scene changes - Peter and Svera, on a bench in a park. After the wedding ceremony in the Town Hall, Peter took Svera to the famous Theme Park, the Tivoli, to celebrate. Svera is eating an ice cream with chocolate flakes. Peter is holding her hand looking into her big brown eyes.
"I will always love you, Peter."
Svera puts her head on his large shoulders and looks at the orange sun disappearing from the sky. They kiss as the carousels circle joyfully behind them.
"I will never in my life deceive you, Svera, I promise you that."
Sincerity flickered through his big blue eyes like fireflies shimmering on the water of Sukhna Lake. The horizon suddenly appears blocked by clouds. Svera shudders for a moment. She shudders, while counting. Seconds, minutes. One, two, three. Ek, do, teen. Tick tock, tick tock, tick tock. If he was the man in love with Svera, he wouldn't...Waiting, wanting, desire, hope, faith...

On the bookshelf before me, as I write about love, faith, hope, deceit, is a cardboard box bound with glossy paper with a picture of bougainvillaea bush with fireflies glowing in the dusk. It contains birthday cards, letters from your Mum, dad, notes, identity cards from Denmark, diplomas, old passports, certificates and Peter's letters. After telling me of his affair, mid June, he went back to Eritrea and wrote a letter dated 25th June 1994 saying that he had finished the relationship with his lover.

"Thinking about it, I damned myself to have started looking for sex and women here in Eritrea. When I met her yesterday, there was nothing left of the initial feeling I had. I simply said to her that we could not meet anymore. She accepted it without a big fuss and took the

cigarettes I had bought for her in the plane. It was so undramatic and emotionless that I cannot help cursing myself. An old fool I have been."
"It is true I have not been very romantic with you for a long time (have I ever?), but I am actually a very emotional person. Look how I have thrown myself at that young girl here in Eritrea. I have a lot of feelings inside me. I am just emotional in a different way than you are, Svera, that is difficult for you to accept. I love life. I love to work for other people. I cannot restrict my feelings to you only. I always mix my commitment to you with rational ideas. But you are little bit like Clara in the "The House of Spirits'. You do not care so much about the rational. You thrive quite happily on 'kaerighed og kildevand' (love and spring water, love in the cottage). I think I am very confused, maybe..."

Confused? Mr. Hyde? Dr Jekyll? I love life, Peter. I just don't play games with someone who is committed, faithful, emotional and as passionate as Svera is. I am not in my favourite bedroom, but in front of my lighted memories, having the company of Joseph's shadow, enabling you to see through words, while Svera is eating an ice cream waiting in anticipation for Peter to tell her that he will never deceive her.

The night has engulfed Tivoli in its arms. Svera, sitting beside Peter, listens to the beat of her heart, listens to Peter's words, trying to understand him.
"The comrades from the group are very dedicated - meetings, mobilising, publishing *Manifest* and so on. We always go away on a weekly seminar together."
"Oh."
"This one trip away from you is important."
His face advances slowly towards her but she moves away and his kiss lands slightly below her ear.

A pause. The Moon is slowly going to expose secrets of the dark shadows on the earth. Svera feels cold, shudders and waits.

"The struggle must continue. People get married. People die. The fight against capitalism is greater than all that. I thought you understood, Svera. The comrades have arranged to stay in a beautiful summerhouse in Sweden. There's a lake nearby, we even train Karate (he made a comical chopping gesture). I am no Bruce Lee, but, so all day we study Marxism. It is very good for us to be together. I have to leave you darling, but only for a week."

"In Sweden? Well you have to tell me when you are going, Peter?"

"That's what I'm doing - telling you. I am going tonight, Svera."

Svera now closely watches his face. His black hair shines like copper in the departing sun and his eyes reflect with a mysterious glow. They seem to widen as he speaks of his comrades. In his big blue eyes, she is trying to find a glimpse of passion, she had once seen in Deep's blue eyes. The honeymoon evening was going to be spent at Rosa's house. This is Rosa's kitchen. Peter found some sausages, his favourite food. He is frying them. Svera is cooking vegetable curry for herself. She never liked sausages. But you will see how she learnt to cook them for him. No shopping for the occasion had been done. However, there is plenty of wine and beer in the fridge. Peter has had a few Carlsberg's, already. He is on his sixth. The strong odour of the beer mingles with the silence of the room. The sound of the cutlery seems too loud. The crystal glasses and the glass bangles on Svera's arm are as soundless as her thoughts. She seems to be in her usual dreaming state as she always was. Can you imagine what she might be thinking? I shall tell you.

A big majestic bed with carved pillars, silk dupattas hanging as canopy. Rose petals spread all over the velvet bedspread and on the floor. A woman wrapped in red sari with golden jewellery sits silently waiting for someone. A man maybe a groom enters the room, lifts her chin up, looks into her eyes.

"Svera, I will make this trip a heaven for both of us," he moans.

"What heaven? Where? This is our wedding night, Peter. You are going to Sweden? Did you just say heaven, Peter?"

Svera is back to reality. Her trance is broken momentarily. It's Peter. It's Rosa's kitchen. It's Peter's trip to Sweden. Svera's hunger has disappeared. They both sit there silently eating their own meals. You must be wondering, like I am, why the hell did she not question him?" Surely the fight against capitalism will continue without Peter's slavish devotion 24 hours a day, seven days a week, 52 weeks a year? Yes, why is that woman not questioning Peter? We see her smile at groom, assuring him that everything will be all right. It's unbelievable, mind you, but true. She is in his territory now. Peter takes a can of beer and opens it. He fills a glass for Svera with Liebfraumilch, Liebfraumilch for thirsty passion, spiced with verses from Mao's red book, were the tokens of love from Peter to Svera.

Let's move in to the lounge and join the others where the tobacco of communist spirit burns interrupted only by the summer breeze which wafts gently through the half opened window. Svera holds tight on to Peter's big sweaty hand. Yes. It hasn't taken long for Peter to perspire as though he was hiding a guilt, a secret. Loneliness crawls over Svera's shoulder like a black widow spider. At last the moment of parting arrives. With one hand he tightens the grip, ready to depart from her, with another he draws her face closer to part a warm passionate kiss on her lips. Bon voyage comrades - Lenin, Marx, Engels and Karl Liebknecht. What wonderful wedding night companions you will prove to be for Peter.

Svera closes the door. She paces up and down from one room to another, switching off all the lights. She lights a candle in her bedroom, sits on her bed and folds her hands in her lap as if in prayer. She thinks about Peter. Outside, noises, lights, people, traffic move with a strange rhythm. The invisible moon in the sky doesn't appear again. She tries to sleep holding on to the pillow. Her body moistens with the heat from Peter's hands. She takes off her bangles and places them on the side table.

I can't continue now. I too get drawn into Svera's agony. I am not supposed to. You understand I am...I am...only the other Svera, have to stop, draw away from one Svera and be the narrator. Be objective. It is not so easy. There's no one telling me to do so, like some psychologist would command me to sit on that chair, be the other Svera and talk of my trauma, then step aside and sit on to another chair and be the other Svera. No, it isn't so easy to step aside, have to sit on my rug to perform the Lotus, my favourite Sukhasana pose, one more time. I can hear the sound of thoughts splash like sea waves, creating ripples in the lake of Svera's memories. I can see the images behind my closed eyes as I find myself gazing at the point between my eyebrows where my 'third eye' is supposed to be awakening, Kundalini. I am thinking of you, mother. Mo...the...er? Are you here with me? Why are you walking away? Are you mad at me? Come back. I can almost touch you, smell you, see you, want you, want you to hold me in your arms like a baby, cradle me, comfort me. Oh, mother not again, watching over me with your wings, you are crying. Don't cry for me mama. Be brave. You have taught me to be. I am so very sorry, mother. I shall retire to my bed. I shall continue dreaming, looking at my past, memories, the flickering silver around clouds. My thoughts will communicate to you in my sleep. You know they can. Thoughts are very real and alive. Sometimes they kick our guts in rage, as if they want an outlet. They can drive us crazy. They grip us like fever. They can't be static. They can travel across boundaries, seas and territories to reach anywhere the other person is/ are. It was the night of the 20th July, 1973, that I slept alone without Peter - the night of my honeymoon.

Next morning, I resisted getting up from bed. It was still early and the dawn had not broken. Looking in the room with my half-opened eyes, I saw a reflection near the long red silk curtains. A young woman in her early twenties, wearing a blue cotton blouse and denim flares, stood watching me. If my daughters saw her now they would perhaps laugh at her 70's clothes, but I was amused by the thought. She looked slim, self conscious and sexy. Before I could figure out who she might be, I saw her lips move.

"Hey you! Feeling lonely? Why don't you phone your Mum? You always do when you feel lonely. Missing Peter? Don't. He will always leave you like this."

"Hey! Who gave you permission to enter my room?" I shouted.

"This is a bad start for us to know each other. It was a bad start girl. You shouldn't have let him. Be positive, give, give, give, this is how you would like to convince yourself, tch...tch...tch...I need to teach you one or two things. Now get up and get dressed, you have some errands to run."

Speaking non-stop, she walked towards me, sat by the bed and started pulling my legs out of the bed.

"Leave me alone!" I shouted, rubbing my sleepy eyes, not knowing who I was talking to. I pushed her creepy hands away. Yawning, I got up from my bed, looked at Peter's photograph with his full mouth and planted a kiss on his lips. My lips felt his warmth. My body had a strange craving. The room felt cold.

"Mao Tse Tung's 'Little Red Book'. You can now study this mindless volume thoroughly for the whole week, my dear. How romantic an experience you would have with Mao's holy hymns."
The voice continues. I turned my face and found her sitting on the window sill with a naughty twinkle in her eyes, in her hand, she held the 'Little Red Book' that Peter had given me as a wedding present.
"What a fool you are, Svera Jang. Whilst you thrive on the illusion of love, your Viking prince has gone away to a bloody Marxist conference with a group of pie-eyed young women and earnest young men," she said.

Oh, my God, I suddenly panicked. My wedding night was gone. I was going to be on my own. Has Peter really gone? It slowly began to sink in. I looked at the mirror and saw a sexy, young woman of 25, who was still available for Peter. Here, now, anywhere he liked.

Peter, Rosa, Niels and all his comrades were gone. I looked at the girl of my own age and looked at Mao's podgy yellow face which was as much of a turn on as the fat, bald guy I met through the dating agency who made a fumbled pass at me in my car outside the Little Chef on our first meeting. But I digress.

What the hell was going on? I take a break from my writing, sit back, stare at the lighted screen, one hand under my chin, leaning on the table, looking at my typed words, thinking back for a long time. I realised that already at that time, I had started to imagine things, spectres, ghosts, spirits and even my own shadows like that one. Not a bad idea to have a companion. I mean myself to be my invisible friend. Children do that when they are left alone in the house. In order to cope with their loneliness, they invent ghosts, creatures from the 'other world', sometimes these creatures take their hands and go for a rough ride, step inside that wall, that mirror and you are inside the other world, like the girl in Poltergeist film.

Me. I. I am an honest, objective narrator who sometimes does the trick of turning around things, pulls the arm of one character, pokes the nose of another, teases the reader, who likes to be in suspense, who likes to be reminded, be twisted. Truth can be subjective, but a card shark can have an ace up his sleeve. You might believe when a lie plays the trick. You might not believe when the truth screams in your face. Well, then my friend, my mother, my lover, my daughter, my Sssssssss...weet fantasy, my truth, my fiction, believe me, Miss Ghost and I did go together to the kiosk in central Copenhagen to buy a copy of the newspaper "Det Fri Aktuelt". We sat in a café and flicked through the pages for jobs. I realised that it was going to be really tough to find a decent job without being able to speak Danish properly. Carefully packed certificates in my suitcase were useless.

"Du skal laere Dansk, kvinde," Miss Ghost irritatingly whispered in my ear again.

"You have to learn Danish woman."

"Tie stille," I shouted at her - keep quiet.

People watched me silently, probably thinking about themselves in my situation. I liked talking to myself. I even do it now. Sometimes I am walking down the street, climbing a spiral staircase of my own illusion, having a conversation with myself and I see someone crossing my path, stretching the hand of friendship, pulling out a tongue to tease, looking at me as if I am mad. I even talk to Josef Strauss in the cemetery. If people don't like it, blow them, stuff them. I don't care what people think anymore. That's the beauty of getting older. They can say what they like. They can think what they like. Are other people so perfect that I should crucify myself for my idiosyncrasies?

"It's enough. Next time, you'd better stay home. I don't want you to tell me things. If you want to come out with me, you will have to behave. I will be the boss."

I decided to be tough with Miss Ghost.

"I wish you could tell Peter that. Tell him off. How could you let him leave you alone by yourself? This is a new city, a new country. Can you manage?" she persisted.

I didn't know what to say to that and continued looking through the job section, ignoring her presence. Peter's letter arrived on 24th July.

"Every day we spend seven/eight hours discussing materialism, dialectics. We read 'On Contradiction', articles of Engels, Marx and Lenin. We want to use Marxism as a method of analysing phenomenon of the world-and a tool that can enable us to better change the world in direction of socialism. The rest of our time we do exercise, swim long distance, we train Karate and shooting the pistol. It's very good for us to be together-we are eight comrades. I personally think it will be good for us to spend time like this together every year. The house is in a forest and is quite deserted. I used to live in the countryside, when I was a child, so being here pleases me."

A whole week dragged by, like a month, but I enjoyed the monkey company of Miss Ghost on my back. I went to a bookshop and bought some basic books on Danish in the hope of becoming integrated, making friends and communicating. If I wanted a nice job I had to learn Danish. When Peter came home, I hid Miss Ghost under my bed.

My very first job in Denmark was to wash dishes in an inner city kindergarten with lively and unruly working-class children. I wasn't really looking forward to that kind of a job you know, but it did help me learn a bit of Danish and naughty working-class slang. One day when Peter came from his work I was sitting by the table with a thermos full of Indian tea for him. Rosa and Niels had not come back from work.

"Pack your things, Svera. We are moving to my place," he commanded.

"What about tea?" I asked.

"Just leave it. I've had enough, having no privacy. I want to be alone with you, Svera. Let's leave now."

With that he left the room.

In fifteen minutes I had packed up and was ready to leave thinking it would be a paradise having a place, totally for us. He unlocked the door to the stairs and kissed me. We walked all the way to the fifth floor of this ragged looking building in the inner city estate with small flats called 'club rooms', suitable for single men. Peter led me into the lounge, which was also his bedroom. There were four wooden beer boxes placed in one corner posing as bookshelves. Peter had a couple of corduroy trousers, some underwear, a few shirts and a second hand leather jacket. Peter would wear the same pair of underwear for days and he only brushed his teeth in the mornings. There was a single bed, a small sofa, a fridge all tucked together in that small lounge. Each floor had six tenants who shared kitchen and toilet facilities with no shower. I was forced into this bad habit of taking a shower once a week in the communal baths in town. I felt dirty and disgusted but there was no other choice. I never described the state of the place where we lived to you, Mum. It was a rough working-class area with piss on the staircase, dog shit on the pavements, garbage, porno shops. You wouldn't have approved of me living there. But I knew it was just a temporary place.

I had found work in a factory, packing spaghetti. At the same time I enrolled myself for Danish classes. I went to my work, came home to grab a sandwich, changed and took the inter city train to my language course three times a week. I came home late in the night and walked all the way up to the fifth floor. Peter would sit up waiting for me to come back. He would always meet me down stairs with a smile thinking I wouldn't be able to climb all those stairs since I was a middle-class 'softie'. In August we were offered a small council flat near Orsteds Park.

Peter went for his one year military training in August. He came home only for holidays. That year there was a fuel crisis and the winter was extraordinary cold. Fuel for our only heater was rationed. I would carry two jerry cans three times a week from the shop.

"You'd better come into my office. There is an emergency phone call for you from the military camp," my boss said to me one day.

Peter had broken his right arm while he was training with a hand grenade. I grabbed my jacket and rushed out to catch an intercity train to the military hospital in Holte town. His arm had already been operated on by the time I arrived. He lay in the bed with his arm wrapped in bandages. He could hardly recognise me. I bent over his pale face and stroked his hair. He spoke slowly with gratitude in his half-closed eyes. He thanked me for being there by his side. I would go to my work, come home, change, pack a thermos of Indian tea and catch a train to Holte to be with Peter every evening. He waited for my visits anxiously and as we sat together drinking tea we would plan our future.

"I would like to learn Punjabi, Svera. After staying some years in Denmark, we shall settle in India. I owe you that and promise we will, Svera. You are a good wife to me," he would say looking into my eyes.

I bought him a Teach Yourself Punjabi book the next day. After a week he wrote me a small love letter in Punjabi. He got discharged from the hospital two weeks after that and when his wound healed he had to go for physiotherapy at a local hospital in Copenhagen. He had already spent nine months in the military camp, they let him go home in May 1974, after the treatment in Holte. At that time we were offered yet another flat from a private housing company - two bedrooms, a spacious lounge, a large kitchen, a toilet and no bath. The luggage from Peter's clubroom hardly filled one of the bedrooms in the new flat.

"We shall never buy things on credit Svera. Once you start it never ends. My Grandpa used to advise me not to be sucked into that vicious circle," Peter warned, as he set the four wooden boxes in the corner of the lounge, whilst I unpacked the few kitchen utensils into the many cupboards of the kitchen.
"I'd hate sleeping on a fancy bed, sitting on a luxurious sofa, owning a colour T.V, driving a fancy car and walking on a soft carpet. These are the symbols of a petit bourgeois, you know," Peter lectured.
I was surprised he ate so well. Those choice cuts of Danish bacon and large knobs of Danish butter on his bread were very bourgeois, I often thought. But I never took issue with him. What Peter said, went. If he

told me the moon had been made of green Danish cheese, I would have believed him. In my eyes Peter was a mini God. He'd flown down from a Nordic heaven, landed in the deepest hills of Punjab and swept me off in his angelic arms to a Northern Valhalla where only heroes lived - fighters, strugglers, leaders. He was grooming me too, I was convinced, for my role in his great struggle. I was on a mission led by Peter, my Guru, my hero, my God. What a naïve Indian middle-class girl I was. Stepping out of the shadows of my brothers and father only to be eclipsed by this false Danish Moon, who didn't even have the decency to practice what he preached.

"I will always be happy with you, Peter," I confirmed, wide-eyed, gazing into his revolutionary eyes.

We found an old fashioned T.V. from an antique shop. But where would we sleep? Where would we dine? Two weeks after we moved into the flat I convinced Peter that we had to do some shopping. Shopping of course was for the petty bourgeois unless Peter's mother was doing it for him. In which case it was a revolutionary task to feed the mouths of the heroic fighters of which Peter of course was one of the most glorious of all. I did need a rug for my bedroom. I did need cutlery, some chairs, a table, a double bed. In the end he gave in and bought a few "essential commodities", as he put it. But having done the necessary shopping, I started pestering him to buy more. Of course we needed them, I reasoned with him. But I got so addicted to those shopping centres that Peter started getting annoyed. He wanted to buy cheap stuff. "But they aren't solid and they don't look good," I would argue. Peter would argue back saying we couldn't afford the expensive stuff. Still I managed to persuade him. What was next on our agenda? I did not know what Peter had in mind. But, I now wanted a small family of my own. "If you are not a member of the Communists' Working Group, you are not supposed to take part in their meetings, even if they are held at your place. Having children would distract your commitment to the party. Party members are not to socialise with others, not even with each other," Peter said, repeating verbatim the party rules by the party's organising committee.

One day however Peter was asked by his party to travel to India to write a report, back to the country of my birth, with my European husband on my arm. So we set off just like that!

CHAPTER 13
The Flicker In Her Eyes

FEBRUARY 1975. The Deluxe 145 of the Indian Transport system did not exactly fit the criteria of a luxurious European bus, but it had tinted jade windows, saffron velvet curtains to match with soft comfortable seats and a screen showing 70's Hindi movie with all their masala ingredients. Mithun Chakraborty, with his karate kid kicks and dirty dancing steps, was a jumping Jack enticing the heroine with her flirtatious eye movements. I found myself drawn into the melodramatic love scene imagining how I would cope with Peter's bold approach on exhibiting gestures of love in public. I felt a sweet craving in my belly to show Peter my town. I found a young man with a pair of naughty black eyes staring at my direction as I rested my jet legged body against Peter's tense shoulders. He was totally absorbed with the dancing sequence of the heroine, singing under the pouring rain with a wet sari explicitly showing her body curves. On this four and a half hour journey from the airport of New Delhi, I slept most of the time, dreaming about the extra ordinary city of Chandigarh, where I had spent my volatile teen years. The French artist, Le Corbusier, designed Chandigarh, the town with my inspiring Sukhna Lake, a town where I had left Jaz, my brother, my sister and you mother.

You, on the wicker chair, a cup of Darjeeling tea, having a pink bed linen sheet on the balcony to dry under the mild February sun made a perfect back drop to my youthful yearnings for change. The vision was trapped so clearly behind my closed eyes that I thought for an instant, I was already there with you, in your strong arms, sobbing with delight. The hospitality, the energy of the house with its fragrance reminded me of the family harmony I once dared to depart from.

The city divided into sectors, open spaces, long distances from one sector to another, created partition between social classes distinct. The urban plan for the city with its intersecting axes was reminiscent of the infinite development of knowledge and social progress. Your house, a three-story building, was only fifteen minutes walk from a modern bus terminal where we were arriving.

The house proudly exuded a middle class glory with two bedrooms, two spacious lounges, a kitchen, a veranda on each side, a decent bath with toilet and a room upstairs on the roof with open space. When we approached the iron gate of the house, I could see your sun tanned arms flexing with anxiety looking across the street, waiting for my arrival. Dad had come to pick us up and it was a Friday afternoon.

"Guddi!"
You crushed me in your strong arms. I smelt the Jasmine warmth of your embrace and buried my face in your soft bosom which once had taken the thorns off my inconsolable youth. Peter clumsily folded his hands to say "Namaste." You took his hands into yours, watching his kind pale, Nordic face and said in Punjabi:
"He could really do with a little sunshine, darling. His skin is as light as my Lux soap!"
"The hot water for your bath is ready. Then we will have lunch. I have prepared the room where you used to sleep with me and Jake, a room only for you and Peter, Svera," my sister said, taking the bags out of our hands.
My father led Peter into the living room.
"Cheers, and welcome to our humble home, Peter. I hope you will find your stay pleasant in our country."
With that he offered Peter a glass of barley beer. I stepped into the living room as the ghosts of the past jumped out of the closets to welcome me. I felt the nostalgic skeletons of memories tightening their grip on my pulsating heart. This was where I had spent minutes, hours, nights, reading, drawing, writing and listening to Amar and his friends talk about the Naxalbari movement. This was here I had to part with Jaz. I could still hear the echo of your voice coming from the kitchen where you then sat frying parathas for the boys.

"Hurry up, Svera. The food is getting cold. Add some salt to this curd. Take this tray to the room now. Don't stay too much in the sun, beti. It's not good for you."

Here you were, wrapped in the spicy aroma of your kitchen, frying parathas and making tea, this time for your precious doll, Guddi and her husband Peter who was already enjoying a cold beer with dad, gossiping about the welfare system of Denmark, Carlsberg, Tivoli and fashionable old ladies. I sneaked upstairs to the roof leaning on the low brick wall around the 24 square feet area, looking 15 meters down at the row of identical houses with courtyards and gates. The street hawkers with their over filled trolleys of fresh fruits and vegetables struggling to get a few rupees more out of the pockets of aggressive fat middle aged house wives. As I was breathing in the psychedelic February foliage, the chirping of the pretty grey sparrows who try and steal chapatti crumbs, the black crows in trees tops, the approaching footsteps of the Holi festival played drums in my imagination. My eyes wandered to search for the teenage Svera's familiar face in the translucent pale tone of winter sun. I saw a young girl hanging clothes on the rooftop of her house, listening to a Hindi film song on the transistor radio. Her Mum is downstairs on the balcony, trying to spot any young men, in the fear that the girl might start flirting with them. Nothing had changed much. I smiled. Chandigarh - harbinger of modernism, development and love. Rendezvous! Closing my eyes, I stepped back to fill myself with aromatic smell coming from your roof top garden of dahlia, rose, mint, fennel and jasmine. I had been away from this paradise for not more than a couple of years and yet it seemed centuries. My soul was thirsty for the smell, colours, sounds and heat. As if I had never left this scene. Denmark seemed like a dream, I had the previous night. Your voice brought memories back when I used to take the washing to hang in the sun. You were calling for me, just the way you used to, just the way I wanted it to. Come back to the present my past, I wished I had been in a time machine of Michael J. Fox.

The curious neighbours had started to line up for their customary visit to see your daughter who had dared to travel alone to a foreign country on her own and had brought home a handsome Viking. I had half expected the line of their suspicious questions, even before I had touched down in the Indian Territory with the British Boeing 747 from Copenhagen. How did I meet my European husband? Did we have any children? How were my in-laws treating me? Were we living in an extended family? Did I get golden jewellery from my mother in law? Was my husband of high cast? What was his job?

Mrs. Dutta, the woman in house number 44 came particularly to enquire whether it was possible for her son to emigrate to Denmark. With a georgette sari wrapped around her broad waist, a shiny stud in her long nose, twelve golden bangles on each of her thick round arms, and a large heavy necklace dangling around her neck like a noose. She was a walking copycat of Indian traditions. Nosy, curious and boisterous she didn't hesitate to question why I was dressed in jeans and t-shirts and wasn't wearing a Bindi on my forehead as a married woman should do. No make-up, no lipstick, no jewellery. What type of a 'girl' was I? While she greedily gulped down the round yellow sweet ladoos with cinnamon tea that I had specially made for her, you looked at me and replied,
"Well, if Svera feels comfortable in those clothes, I don't think it's anybody's bloody business what my daughter wears."
I must admit I didn't expect you to be that blunt, mother. I didn't have the patience to tell her off. I kept silence just out of respect of course.

A group of young men stalked us as we strolled down the streets of the fashionable city centre one afternoon. I watched them out of the corner of my eyes, half-listening to Peter's crooning of love. I heard their taunting remarks about me walking shamelessly with jeans and T-shirt having a foreign lover.
"Who does she think she is, walking with a gora in public," one of them said.
"We ought to teach her a lesson," the other one replied.
I felt the blood gushing towards my eyes. It was good they spoke Punjabi and not English, and waited to see how far they would go. I waited for them to come closer as they continued with their rude remarks. I knew where they were coming from. They were brainwashed

by typical junk Hindi movies often produced by drug barons and were behaving like the screen gundas (ruffians).

"Have you lost all your dignity? Is that how you treat your foreigners in your country? How low can you stoop boys?"
I suddenly turned around to face them. They had left me with no other alternative. I saw the look in their eyes. They were stunned with humiliation of being told off by a woman. They had no idea how to react to my bold rebuke. They stood there like a bunch of pussycats with tails between their legs. They had certainly never come across such a woman who could openly challenge them in broad daylight while other passers-by were listening. A shopkeeper, who had watched the whole scene, came to apologise on their behalf.

"These young men don't have anything else to do than harass normal people, especially women and foreigners. I don't think they had any idea who they were dealing with!"
He spoke Hindustani.
"Thanks. This is my husband," I told him proudly and watched the young hooligans walk away timidly. They looked back before disappearing from our sight with a mixture of suspicion and bitter look in their eyes thinking who the hell is this woman? Where is she coming from?

"Where are you coming from boys? You have no right to harass people like this. You should be ashamed of yourselves."
I hear a meek voice speak, but see a man with soaked clothes shake his head and walk away. He is intimidated, humiliated. And yet he is afraid to speak up, of being labelled as a racist. Those young boys on the pavement of Bradford, with water pistols love to play 'hot guns' splashing mud on decent passers-by. Given the chance, they wouldn't hesitate to turn the virtual realities into real action where lethal weapons create fire havoc.

"Where am I coming from?"
As you can imagine, standing in front of a broad window of this tall house on the hill, watching these boys, I am trying to reason within

myself, asking the question, why in a time like this, the summer of 1995, this town is bleeding with hatred and not accepting the cycle of change? I'm trying to catch myself between the shadows of cultural animosity. Instead of slaughtering cows, I wish people would slaughter prejudice; to bleed its dirty blood so that pure light can gush out like a rainbow. The day is soon going to fade. Here and there stars twinkle their light over this beautiful city. In my confusion, I pray for rain to wash away ignorance, prejudice and racism down the drain. I shake my head and try to grab the dispersing trail of thoughts between the stars. I hear Peter's voice.

"What can I say, having a woman like you beside me? I'm sure I am going to love this town, Svera. I could easily pick up the language. Your Mum is great and you are fantastic."

Peter squeezed my hand. Head held high. Flicker in my eyes. Smile on my lips. I walk with the man who loves me in the middle of my own beautiful town, Chandigarh. Pearls of affection that Peter has garland me with, fall to the ground like rose petals spread before a queen. I fly high on the illusion of love. On a night in February, 1975, I conceived a dream.

The amoeba of curiosity was constantly gnawing the inside of my brain to visit the 'red tiger' of East Bengal. My vision of the city Calcutta was red flags, workers, Marxist government, Sikh taxi drivers, extreme poverty and slim, handsome intellectual men and women speaking soft Bengali. We decided to travel by train and booked ourselves in a Hostel.

Peter was anxious to meet Mr. Sen, the editor of a Marxist magazine 'Frontier'. The office was on the second floor of a building in a dark, narrow and dirty street called Mott Lane. Bengali magazine, 'Darpan', had their office on the first floor. Mr. Sen was out of office but the typist, Mr. Thomas asked us to wait. The office was small and piled up with books and old copies of the Frontier. It was 30 degrees C. I suddenly felt very unwell. Thomas ordered some cold drinks for us while we waited. Mr. Sen finally arrived and we talked for about half an hour. I was still feeling unwell, and Peter asked Mr. Sen if he knew any doctor who could examine me. Mr. Ghosh, the young doctor arrived with half an hour notice, leaving his busy surgery for Mr. Sen's guests. The doctor checked my pulse, and asked me a couple of questions. Then he smiled,

"You are probably pregnant. But come to my clinic, we will have to examine you."

We took a cab to the clinic, which was actually in a small hospital near the city centre. Peter went in to drop off the urine sample. We had to wait for about an hour. We decided to stay and get the result, before going back to the hotel. The waiting room was an open yard with big shady trees where twenty to thirty people sat on the wooden benches. Thin, dark skinned anxious faces of children, women and men swarmed around in the yard like a black sea, all waiting to be treated for their ailments. They spoke Bengali, which sounded like sweet rusgulla in my ears. I closed my eyes and saw a baby girl with thick dark black hair, a little blue wrinkly nose and maybe Peter's blue eyes. I could have held that vision in my mind for hours if Peter hadn't have shaken me with his strong hand.

"Yes, it is positive."

"What!" I shouted.

"You are pregnant, Svera!"

Peter spoke as if in a dream. I could not make out anything from the blank expression on his face, whether he was happy or sad but I did not care. I wanted to have a baby. I knew Peter was not totally convinced of having a baby at that time. It was a taboo, an obstacle to people's active political careers. None of his comrades had children. But there I was pregnant in the red hot town of Calcutta! What could Peter or anybody else do about that?

On our way back, we could not find a cab. We decided to take a rickshaw. This was a means of transportation I would never feel comfortable with coming from the Punjab. Human beings running in front of the carriage pulled these rickshaws. Calcutta was the only city where you found this type of vehicles. We had no choice, then to take this option due to the taxi strike. We commuted through the densely populated city, carried by this strange inhuman transport, we noticed the streets slowly filling up with people carrying red flags. The broad tarmac road was blocked with five kilometres long demonstration of the jute mill workers demanding higher wages and decent housing led by the communist party. Calcutta, the third largest city of India was founded by The East India Company of England in 1690.

Our hotel in Esplanade Street was situated near the city centre, with wide streets and modern houses. People sat outside small restaurants, eating as late as midnight. Young people strolled the streets in groups or in pairs, families having their tea on verandas. Summer nights in Calcutta (Kolkata in Bengali), the capital of West Bengal, like Bombay or Delhi where the majority of people slept in the streets or slums made of scraps and metal with no electricity and running water. People, heat, aroma and smell.

Jasmine flowers, the oil of the traffic and multi-religious voices. Bright shining stars made dense demarcations against the silhouette of this densely populated city. I woke pre-dawn with the feeling of sinking into the dark depth of the room. I felt   something slimy on my leg. I got up from the bed, went to the bathroom and was horrified to see myself bleeding. I came back to my bed, sweating with fear and heat. The fan on the ceiling was making a ghastly rotating shadow on the wall. The thin curtains on the iron barred, shutter less windows, moved with the wind from the fan. Silently, I slid on the bed beside my husband and tears started to roll from my eyes, soaking my nightgown. My wet sari Bollywood scene had turned to sadness!

Peter, who I had thought was deep asleep was stirred with my gentle sobbing and looked bewildered.
"What is the matter, Svera? Why are you crying? Do you miss Punjab? Do you miss your mother?"
When I told him of my bleeding, he took me in his arms, wiped my tears and laid me gently down beside him. We decided to wait for a doctor to check me in the morning. In his arms I felt secure and relieved. I tried to sleep, wrestling with uneasy thoughts whether Peter would turn out to be like his comrades, blaming me for wanting to have this new human being in our family. The dawn broke gently between the white linen sheets and the sooty sky outside. I could hear the sound

of thousands of feet as they eagerly trampled the roads of this spectacular city of contrasts with their yearning to find a destination.

The fast-moving feet of restless travellers. Job-seeking feet of youth, vigorous feet of vegetable hawkers. Suspicious feet of consumers. Restless feet of builders. Yelling feet of pedestrians. Worn out feet of the beggars. Arrogant feet of car drivers. Racing rickshaws, bicycles, taxis, trucks, wooden carts and even animals trotting along in this huge jungle of feet. Peter woke me up. My bleeding had stopped. I stepped down lazily from the comfortable bed on my heavy feet. We walked to a restaurant cafe' for breakfast. The early morning air was dripping with dewdrop expectations. The smell of curries, sweat, sandal tree, garbage and petrol spiced it up. We were now ready to leave this enormous historic city with its famous Howrah Bridge over the River Hooghly.

The station was over-crowded. I notice that in contrast to Bombay city, where irritating beggars would pull your sleeves for some pennies, there were only a few children with their dark black eyes asking for food. As I stood waiting for Peter who had gone away to find out the schedule of our destined train, I saw a one point four meter skeleton walk towards me with the speed of a tortoise. It had two huge black holes popping out of sockets fixed on its head looking like a human face and something very skinny clung to its body. When the creature saw a basket full of colourful fruits in my hands, its limb stretched towards me. I found myself in a state of paranoia and shock as it dragged itself closer, facing my eyes.

It was a skinny girl of eight or nine years old, looking deep inside my eyes, pointing fingers to the shape clung to her chest. I could now clearly see it was a baby boy who seemed asleep with the exhaustion of starvation. Instantaneously, I handed over the whole basket of ripe mangoes, yellow bananas, green grapes, delicious Simla apples and yellow papayas to these hungry children. The girl's eyes stretched even wider and I was scared that the delicate skin around them might burst. She was as shocked as I was and a reflex of gratitude spread like cherry blossom on her baby face. I felt an acute wave of pain in my heart and when Peter returned he found me empty handed and baffled. He took my hand, led me towards the majestic red Indian Express where I sat staring in a vacuum without uttering a word, for a long time. He was busy looking after our luggage, checking in and ordering a cup of hot tea from the tea stall. Unable to describe the beggar girl and her baby brother, I just told Peter that I had given away my food as alms. On that whole journey from Calcutta to Delhi and from Delhi to Punjab, I couldn't eat anything. Peter thought it was due to my pregnancy. After spending three long weeks in this city of Bengali intellectuals, jute workers with their red flag demonstration and Mother Theresa's charity projects, the silhouette of that starving girl became a constant reminder that exploitation is universal. Even now ,as I edit this manuscript for the final time, my eyes well up.

We were back in Chandigarh, in your house with your warm hospitality. With an expert look and an anxious face, you provide me with fantastic food, love and care. The more the day of our departure drew closer, the more I became sad to think that soon I would be back to the crude reality of a foreign welfare state having no family to guide me through this tough period of my motherhood. I didn't feel the need to explain to you that your dainty Svera, whom you had nicknamed Guddi, meaning a doll, was soon going to have a living doll of her own. "You look pale and thin. Everything all right daughter? Any news?"
You had a hint of knowledge in your voice when you asked me this question on my arrival from Calcutta. You knew something important had happened. I knew that you had already guessed. I was pregnant. I did not need to say anything. It was hard for me to tell you in straight words.
"Look, ma, I am pregnant."
You understood my silence and started giving me advice on healthy diet, care and rest. We were already in the middle of May. We decided to spend the last two weeks in the house resting. Peter had developed a ritual of getting up late in to the morning, have his breakfast, and only with a newspaper to cover his eyes, he would lie down on the divan in veranda with his boxer short to have his daily ration of sun bathing. His pale hungry body consumed the extremely hot vapours from the glowing sun. I would sit down near your wicker chair in the shade to watch you prepare vegetables for lunch. Now and then you would

glance at Peter, frown and worry about his pale skin being basked in the heat like roasted chicken. In between the smell of onions, okra, lady fingers, mint and the loud chirping of sparrows, I would get lost in my thoughts of going back to Copenhagen where I would have to rearrange my entire life for the arrival of my baby.

You, the full circled mother earth with your life experience. I, the expectant mother with my limited knowledge on childbirth. It was an unusual relationship that we had nurtured between us. Your tone had changed from the usual prohibiting of don'ts to the one of do's.

"Do drink plenty of milk. Do eat green vegetables, fruits and take a lot of sleep. Doing some light exercise is good for a healthy birth," you would say.

You would make curd every day. It was good for me as well as for Peter to cool him down after his sun-baths. You would even insist I drank a hot glass of milk with almonds that you prepared for me. It was good for my baby's brain. My sister brought us tea in bed every morning. You would cook special meals for us with meat dishes for Peter who tried to communicate with you in Punjabi. You were so thrilled and enchanted by him that you would tell all the girls and women from the neighbourhood how he made gestures in order to communicate with you in Punjabi.

My father had now retired from military service and was proud to have found a job as a transport officer in the biggest car showroom in town. He wanted to stay active during his retirement. In the afternoon when he came from his office, he would sit with Peter on the cool balcony with Indian beer and a man-to-man chat. Sometimes he would also invite me to join in for a small sip. I can still visualise the way you sat, watching the two men, frowning with disapproval in your eyes. My father would argue that the Indian beer made from barley was no more than a soft harmless drink.

Peter and I often went out shopping before noon. The sun would get too sharp in the middle of the day. The heat had started to affect me in the early stage of my pregnancy. One day we found a bookshop with an exhibition of Russian books on sale. We got excited, like kids. We bought all sorts of old classics of Maxim Gorky's ten volumes, Marx and Engels' collected works and Russian fictions. One afternoon when we were going through titles in the bookshop, I felt dizzy and almost fainted. We ordered a three-wheeler scooter to come home and everyone in the family gave me the utmost attention. After celebrating the Holi festival, we left India. Looking out of the aisle window of this Russian Aeroflot, I sat thinking whether I had left Svera back in Chandigarh.

CHAPTER 14
A Heaven Is Born

I had left a Svera back in Chandigarh. Who was I? Where was I? Was this still a dream? Was I still in a trance? Have you ever felt the way I did? Living the life of someone trapped between the hollow depth of thoughts, constantly thinking, I didn't exist as Svera, but I did in order to tell her story. I had to play the role of a narrator. I had to be there at that particular time so I could witness the whole plot. The only thing, which was out of control, was my thoughts, they flew freely like magpie, all over the place, only when I was the narrator could I control them.

Did you know that unlike alpha, beta, gamma and X-rays, thoughts can travel across the globe, invade cultures and break barriers? Thoughts never stay in our minds. As soon as you conceive a thought it may be born as spoken or written word or even an action, which goes out of our minds to play games of shadows and lights. Once your thoughts are born, you can't retrieve their actions. My thoughts travel from this present to where the main character of this story Svera was, all the many chapters of her life in the past. You, the reader who may have ventured into the illusion of his or her own mind by reading this story, may need a recap.

Welcome. You are now about to enter a mighty time machine, ruthlessly driving you back to Copenhagen, May 28th, 1975. It's the midnight hour when witches and skeletons come out of their closets, rattling their bones, sharpening wits, casting spells and dusting the broomstick ready for actions. They will hit you with havoc. So please keep all your personal belongings under your seat, hide your identity in the pocket of your consciousness, put dark glasses on as if you are going to watch a three dimensional movie in the Imax cinema. The heroine of our story, Svera, had gone into a deep sleep, a baby inside her womb, slowly shooting up like a winter aconite on the wet spring soil of love's dreams, making Svera's stomach stretch like expanding foam. Scratching her belly she would suddenly wake up in the middle of the night and notice long red marks appearing on the soft skin. The belly has been growing bigger each day like a huge gourd. A sweet itch forced her eyes wide open. Peter lies asleep at his desk. The dim light from the bed lamp makes shades on the Political Travel Report he was writing.

Svera longs for him to listen to her weird thoughts she had about the baby inside her. She has been feeling haunted by the face of the starving girl from Calcutta. She feels scared. The boredom of reading his own report sent him into a coma, where perhaps he is dreaming of babies born out of his ravelling actions, out of sight, out of mind, out of the party procedures like Rosemary's babies!

Svera, Svera, oh Svera. You were the ignorant village fool from the Punjab, day dreaming and giving yourself to fantasies of love. Where was your own consciousness? Had you wrapped it up like a gemstone in the silky threads of love? You should have taken care of your own thoughts, words and actions, girl. Your thoughtless words, mindless actions indeed played games with your mind. I am thinking now, pointing it out to her. I have the ability to analyse thoughts, look through, reed between the lines and beyond.

I hear voices, see things, and become depressed to think that I could again be caught in the illusion of love, like I did when I was Svera. Oh Peter, yes you did love that innocent village fool, when she sailed with you on a big boat on the North Sea from Copenhagen to Bornholm to visit your mother. You held her tight in your strong arms when she felt seasick. You rested on a narrow seat comforting her all night. You drew her slender body close to yours as she swayed in her African khanga with her gypsy smile on the white sands of Oyster Bay Beach.

You wrote poetry in praise when her sensual, ragged body made love to you vigorously, giving you the beat and the rhythm, her entire soul. You drew her sexy body on the canvas of love. You offered flowers on her alter as if she was a Goddess. Her loyalty baffled you. At times, you got frightened of her strikingly honest soul. You became ruthless, reckless and put your own aims before the family - a selfish act to put the saving of oppressed women before your own women. How could you not have loved Svera, Peter?

I now move back and look at Svera who is scratching her belly. Midnight hour strikes. The red silk curtains slide aside allowing the light to enter the bedroom. Svera's gaze wanders in the room to fall on an old stained picture on one of the walls, which shows a tall handsome Sikh soldier, in British army uniform, standing with three other soldiers, on the soils of Borneo. He looks down at Svera with his tough exterior. The light moves on to another wall with fairly tale tapestry. Let's go closer. We see a figure of another woman lying on a huge bed. More lights please. Now we can see the woman clearly. We can even see her eyes through our thoughts. There is a slight fear in them, of anticipation. She has a tiny little baby beside her. The man on the picture stands besides her, making a gesture to the midwife who takes the afterbirth and steps outside the room. Now he bends to kiss the tiny forehead of the baby. He looks at the woman with his heavenly smile.

"Here, this is for all the pain of bringing this beautiful little girl into this world for me," he says and blesses the woman with his words and a magnificent golden necklace.

Not many such men existed at that time in that village, in that particular country. Our dear Svera smiles at the picture, even in the middle of her agonising thoughts. She can always smile. Are you smiling? That night and many other nights Svera woke up with some terrible troubling thoughts. She wondered how Peter would react when the baby was born. She remembers the woman in the picture who had once held that same fear and told Svera about it when she was old enough to understand. The woman, Joshili, had told Svera that she was scared of the reaction of the man in the picture if she gave birth to a baby girl and not a boy. Peter lying beside Svera hadn't expressed any joy or disagreement of her pregnancy but she fears his reaction. Would he accept the new human being if it was a girl? Naaaaaaaa, stop it Svera, she said to herself. This is not your mother's village of Punjab in that particular country, India. This is Copenhagen, city of freedom.

In order to let more light into her sullen thoughts, Svera would go for long walks in the park on bright afternoons. In order for the birth to be smoother, she attended antennal classes twice a week. In order to become wiser she read many books on pregnancy. She bought baby clothes and other accessories. There were only five months left. One day she sat down to rest on the bench in a park. A beautiful Robin landed softly on her out-stretched palm to eat the breadcrumbs she held. Without any fear, the little devil sat there, eating crumbs, "a sure sign of a baby girl," prophesised Svera's mother on the phone that evening.
"She is so thin and ugly," mumbled a startled Svera, looking at the thin, pink bundle of human flesh by her side, not imagining how she would grow into a beautiful swan.
"She is a little doll with beautiful hair. You'd better ask your husband to buy you a baby brush, Svera," said the midwife, admiring the black shining hair on the baby's soft head.

The baby, her first dream-child, was born in Rigsehospitalet, in Copenhagen. Svera wondered whether she might have committed a good deed somewhere in her previous life (a belief, from Hindu mythology, that she would usually have dismissed as superstition) since she had been so lucky in having a smooth, painless birth. It took only three hours of pangs before the tiny little creature was brought out to be put onto the cold scale for weighing. Svera was so relieved she did not bother to hold her in her arms right after the birth. Peter took care of that. He was cautiously touching her body, counting the ten fingers, ten toes, ears, nose and the soft plump head.

"Du er en fin pige. You are a fine girl," he giggled with relief.
The nurse brought light supper with a cup of tea, a well-deserved present for bringing a human being into this world. Svera waited

patiently for Peter to bless her with a golden bracelet, a ring or even a little petal of a red rose. He might have forgotten to offer her a present, she thought as he started putting his jacket on, avoiding her searching gaze.

"I must go and buy a bottle of whisky to share with my comrades, and I will phone my Mum to give the news."

He bent to part a kiss on baby Nina's forehead and was ready to leave.

Svera closed her tired eyes and her thoughts travelled back -the golden words, the grand necklace, the year 1947, a tiny girl being kissed by her dad. Svera's thoughts came back and a smile crept over her face.

"Remember to buy a hair brush for our daughter," she whispered to Peter as she closed her tired eyes.

A crib with mobile decorations and toys that Svera had bought during pregnancy was placed near the double bed with its pink rose-petal quilt in the room that had red velvet curtains, a room in a totally different setting, culture, city, country, the room where Peter had left her on their wedding night, the room where Svera had met her invisible friend, Miss Ghost, where Svera was now bringing her own creation, another little baby doll, Guddi.

The room filled with this new creature crying, screaming, giggling and making her forget the shadows of postnatal blues, being the tiny rainbow through the rain and wind of the cold winter of November 1975. All those negative factors were irrelevant for Svera. Breast feeding, bathing, changing and washing the nappies, ironing, sitting by the crib, watching her sleep, reading leaflets, listening to every word of advice from the health visitor and watching the pale shrivelled-up tiny human slowly awakening became Svera's whole world. Svera was on maternity leave and Peter worked full time as a lab technician. After breast-feeding Nina for two months with all the other normal chores of the house, Svera started to get tired and irritable. She didn't have enough milk to feed the baby. Oh, how she longed and wished to be with her mother who would let her rest and nurture her aching body for forty days according to the ritual. Peter had not planned to take a vacation for the occasion, on the contrary being the only family person in the organisation, he had to get more involved with his political activities for both of them. It was the most active period in his life when secret meetings, visits and trips were taking place and Peter was determined to stay loyal to his party. Whenever the baby cried in the night, he was the one who got up, changed her diaper and put her by Svera's side for feeding. The baby slept in the middle of the two parents, enjoying the close contact and their body heat.

"Your brain is a devil's workshop."
Svera teased Peter about his hyperactive mind, a live factory producing ideas at full speed for twenty four hours. Not all of them would materialise. They were like premature babies born out of misconceived thoughts. Working in the paint firm, he invented a wooden bath-box to be fitted outside the toilet, painted with a special blue water resisting paint, used for swimming pools. A pump would drain the water from the box that was connected to the waste pipe of the outlet of the toilet. The wooden bath box was one of the rare luxuries in Svera's life. Three month after Peter had placed the bath in the house, an accident occurred. Peter was away at his work. Mrs Madge, the old lady downstairs knocked at Svera's door.
"It is terrible. There's a leak through my ceiling. It's somewhere from your kitchen sink, I'm sure."
She sounded unfriendly and annoyed.
Svera was terrified. What if she complained to the housing company, since it was not legal to build or add any modifications to the flat. The pump used for draining the water from the bath box had already stopped functioning. You had to stand in the dirty water while taking a shower. It was disgusting. On the one hand Svera hated it, but having a bath in their own flat was a real pleasure for Svera and she was proud of Peter's invention.

The entrance to the flat was through a small corridor that then led into the living room from the third floor of the well-known Solv Torv by the lake. Another small passage from the lounge led to the kitchen, so there were no doors between the living room and the kitchen. And since the windows were not double-glazed there was always a draught in the flat. In the winter, Peter would paste transparent plastic to cover the broad windows where Svera had all her lush plants, crystals and ornaments. She hung a thick woollen cream curtain to block the draught from the corridor. The living room had Chinese and African posters, pale yellow thick curtains, a piece of green rug on one corner of the room, a wooden sofa, a round table with four chairs and a television. Peter did not own many books at that time. Four small wooden beer boxes were all he had brought when they moved. The bedroom had red silk curtains, a huge pine wardrobe, a double bed and a baby crib.

Having a baby did not restrict Svera from other activities. She would pack Nina in the pram with warm clothes and go walking from one park to another around Copenhagen for fresh air. She bought herself a baby bag in which she could carry Nina and travel in buses to attend her other appointments. She managed to do shopping, prepare meals, take rest and keep in touch with her group members. Peter carried on his work and his commitments as if nothing had changed in their lives. He went to his work as usual. He came home. They had tea. He then watched the Danish news on T.V. They had their dinner. Svera would take care of Nina and then go to bed. Peter would often go to his meetings and would come home late at night. Minutes, hours, day nights and months passed in this fashion with the exception of one little miracle.

One day Peter bought home an antique movie camera with lamps and so the filming of our baby's each move started rolling. Nina sleeping, crying, in the bath tub, smiling, playing in her crib, first time she sat on a chair, first time she started to walk. The baby was growing up. She was five months old and since her birth Svera and Peter had not even been together for a walk. It had been months since they had been to the movies or for cappuccino at the new Italian café on Vestergade. Svera was on maternity leave and most of their money was spent on setting up the baby room. It was Peter's political life and the baby that consumed all of their time. Then suddenly Peter announced his plan to spend his week-long holiday in Paris, with Svera. Yippee! She agreed. At the age of twenty eight she had had her first child. She had always dreamt of having a family with children. She was in love.

Let us leave Svera with her own illusionary world to dwell in. I, the narrator, will now describe the sweet sour happy moments of this woman's life in my own words, as if it's mine. Let's see whether you can figure it out.

Yes. I said yes - instantly, without even blinking an eye. I was in fact pleasantly surprised by his offer and suggested his Mum could look after Nina for that one week. I'd always heard about the famous Mona Lisa picture and dreamed about visiting the famous Louvre since my Art College days in Chandigarh. Maybe the city would instil the feeling of romance into his dry heart, I was hoping. There wouldn't be any political report writing. Paris was going to be pavement cafés, holding hands on the Champs-Elysées, making love in a luxurious hotel bed and dining in restaurants with glorious French wine. My dream of travelling to Paris was fragrant and as thick as Kahlua liqueur. What made my nights restless and sleepless was the fear of leaving Nina with a grandma who had her doubts about taking care of Nina.

"I don't think I can handle that little devil all alone. Could Svera's brother not come and stay with me? It would ease the burden," she said.

So Nina was driven from Copenhagen with all her accessories, and an unemployed uncle, all the way to Naestved. We took off to Paris on the 20th April 1976.

Our window at the hotel overlooked the Arc de Triomphe, that insane circle of traffic in which French men would madly honk their horns and disappear into the different *arrondissements* of Paris like a ball in a roulette wheel. While the pale green foliage of trees was still waiting to bloom, one felt almost lost in the colourful crowd of people roaming through the streets of this international city. English, French, Americans, cars, motorbikes driving crazily hunting for the already filled parking spaces. Peter and I went looking for Indian, Chinese or even Danish restaurants, never even for a minute letting our baby Nina out of our minds. Restlessly, we would enquire about her over the phone. One evening when we phoned to ask how she was, we were told of her first baby tooth by her proud uncle. She was six months old that day. Peter had been strange during this trip to Paris. I couldn't put my finger on it. There was something disturbing him. Although he joked and smiled with me, I detected a strange undercurrent in his behaviour as if I, in some way repulsed him. As if he did not want to be there. Yes we made love on the strip, but it wasn't the romantic lovemaking I imagined in Paris. Despite the perfect backdrop it had a cold mechanical air as though Peter was going through those emotions, performing his duty before turning back to his comrades in Copenhagen.

For me Paris was an adventure, but for Peter it was a tiresome chore. Whilst I looked at the buildings and the squares with awe, he seemed more interested in the trivial events, which were taking place in Denmark. Soon Peter's wish was granted and we were back in Copenhagen. The grey doves had already started dwelling outside the lounge windows and the sun stayed a bit longer in the evenings. You could even walk from Solv Torv to the biggest fashionable department store, 'Magazine', in the city centre through Kongen's Have where children, men, women strolled late into the evenings, breathing in the mild April air. My sister Gulu had arrived from Canada to visit me.

One afternoon Gulu and I went for a tour around Copenhagen having Nina in the pram. We visited the finest Museum of Art in the park. Then we went shopping at the supermarket. Gulu needed a jacket from 'Magazine'. We ended up buying a dress, two tops, a cardigan for her, and I bought a woollen sweater for you, Mum. We got back in the house around 7 in the evening and Peter had yet not arrived. He was supposed to be back by 5.00pm. Gulu had bought some ingredients for a cake. She wanted to please Peter with his favourite coconut chocolate cake. In a very good mood, she stood listening to a cassette of Hindi remix music in our spacious kitchen, mixing the dough, when Peter returned home. His eyes were red and from his uncombed hair it looked as if he had been fighting with somebody. I silently let him through the door. He tried to explain in his trembling voice that he had gone shopping after work and the shops had been crowded. He had wanted to buy fine pork chops so he could cook supper that night. No mention of the dishevelled hair, although I knew from his demeanour that something had gone wrong. I told him that I had already done the food shopping and saw that he hadn't brought any shopping with him. So where were the pork chops.

"Oh my god," he said, "I must have lost them in the bus."

I didn't want to make a scene in front of Gulu and waited for the night when we would be alone to have an explanation for his lie. At last we were in the same very precious bedroom where Peter had left me on our honeymoon night to travel to Sweden so he could study Marx with his comrades. He admitted to having been with a woman in the Vesterbrogade area of town which was famous for prostitution. Peter was extremely ashamed of his act.

"You'd have guessed it anyway," he said.

He yawned, groaned and told me not to wake him up next morning, as he wouldn't be going to work. This was the first night in our marriage when I had to sleep by a man who had committed adultery and openly admitted it. I lay awake in that precious room thinking of all the nights he had left me alone. On that particular night my thoughts got muddled up in a gullible wet mixture of confusion and reality. The confusions were of shame, dignity and the fear of trying to save my honour. The reality was of being cheated by the man I loved. I realised that not only one but many walls were slowly being built between us. Peter had laid the foundations, the first few bricks. He had supplied the mortar, dug the trench and placed the solid base into the ground of the relationship. The most upsetting thought of all was how breathtakingly indifferent he was about the whole situation. One quick explanation, a yawn and a mumbled apology were all that were needed in his eyes. Peter lay on his back with his closed eyelids, behind them two cold blue marbles shut away.

I listened to his heavy snoring and to Nina's light breathing in her crib and the silence of the night became my friend and in that silence, you might think that I dutifully accepted because I was an obedient little Indian wife who knew better than to ask too many inconvenient questions. Let me reveal it to you, dear. It was a mild spring night, without thunder, storm or lightening outside, but the first seeds of a revolt were sown in my heart. I couldn't tear up the protocol of my marriage. Why? Because of that sweet itch on my skin, because of a human life growing inside my belly. Because...because.....hell....

Ah...I know. Someone up there was pulling the strings, making me dance like a puppet, a Kathputli. I was willingly dancing on the tunes. Because a little voice at the back of my head, or maybe my higher conscience, unconsciously kept on telling me to hold on. Someone was brewing a plot at my expense. Svera had to hang on as the story was being built like builders' stones, brick by brick, step by step with all these thoughts, actions and characters. A stage was set: lights, cameras, plots. I had taken an oath not to reveal anything to anyone. Gulu never suspected a thing and neither did I mention a single episode to you, mother. How could I? I saved the honour of my own little family as you always did yours, mother. I saved the plot and stepped aside from the foggy thoughts of mind to give way to the future narrator - the I.

CHAPTER 15
A Hell Is Loosed

Time runs by chasing the future and dragging the past into the endless. Perhaps time is a river, running in a line. Perhaps it's an ocean and we sunbathe on its beaches, so come on, hold my hand, take a leap of faith and swim from June 1981 when Svera was in Denmark to June 1994, when I, the narrator, was here in this city, Bradford. My thoughts were stretched on my bed like aching requisitions, while my body on the rug tried to perform 'pranayama', a yoga therapy breathing exercise, to calm my nerves. I was scared. I was very scared, because I had discovered Peter's shopping list of items for a baby and it wasn't me who was pregnant. The thought of him being promiscuous was turning into a nightmare. My values were acutely different from his. Having a child outside marriage was not acceptable in my family. I didn't want it to be true. I wanted him to finish his writing and tell me that it wasn't true. I needed his assurance, his soothing words, his touch. I was reminiscing about those good old golden days of mad youthful passion, and, writing about it now, I realised that I was trying to pull the soft silky sheet of hope over my head. Writhing on the illusionary pangs of sweet sorrowful listening to the sound of Peter typing, I remembered a poem, the incenses of which became a soothing ointment:

I came to you
With my Eastern
Poetic mysteries...

Finally, Peter entered the room. He had now finished his report, "Letters from Africa" for a Danish newspaper. He came straight to the point,

"Svera, I have to tell you something. I have met a girl."

He drew the wicker chair beside my bed to sit down. His elbow resting on the arm of the chair, I remembered when we used to relax arm in arm, his eyes vacantly moving away from me, looking into the distance as he spoke. I saw his large hands tremble. I could smell the aura of another woman from his open mouth and I waited for the venom to spit from those thick treacherous lips. The same lips that I once gazed at, hypnotised, for hours now waited for him to paralyze me with his forked tongue.

"I don't know how it happened, but I am in love. She is so young and full of fun, Svera. Try to understand."

I understood nothing. It was so blunt, so cold, so deliberate. Whether he had been stealing himself for this announcement, I didn't know, but there was a rehearsed quality about the way he said it, like a third rate actor mechanically delivering his lines in the local amateur theatre.

"She is so young, Svera," he had said and I saw two faces in front of me, Nina and Minna - fresh, innocent, white teeth, black aubergine hair, fun, vigorous, exuberantly tiptoeing through their reckless teenage years.I saw the black cloud of his confession corrupting their dreams like a noxious poison emitted from a badly maintained factory. It spread over the beautiful village where my family was, poisoning, suffocating, polluting. Our own personal Bhopal, except this was no multi-national company poisoning its workers, it was a champion of workers' rights, poisoning his own relationship. It's hard to describe in words the state in which I found myself after Peter's revelation. You might even find that the depiction of what was happening sound as if I am trying to turn myself into a heroine. My truthfulness is like the layer of skin on my skeleton, visible, transparent, see-through, easy to peel like the thin layers of an onion. Peel the onion and my whole world falls away, layer by layer.

When Peter peeled the skin of his truthfulness, I couldn't handle it. I started to tremble in fear, fumble about blindly, trying to catch sense, from somewhere. Thoughts were slipping away from my mind like an eel. I was falling into the void in my own illusionary world, disabled, numb with agony, forgetting how to project words. His voice dragged me back to reality.

"I met her in one of the bars in Asmara. Please, Can you help me? Tell me to stop seeing her. I don't believe God intended this. Do you Svera? It's love. I couldn't prevent it. That's how it is, Svera."

His grey hair shone white under the square lamp, his wrinkled eyes as pitiful as those of a 15 year old boy, caught stealing toffees from the local shop. This was the vulnerable side of Peter that I always found hard to resist. The look that kept me attached to his selfish life. Even now I felt I couldn't break free. My wrists held by the skeletons in the cupboard.

"This is life, Svera. A reality," says Peter.

Break away woman. Get over your trance. You have to do it yourself. I heard a little voice. It was the girl in my car with her cute mouth and a self-assured attitude. Maybe you mother? Tell me. Where is that girl who used to rebel against your norms? Who used to mock the hypocritical behaviour of people, of democracy, of religion which oppressed. I imagined myself in his place. What would my daughters, my dog, the milkman, my neighbours, my father, my mother, my Guru Nanak have thought of me, if I had an affair while he was away at numerous meetings for good causes which caused his family to be neglected. Imagine the scenario if I had gone out to one of the nightclubs with my friend Anna. Maybe it was the girl inside me, who did it. I can throw the ball of blame into her court and tell you about it.

Svera had met him at the Midland Hotel. It was singles evening. She had started to go out with Anna. Everybody knew why he or she was there. Self-conscious men would hang about uncomfortably eyeing up available middle-aged ladies scattered variously around the room. At 11 o'clock Svera and Anna would retire to the dance floor in the adjacent room. Pie and peas, the Yorkshire speciality, would be on offer together with pounding disco beats and the possibility of perhaps a little more?

Svera might have gone there when Peter was at one of his communist meetings in Brussels.

His name was Neil. She had seen him on two previous occasions, tall, muscular, sensual, half her age. It was clear that he was interested from the first moment their eyes had met. In fact the first time they spoke, his hands shook nervously as he lit the cigarette with the lighter he had borrowed from her. She felt maternal, protective but most of all she had come over with a savage lustful desire for this man. Her body was so hungry for vigorous love making after the barren years of her marriage. She knew the moment he asked for a light that they were destined to make love. On top of this it was the thought of Peter's reaction, if he could see Svera in the arms of this young man. She felt as if she had added extra spice to one of the curries that Peter loved to wolf down. This was her dish, a recipe she had created for herself and yes she felt guilty despite all the things that Peter had done. She just simply couldn't resist it. She spent those nights at Neil's apartment.

Peter's affair hit me like a cricket ball with its sharp speed. I felt a peculiar pain on my face. Felt as if my nose was bleeding. My eyes were wounded. My lips were swollen. My skin was stretching to break. I was about to faint when I heard voices - my children, Peter, you, Mum.

"How could you do such a thing, Mum?"
"Have you gone nuts?"
"You should be ashamed of yourself, at your age!"
"How could you ever think of such a thing?"
"Where is your dignity?"
'Dignity', 'Shame', 'Wife', 'Mother', 'Woman', 'Honour' - these words were not screams but orders of morality imposed by society and culture. But the loudest order came from you, mother.

It might not have happened. Sometimes, the fiction becomes a reality and the reality a fiction. You are the judges. You are going to judge me, despite my honesty. So, I admit, it didn't happen. The reason that this affair I've just described never happened, is that faith and trust has been part of my upbringing - my mother, my father, my own belief in the sanctity and faithfulness of marriage, to be committed to one partner. You must trust my integrity.

Out of my imagination, I looked at the tie-dye version of the Kama Sutra on the wall, designs copied from the famous Ajanta and Arora caves of India. I continued counting the years I had spent, yearning for love. My marriage was an investment. Twenty one, twenty two, twenty three, twenty four. I realised, we had spent all those years together and yet I was short-changed. My life was stolen.

Peter still sat there in the chair. He had become a phantom. He looked at me puzzled as if my train of thoughts had aroused a suspicion in his mind. He spoke with exasperation.

"Well? Aren't you going to say anything, Svera? It is not that I have left you. Speak to me Svera...Svera..."

Now he looked at me with his questioning eyes. There was a hint of pain in them as if the card had wronged him that nature had dealt him. I was still strangely transfixed by the hollow depth of his eyes. My fingers reached out to touch that burning flicker which once ignited his love for me. In them, I caught an object of desire for another woman. Electrocuted by the cruel reality, I fought my way back to gentle memories deep in the crevasses of the silky web of my trance. How well I had learnt to thrive in my own isolation. It somehow saved me from the cold reality of this cruel world with its self-centred characters.

It was Peter's treat. We took a trip on a Boeing 747 from Copenhagen to London in the summer of 1974. Driving on a coach huddled together on a seat, I slept with my head on his shoulder - to Victoria station, King's Cross and Piccadilly, I dreamt about the crowded pavements, double-decker buses and the railway station at Bombay.

He woke me up gently as I dreamt of Punjab, you mother, and Jaz. The coach had arrived. With a long kiss on my forehead, Peter spoke as I slowly opened up my eyes. I saw a tall man who wore scruffy overalls with stains of paint, a blue rucksack on his shoulders and a pink hat with a red stripe. I saw his glaring eyes looking in my direction.

"We are here, Svera. Get up, darling. Remember it's the second anniversary of our wedding."

Peter was shaking me and the tall raggedly handsome man disappeared from my vision. I got up from the seat, still dreaming, thinking about him. I reached out to touch him and found Peter's hand. We walked with our bags on the crowded pavement of this endlessly fascinating city. Suddenly Peter stopped in front of a floral shop and bought a huge bouquet of lilies. He took two white flowers to put on each side of my hair near the ears.

"Oh! White suits you so much, Svera. Welcome to the city of love. I love you Svera. We are going to grow old together. One day we shall return to India."

I looked up towards the sky walking with not so tall but dashingly handsome Peter, with the striking deep blue eyes. I could see myself with his children, a nice home, growing old together with our children's children, finally settling down in a small tranquil village, drinking Darjeeling tea sitting on the open veranda with you on your majestic chair eating your favourite dish of kheer with almonds, mother.

What a golden dream. I would do anything to hold on to those shimmering fantasies of mad romance. Billie Holiday is singing with her rich, golden, tragic, melodramatic voice, while I write remembering, "Yesterday...days of mad romance and love."

Yesterday...that transient weekend of love in London, where the world was but a dream that had now been lost forever. But the soft truth is that I have probably lost the chance to meet that tall handsome man of my vision. The harsh reality is that I am here in this city, June 1994, listening to Peter's cruel revelation. He was sitting on the wicker chair looking sternly in my direction, trying to get an answer from me. I was lost in yesterday when I would do anything for him - anything from holding a dead embryo on my palm when I was lying in a hospital in Kenya, to believing that he would love me forever. I had been travelling to unknown destinations wherever he wanted to take me. Wouldn't you do the same for love?

"Sige noget fa helvcde kvinde," he suddenly shouted in Danish.

Damn it, say something woman. This was Mr. Hyde speaking. I didn't want to look at him. I was wrapped in the comfort of yesterday. I felt speechless, couldn't form words, lying there making myself helpless in front of him. I started to fumble about, trying to formulate an answer, feeling clumsy. Then I heard voices again, sharp, clattering, determined and clear voices of other women. They seemed very close. No, I am not schizophrenic. These were real voices from the past.

"Do you have anything to say?" asked the women, reminding one of the men of a specific episode years back.

"Can't you remember?" the man was asked.

If he could, it was bad enough. But if he couldn't that was really bad. They were interrogating all the men in the organisation. They would ask men's lovers and wives as well, how the men had behaved at home.

To explain this incident, we have to do the hopscotch. Backstage, Denmark in the late 70's. Peter became more and more confused as his political studies became more complicated. Confusion forced him to take up hobbies he had neglected in the past.

"I think it's in my blood. I am always restless. I always wanted to do something meaningful. But now I want to delve into my artistic talents. Maybe I will feel happier," he declared.

To fulfil that side of his character he took three months leave from his work to invest money and time on art, lots of money. As a faithful partner, I supported and encouraged his artistic vision. The result was an exhibition in a small, private art gallery. He received no publicity, but many people visited the gallery. His mission completed. His artistic desires satisfied. His style was purely surrealistic and that wasn't the trend at that particular time, but he was a good artist. Many of the paintings were then given away as gifts to family and friends.

Meanwhile the crisis in the organisation KAK became more and more visible. Members started questioning the leadership. In order to divert their attention, Anna started campaigning and mobilising the female members. She raised the issue of women's roles in the organisation.

Most of the female members took up the fight against their male comrades for being male chauvinist. It was decided, they needed to be reformed and the reformation strategy was put in to practice. All the male members would be invited one by one to face their female counterparts.

"Do you remember that evening in the meeting when we were in Sweden, you forgot to mention my name? You bloody male chauvinistic pig!" Hanne asked Niels.

All men would be reminded of their bad behaviour in the past, given examples of how they had disrespected their women comrades. The men had to go through criticism and self-criticism and had to show the willingness to reform. Apology and contrition was mandatory. The meetings were five women to one man. Women members would note down every sin the men had committed. The men had no chance to prepare themselves against accusations. They didn't even dare tell each other what harsh methods were used to extract their confessions. None of the men dared to alert other male comrades for the fear of being exposed in public as a male chauvinist. Marxists being male chauvinists? That would be the biggest shame for them to admit. Instead they let themselves be insulted throughout the meetings and promised to reform themselves.

The women physically beat up most of them until they gave in. Peter was considered one of the worst male chauvinists who needed that reform. Some of the men were so clever that they devised tactics to get away with having only the 'mild' treatment, which meant they only attended three or four of those terrible meetings whereas others had to go through 20 to 30 of them. Peter attended about 15 of those meetings. He was interrogated and beaten up, physically with fists and slaps by his own dear women comrades!

Oh, Peter how ridiculous you looked returning home tearfully from those encounters. Just as you were beginning to slap me, you were being slapped yourself. Dr. Jekyll was slapped by the women and Mr. Hyde was slapping Svera.

Those women were not physically big, yet Peter submitted to interrogations through a warped sense of duty. What a pity that duty never extended to his wife and children. He would come home to me every night, frightened, crying and humiliated. I was furious to witness my husband in that state. I took to him as if he was a child. I nurtured his soul, like a mother.

There were some men without support from anybody. They simply broke down. One of them committed suicide. The leaders were ruthless, hardcore, aggressive Marxists. After several clashes during factional fighting, some of the members rebelled and formed a new group with new leadership. I protected him. I gave him the courage in my blinkered state. I couldn't believe that my own husband was a male chauvinist. How wise those women were!

How strange I felt in front of this man sitting here sheepishly not being able to utter a word, only reviving memories. I couldn't express my anger while he was interrogating me.
"Answer me, Svera. Have you nothing to say about this?"
The strangeness spread further upon my soul. I could not conceive, I know that, but I couldn't even conceive words because Peter's unzipped fly had zipped up my mouth. I became weak and mute. I gathered enough strength to rise and left the room, leaving Peter in splendid isolation. Well, wankers are usually alone! Perhaps he might beat himself up if he spent enough time in his own company. I stood outside the door feeling unable to walk but amazingly my feet then dragged my weight downstairs, towards my favourite lounge, to seek commune in isolation. When I am alone, it's a comfort zone. I needed to ponder over things, to wonder, to gather together my strength. I couldn't. I couldn't meditate. Neither could I seek advice from my inner superior conscience, nor from Guru Gobind Singh.

I found myself outside the house, on the patio. I looked above. The night was blue. Mad clouds hung down over the garden like giant dream catchers. It was cold out there, but my body burned slowly in agony. Quivering in a dim, silent fire, I started shaking. Then the flames began to rise higher, higher and even higher. For a moment I saw myself turn into a wild crazy woman with a huge dagger in my hand, cutting Peter's body into pieces and then jumping into the burning pyre, like a Sati. The whole house was caught in those flames. Everything was burning. Ebony statues of passion, rainbow marbles of love, a million pages of a trillion books in the shelves of wisdom, broken pieces of porcelain scattered with disharmony, silk, cotton, woollen tiers of protection, everything collected through the years was on fire, slowly turning to ashes. I saw myself sitting on the pyre, watching in awe, the whole spectacular scene. Then I heard voices, the sobbing voices, crying and screaming frightened humans from the attic windows. I jumped out of the fire. At first I ran to one direction, then to another. I could smell flesh burning. Was it I? Was it my children? I had to save them, and the thought kept me running towards the smell, like a hunting dog. Then I felt a hand on my shoulder. I almost saw a shadow of another man I had seen in London. A face with big kind eyes, a face with thick sensual lips and a pink hat with red stripe. I felt like putting my head on his broad shoulders, but the hand I felt was rough and harsh, shaking me violently. It was Peter's hand.

"What are you doing here? Have you gone mad? Do you have any idea what I just told you?"

Peter had come down looking for me.

"Don't touch me!"

I jumped and squealed like a wild pig, coming out of my state of insanity. I felt like vomiting. So I did. It felt good. My stomach was churning in pain.

"What can I do, when you are in this mess."

He shook his head. I was in the bathroom, facing the mirror, trying to wipe my face. The mirror reflected back the pain that had overwhelmed me. Slowly coming to my senses and wishing to find something soothing I felt the darkness of the night like a silk dupatta, my honour, rustling against my skin, soothing. I covered myself under this blanket, which was able to put out the fire and at the same time acted as a coffin, smothering the reality of what had just happened, an ironic haven for the death of my love.

Your face reappeared. Oh how I wished you were here to hold me, Ma, to drag me out of the cold box. Like the many other times, I did not want to hurt you. You didn't deserve the hurt. If you knew how much my heart ached, you would have felt it in your own body, you would bleed. I did not want you to. The soft image of your face was enough of a soothing balm. Covered with its odour, I slipped into a deep tormented sleep.

It was early Monday morning and I tried opening my eyes only to find that I had a painfully stiff neck. I heard snoring. It must have been a dream, I thought. Could it be a nightmare? My arm stretched to touch the other half of my bed. He really was there, warm, snuggled up on one side. A loud noise came from the clock. It was 3.00am. I must have only slept for a couple of hours. The lilac Batik curtains on the window were drenched in the pain of my confused slumber. My face was parched with dried tears. I wondered why I was still moving, alive and ticking, like a dead woman walking. I could still smell the burnt flesh of my dreams. I could see the scattered pieces everywhere. I was frightened. Something was stuck in my throat. I needed water, ice-cold liquid, the lifesaver of those who thirst. I was curled up in the corner of the bed. Holding my breath, I straightened my bent knees and lifted myself. It was an effort to go downstairs. After pouring eight glasses of water down my throat, I made a cup of black tea and went into the lounge. For a while sipping the tea and not knowing exactly what to do, again, I tried to chant a few verses you had told me to repeat whenever I was in trouble. They used to help. This time they didn't.

It was six now. Holding the warm strong cup with both hands, I sat on the chair thinking about Ruby. We knew her from Africa. Now she was just a phone call away. I grabbed the phone.
"Hello..."
A drowsy voice. Oh, God, I shouldn't wake people like that.
"Hi, Ruby, sorry to ring you so early."
"Oh, is that you Svera? What's the matter? Are you all right, dear?"
Her concern sounded genuine.
"I have to tell you something. Not a pleasant thing to announce over the phone," I said and talked down the line for an hour.

She was understanding. In fact she went a long way to calm the situation for me. Ruby was a deeply pragmatic woman. She could put these things in perspective, and the despicable behaviour of a man was low on her agenda of the calamities that life can throw up.

"All men make such blunders at one stage or another in their married life. It is so common these days, especially here. All white people here have bastard children. What a messy society. Now I have witnessed it myself. England is full of poufs. Even Africans, I have known plenty of them who've had affairs. They have a child here and a child there without necessarily destroying their marriages. You shouldn't have sent him to work out there, alone, Svera."

This last barbed comment shook me somewhat. As if Peter was a child who should be supervised, incapable of keeping his marriage vows simply because his wife wasn't there.

She continued.

"Men! You simply can't trust them. It's like they have a wild animal between their legs. You should know that by now Svera. That's why I follow my husband everywhere. Men created chastity belts, but they got it wrong. It is women who should have created some medieval shield to control their roving manhood. Every wife should have the only key, Svera. I hate to sound clichéd, but all men, really, are bastards and I knew all along that Peter was the biggest bastard of all."

The venom of her judgement took me aback.

Ruby promised to talk to her husband Om and agreed that they would visit me later. Strangely enough the phone call worked. Ruby's hard reality always brought me back to earth even in the darkest moment. It was difficult to suppress a giggle at her comments. Peter went back to Africa. Comfort from my friends was just a mildly cooling breeze of reassurance, when it had passed my pain returned to pester me further.

The fire of humiliation burned inside me, killing me, but I kept it buried because I did not want it to infect my daughters. Nina was doing her A-level exams. Meena had just entered her vulnerable teen years. I could not even write to you, mother, because I was so enclosed that I shut my own book and yet I saw something flashing in the darkness. The sword of Guru Gobind Singh. The symbol of struggle.

Bless my soul, to any length
Show me the way, rescue me,
O, mighty sword of strength.

As a last resort of communication, I wrote a short story. I sent it to Peter, so I could communicate through words. That was the only weapon left in my armoury.
He wrote back:

"Instead of being so self-centred, why don't you concentrate on other peoples' problems. Your problems are nothing compared to others. I have finished my relationship with that girl. She came to Asmara again and contacted me, but I told her, that it was over. The first week I was feeling strange, that I had thrown myself into this affair and I was a bit disappointed that she had gone. But then I realised how foolish I had been, because she obviously did not put the same in it as I had. Why should I, an old man, risk my marriage and everything for such a young girl?"

Peter invited me and the girls to visit him in Africa. I wasn't sure whether it would be an effort to save the marriage or I should just take up his invitation to see yet another African country. I was confused. I couldn't make up my mind. When his London office asked me to send some documents, I kept on delaying. Peter thought, I was refusing to accept his offer.

"How can you refuse such an excellent offer to visit a country like Eritrea. How can you even dare to? Who the hell do you think you are? Such an arrogant, self-indulgent middle-class woman," Peter wrote back.

Gathering together moans and pieces
Gracious storms of these riches.

Could I find advice in the words of Guru Gobind Singh? What advice would he give me? After twenty-two years of marriage it would be churlish not to go.

CHAPTER 16
Crack In The Glass House

Trials, errors, the madness of trying again, thinking you would learn from the old, thinking you might have become wiser. Or shall I say, we all become blindfolded by our wild urges. It can be anything. Passion, lust, love, hate, you name it. For me this was a perfect excuse to let Svera get away from her screwed up life. There was a possibility to mould the plot, to make it more adventurous. Send her to explore a new territory. She had done that before, when she left you to pursue her journey, mother. It was in her blood, after all, to wander like a gypsy, to travel, to tread on new horizons, to find what she was looking for - change. It could easily turn out to be another desperate attempt for reconciliation with the man she had spent the most vulnerable youthful years of her life. My mind told me maybe I was taking a risk. Svera didn't want to be left behind, so I put her in a secret compartment of my suitcase and found myself with swaying arms, closed eyes, closed palms, in a position to fly.

The local people warmly embraced me when I touched the soil of Asmara. A bouquet of tropical flowers was placed around my neck. This warm welcome spread like a marquee in the air over my head. Somebody spoke to me in the local Tigrinya language. I must have looked like one of the many 'tourists' from the Diaspora, returning home from Europe and North America for my summer holidays. Holding back a nervous grin, I doffed my black beret not knowing how to return what was apparently a warm local greeting.

We were driving, a few miles from the small airport. Together with the wheels of this mighty vehicle, my mind swooped across the streets towards Asmara city, an oasis of racial harmony, they had told me.

Could Svera really rescue her relationship with Peter? Would she find her peace, her harmony in this Haven of peace? Or was she being the naïve village fool after all?

Your voice touched my skin rustling like a breeze with sand.
"Have you gone all the way to Africa to see that bastard? After what he has done to you - hit you, spat at you? Oh, Svera, how could you. Have you got no self respect woman?"
"It's not me, Mum. Svera is in the suitcase."
"Who the hell are you? You look like Svera to me. What the hell. Svera or not Svera, tell her, what I said. You are mad. Let Svera out, do you hear me?"
The old woman was annoyed.

I suppressed your hectoring voice by putting earphones on my thoughts. I pondered over events and decided to let Svera out. My job was to observe her and take notes of her every movement. She looked sad, tired and pale. She had a lot to think about. The sweet sour pain she had gone through was everywhere in the atmosphere, hanging from the blooming trees, peeping down from the broad balconies of this African city, hidden in the strong aroma of flowers and freshly baked bread. I saw it so vividly - the pain.

Peter, dressed in his expatriate pride, appeared aloof from the nostalgia of Africa. I couldn't stand the sight of him. I was just on the verge of exploding in anger, but in fear of being found out, I decided to disappear from the scene and be invisible, watching, taking notes and letting Svera be herself.
"Guess what you are going to have for dinner tonight children," he said. I glanced at Peter who had not exchanged any words with me until now. Nina and Minna were both huddled together on the back seat smiling wearily, half asleep from the long journey. Two hours later as the sun glided down over the rocky African city, we crept up the hill in the four-wheel drive to meet the barefoot bankers. These were the former freedom fighters that were now going to learn new skills in order to adjust themselves to a society without war. The road was bumpy and the mountains ahead expanded on the horizon. The moon

had now risen up like a huge yellow daffodil over the hills ahead of us swaying majestically to guide the way. We drew up beside a newly built brick house, which was used as a training centre for educating men and women who had fought the war for the last thirty years.

"Welcome to Eritrea," Genet and Julia stepped forward together to greet us in soft, clear English.

"Can you imagine how these light brown, oblique faces with tall slim figures could carry guns for 30 years?"

Peter brought the suitcases inside the room. There was only one little window, covered with a mosquito net. The children had already changed into more casual clothing, ready to enjoy pizza in the only restaurant in that village. This ex-Italian colony still had some remnants of its former colonial masters.

"Svera, do you remember the video film we saw in Dar es Salaam? Watching them in the liberated area fifteen years ago and finding myself face to face with them now, I wondered how they were able to retain their gains in terms of gender equality."

He was always so very verbose when he discussed politics. He couldn't resist talking down to me as if he was the senior lecturer on one of his development courses in project planning. However, his blue eyes flickered with passion. Politics was still his first and only love. He pulled out a light green shirt to wear. I swallowed the bitter aftertaste of inequality between us in that dark coffee offered to me by Genet. I had to freshen up. I finished my drink wondering whether Genet and Julia had won any grain of equality for themselves together with the freedom. Peter continued his lecture.

"You should be happy, Svera. You have nothing to complain about as I told you before. I come to see you at least twice a year. I can't speak their language but I know how to communicate with these women. They are so wonderful and strong."

Strength is not an emotion I feel at this time, I wanted to tell Peter. But he continued.

"It would be really worthwhile for you to talk to them. You can learn from them. Many of them live alone, while their husbands have to work in other towns. They have one or two children of their own but many have also adopted children whose parents died in the war. I wouldn't mind having one of those adorable boys," Peter sighed.

I could sense the urgency in Peter's voice. He had always wanted a son of his own. For a while his voice became a chatting clock, non-stop. I had to adjust my sullen mood and try to wake the inquisitive thirst to explore within myself. I shut my pain out and imagined myself in my turquoise Indian Shalwar Kameez I had chosen to wear in the blazing red-hot weather. I could hear the familiar clicking of the lens of my Minolta 3000i. The zooming in and out in my mind became more objective than my subjective sadness.

Next day.

"Demobilisation of the women is a great job for those boys in the government. We have only been given one thousand pounds as war compensation. We want to live a normal life. Children have to be looked after if we go to work or to school. We don't even have proper housing."
Janet added words as if she was one of Peter's trusting Lieutenants whilst mounting the motorbike. It was the afternoon. We had spent a night in the training camp of the village. We had gone back to Asmara. I was taken to photograph women learning to drive the black motoguzzi. I hit an amazing target with my camera: the silhouette of two teenage girls on the hill with their curious eyes. The magnificent orange sun splattered African rays across their baby faces. My daughters had gone to town with the children of Jeeday, a friend of Peter. Another soft ebony night approached and images of the day became nightmares of the airless evening.

We were booked into a two-roomed flat in a posh hotel in the Italian quarter, north of the city. Jeeday came for a chat. They settled for the evening demanding whisky, beer, and roasted chicken. Sitting with them for some time I gave half an ear to their sick jokes and gossip about the other expatriates. I decided to retire to another room and I heard Jeeday whispering,
"You can't meet her when your wife is here."

"Is he still having an affair with that young woman - even now, when I am with him here?"

I came straight to the point and made eye contact. He looked away guiltily and stood embarrassed.

"Look. I have to get back to my family. I will see you in the morning, Peter," and without answering my question, Jeeday left.

There was a long pregnant silence as I ruminated over his words.

"So you really haven't stopped seeing Kika, have you Peter?" I demanded.

Peter taking a nonchalant gulp of his beer was caught in the puddle of his own lies. He looked like a wet Tom cat with red eyes and responded,

"Yep, I suppose I like her, because she doesn't object to anything. She doesn't ask questions. She is not complicated."

There was another pause.

"So I am complicated, Peter?" I asked.

"You know the bloody Indians. You are a complicated race. It has taken me 25 years to realise that. I suggest you find yourself a bloody complicated Indian man. Nothing is ever that simple in your culture."

He finished his bottle of beer and tossed it in the bin.

"And if you will now excuse me, Madame, I have to take a shower and get my beauty sleep. I will be sleeping in the next room. You can sleep with the children. I will be late tomorrow, so don't sit up waiting for me."

With that he began to depart. Left behind were the shredded thoughts, crumbling to the floor, trying to find an outlet from the hot African night. I looked at Peter's back, which disappeared behind the door he had slammed on me. I started measuring my footsteps, looking out of the window. Words had abandoned me, evaporating from my mouth like water on a pan that had been left simmering for too long. Stars sparkled clearer. I gulped the mild breeze and sensed the death of my passion on this humid air. A stranger in the land of Freedom. Peter's land. Peter's world. Peter's freedom, Peter Pan. I closed my eyes and thought. Why am I not dead with humiliations? Was I deathless? A deathless goddess with my eyes tightly shut. A delirious melancholy triggered memories.

It is in India, an evening in 1975. The stars in the sky are a million luminous clay lamps. The whole universe flickered in their glowing warmth. I am caught in a fire of longing for Peter. You are cooking in the kitchen, Ma, as I hear his footsteps. I can smell his broad chest moisten with lust. He is quivering over me like a tropical firefly. I breathe him in through my skin and take his sweating hand to touch my neck, my hardened breast, my stomach, my thighs and we both fly high on tantric illusions of love. The wind ruffles with my wet body, clinging to my hair like butterfly as I cling to his skin as I sob in my sleep, as I cry with pleasure. I cry loudly in the state of half awake, I sit up in the darkness of the room, returning to reality, the African reality. I hear soft footsteps, somebody opening the drawer. I switch on the bedside lamp. The light falls on the thin body of Nina standing with a knife in the middle of the room with red eyes.

"I cannot bear it any more, Mum. I heard you screaming and crying in your sleep. If you two don't make up tonight, I shall kill myself, now."

I was awe stricken by her determination. I felt both fear and admiration for her.

"I can't bear it anymore, Mum", she sobs.

And neither can I, mother. If I could only talk to you face to face. You could have given me the courage to resist. I know you would, mother. I am soaked with the sweat of guilt. I put my arms around Nina. I kiss her forehead. I take her to my bed, lay her down gently stroking her hair. She smiles back. She is tired, exhausted. I lie awake. In my chest, the night gasps like a dying fish out of water. The morning will give birth to a new sunrise. I try to sleep holding my two daughters close to my body. We will be leaving for home in two days. I feel nostalgic about my city. The city which now had become my home was far away. Wrapped in the blanket of its memories, I was about to sleep.

Hold on, before I eventually fall back to sleep, there's another scene for you to watch. I almost forgot this important one.

"So, you are Peter's wife?" a woman asked me when I was invited to a party at Jeeday's the other night.

"Yes," I said.

"I did not know he had a beautiful wife. He never told us about you."
She looked across the room towards Peter who was standing talking with others, a beer bottle in his hand.
"Can I tell you something?"
I tried to hold the glass of wine firmly.
"Yes."
She drew her face closer to mine.
"I have been living in an illusion, a trance... a glass house of love with Peter for the last twenty-five years. He has smashed the facade totally. The broken pieces have hit me hard. Can't you see I am bleeding?"
She scrutinised my face closely and said,
"You are certainly talking like somebody very hurt. But by looking at you, it is hard to judge. You look so innocent, almost...almost.... I wonder why Peter..."
"What? What has Peter done?"
Before the woman could answer, Jeeday's wife appeared from nowhere to save the situation. She stretched her thin hand with long nails with white nail polish in front of her lips and made a gesture to that woman.
"So here you are my dear. Let me introduce you to my family."
She had a wicked smile on her face. She had painted her face so much that it was hard to see her real self. Her eyes were dark and big, looking like a witch. She led me away with her long thin hands. I felt her long nail hurting my hand. She was pulling me towards the crowd of people. I was more inebriated when I returned a bit later to speak to the woman. She seemed to have merged into the mass of beautiful faces, disappeared like a ghost. Was she a she-devil? As I walked, the fringes of my long dress get caught under my left high heel. I tried to hold the glass of liquor steady in my right hand my body tilted downwards and I felt two strong arms around my waist. Somebody had straightened me up and my left hand rested on their broad shoulder effortlessly. Two wide bespectacled eyes looked at me.
"Sorry!"
I felt the male aroma encompass my body and a whinnying laughter exile out of my throat.
"Are you feeling all right?" he asked and took his eyes off me, leading me to a sofa.
We both settled down for another drink.

"So tell me, what is going on?" he said.

"I don't have a clue, stranger," I laughed.

"Who are you and why are you alone in the middle of this big crowd, and why drunk?" he asked.

"Who am I? Where am I? Who are you? Who are these people? Where are we? I am so confused, really."

I laughed hysterically.

"Look, I can only guess. You must be with Peter," he said.

"Hang on - now it all makes sense. You must be his wife."

He looked at me triumphantly.

"Do I look like a wife? Well, full marks for deduction," I said.

"I am Holger, one of Peter's German friends. We met at the project-planning workshop in Stuttgart. He told me he had a beautiful wife, but I did not know he was such a master of understatement."

At this he made firm and prolonged eye contact with me. He then looked hesitantly towards Peter who was engaged in conversation.

"If you want we can go outside and watch the moon."

He took my right hand stroking it gently.

"The moon is a metaphor for a lover. I love the moon. But you know I am a wife, maybe Peter's. Who cares anyway?"

At this he winced a wry smile.

"Peter has been very busy since he has been here in Africa. It must have been hard for the marriage to continue with such distance between the two of you."

His statement was patched with a lie holding no weight.

"A woman like you will not remain alone for a long time. Of that I am sure."

"Who is alone? I have this. We are here, somewhere in the middle of the beautiful people. There's plenty of food, Arabic music. I can hear them chatter as they queue up like greedy monsters. We are all monsters. Let's have a monsters dance. You start."

I lifted my glass in the air, the wine simmered inside me, I laughed and a conversation followed which lasted for hours and I hardly noticed the existence of Peter who had disappeared from the scene for the whole night.

I tried to drown the pain of dejection but felt lost. There was I, Holger and the crowd and I was lost in the rim of the bottle. My children were tired. They wanted to leave, so we all went back to my hotel room. My suitcase was packed and I immediately regretted not accepting Holger's invitation to visit his room later that night. I tried to phone him but it was impossible. The infrastructure of the country was still threadbare and tentative enquiries on the telephone produced just a confused babble in a foreign tongue.

Next day, it was time to fly home. Finally I packed Svera in the suitcase, sat on the static aeroplane watching Peter outside with his friends cavorting on the makeshift runway. A young girl, probably his new woman, in her twenties, stood by him, with greying hair in his late forties. I felt disgusted. I took my diary out, looked at Nina and Minna of nineteen and fourteen sitting beside me. I imagined the shock I would feel if they came home with men twice their age. They were oblivious to the events around them. The Simpsons flickered onto the screen. The long arm of American culture had even spread to this newly liberated country, Eritrea. I bit my tongue and my mind wandered in a wild stream into the Red Sea, colour of my bleeding heart.

CHAPTER 17
The Time-Lapse Film

Time is a forceful ox raging through this universe with its mighty horn,
its broad backside slipping away through the mist,
leaving behind its cow pats, strong odour
and the ruthless footprints of all that it has trampled on.

As the airplane picked up speed, I looked out of the small window. Peter's broad back started to disperse in the sharp sunshine spread over Asmara. The wondrous city, a Haven of tranquillity was a soothing shadow to Peter's disturbed psyche. The big roaring bird of iron and steel sped on the runway banging hard against the wind, pieces of shattering metal hit my hearts' glass frame. I shrank back to seek comfort in the soft white pillow of the seat. Love, that forbidden fruit I had touched, smelt, tasted, absorbed in my skin so deep for twenty five years, had exploded, with one cut of the dagger of deceit. Somehow, a shapeless spirit within me desperately fought to keep itself alive, compelling me to look closer at my inner self, closer to your wisdom, mother, closer to my essential beliefs, some of which I could face, some I buried like the graveyard. Words were my attire. I dressed myself in them to cover up my naked, wounded soul. Words. I drank to quench my thirst for more. Words I slept with, made love to, gave birth to new courage. At last. Yes, mother, I was now home and home in Bradford. I was here to find my peace in the company of this house with its ears, eyes and senses. The ghosts of the past and present were there, to help me to slay the demons of disturbance.

My house sits on the hill overlooking the famous Cliffe Cemetery.
A wonderful place of rest, resplendent in reflected glory,
where obelisks point high to a hopeful God
and the bones of merchants lay in tombs fit for Caesar,
where undergrowth spreads gothically in the unexplored parts.
Vast expanses of bramble bushes arched over like cathedrals
providing the perfect hiding places for insects,
spiders, small animals and dope dealers,
like the underworld spreading through this city
of intolerance and separation,
of fear and suspicion,
of words that should not be spoken,
of issues that cannot be raised for fear of that midnight knock,
of segmented ghost towns which lie cheek by jowl
with the net curtain clipped accents,
of gypsies and thieves,
of long gone Germans and Irish men
who rolled up their sleeves and dug the canals,
those flat, straight works of art,
of Asian nightshift workers who toiled on dangerous machines,
of penniless Ugandans who dragged themselves up by their bootstraps,
of fading trolley lines and fumed up bottlenecks,

of sixties white elephants and exotic back alleys.
This city has it all.
It's where they burnt the book against the words of the Prophet
where cappuccino drinkers admire Hockney,
where Charlotte and Emily penned their rugged books
on moors that look down from a parallel world.
This city is where I continue my search.
Why here? For what reason?
For one, it was here that the ghosts would depart from me.

I strolled through the cemetery, delving inside the soul of that lost girl, woman, Svera. I looked at her as she stroked the feathers of her life, shining, strong, bold colours. Love is tarnished, but not Svera. I looked at a magpie, flying freely in woodlands. Words of a poem someone had written about magpies sprung to my mind. "Ruthless creatures amongst birds, who stole." Every time I walk through this place I see magpies, pricking the conscience of humans. Magpies, Foxes, ghosts peacefully perform their own rituals. Who are the thieves? Ghosts or the humans who plunder in order to build their own empires? It is the humans I fear and see hunting for more, thirsty vampires, sucking the blood of others to quench their greedy thirst.

It's late afternoon - Undercliffe Cemetery in the twilight of autumn. Yellow, brown, golden leaves falling under my feet like showers of memories, making a soft rug for the thunderous storms, winds and the snow yet to arrive in my life. I am the observer, a venturing traveller in a state of hallucination, watching Svera climb slowly the steep path. While she makes small stops, I listen to her gasping breath. She had wanted that moment so much, she was pregnant and in pain, was going to give birth, to nurture the baby of higher consciousness, feed it, let it grow.

I was playing the role of a midwife. There would be many years of labour before the strong Svera is re-born. I was waiting for it to happen. There is a long way to go. There always will be. You had gone through your pain, the birth of your search, your journey, your choice. Why couldn't I? Don't you see what it is all about, mother? Minna, Nina. You?

My doctor would not prescribe more drugs.
"I have observed your life. You don't need tranquilisers. A woman like you..."
I did not hear him. The sound of his voice became a blanket covering my ears. I knew my body more than he did. I needed to open my heart to someone. The way out was therapy, but it would take a lot of thinking and courage to enter that door.

Wednesday afternoon, 1st September 1994. 4.30pm.
"Hi, my name is Lola, please make yourself comfortable."
She spoke softly.
"Let's fill out this information first. It will only take a couple of minutes. The actual session will last about three quarters of an hour."
The young female psychologist seemed to have control over things. I felt restless, a bit intimidated by her power over me. I sat in front of her in a big armchair, its arms wrapping me to shield my embarrassment, shyness. The room was a comfort zone womb: a table beside me with an ashtray, water and a box of tissues to wipe the traces of hurt. The pale concrete ceiling offered the material dimension, a balance to my wandering spirit. In panic, I grabbed the glass of water. She spoke again.
"Well then..."
Lola with her long grey skirt and piercing oval eyes watched me, "Would you like to tell me about yourself?"
"I don't really know where to start. I have just been to Africa, visiting my husband. Things have deteriorated between us since I found out he had an affair with a young woman out there. I'm..., I feel I'm, going crazy.".
My hands were shaking. I tried to keep them still. Like an innocent victim of circumstance, I continued.
"I see no choices in front of me. I am so bitter about everything. I even made long distance phone calls to Peter, humiliated, angry, threatening to expose him, thinking things would work out between us. But all that

effort I made to visit him seemed in vain. I've lost my confidence. I do not know what to do."

"This is a safe place to be. No pressure. You are free to tell me anything. Here you have the choice. If you don't want to talk, it's ok."

A self-assertive smile oozed from her face like milk from a cactus. A pause hung between us like a starched piece of Khanga on my bathroom window, keeping the pervert from peeping in. Holding my stomach tight, I spoke in a low voice as if frightened, as if dreaming.

"If infidelity was a sickness, I would ask my doctor to cure it. This cancerous virus is going to take my life. I would willingly swallow a thousand quinine pills if only my relationship could be saved. But then, I'd be dead. I have two daughters, they need a father. I am growing old, I need a man. What am I going to do?"

"Tell me what you do, Svera. Do you work?"

"Not at the moment, but I write. In fact I have started writing a lot these days. I cannot sleep, so I write."

Why is she not telling me what I should do? I feel the blood in my veins slowly racing towards my face.

"What do you write about?"

"Oh, it's... I mostly write poetry. Well I used to write for a newspaper, the 'Daily News' in Tanzania."

I try to breathe steadily.

"Oh, so you've been to Tanzania?"

Lola looked intense.

"Yes we came to Britain two years ago."

"My Mum used to live in Arusha. Oh, the beautiful Mount Kilimanjaro. I was born there. My parents moved here when I was only six months old. My Mum can't speak English but she can speak a bit of Swahili. My parents are East African Asians really."

"Well, I can speak Swahili and Danish."

"Ah so you have travelled around."

"A bit, yes. I was married to a Dane. Well, I still am."

"Ah, that's interesting. We don't see many Danish Asians here in Bradford. So, Svera, you write poetry."

She looked through her files.

"Actually, I know they need someone like you at the college to teach young Asian women bilingual poetry. I have this leaflet somewhere. Tell you what Svera, I will find it and post it to you."

She leaned back in the chair looking at the huge statue of Hanuman standing in the corner of the room. Then she looked at me. I looked at Hanuman.

"After this meeting it's important we meet regularly and I'm sure we'll find an outlet - leaving India to travel to Denmark, married to a Dane, in Africa and now here. Svera, you have been through much. No wonder you feel the way you do and you still look as if you are going to make it. You don't need tranquillisers, doctors or a therapist. A woman like you..."

She was looking deep into my eyes. I closed mine and heard her voice disappearing behind the sound of her words. My mind drifted away to a distant place.

A woman like me? Who is she talking about? Svera? Does she mean Svera? That girl, that woman who was once very strong, bold and determined. But who am I? Been through much? India, Denmark, Africa. Where am I now? I felt I was in a dark tunnel. Oh, God, I don't want to be here. Please let me out. I wanted to scream, but sat glued to the chair, staring into the dark emptiness behind my closed eyes. My head felt light as if I was flying. I tried to concentrate on listening to her words, which began to flicker like beacons in a vast airfield, dotted along either side of the runway waiting for my jigsaw life to touch down. Continents, places, cities, people, pictures from the past, like time lapse film, instant replay, my life running backwards, fractured images, watching my existence as a random series of events dropped into a fishbowl. In my vision, I saw Hanuman, the monkey god, slowly walking towards me, wagging his long majestic tail, carrying his sceptre on one shoulder. His big round friendly eye winked at me and he held my hand, gently pulling me up to stand. I felt like we were floating through the room as we walked, like being carried up, out of the window, where he took hold of a rope vine and we swung through the air, disappearing into a hole in the sky. My eyes were wide shut as I heard him whisper my name.

"Open your eyes Svera."

"I'm scared."

"Don't be scared. I want to show you Svera's life. Take notes. Record events in your mind. You have to tell her story."

"O.K, show me."

"Ah, this is Copenhagen, look down, there she is - Svera in her late twenties. Hang on, this looks like a flea market in the outskirts of Copenhagen. Strong, energetic, positive and determined, we see Svera waltzing through her hectic and complicated life. Take a closer look, you will see, she's walking with the illusion of love in her eyes, ready to do anything for Peter."

"Even carry a dead foetus on her palm."

I interrupted and looked down, watching Svera.

I clearly remembered the flea market. I remembered TTA, a splinter group from the main Communist Working Group, consisting of twelve members. The group was like a garden of budding flowers. They were devoted, well organised and were maturing into strong personalities. They made posters illustrating the need to support Liberation Movements. At that time in the middle of 70's, FRELIMO in Mozambique, MPLA in Angola, ANC in South Africa, ZANU in Zimbabwe, PFLP in Palestine and SWAPO in Namibia. Posters were distributed from house to house. Twice a month, a truck would drive and collect hundreds of bags of clothes within a very large area. TTA was a sincerely active group of young people. In the cold winter evenings, they would stand with their thick jackets, working for two to three hours, drinking hot tea and coffee to keep warm - young, committed men and women in solidarity for a cause. It was a productive way for Svera to get out of her isolation. Every week they participated in study circle, talking about how to organise and make them politically conscious, studying Marxism. The main activity was the practical support work. Did they see themselves as modern day apostles? Once a week clothes were sorted and packed in a big factory hall. Sorted clothes were pressed through machines to reduce the volume. Hundreds of bales together with medicine and shoes were sent to liberation movements in the third world.

The money from the flea market was used for transporting clothes, medicine and shoes. Sometimes sending weapons was a 'trend' at that time amongst the middle class Marxist intellectuals. Of course Peter was sending clothes to the whole of Africa. That took precedent over everything. His wife, his daughter, the new shelf he should have built for the living room.

Svera never missed going out to collect and sort clothes, or to meetings. Before leaving the house, she would agree a time to return, in case something happened. She would arrive at the promised time. Peter would read or watch T.V waiting for Svera. He would have tea ready for them. She loved to sit and sip tea listening to Peter's thoughts about the working class, Marxism and his longing to do something 'meaningful' in life. Peter frequently attended CWG meetings. Svera would return the favour by waiting up late with a pot full of Indian tea for him. He enjoyed listening to her discussion of the TTA.

At first it was fun, distributing leaflets and then collecting big bags full of old clothes. TTA members were proud to support the movements in the Third World. It was a drop in the ocean. But it made a difference. People threw out nice clothes, shoes and furniture. Svera thought it was very affluent and bourgeois. But if they did not throw them out, what could be sent to the people who needed them, she wondered. At times Svera despised going out for sorting and packing. She hated to touch the dirty, smelly, unwashed clothes and the ice-cold warehouse would make her shiver, but she was afraid of offending Peter. He forced her to go. She began to wonder whether she really was being petulantly middle class. Sometimes a member of CWG would come and honour TTA (Clothes to Africa) with a lecture. Svera particularly liked the young, tall handsome Jan with golden hair. His beautiful smiling eyes always flickered with energy. He always probed Svera why she had come to live in a strange country like Denmark. His two sisters adored Jan like a hero, just the way Svera worshipped her brother Amar. Jan and his sisters played an active part in the political struggle of the group. Jan was clever with words. With his good looks and angelic eyes, he could easily persuade the young generation to support the liberation movements.

"They are fighting for their liberation. They need our help, any help we can offer them, comrades."

Jan would speak with a twinkle in his eyes. He died a very tragic death. It was a strange accident, a head on collision with a truck.

People wondered whether it was a deliberate act of murder planned by the secret service of Israel, Mossad. He was one amongst a long list of guys who were ready to help when Svera needed a green card. Svera would have married him. It was her fate not to become a widow. Do you believe in fate? Before Svera realised, she had become seriously committed to meetings, collecting clothes, sorting and packing them to send away. Sometimes she would demand that people in the group spoke English. She wanted to understand everything. Out of politeness they would do so, but the conversation would be switched over to Danish automatically.

"Look, Svera, look at the comrades, how they are working. You are very privileged to be working as part of a great cause. If you hadn't met me, you would've stayed in your middle-class fantasy world somewhere in a small village in Punjab. We must give everything, even our clothes. This is the front line of the struggle Svera. We are soldiers - ideological soldiers, fighters."

When Peter had finished speaking, Svera proudly picked up the small moneybox and took it to the stall she was supervising. Despite Peter's speech, this was something she wanted to do, something she could identify with. Svera's mother had taught her to support less advantaged people. Joshili always gave away her clothes, food and even money to poor people.

Peter's Communist Working Group (in Danish KAK, referred here as CWG), was one of the many such Maoist groups in Western Europe at that time. CWG consisted of former communists that had been excluded from Danish Communist Party because of their support of China in the ideological battle between Peking and Moscow. The slim, tall and staunch leader of GWG, Mr. Anderson, and his shapely younger wife Dina, started the group in their huge villa in the outskirts of Copenhagen in 1963, ten years before Svera arrived in Denmark.

Mr. Anderson and Dina managed to brain wash 20-30 young activists, who became committed to anti-imperialist work. Sometimes these young members were sent on a mission to investigate the working classes in different countries. India was one of them. Svera would often ponder over their intention of choosing India, when they had such anti Indian attitude. Why would they travel to India?

The Communist Working Group sometimes held meetings at their flat. Peter would persuade Svera to stay as an act of politeness.
"I am so proud to show my comrades how beautiful and intelligent you are, Svera," he would whisper in her ear as she uncomfortably sat listening to their debate on Emmanuel Arghiri's 'Unequal Exchange and the Prospects of Socialism'. Svera had learnt enough Danish to communicate but was shy to express her thoughts. There were words like 'roed', meaning red, where you had to role your tongue to pronounce as if the sound came from the throat. She would feel embarrassed but would stay at the table to please Peter. He would smile at her from time to time. He knew it was hard for her to stay on listening to their barely comprehensible Danish conversation. But he was proud to have her around, by his side. Out of politeness Klaus or Svend would ask Svera whether she liked the Danish food or how her job was going, but she wanted to tell them about what was happening in India. They were reluctant to talk about Indian politics. She was not a member of the CWG. They were too busy debating with each other in Danish and she would fill the thermos with more coffee. In the end she would give up being a mere piece of decoration and retire to the bedroom. Peter was sometimes irritated to be caught between his loyalty to the organisation and his wife. Members were not allowed to have children. Neither were they supposed to socialise with 'ordinary' Danes. On their trips to other countries, they were not allowed to come back before they had done their work properly. When they returned, they had to deliver their findings in the form of long reports.

Discussions were held weekly and members were often laughed at by the leaders if they couldn't present their arguments properly. Once a member asked Mr. Anderson which books he would recommend for reading. He was given a hundred titles. Some of the books were for pleasure reading with titles like, 'The Fascists and Revolutionaries in India' and 'Mao Commintern and Liu Shao-Chi'. In 1978 one of Peter's friends from Tanzania wrote an article for a small Indian Marxist magazine. He wrote that the European working class was oppressed and were soon ready to start a revolution. Svera had witnessed the European working class herself. She didn't see any oppressed workers. Svera was not a village fool after all. Peter suggested she wrote an article in response. Eventually she did and it was published in the same magazine. Svera saw the working class in Denmark living in big houses with expensive cars and other luxurious commodities. They had an excess of material goods. Those collected clothes were thrown away by the so-called 'oppressed' working class.

"Svera, are you listening to me? Svera, open up your eyes. You are still in a trance woman. It has caused your defeat." Hanuman became angry. He banged the air with his sceptre so forcefully that it made a thundering sound like clouds wrestling with each other in a battlefield. The sound woke Svera up. She looked away from the screen of delusions and saw two hands, eyes and the face of a woman.

"Svera, can you hear me? Come back, here, now, in this room". Two lips called my name and I heard the snapping of fingers keeping time like rap musician talks his way into meaningless oblivion. I found myself sitting in front of this other human being. My therapist!

Svera? Who is she talking to? Svera - a woman like me and yet not me. If I am not Svera, who am I? What is my purpose? What am I doing here, in this city, here in this room, where I sit helplessly in front of this person? Where was the Svera I saw with Hanuman? While Lola scribbles down some names and numbers for me to contact, I am trying to make sense of my confrontation with Svera, looking at Hanuman in the corner. I could see he was winking at me again. Wicked. Monkey business!

I observed Lola's well-sketched manner. What were her thoughts behind those rehearsed words? She could be saying the same things to all the other clients. I wanted to believe her, but feeling weak, timid, tiny, so very meek, I couldn't. Believing in myself was the last thing I could do.

My visits to Lola continued for some time. The trip with Hanuman into my past and the conversation with my therapist helped me to realise there was yet a struggle to wage, a path to tread, a search to pursue. Questioning. Finding. Minutes, hours, days and months were fleeting directions on a train moving like a toy on a circular track in the living room. After the eighth session she referred me to a marriage therapist. That, she concluded, was what I needed

A letter from Asmara arrived this morning, October 1994.
"Thanks for being so positive about everything. Thanks for the beautiful photographs of Eritrean kids. We might be able to use them to raise funds for the project we will be setting up for the war-orphan children. Sorry for all the trouble I may have caused you. You just have to make up your mind. I will agree with anything. If you want a separation, it'll be arranged. Love, Peter."
"If you want separation," he writes.

Fuck. What is this? One of his well planned manoeuvres? It was so formal, this letter - detached, like he was addressing an audience in one of his workshops. I had evidently become another tiresome chore in his revolutionary work. I thought that maybe he was trying to be nice to me. Maybe he regretted being harsh? Maybe there was a hidden meaning in everything he said. Maybe, maybe, maybe...Again, my trance, made an obstruction in my rational thinking. The illusion of a woman who was struggling to come to terms with her broken vision of love, harmony and family, faced with the harsh reality of departing from all this.

It was already December. A little pause for celebrations. Time to forget the vision of setting fire to my house that night, standing on my patio. I bought a huge fir tree that my children helped me decorate. I had done that for many years.

Small red and white candles were spread on the floor, soon to be burned to commemorate the family harmony. Stars, clay birds, round yellow, green, silvery balls, glass figures, straw dolls dangling on the branches, waiting to be lit with love. A huge turkey in the fridge ready to be roasted, sweet and sour potatoes, red cabbage, and, most precious of all, my children's anxious eyes wandering around the house, searching for a glimpse of the hidden-away treasures in the glossy wrapping of hopes. Christmas had started. Let me narrate the tale of this Christmas to you. I am after all the narrator here. My house seemed pregnant with thoughts, heaving and sighing with its own spooky pangs, ready to give birth to words in its own peculiar style

CHAPTER 18
She's A Dream Junkie

Now I borrow minutes, hours, months and years from the time machine and invite you to the scene where Svera and her family celebrate a traditional Danish Christmas. It was 24th of December 1994. Bradford, Yorkshire. The sky glittered with the dust of festivities, everything shining, everyone in the mood. Shops, streets, buses, cars were all buzzing, jam packed. You could walk alone late at night after shopping. Presents were bought, wrapped and placed under millions of plastic or fir trees. It seemed the whole forest had been cut down to light the human hearts in the winter dark.

Christmas Eve was in an old terraced house on the hill, overlooking the cemetery, like the dead overlooking the birth of Jesus - a festival symbolising rebirth and celebrations, new hope and peace between people. In the house on the hill a father, a mother and their two beautiful daughters, Minna and Nina, who were running around like wound-up clockwork toys. In the kitchen of that house, a pan filled with small rice corn in thick luxurious creamy milk slowly simmered on the fire. Father Peter, stuffing the big fat bird with cabbage, honey and oil looked like a huge goblin in his red gown. There were sweet potatoes frying, white potatoes boiling, green peas and brown gravy simmering. The atmosphere was enveloped by that delicious aroma which only brought bliss on special occasions. Mother Svera did the cleaning and took out the special blue porcelain set for the occasion. Tall crystal glasses of Piesporter Michelsberg for herself, medium ones for Cockspur, Old Gold Barbados Rum for him, a small bottle of sherry and bright, sunflowered short glasses to fill with apple cider for the two small gems of the house.

Proudly with his two big solid hands the master of the house, Peter, was half way up the staircase carrying the pan of hot pudding. This was also part of the traditional Danish hiding the pudding in a blanket until dinnertime.

"I hope you have remembered to buy the almonds, Svera," he shouted to her.

"Oh, God! I haven't. I am so sorry. I have completely forgotten about it."

"Faa helvede kvinde."

In a flash, Jekyll had again become Hyde.

"Faa helvede kvinde." He repeated his Danish curse. How Svera had come to dread that phrase. She knew he would be unstable for half an hour, two hours, three hours. Then there would be the sullen silence as he munched his favourite chocolate cookies and listened to the Danish Radio.

Svera offered to buy the almonds immediately. She was lucky this time, because it was Christmas. The Danish radio succeeded in calming him. "Greetings from Copenhagen. Happy Christmas," the presenter said. The message brought a child like longing to Peter's face. After sulking for sometime he calmed down and said,

"Ja, ja. Go and buy them now."

She put on her jacket and returned with the almonds by which time Peter had visibly lightened. Mr. Hyde had returned from his laboratory, peace reborn. At last everybody sat around the table to dine. The first dish was the white creamy rice pudding, traditionally served before the main dish.

"Who would like to throw this little almond in the pan," he asked.

"Let me, Papa," pleaded Minna.

When the white almond had been well hidden in the pile, they started eating and would eat until Nina crunched the nut between her teeth.

"I got it! I got it!" she screamed, taking it out of her mouth to prove. She was proudly pronounced the winner.

Second round, the main dish. The voluptuous turkey decorated with vegetables, nuts and cranberry sauce. Minna and Nina gulped their food eagerly.

"Not so fast, darlings," Peter said.

The tradition was that when the family finishes their meal, the mother and the children would wash the dishes, tidy the kitchen and only then would they be allowed into the lounge. Meanwhile the man of the house would place all the parcels under the tree, light the tree and ask them to come in.

"To do all these dishes is so boring, Dad," interrupted Nina.

"That is the Danish tradition, Nina, I'm afraid. The man of the house will now prepare the tree for that last final sparkle. Imagine all those glittering parcels waiting for you to unwrap them girl."

"Oh, Daddy, you are mean," they shouted in unison.

"You are a swan, Nina, and you are a sparrow, Minna. When I say fly, the swan takes the item from my hand to wipe. When I say chirp, the sparrow does it. If we play this game, we'll finish in no time," Svera said to the girls as they started washing up.

"Ja. Let's be fast Mama," they both shouted.

"I can't wait for my gifts. What about you Minna?" Nina asked.

"Ja. Neither can I," they giggled excitedly.

As soon as the dishes, forks and knives, spoons and utensils were sparkling clean and the whole kitchen was spotless, they eagerly went to wait in front of the closed door which would be opened by Peter who had lit the tree and placed all the presents underneath. He finally came out and asked them to close their eyes. They were led inside and were then allowed to look. Wow! What a sight! The green tree had been turned into the eighth wonder of the world, alive with dangling red and white candles, golden, silver objects, lighting the whole lounge. It was a spectacular beacon of glittering lights. They all flocked around to perform the ritual dance.

"Nu det Jul igen. Nu det Jul igen," all four of them holding hands, singing the first song of the evening, 'It's Christmas once more! It's Christmas once more!'

According to the Danish tradition, they had to go through at least ten songs. Then the grown-ups sat down while the children crawled under the tree to look for the gifts. Svera sat watching her children, her hands folded on her knees as she juggled various rhymes in her own imagination:

The sound vibrates
Rapturous music
Tightening its grip on my skin
The fir tree is laden with the winter leaves of gold
The midnight moon slides graciously
Into my lap like a puppy
Words collide with clouding thoughts
Words form pink, purple symphonies
And this restless night exposes its chest to
Philandering realities, smudged kisses
Departing travellers and the hope
To meet new ones
My sorrow might be washed away
In the darkness, never to return again

She can hear...I can hear...

She can hear...I can bear...
No more sor.....

In her anticipation, she did not hear or see any sign. Words did not flow in her own heart as they used to. No gestures, nor encounter, no union of souls. She tasted the bitter sweet liquid that kept on pouring into her writhing heart. She looked outside the window, beyond city, beyond shadows, towards light. A face flickered like Chandra, moon in the sky. The face she had seen before - two wide, blue-grey kind eyes with sensual lips, calling for her. She could hear a vague whisper. Was that face of a stranger calling out for her or was she a dream junkie?

Peter's heart was a log of soaked wood that no flame could ignite. The night was slowly burning in the ashtray like a discarded cigarette. Peter had been on his best behaviour just for that one evening. The night was withering away in his eyes like a strain. His mind was elsewhere - in Africa probably. Even Christmas couldn't bring the two individuals closer.

CHAPTER 19
Two For Joy

"Resting under the shade of a dry bare tree?"
A voice suddenly shot in the dark as my thoughts lost the ability to see the logic in passion. Voices from the past came to me in all shapes, phenomena and sounds. I wish they would bounce back to the place of their origin, into their own shadows and let me travel towards the light. Strangely enough not only could I hear voices, I could also see their fluttering wings like angels. Voices flew around me and everywhere they wanted to. Whenever I felt week, they got the freedom and went berserk. I wished I was a magpie with shiny wings and had control over things as she did. I am once more beginning to lose control. So I hear voices, see things and touch abnormalities. I get frightened, when I do, so I have to write. I write to fight my fear. I write words that I could not tell nor speak to anyone. Even not to you, mother. I write to tell, to influence, to change, myself and maybe others in a similar situation. I have to write. Sometimes I write without sleep. I write all night, surrounded by ghosts of memories. This ghost was tapping my shoulders to remind me that the time had come for me to grow new wings.

It was a Christmas tale I narrated to you - December 24th, 1994.

Five years, splashed like waves on the coral reefs of time. The sharks and piranhas showed their teeth between ripples of trouble and sunshine. The time was a pirate fleeing on a ship, after having stolen some of the gold from my youth. Peter had control over time. Peter and time, had joined hands to rob me.

This is the night of October the 10th, 1999.

The smoke of Silk Cut mingles with Dewberry vapours in the oil burning like my heart. I must have inhaled at least ten cigarettes. This is my bedroom. The fumes of the incense force out the ghosts of those days with Jaz and Peter. I can even feel the third eye of this house as it watches me constantly, helping me revive memories. It is tough letting memories prevail into the present and then commanding them to disappear. It is the hardest task one can go through. I let my words mount the horses of my thoughts, enabling them to ride against the winds. They also teach me to survive. Sometimes the horses get too wild. They run amok on the highway. I can't hold them back. I want to survive. I want to be the survivor. I don't want to fall down and cry.

Curling snakes of smoke are like memories, helping smooth my journey. I miss both Jaz and my daughter of nineteen, as I write, shedding small fire balls in the ashtray. She didn't want me to smoke, yet I do - a foolish addiction. Sometimes the story swirls in the darkness, struggling to come out into the light. My daughter is the flicker of my life. Memories, words, and hundreds of books are everywhere - in the lounge, in my daughters room, in the spare room, on the landing, in the kitchen, in the bathroom, in my bedroom, in the staircase. My desk is cluttered with papers, scraps containing poems, notes. Magazines and files are everywhere. Books and items of artwork from Africa, Canada, India and Denmark seem to be the only possessions I am left with. I like to be surrounded by these bits and pieces for memories. No one can take them away from me. I would rather live without owning a wardrobe than without memories. I chose to throw away the one Peter bought for us. It was dark grey, the colour I hate the most. Finally, I moved it downstairs, to the cellar. It is buried alive, like other memories of him.

There are other spooky items in the cellar. Last night I went down to switch off the boiler when I came across a small cupboard, hidden behind the shelves. It had a rusty padlock, looked almost ancient, a hundred years old, maybe. I tried to open it. It creaked as if it was alive. It was dark in there. I went upstairs to find a candle and then the telephone rang. My friend, Ali Somi, wanted to know whether I would be interested in going for a ghost walk in York with her and a few friends. I said no, that I had to deal with the ghosts of my past at home. She laughed and said I spoke in metaphors and that I was becoming weird. She was hoping to meet a man that night. I thought about the man in pink hat. Would I see him there? I forgot all about the cupboard in the basement and tried to find someone to turn the tiny little room beside the bedroom into a wardrobe instead, a trendy modern walk-in wardrobe where I would have all the new clothes I was planning to buy - fashionable sandals, high heel boots, a pair of leather trousers and a new dress. It would be like walking into the present.

Time has this breathlessness, ruthlessness and deathlessness about it. It doesn't stop for any one. It changes people completely. It has changed Peter. I can't believe I ever lived with that man. Of course it was the other Svera, the one I write about. Sometimes she is a complete stranger to me. Time has no colour, race or religion. It's cruel but treats people equally. When you don't know how to tackle it, it will pass you buy. I still think about Peter and smell his broad shoulders where I had once laid my head on our first trip to Germany. Should I wish I hadn't done that? He must be thinking or having similar feelings about me. If time was a magpie, I could perform some black and white reasoning with it, tame it, tell it to fly backwards. But you can never reverse the past. This moment will become the past as we step into the future, our present. We choose every moment that we are moving into and everything that's gone then become inevitable.

One for sorrow, two for joy, three for a girl, four for a boy, five for silver, six for gold, seven for a secret...never...told...gold.

This early morning, I saw seven magpies in a flock. Walking in the cemetery with my dog, Simba, had become a ritual. The grass was wet and quiet - an October day, cold and healthy like a dog's nose. The pale autumn sun was trying to push the mist away, but, like my recovery, it was a slow process. The lazy magpies flew away towards the tree as we strolled onto the narrow path. Simba chased them. One remained sitting on the ground alone, not lonely, but solitary. I love this bird with shining blue black feathers and a majestic tail. I envy her. Maybe she has the freedom to move anywhere she wants to. Where is the sorrow?

An arbiter magpie
The long autumn
Flutters its wings
On the lonely hibernating
Bird of my
Aspirations
You can shrine the twittering
Truths of
Her anguish, Moon

Yes, where is the sorrow? Certainly not in the magpie, but in my heart. Let the bird of sorrow fly away, walk through the misty path. Something was shining ahead of me, enticing me to keep on moving. A breath of fresh air brushing against my shoulders, pushed me forward. I can see the town from up here. How beautiful the grey shades were, soon the chandra, the moon, will come up. Remembering the many undone tasks, I finally return home, pick up The Guide from Saturday's Guardian, put the kettle on, make a cup of cappuccino and press my answering machine to listened to my messages.

"Hi Svera. It's only me, Anna. I was wondering if we could go to The Pennington tonight. I am really bored...,"
"Hi, my name is Suzy. I saw this leaflet about your group. I was wondering if I could join..."
"Hi, my name is...let's leave it at that. I will tell you my name when we meet. I am sure we are going to. I am not from your city. I got your number from a friend and was intrigued enough to make this call. I have seen you before. My number is..."
"So how was your Sunday?"
Out of extreme curiosity I had phoned him, thinking he may be the man with a pink hat. His voice sprinkled the embers of sound in my ears, trying to overtake my solitude, my freedom. It was only a voice, a

very sexy voice. I caressed the phone. The sound sails on the air. I had seen him earlier, somewhere.

The kettle makes hissing sounds. I make another cup and go upstairs. I continue to write and time flies. My phone disturbs me. I extinguish the cigarette to steal a pause from the eroding flow of my memory. I have only started smoking recently, since my eldest daughter, Nina, didn't come home for her twenty-second birthday.

"The man with a pink hat?" A shiver of sensation runs through my spine and in my mind. In desperation, I try to catch an image from the voice. I even feel the warmth, momentarily.

"I said I will tell you one day who I am. Not now. I was trying to enlarge your image on my computer. I am sorry you couldn't open the file. I'll try again later. I am not very photogenic. I am anxious to meet you."

"I will now baptise you with a name – Johnny - that's what I will call you until ...well, until, we meet. I do not seek your approval." I said with determination.

"I know I have seen you before, many years ago, in my city. I had been searching for you. Why didn't you come to me, Svera? We have to meet, Svera. We have to, Svera Jang."

"There's some fear in your voice."

"Do you know that when a kettle is put on to boil it seems to take ages. As soon as you step aside, in no time at all it starts to boil," he said.

How did you know I was boiling a kettle?"

"Be patient Svera, you always ask too much. Enjoy the moment. You are creeping into my mind like an illusion. You run through my mind like a lake. The wait is like a shadow, so I chase your light."

"I thought I was the only one who talked in metaphors," I replied, thoughtfully.

"Who said?"

"Does it matter?"

It was Joseph, I whisper in my mind.

It was getting dark. Soon shadows of memories will start to chase me. This man could be a ghost but he seems so close, though far away. I had only spoken to him on the phone. He was just a voice from a distance, the midnight caller, holding sessions of steamy conversations on the phone when he needed to have some fun. He thinks I don't know that. Maybe he had a lover. Maybe, he had a child with her. Maybe this, maybe that.

All these men you meet or bump into, these days – old-fashioned, divorced males in search of love and passion, names on a typed list: smokers, non smokers, junkies, old hippies, good looking, short hair, long hair, bald, big dicks, shrivelled penises. Men with children, ex wives, depressed, abused, physically unfit, with a mysterious past. Men looking for a bit on the side, a spicy affair with a woman who can teach them the Kama Sutra - the 'art of love'. The mail order romance that invariably disappoints. What are they looking for? A woman like me, attractive, but perhaps too intellectual for them, too clever to know of their cruel intentions? Is it conceited to think that? I am a poet, a writer. I can see through some of their intentions. I can surprise them with words, poems, pictures, thoughts. These men are invariably office workers, computer operators, musicians, poets or travelling salesmen selling their hearts to the highest bidder. But even they don't know what they are searching for. I always meet them at the top of the motorway - me in my car, they in theirs. We look at each other across the car park and make instant judgements. First impressions really do count. Then they invite me for a drink or a meal. They always pay on the first date. We talk, laugh, make earnest eye contact and decide whether this is the love that will endure and make our subscription worthwhile. On rare occasions, I like to invite them back to my house. Most of them are never seen again, other than a midweek phone call. Maybe this was not what I wanted. I am still searching. It is not the Mr. Right that I seek, rather a filling of an emotional gap and the sensation of waking in the morning with sheer enthusiasm for the twenty-four hours ahead.

"I was pleasantly surprised when I got your picture," said Johnny.

"A few times, I have talked to women on the net. They describe themselves as something, but when we exchange photos, or meet in person, the picture changes completely. I didn't realise such beautiful women were available on the other side of this screen."

They all fell in love with my picture. I did not know what other kind of women he was talking about. It was evident that I was a catch. But it was I who was doing the fishing and enjoying the thrill of it. Was he really a catch for me?

He continued,

"They should be coming through the net now. My photos are coming through..."

I fiddled with the mouse and clicked on the attachment. And there he was in all his mature splendour. Five images of Johnny, 6 foot athletic build, loves music, art, women, sports, acting on impulse, and above all, life. How could these men describe themselves as if they were commodities for sale in a supermarket? That was exactly what you once tried to do for me Mum, Uncle Karl. You sent my picture to a man in exchange for his picture. That was exactly what I was doing too. My rational voice told me that in this day and age it was normal to meet like this. Work schedules, the fear of going to a bar alone,- they are why net chat is taking over.

"Listen Svera, I want to make a confession," he intoned over the phone. "I saw your photograph. If that's really you, I am stunned. I promise to worship you as the goddess of love. You will be a rose, Svera, in my heart."

Not your white English rose sucker, I thought to myself and was amused with the idea of him calling me a black daffodil instead! Ha ha ha!

"I could cross all this distance to come and see you soon. I know we will get on well," he said.

I hesitated. An excuse came quickly into my head.

"I can't pin myself down to a specific date at the moment, but give me your number and I will ring you next week."

I imagined a frown of surprise from Johnny. He did not know whether he had me yet.

I wanted to play the game of cat and mouse. That he had fallen madly in love with me just after seeing my picture was a bit too far-fetched reality, which made me shiver with an unknown pleasure. I put the phone down, sat for a while and felt strangely liberated by my rejection of this man. But could I reject him? I took my sheet of men from the agency, crunched it up and tossed it in the bin. A thousand needy stories jettisoned from my life. How good it felt. I wrote Johnny's phone number down in my notebook, just in case.

"You never know," Anna my friend would say.

Yes, you never do. She was dating four guys at the same time – a clever move indeed.

I logged off from the computer and returned to my letter. My words tumbled out as if energy had been blocked and I was free to pursue my true vocation. I wrote through the night. The tale of Peter's betrayals was still not finished but I felt I had begun the healing. Now I could remember him not with a bitter taste of Quinine in my mouth, but lemon with salt.

It is 5.00am, Monday morning, November 14th 1999. I, Svera Jang, once a true believer in love, romance and dreams, in the company of my memories, am trying to find the meaning of this four-letter phenomenon called love. How can I? Can you tell me, mother? Can you Johnny, Jaz, Johnny B my Jaz, oh, please be here, Johnny, Johnny. Johnny?

You have to find that inner...Is it you Johnny? A voice is speaking and disappearing like dewdrops with the first morning ray of realisation. I stop for a moment to place my right hand on this palpitating roundness in my chest to touch and feel the normality of life, to come out of the abnormality.

"Aa ke dard jawan hei." Lover come back to me, my pain is young.

Sunrise radio is blasting the melody. Johnny's voice echoed in the mild air of my room. I opened the window to let this trapped energy out like a Genie from Aladdin's lamp. The breeze came in to pay her tribute. The mild dewberry vapours, reminded me of your soothing fragrance of strength mother. I sit on my double bed to perform Salvasana, a duet of the body and mind.

The blue and pink coloured quilt falls over me. Like a feather, I float in between the colours of reality and dreams. The house breaths in its own peculiar harmony. While it does, I shall enjoy my sleep.

CHAPTER 20
Upside Down, Inside Out

This is, well, this is me. I am a no word wizard, but a solid terraced creature, immobile on the hill, a tower of some fifty four thousands moons, a hundred and fifty years ago - a mindless series of brick walls standing for centuries, protecting the innocent and the abusers and whose fate might finally be to crumble to the dust, perhaps to be hurled by the homeless at a policeman in some urban riots.

The main character of the story discovered me on one of her walks in cemetery. She polished my interior so much that, I started to gleam in the darkness as an inspirational wall, perfect on which to graffiti your life story, Svera's story where she is acting the part, playing the role, writing the script, all simultaneously. In the process, I noticed she had started to delve deep into the abnormalities of life. I dragged her back to reality. There were times, when I saw her press her belly so hard as if she was trying to let the trapped northern wind of pain out of her womb. Agony of her existence aggressively messed up her psyche, made her confused, was turning into unproductive thoughts. In such situations, I was the midwife, giving that final push to let the devils come out into the light in the form of words. Her entangled thoughts needed an outlet, a flow in the right direction, like water through a hosepipe, umbilical cord, life vein filled with millions of molecules, mental electricity moving in the path of least resistance, re-connecting the threads, to let the story meander like a river.

This was one of those moments, when she was lost in her own dream world. She wasn't going to interfere with what I did with this script. I got the free hand. I did my best to create suspense by keeping a few things removed from reality like giving myself a fictional name, The Cliffe House. How's that. We've met before, in and out of chapters. I'm the wall at the end of your blind alley, the logical place for us to finally catch Svera as she chases herself through a maze, wandering from one place to another. Like Johnny, I wouldn't want to reveal my identity yet. So I welcome you. Step into my vicinity and share with me the secrets hidden behind my obstinate walls. I have been here all this time to be a witness so that Svera can continue to form words, running through chapters, paragraphs, making a mess of lines, cut and paste, rewrite, go back and forth, delete, add, discard. The delicious irony of describing the violence inflicted upon her gives the story its punch.

My senses started to develop fast as I slowly became part of the script - a character in a story with eyes, ears and a nose. I could smell trouble faster than time, ahead of time, before time. What I didn't know was that I had finally grown a soul within myself. Don't be shocked - this is as much a surprise to me as it is to you. I creak when the children jump on my floorboards. I bow to the power of a tornado. I acknowledge when I see something that I respect. I stand firm against the winter wind. I frown when I hear the arguments, the beatings. I blush when they make love and rattle my windows. I whisper when I hear her name called out in an orgasm. Sve...ra...aaa...I hope you are itching to hear me out. I love to describe events and express myself. I am going to let you into Svera's story. Let's draw the curtains aside, so you can see. This is a scene from early March 1995. Remember the storm in June 1995? We are only going three months back.

Soft, white flakes of floating cigarette papers fell from the vast heavy Western sky landing on my roof top, making me look like a giant joint as my chimney gave off a little smoke, I was hoping that no one was getting stoned by smoking me. Oh, I hate these winters, when I look like a ghost. I could do with a bit of sunshine to colour my skin and an extra wrapping of paint on my windowsills. Svera is afraid of the height, so she was probably hesitant to climb up and do the job.

The more I grew fond of Svera, the more she turned into a moody witch, filled with contradictions. Sometimes, her brain was a breeding ground for volatile thoughts and she created wonders. Two years ago, in March, there was a winter like this with heavy snowfall. The whole of

West Yorkshire had become a frosted field with a thin layer of sunshine glazed over Bradford and a mysterious glow. Svera went berserk with her camera. She drove miles to find images for her photography. Let me show you one of the rare scenes she caught. In this majestic cemetery a woman stood on the heap of snow with a little fellow by her side, maybe her son. Their black faces bathed in the orange lustre against the white snow. As if the heaven had created the scene. The mother and the son were so still that they looked like ghosts. Maybe they were lost in nature's backdrop, but there was something unusual about the two figures. Their eyes were shining, calm and didn't move with the click of the camera. There was no one else in the cemetery.

Another day in March, 1995. Svera came home from her work, parked the car on the pavement with heaps of half melted snow. With a pink shalwar and kurta, matching earrings and bracelets, she stepped out of her car. A shining bright light formed against the drizzling sky reflected on her face as she walked through the muddy slush.

"Wow - You look great."

Nina opened the door for her Mum. Peter's head turned to look as Svera entered the lounge to greet him. He was munching his favourite cookies. The room was filled with disorder. Books, papers, files, press clips, holiday brochures, newspapers, cups and plates were bubbling on the floor like warts. Mr. Bean's crazy eyes popped out from the T.V. as Minna sat on the sofa, her eyes glued to the screen. I hate this funny little monkey man creature. The kitchen had accumulated heaps of dirty dishes, clothes and music cassettes. Svera's own bedroom needed a face-lift like a mature woman who had been neglecting to go to a beautician. Svera was annoyed with herself, with children, with Peter. She paced up and down from the living room to the kitchen, back and forth, until she heard Peter speak.

"What do you think you are doing?"

"I am just trying to figure out what is going on here. Where is lunch?" she said.

"Honestly, I don't know what you want from me."

He looked at her shaking his big head, munching his favourite cookies with crumbs falling all over his sweatshirt.

"I think you do," she imploded.

"Well, since you insist, let me put it this way. I didn't want to prepare that lunch you ordered on the phone. I haven't come all the way from Africa just to follow your bloody wishes. Do this, do that. What do you think I am? I am....I am..."

"You're a sly old bastard!" I shouted at Peter on behalf of Svera.

No one could hear me because this was not part of the script. I observed Svera while Peter was finishing his sentence.

"I am the director of an important project in Asmara and I am here to relax and not follow your commands, Madame. Do you understand?"

Startled, Svera returned to the kitchen. Not knowing what to do, she took the pastry out of the paper bag. She took the knife out from the drawer, held it in her hand and thought of lashing out at Peter. Instead, she cut the cake in four pieces. Licking away the sugary crumbs from her fingers, enjoying the taste, she watched her face in the glass door of the cupboard.

For a moment, she saw clouds, fog, patches, and chaos peeping out of the mirror behind her reflection. I watched her and instantly stretched my hand to comfort her. She sensed something slide behind her back. She thought it was Peter's rough hand trying to reach her in his desperation or his whole personality disappearing like a ghost of the past. It could well be the shadow of her future, Johnny, maybe. She was frightened to imagine and so was I. Her hands started to tremble. She looked away from the mirror to rinse them in the sink as if she was trying to wash her fear. The sound of the clock on the wall was a reminder. She was losing it. She was losing her sanity and the synchronised beating of her heart and the wall clock was ruthlessly reminding her of the loss. Ruby's words echoed in the air.

"All men have affairs. Don't take it too serious. You can't trust men. You shouldn't have let him go alone. They have a wild animal between their legs. Men created chastity belts. But they got it wrong. It is women who should have created some medieval shield to control their roving manhood. Every wife should have the only key, Svera."

Reluctantly, she stepped out of the house into the pouring rain. From the roof top window, my eyes became the lens to watch over her while she drove back to work. She was lost in herself, trying to ponder over things - a wise thing to do. She felt weak, unable to fight the arrogant bastard. Her eyes were filled with tears and her vision became blurred. The drive to her work took longer than anticipated. Life without Peter seemed a barren land spread miles and miles ahead of her - life without a partner, a lover, a man, her soul mate. Teaching the students in the college was the in-between thing, merely a mechanical action. But it was between loves that we learned. It was beginning to get dark. Svera hadn't returned home yet. I anxiously waited for her return. It was still drizzling outside. I was soaked. The city lights dangled through the rain like the broken wings of thousands of fireflies.

At last Svera came back. Silently, she turned the key to the front door, stood near the window, looking outside, listening to the soft sound of the rain, looking at the lamppost. Voices from the many storms. Voice of her mother in the village. Voice of Uncle Karl. Voice of Jaz. Her inner confused voice. There were voices from the attic room. Nina had her friend Trish visiting. In the lounge, the ITV news was on. She drew the curtain on the window and headed straight towards the bedroom. The mirror on the wall was filled with vast blue sea of coldness. The carpet, a stripe in the ceiling, her tight fitted kameez, everything got reflected in the mirror through light, like an artist had splashed blue paint over all the world's worries. Peter's eyes, Nordic blue and cold. The clear blue sky with patches of sunshine and the rainbow were lost, far behind, in her childhood. She was now looking up into the flashing mirror.

Wait a minute, the mirror is cracking. A negative omen. It opens up to a sharp blue sky and another house, placed in the huge courtyard of a small peaceful village. Peaceful because it looks deserted. A little girl who has painted a rainbow with crayons on the cardboard dollhouse, sits beside it in a cross-legged position, crying. We see a four-wheeled wooden vehicle with two white horses, a rath, approaching from the horizon. We see an old wise woman with silvery hair driving the rath, which is stopping near the girl. The woman dismounts to sit beside her. The girl seems lost in her own little world. The old woman puts her hand on the girls shoulder. Now the girl lifts her big black tearful eyes.

"What's wrong, Guddi?" asks the woman.

"Nan, Ritu has snatched my doll, she has taken some of my toys, and now I can't play."

Guddi cries profusely, thinking the woman was her Nan.

"There, there, hush now. Look what I have got for you," says the woman, taking out a beautiful dolly with two long plaits in her hair, a sari and some jewellery.

"Ahh," gasps the girl in awe, admiring the doll. There are twinkles in her eyes and her tears dry away. She takes some utensils from a yellow brass box, which had been sent by her aunt in Bombay. She loves her dolls house. She starts cooking food with the stainless steel crockery to feed her dolly. She is dreaming of being a grown up woman, having a husband and children of her own, a nice cosy house to live in. This little girl, Svera had always been a daydreamer. The old woman has disappeared with her rath from the scene. Another voice appears.

"Svera, go and look after Bally. He is crying."

We see a middle-aged woman approach.

"O.K. Auntie."

Svera obeys at once, goes inside a room in the house. Now we see her rushing out of the room crying, holding her cheek. The mother steps into the scene to take Svera in her strong arms.

"There, there, hush now. Don't cry darling, what's the matter?"

"Bally bit me, Mum. He bit my cheek."

Svera is in tears again, sobbing, holding tight to her Mum.

"That little rascal. How many time have I told you not to go too close to that demon. You are always trying to be nice to others. You have to learn to take care of yourself, Svera. You must learn to tell the difference between evil and good."

"I am not scared of the demons and fairies, mother. Bally isn't evil," Svera insists.

The vision ends.

We see Svera in her bedroom, about to doze off with tiredness. She looks like that little girl from the village - tiny, dreamy, in a trance, vulnerable, weepy. She slowly undresses. Wow! What a body. Smooth brown almond skin. Any man would bring a dowry of heaven on earth for such a woman. I couldn't resist looking at her either. I wished I was the man of Svera's dreams.

I am getting personal. I shouldn't. I am the narrator here.

We see another doll with her blue dress, blueberry black hair, and a wide smile sitting on the shelf of a bookcase looking down upon everything including Svera. We hear the doll hysterically laughing at Svera, "Where is your rainbow?"
Svera is disturbed by that. She is trying to bury her face under the quilt, trying to hide from that wicked laughter. I heard another noise. It's the telephone interrupting the tranquillity. Let's hear who the intruder was this time.
"Svera, what happened? You were supposed to see me tonight. Are you O.K?"
It's Svera's counsellor, Lola. Svera had forgotten to attend her session.
"Oh my God!" Svera screamed.
"Everything is a nightmare. I heard someone laughing at me in my dream. Peter and I had an argument, and I'm right down in the ditch. I don't know what to do."
"I'm sorry to hear of your problems but you realise you do have to keep your appointments, Svera. Let's meet next week. Why don't you ask your husband to get counselling as well. It should be for two people".
"He will be angry if I ask him to. I'll try."

She puts the phone down and slides back under the silent purple of her quilt. She could still hear loud voices and laughter. Who were those people, downstairs? I sensed they were going to become characters in a story or a play. They couldn't possibly be Svera's family. Why was she alone in her bedroom if they were? She could smell frying onions and hear the chopping of tomatoes, the opening and closing of the large fridge, the Danish radio blabbering. Were they preparing a ritual? Someone must have slaughtered a goat – a celebration of the death of Svera's love, celebration of Peter's new wedding. The ringing of phone disrupted her melancholy once more.
"Can I speak to the poet?"

The person on the other end of the line had sarcasm in their voice. It reminded her of Peter and his lack of encouragement

"Can't you see your own self-indulgence in your poems? You are too emotional. Use logic. You should write about the people, for the people. Not about yourself."

Her anger vibrated in my walls. I started to shake - anger, empathy, watching over Svera.

It is all too much for a creature like me. I have started to become depressed, recently. I hadn't planned to do any thinking, so it has obviously become complicated for my poor soul. I can't think of anything else to say now. I shall retire within myself once again, to gather my thoughts, to fit myself into another chapter. See you some other time, people. I will let Svera step in. Au revoir, Kwaheri, Farvel, Phir Milenge dosto.

I have been in between the fractured images of dreams, trying to put the broken pieces together. Thoughts kept on walking behind me like shadows, sometimes turning my whole entity upside down, making me do things, think, create, forward, backward, static, moving, flashes of lights drizzling through the sieve of my memories. Having just awoken from a deep sleep, I can feel the beat of their footsteps. Maybe it isn't Jaz this time but the soul of a man I saw in London reaching out to me, a stranger, with a funny hat who didn't want to reveal himself. I gave him a name, as I do with other characters - Johnny. I am getting so used to penetrating into this world on the other side, a world where Svera once lived, where she often loses her direction, gets stuck in memories, ghosts. I am getting sucked into the tunnel of her memories. Let me perform the Surya Namaskara - obeisance to the sun pose. My bones are stiff. I shall continue my asnas. Johnny's always trying to put his hands on my asnas. I dream a lot these days even when I am awake. Last night I dreamt that I saw my village in Punjab, the big house where I used to live with Amar, my Uncle Karl and his family and you, mother, one of my baby cousins, Bally, all of us together. My father wasn't there with us. He was on the Indochina borders, defending his country. I have fond memories of Bally who is no more a living energy, but a ghost from my past. A stream of events, places, faces, is running through my mind.

Once I travelled to the island of Zanzibar in East Africa. I had to complete an assignment. I walked around, looking, listening, touching and tasting everything. There were faces, voices, the sea breeze, the sun. I wrote this poem, inspired by the landscape, the city, its people, a crowd which had gathered to receive their beloved leader. I always get inspired by my surroundings. I give them an energy. Anything that happens around me makes an impression on me, forces me into writing.

Bahari streets
of this stone town
cast majestic spells
over my perturbed travel
Blessed in their insouciance
I walk upon the footsteps of
an old Arab dynasty

There, against
an elusive sunshine, the castellated towers
of the Afro-Sheeraz rattling in
eucalyptus harmony

In between the vivid folds -
black clad beauties,
a stranger. I am caught up
in their coaxing fires,
sneaking my bare smile,
crossing the Forodhani Front
Too deep the water crimson
Too high the orange sails
Wind by wind they fly away
wavering in the sky
Now to the humming gathering
on the island of Zanzibar

it is the signing up day
of their patriotic fears
It is the chanting up time
for their hunch backed grievances
Inch by inch, taller than the crowd
the face of a beloved leader
floats like a black ivory icon
To join
Or not to join
Sitting on my
meaningless polite surface
writing these lines
I ask myself
a question

Poetry has always fulfilled a longing for exploration. It contains emotions, the desire to spread across cultural boundaries - love, hate, pain, empathy and the wish to change. The power to express eases the pressure on my mind. Words scripted on the pieces of paper, give me the strength I need to strive. They allow me to stay sane, intact. They help me to understand my own bewildered state. They prevent me from wandering in the rubble of sadness. So I won't break down completely. I compensate my isolation by writing.

I had a busy day today, teaching. The footprints of yesterday got somehow washed away with the rainbow flood from my childhood. You know very well, Mum, I used to sit up at night writing verses. I continued that habit. Even now in my solitude, I sit in my bedroom in front of this computer, writing. Most of my poems were kept behind their fear masks, not yet ready to jump out from their hiding place, in one of the many files, Peter had in his computer. I did not have access to his computer, as he needed it for his study. I was convinced that I did not write good poetry, thus the voice on the phone sounded like a threatening finger in my solitude, as unfriendly as Peter's comments. "Who is this?"

"My name is Tina. I got your number from Steve who works in the library. He told me you had a collection of poems for publication. Would you be interested in getting published?"

I at once recognised the woman on the phone. Months ago, I had met her at one of the workshops organised at the Central Library. Recommended by Steve I had attended one of those sessions, bringing the manuscript of my poetry. Here is the scene.

I arrive late. I enter 'the exchange', a small room on the ground floor of the library. Another young Asian woman in typical traditional clothes with a scarf on her head exudes confidence and determination. She is in conversation with Tina.

"..........I now live in a women's shelter in ...town. It is so difficult. If my brothers find out about this, they will kill me. My mother doesn't understand me. During my college days, I used to change my traditional dress to a short skirt and put on makeup in the toilet..."

I see Tina's shrivelled face filled with empathy for this oppressed Asian woman, a young Asian woman in need of recognition in the racist society of Britain, a white liberal community worker in need of presenting her case to draw funding from the social system.

At the end of the meeting, the young woman spoke Punjabi to me,

"It's easy to cheat the system. Goras sympathise with you when you show them how oppressed you are as an Asian women. Good luck with your project."

At once I saw that my chance of getting the grant would be unsuccessful.

At that time I did nothing to protest, because I, the character Svera, was not nearly as confident as that young Asian woman. I also know what I write here may be misinterpreted. Tina did not have the ability to see through my eyes, my experience, my consciousness and yet I felt betrayed by her not taking my book for publishing because I was not an oppressed Asian woman. I felt as if I was pushed to a corner, like a weak animal, by the hunter. Ironically, this made me an oppressed Asian woman, at least a neglected Asian woman.

"Those who have eyes will see. Those who have feet will walk. Those who have mouths will shout. But sometimes we are silent because we don't see ourselves putting our foot in our mouth". George was sitting on the pavement in front of the newly opened Cafe Red, in Portobello Road smoking a spliff, speaking to himself.

She might be wearing a shalwar kameez, but she's the one who climbs on top when she makes love to her man. She may be wearing a Burka but she's the one who leads him by a ring in his nose. She may have brown skin but she has a doctorate in metallurgy. She maybe a sweet looking delicate Chinese doll but guess who runs the heroin factory? She maybe a West Indian but she resents Africans. She may be a Filipino but she won't live in a neighbourhood with too many Blacks. All nations, all colours, all races, all classes have prejudices. Some Asian women are oppressed. Some take advantage of being oppressed. Humbleness can be taken as weakness, silence for complicity, innocence for ignorance. Every situation has a different answer. There are so many sides to examine.

For Tina I was a westernised woman who was a threat to her livelihood, because I was an intellectual middle class capable articulate Asian woman not prepared to be subservient or needy, nor did I have six children hanging on my breasts. I am a threat. Not all Indians believe in the caste system, or will tolerate being pushed into second-class citizenship. We are strong. We are female. We are equal. We will proclaim it. We are a threat. Asian women should be judged with compassion. We must trust in the ability of people to overcome the difficulties of their upbringing, their cultural prejudices and their economic circumstances.

Tina never contacted me long after the workshop had taken place. Now she asked whether I would be interested? Of course, I would want to get published by a proper publisher - my poetry, my photographs, books, this book. There had been a great jump from that time to where I am now. I had been busy chasing the illusions in this unique town of alleged cultural harmony, trying to figure out what was real, what was fake, what and who needed their false facades to hide behind, trying to sort words, the sequences of events, which occupied most of my life. Of course, sometimes I lost the logic of seeing through her eyes, what she had been through or touch the nerve of pain she had suffered, because I was slowly developing the ability of an author who had to ruthlessly cut the existence of subjectivity like the cutting of an umbilical cord from the belly of a mother, from her own flesh. I found myself busy wiping up blood that I had spilled in the process. You beat me, I bleed, yet still I have the subservience to clean up the mess you've made of me.

I am no longer interested in the tragedy of the community workers trying to pursue their own ventures by publicising oppressed Asian women for their own personal development. Excuse me - whoever you were, are, wherever you are, then, now, here, trying to help me whilst others ignore my existence - how dare you? Have I offended you? Tough. I can see through dishonesty.

So the excuse I made to Tina.
"I have visitors at the moment, but I will contact you later. I might be able to send my manuscript."
At that stage she was not very clear whether the project would ever materialise. That's exactly what she'd said at the end of the workshop. At least she had acknowledged my existence, I thought, and she was interested in my poetry. An hour ago when the phone rang, the sun was shining on the windowpane, suddenly the overcast spread and the sky became foggy, seemed it might soon throw showers of rain. Maybe I won't see a rainbow but I felt good and went down for the dinner prepared by Peter.
"We have been waiting for you for a long time, Svera. The food was getting cold while you were chatting away on the phone."
Peter frowned.

I wanted to keep the image of the changed sky on my mind, I wanted to run outside to go for a long walk in the cemetery where I could observe, think, thinking what Peter's intentions might be. I had decided not to become angry. I wasn't going to put my calls off just because he had prepared dinner for a change. I restrained myself from saying those words and observed Peter sitting on the chair with the authority of a host. I sat near Minna. We had finished the main course. The sweet dish was a big oval green fruit with freckled shell. Cutting the thin slices to put on his plate he smiled at Nina.

"This is quite a unique fruit. I didn't think you ever tasted anything like this before. It is delicious. Try some. It is from my own garden. I have oranges, strawberries and bananas," he said.
Nina took a bite of the strange fruit.
"Well, what do you think, Nina?" asked Peter.
"It tastes awful."
She spat a mouthful out in the serviette.
"How could anybody eat that?"
Peter flinched but maintained his air of a moral supervisor, saying
"You should come and visit me again. I have chickens, two dogs. People are so different. Unlike Europeans, they are friendly and helpful. My garden is big. You should see the kids, they are adorably funny creatures."

Peter always adapted to the culture in which he lived. In that sense he was flexible, it had to be said. Or perhaps the word that I am looking for is unassailable. I still kept quiet at the table, receiving no emotional contact from Peter, turning myself more and more inwardly, looking on, feeling sympathy with myself, not knowing at that time that my mind was working like a camera, storing the images happening around me. I hungrily gulped images in my silence, digesting food, letting thoughts render themselves. Nina's friend left. Nina and Meena went upstairs. Peter left the table to go in the lounge. I stayed for a while slowly gathering myself, putting the dirty dishes in the soapy water. I felt isolated, afraid to lose this precious commodity – sanity.

Do you remember, Ma dear, when my father came home from the border, how happy he was to be with you and us kids? I didn't know why I was comparing my situation with yours but I felt hurt, so decided to take a steaming hot bath. I had done the dishes. I had emptied the trash outside. I needed to empty my mind of all this cluttering thoughts. They were contradictory. I took a green crystal glass from the cupboard to fill with vodka and tonic. I cut a thin slice of lemon and added two square pieces of ice, held the drink in one hand and whispering a Hindi tune went upstairs to open the tap for the bath. I looked in the mirror. I stretched out the lines from my forehead. I loosened my black curly hair and vaguely smiled at my reflection.

The drink slowly mingled with my blood making the temperature of my body rise as the steam from the hot water filled the room. I stayed in the tub as long as possible, listening to a strong urge rising within my body for a male body contact. In my bedroom, I had lit the pink scented candles to warm the room temperature. With my drink by the bedside table I started to rub Nivea on my body. Instead of soothing my dry skin, the gentle silk cream made my body writhe for passion. When I heard a knock at the door, I felt uncomfortable. Who dared to disturb my sweet melancholy? Nina entered the room.

"What are you doing here Mum? I thought you guys were downstairs." Nina's head peeped in.

"My husband is in the company of his lover, Mr. Bean. I am sure that the Danish Radio will provide appropriate entertainment for him. I am sure there was a very important shoplifting incident in Copenhagen this afternoon, or a bank robbery. You know how Peter can't really let go of his roots."

"I shall send him upstairs."

I could see a flash of crimson over her face as she glint my half naked body. Then she shot off like a whirlwind. Two hot-blooded women. Ah, the poor man amongst double femme fatales.

Peter came up and walked into my room.

"Anything important you have on the discussion menu, right now, at this very minute? Can you not keep your usual petty talk to yourself? I haven't come all the way from Africa to listen to that bullshit you know. I can't say that your behaviour at the dinner table was dignified," he said with the air of a wronged defendant in a crown court trial.

"Why? What's the matter with you, darling? Have I been a bad girl? Hmm? Come and sit by my side. I have everything on offer tonight..."

I swigged from the vodka bottle.

"You won't get a woman like this elsewhere. No, no, no..." I slurred as I took my quilt off and revealed my naked body, rubbing my breasts with cream. His eyes wandered over me for an instance, his face stiffened and then fell. The sudden change of expression reminded me of a snowflake landing on the tarmac road in mid May, at a time when we least expect it. The radio clock ticked in a rhythmical beat with each gulp I drank. I got up to fill another one, counting the minutes as my body started to react to the strong alcohol. I was aware that I soon won't be able to hold a rational conversation and will lose control over my senses, but I was scared to have him hurt me emotionally.

"You are crazy, Svera. I am going downstairs," he spluttered, throwing his arms in the air.

"Come back Peter, love. How I miss your Viking body. Come and pillage and plunder in my bed, any time," I said with drunkard-heavy sarcasm.

Peter didn't know how to react. For a moment he stood looking at me. He stared at the bottle and then at my hardened breasts. He picked up my discarded pairs of knickers, and tossed them at me,

"You will become a harridan if you don't watch out," he said gravely.

I tossed the knickers back at him. They landed on his head and hung there. He peeled them off his face and gave me a look of utter contempt.

"Do you want to know why I left you, Svera? Because you behave like this," he intoned in the manner of a 16th century Lutheran preacher. Then he left.

I laughed hysterically, madly. He knew very well I never got drunk like that. I broke down into tears. An hour later when I regained my composure I could hear Peter in the lounge, laughing by himself, watching Mr. Bean's silly jokes. I was not even a footnote in his book. I could hear the stereo from above my room. The girls were dancing to the tune of a song. I could hear my house. It was trying to communicate to me. The flapping of the wind added colour to its rustling, breathing and sighing sounds. I held the empty goblet in between the sullen rifts of my fingers. My ears were buzzing and the voices were becoming frailer and frailer. My eyelids became heavy and I eventually slumbered into the world of fantasies.

When the next morning arrived Peter made notes on the interior of the house. Each item was listed, described and earmarked. The videos, the refrigerator, kitchen pots and pans, the twenty two year old broken sofa, the ragged chairs, the ancient video camera, the T.V, the nicknacks and mishmash, each tiny item. The span of a quarter of a century was condensed on to three A4 white sheets of papers. When he had done the work, he suggested we both add our signatures. What about my daughters, I thought. Shall we compress them on A4 paper too? What if we only had one child? Then it would be A3. Or would we cut two pieces out to divide? Or would it become a child with split personality? Or could it be two personalities, like Jekyll and Hyde...

"Have you read the book about Dr. Jekyll and Mr. Hyde, Peter? It was written by an English man in the last century," I asked mischievously.

He gave me a puzzled look.

"Why do you ask me that?"

"I'll buy you a copy as a going-away present," I replied.

He looked at me uncomprehending and continued with his list.

"It's only for your security," Peter announced brandishing the paper.

Such hypocritical lies. These possessions meant nothing to me, but it was the principal.

Unlike other women, I didn't even own enough golden jewellery for security. What about the money? Peter had all of it in his single account, and there was plenty.

"What about the money?" I asked him.

"Don't worry about it," he said holding a reassuring hand.

"I will make sure that the girls don't go hungry."

So be it, I didn't give a damn about that bloody money. All I cared about was my children and unwillingly I was ready to sign the piece of paper.

"Just do it, Mum. Just sign the fucking piece of paper," said Nina, sick of the spectacle.

I signed blankly, in a daze and came out of the room thinking, how easy it was for Peter to write off the sacred union of two people as if it was merely a contract framed egocentrically with pictures and words. He was acting like a cheap lawyer. He didn't care our twenty-five years of marriage going to gutters. Peter was taking a sadistic pleasure from the scene. Maybe there was something else going in his mind. In the kitchen, I added the freshly cut vegetables to the heated oil and I heard the hiss of whispers from behind the closed door.

"It's only for your security."

These words crawled on the floor like black spider, trying to spread the poison of lies under my feet. Vapours from the frying pan rose towards the ceiling. Even the fireflies fell dead under this spell. Frightened, I tried to hold the vision of live fireflies over Sukhna Lake in Chandigarh when I met Jaz for the first time. I switched on Atlantic radio 205.

We'll be together with the roof right over our head
We'll share the shelter, of my single bed
Is this love, is this love that I am seeking...
Is this love?

The evergreen soothing voice of Bob Marley latched on to the rising smoke from my heart. The document was signed. The roof over my head now didn't seem intact.

The smoke slowly crept out of the kitchen like a thief trying to push its way through the tiny keyhole. Peter was a thief who had robbed me of my youth, my passion, my love. I had sacrificed for him, travelled with him wherever he wanted, to pursue his own career. The pain was rising, making my bones creak, everything wrapped in a thick fog of my cowardly spirit. I was scared of my own weakness. I wanted light so I switched on all the lights in the house and started preparing the dinner. A couple of hours had passed by then. Minna came running down looking for her lost UB40. She threw all my cassettes on the table. Her long fingers moved restlessly and after making a mess on the table she ran upstairs to her own room. Nina walked in with the stream of light, looking agile and shallow. Her pale skin was tightened like a dried peach. Her raised hand told me something was bothering her. She didn't look or speak or explain anything. She was staring towards the void beyond me. Peter entered the kitchen. His cold blue eyes were blood shot. Forcing a smile he tried to explain to me that they were just having a father daughter chat. He then held Nina's hand in his and told me he had some business to take care of and packing to do. They both went upstairs.

Another ritual of silence at the dinner table was performed, without even exchanging glances. Late in the night I remembered that the red patio door was unlocked. Flakes of paint fell on the floor as I shut it. I slowly began to draw the black and white giraffe curtain in the kitchen window. The moon over the neighbour's roof seemed as if it was travelling to a far away land. I looked down towards the fence. Shadows of two cats fighting behind the gate fell horizontally over the wall. Cats are everywhere. The branches on the tree moved slightly with the wind. There was someone in the darkness. I could see a tall, dark figure and then it turned around to face me.

"Josef?" I shouted.

The shadow began to slide towards me. I got very disturbed, frightened. I switched the lights off, shut the curtains and stood frozen behind them. There was no sound, only the rustling of the wind. My hands forced to draw the curtain aside to peep again. There was no one out there, but a huge moon staring at me. Then I heard a bleak knock at the red door,

"Svera, please listen to me. Come out to me, Svera. It's I, Josef Strauss. I only came to tell you that, when one door closes, another one opens. Open the door Svera."

I looked at the red door and for a moment, I thought of opening that door, run away from my responsibilities, embrace Josef. If I had joined Josef at that stage, I would have been free from the consequences of describing and living the life of Svera who was vulnerable. As a narrator, I had to stay, stay alive, stay ahead of my thoughts and not get mixed up with these shadows but play the role of an observer. I chose not to open the red door. I chose not to join Josef. I saw Josef's back disappearing behind the shadows of a tree in my patio. I silently shut all the other curtains in the house, poured a glass of water, searched the old bottle of Amitriptyline to swallow only two tablets and went upstairs to sleep. Not yet Josef. The time is not yet ripe for our encounter.

Peter had arranged to call a taxi at 3 am. He left for Eritrea, while I was asleep. Nina had left too, leaving a note outside my bedroom saying she had gone to stay with her friend, Trish, in Coventry. She needed some solitude, away from what was left of a broken family and a sheltered home. Just like that. A plain message, no explanation. No excuse. It was very unlike Nina. She was on a three month break from university. She was a young woman of nearly twenty now and not a teenage girl. Could I prevent her?

Jane, my neighbour invited me for tea. I feared her inquisitive nature would overpower me.
"How is Nina. Is she doing all right at university? How is your husband? I am sorry I have been terribly busy with marking papers. It is one of the busiest times for teachers. We have to prepare for the results."

I had a strong urge to tell her about Peter's infidelity and that he was going to leave us. I wanted to know how she coped with her two adopted children, especially the teenage daughter who grew up to be a tough and problematic girl. I wanted her to advise me how to cope with family breakdown.

"I really regret not having my own children with my partner," she said.
"I was so self-indulgent. I only cared about my career. I didn't want children of my own. He went back to Nigeria. Later I adopted two children. My foster child, Sara, had grown up to be a very aggressive young woman. She always demanded money for going out, but didn't want to work. She had her moods. She smashed so much in my house. When she was nineteen I had to ask her to leave."

"This one is all right, aren't you, Danny boy? She gave him a kiss on the forehead. Danny was seven and well behaved, obedient. I left her, even more baffled then before.

I woke up to the mild morning of Sunday, 8th of March 1995, thinking about Nina. She usually gave me a card each year on that day. She had been away for the whole week. She hadn't rung or written a note. Later, as I returned home from my work, there was a card on the glass table in the hallway. Without greeting anybody or letting us know, she had come home and gone straight upstairs to her room, leaving a hand-made card for me.

The whole afternoon I sat near the furnace, half awake, half dreaming, looking at the card, her strong words, waiting for Nina to come downstairs and have a chat with me as she used to do. I thought of her when she was born. Peter didn't even want this child who had brought happiness to my life then. She was so close to me, so open, sometimes.
"On this year's women's day, I want to tell you something which you should never forget. I love you Mama, because you have always been there for me - a mother and a strong woman. I cannot ever repay the love, tears and sacrifice that you have given me, but I can give you a piece of my life, and that's why I am alive today. Please keep a part of me with you always so that I can travel this exasperating journey of my life. I love you with all my heart."
Happy women's day! Hail women of the world.

Thank God I fought him on that point. I sat for a long time waiting, not for Peter but for my daughter to come and open herself to me. It was warm in the room and the words on the card made everything glow. The humid weather outside was unlike last winter when it had snowed awfully into March. Maybe the spring of my life was just around the corner. Maybe I should move from this city, sell this house, which always reminded me of my past with Peter. I went to look out from the window in the hallway. There were sounds outside but it was quiet upstairs in the attic room where Nina was. Looking up towards the sky I tried to visualise the whole city with its maddening sounds. Drivers, people sitting in restaurants, students, young loafers loitering outside the Asian corner shops. Then I touched my heart with my palms and tried to listen to any sound of reasoning within myself. I felt there was going to be another gap in there. Nina was slipping from my hands like shifting sand. I could not hold her. No one could. She reminded me of young Svera back in Chandigarh. I didn't like the thought. I knew then I was soon going to lose that girl.

Those days, I tried hard to keep myself busy and pretend that it wasn't a disaster after all that Peter had left. I thought constantly of Nina and Minna and hoped things would improve. Nina had her own agenda but was confused. She would get up late into the afternoon, have a shower, then breakfast in front of the T.V. and wait for her friend Trish to arrive. She was rarely home and the little time she spent with us she would complain of all sorts of pains and aches. Her mood would suddenly swing from one extreme to another. I still stood in the hallway feeling a strange stillness of the house. I suddenly realised that I didn't like this tranquillity. I wanted the sound, the rhythm, colours, rainbows, music. I yearned to hear an old song. I looked everywhere for a Beatles cassette. Running from one room to another I finally ended upstairs on the hallway to Nina's room.

Behind the closed door I heard the music playing...as I approached nearer, I heard some soft sobbing. I got curious to know whether it was the music or it was Nina. I didn't want to push the door open as if I was intruding. She felt my soft breathing through the door and invited me in.

"You might as well come in, Mum."

I stepped into the room to find this pale, thin tall girl sitting on her bed sobbing trying to hide her face with her arm, I saw cuts on her arm. I looked at her face closely searching for an answer. Her black piercing eyes had turned red with pain. She buried her face in my arms and blasted these words.

"I hate this place, my room, this town and everything. I never wanted to be here. Not without a father. Why did he have to leave? The Bastard. I can't sleep at nights. I am mad at myself, with my father, this family that has broken down. I had to let my anger out Mum. Can you blame me for it? Is Peter really my father?" she questioned as I took her arm to look closely.

Her state filled me with guilt. She had recently started going out a lot with Trish who had come back to stay in town with her cousins. They would go out every night and come home late. Was she drinking? Was she on drugs? Was she with men? What was she doing out there every night? These thoughts would keep me awake, night after night. I suggested to her to find a job. She had found a job but after two days, she'd left it.

"Nina, Peter has left us. When a father leaves his wife for another woman he also leaves his children. He has left you and Minna. We have to continue our lives without him. You should pull yourself together."

"I don't need that, Mum. I am depressed. Please try to understand that. I am twenty now."

She tried to confirm her maturity.

One evening she sat in the kitchen with Trish for three hours, arguing. I did not interfere. I had been washing clothes in the kitchen, but left them to be sorted out later. Suddenly, Trish left and Nina said,

"I have to go out with Trish tonight. It is very important. Don't even think about preventing me. It could be dangerous."

"What is going on? Is there anything wrong? Don't you go out with her every night? What is so different about tonight?" I fired all sorts of questions. She looked at me.

"Yes. It is different. Just don't ask a lot of questions. I may even die."

She seemed edgy and nervous. She had a bundle under her arm, which looked like clothes. I got so terrified and suspicious about the whole affair that I thought Trish was going to have an abortion or something like that. Were they going to kill somebody, set fire to someone's house? I knew I couldn't prevent her, so didn't try to.

She left and didn't return until the next morning at 3 am. I was restless, sleepless, angry, hurt and worried for her safety. As I write this I wonder what you would have done Ma, if it was I, your own daughter who behaved the way Nina did. I must have done something similar to hurt you. Daughters don't realise. You must tell me one day. You were the family pillar. Your word was the final statement, not only because my father was the provider, but he made it possible for us to honour your words. Each word coming out of your mouth would be respected. The most crucial factor in my daughter's suffering was her own father's absence in her life. One day I managed to persuade her to go to town with me. After some aimless window shopping we decided to have cappuccino in one of the crowded cafeterias.

"I wonder how these people can manage to shop around, when there are job cuts and the prices are sky high.," I said and looked at her face. Colourless, dark rings under her big, empty eyes. I should have been more wise, I thought, sitting there watching her.

I sensed her irritation. She only seemed to be there half-heartedly. "Why are you looking at me like that?" she snapped.

"There is something bothering you. I can feel it. You are so restless and uneasy with everything these days. You have been very touchy. I know you have gone through a lot lately. But there is something particular. Maybe you would like to tell me why you had to go away, after the heart to heart with your father." I encouraged her.

After sipping coffee slowly, hesitating a bit in the beginning, she told me that she wanted to talk but not there. As we walked towards the car park, she held my arm, tightly. I knew then how insecure she still was in her nineteenth year. I liked it, not that she was insecure, but her holding my arm. I felt like a good old Mum who was still needed by her grown up kid. At times, she would tell me everything. I would be like a friend to her. Sometimes, she would complain.

"Mum, I can never hideaway anything from you. You are like a friend. I need a Mum." But other times she would say, "I wish you could understand me like a friend."
We went home. I made a cup of Indian tea for her. She loved Indian tea. We sat down in the lounge to talk. I had prepared myself for the worse.

"Yes, you were right Mum. Something terrible has happened to us all. I must not tell you, he said he will stop sending me money if I did. I love you so much, but I also love my father. I worshipped him, once. I don't have any respect for him after what he has put us through. What I am going to tell you, could break your heart. I have to do it. I cannot stand the pressure inside me. But the revelation could break your whole life apart." She was speaking slowly looking straight in my eyes.

I was sitting there, watching this young woman, my daughter, in a strange state of my mind. I saw the reflection of pain behind each word she spoke from her mouth as vapours of intense fear engulfed us both. I saw the glimpses of pain on the each limb of her body as mirage of dancing shadows.

Suddenly something snapped like a stretched skin, elastic, hitting my whole existence, waking me up. She was trying to be loyal to her mother and keeping the broken pieces of love for her father who had shattered her faith in him. I was forced to withdraw myself from my own pain and became a listener to my daughter's agony. She sought comfort and support.

"No, it won't. I could sense it long before you had gone away from me. It was the parting of your faith in my strength, which hit my heart. You were afraid to tell me the truth. You thought I would fall apart. Tell me now. Whatever is burdening your soul?" I said.

This escape from being a sufferer to the one who observed other's suffering was very dramatic. It instantly made me strong. It taught me to witness the other, weaker image of Svera, the mother, who was a character in my story. We were playing reversed roles. Sometimes she was weak and sometimes I, the observer, the narrator, was stronger than her. I had to harden her outer shell, the I whose blood inside started to freeze and I could feel the shivers, something which I had suspected was going to come true. I wanted my suspicions to be false. Now I had to act.

"You can tell me anything. What did he say?"

"It is about that secret talk I had with Dad, the day before he left. He did not want me to reveal anything to you but I can't keep it to myself any more. You were right about the shopping list you found in his trousers. He is going to have a child with that woman. It's so disgusting. I trusted him so much. He has cheated you, Mum. What would Minna think if we told her? Poor Minna."

As she spoke, the time stood still. I gently stroked her hair as she became mute, the tears having washed away some of the pressure. It would take years for her grief to be healed. Maybe she would never deal with it. She is my daughter. My own reflection. Another woman. She will come to understand, in the years to come, about her father, in whom she had great trust. The ideal family. Images of love and safety would probably tear her soul apart, but she would survive. Her doubt about my resistance might be right. Her sharp eyes were travelling all over my face, scrutinising my soul. Tension, grief or a shock? She found nothing there, just the pure concern of a mother. Only then was she able to relax. I had to restrain my elf from breaking. It was my daughter who needed my support. I had the choice to escape the consequences by pretending. I could have been the onlooker. I wanted to find a balance between what had happened and how to act neutral. I knew I had to face a long period of anxiety. The anxiety would lead to panic. Maybe I would panic. I was not afraid. Let the events take their toll. I did not have much strength to fight. The little strength I had was used as a shield to pretend to my daughters that I was not affected. It was going to be tough. But I had made my choice

The storm was slowly withdrawing. The soft golden colours of autumn were setting in. There was a thick haze of pollution in the air. Visible only in sunlight, and the pale sunshine was a rare commodity. There was very little certainty in my life. I started to depend on my antidepressants yet again. Nights would approach with an oppressive melancholy to fill sadness in my heart. I had horrible dreams - blood, devils, snakes and dark caves. I would wake up, drenched in sweat. A cold breath smothered like a sticky cover over the white sheets. In between them I found myself awake, perspiring, tossing and turning. For over a year I did not have a night's uninterrupted sleep. Fatigue was constantly with me, antidepressants created a self-destructive cocktail of grief and recrimination. I became like a ghost walking the streets of the city, never far from death in an accident.

I know now that Guru Gobind Singh was protecting me in that terrible state. I know that writing this and writing poetry helped me out of my delusions. During this period I phoned Ruby several times. Foolishly she would reassure me that he never really left me. For her it became a matter of pride. She hated to see our marriage break up. But I was still confused. The man had gone after creating turmoil in his own family.

What could I do? What could my friends do? Nobody could force him back to me again, I knew that. But somewhere in the wounded corner of my heart, I had a small hope. I just wanted to try the last resort. I had nothing more to lose. I couldn't keep holding on to shadows of the past. They would only haunt me. Torture me. Logic insisted that I let him go.

Om, Ruby's husband, phoned back around midnight,
"Well, I had a chat with Peter. He is ready to come back. Let's meet on the 13th of September. We should meet anyway before we go back to Africa. If you are ready of course."
So there she was. Svera, the mother, the woman, the wife, giving Peter yet another chance, for the sake of her children, for family harmony, honour, the devil which was not ready to depart from her. Not yet.

CHAPTER 21
One For Sorrow

"You look smart and young Mum."
Her full lips brushed my cheeks as she entered the car on the passenger seat. It's incredible what you can hide with just a few strokes of make-up, new hairstyle and fashionable clothes. I did it in order to create a fake happiness in our lives, my daughter's and mine. If I was happy, they would be too. When Minna went to bed, I would break down and cry. I had been crying at least twice a day for some time. I didn't have an alternative to my tears like Peter had - a woman who'd give him a son. I couldn't. Neither did I have the choice to pick freedom or another man. If freedom was a mango, I would have travelled to India and picked the one I liked most, from Uncle Karl's grove. In my childhood I would willingly take up the long journey of eight miles, peddling on my bike to my village. The fantasy of climbing on all the mango trees and tasting each one to pick the best would push my bike against wind and the sharp stinging rays of the July sun. My craving to gulp this freedom fruit became more acute as each year rolled by on the wheel of time.

Last year, when Peter came on one of his so called 'visits', (a term he used for those holidays he spent with us), I had the choice between staying home to our usual argument or taking up a invite to a party with poets and writers. I didn't want to be the target of his evergreen anger, which could easily erupt in violence. Strangely enough, Peter offered to stay home and even cook supper for Minna and Nina. I had a wonderful evening at the party and had a fantastic sleep that night until I was woken up by thunderous showers of someone shouting right over my head. I saw two big hands in front of my sleepy eyes, ruthlessly pulling my quilt away from my warm naked body.

"You bitch, how could you forget to renew Minna's passport? You don't want us to go away. Do you? Dit svin!"
He swore in Danish. Now, when I recall this, I am laughing out loud. Pig? I am actually, according to the Chinese horoscope and he is a rat. I could have answered back in Danish, "Din rotte!" Ha!
With a mad rage of other accusations, he stood in the middle of our bedroom screaming at me. It was a Saturday.

Peter had arranged a trip to take Minna to Paris. He had forgotten that her passport was outdated. Her name was on my passport, so she could only travel with me. They were leaving on Monday. The entire house was full of petulant vibrations. I felt the shark teeth of guilt, shame, insult and humiliation biting deep into my skin. I felt bleeding as he stomped up and down like a spoiled brat who couldn't have his way. I want to forget that conversation he had with me, I can't. I have somehow managed to blur my memory. Now he had arrived to stay for a week. This time he was with his baby and a lover, a total man again.

Mina was going to be sixteen that month. She had been irritated with me for some time. She wanted me to go out. Maybe go to movies with friends, a pub, impulsive shopping, whatever. Her definition of me being isolated in the house and not enjoying life outside was depression. She could see through the false facade that I had erected around my identity. She saw me housebound, doing not much but writing. My bedroom was covered with scattered magazines, papers, books, cups and plates. It was here that I spent most of my days and nights in front of a lighted screen writing, grieving, drinking tea, coffee, thinking. Caffeine was supposed to make the process of thinking fast, but it failed to live up to its own credibility. I was working on translating a short story. Images from places I had visited and lived got mingled in my mind with the many languages I had encountered. So it had taken me longer than anticipated. I felt annoyed and tired. Sometimes I slept during the day.

So, when I went to pick Minna up, I freshened up, wore smart, casual outfits, pink lipstick, earrings and combed back hair. I strove for a changed image with fashionable designer clothes, make-up and hairstyles. The years I had spent with Peter, he used to tell me how beautiful I was without make up and smart clothes. I would thrive on his appreciation of my beauty. So I neglected myself. Now that my image in Peter's eyes had broken down, I started to portray an image to negate his belief.

SEPTEMBER 10TH, 1995. It was Saturday. I had an uneasy night. The decision to get out of my warm bed was a battle I could not win. I tried to pull the soft quilt right up to my forehead, smelling the sweet odour of my sweat, pretending it was still night at the same time sensing there was sunshine outside, but I could feel a purple darkness roaming around my room. I wished I could stay in bed. I heard a thud on the tiled floor in the hallway. Curiosity was the only motivation that succeeded in dragging me down the stairs, in the hope of getting interesting mail. Not because I had been busy writing a lot of letters, but I did expect them, selfishly. The Peace Lily in one of my windows had stiffened with neglect. I noticed the soil had cracked. I poured some water onto it. I could hear the slurping sound as if after drinking the water it was waking up. It seemed smoother and softer as I stroked the petals. I realised my whole body was thirsty for something - a miraculous liquid to give me strength. I needed to lift my spirit up. Remnants of the lavender incenses I had burnt last night were still filling the house with their aroma as dawn jumped in through the large window like a naughty little girl, giggling loudly. I added a cinnamon stick to my strong tea with a teaspoon of ginger powder. I inhaled the aroma. My body moistened with perspiration. I read through a letter from Manchester. An invitation to attend a Seminar on Asian Languages. Peter was still sleeping upstairs. Om and Ruby were coming on the 13th.

Yesterday we had gone for a walk. There was a pond with frogs. He sat down to watch those creatures crawling in the water, admiring them. He wanted to catch one.

"Come here Minna, try and touch it. They won't bite. They are so sweet. When I was a kid, I always held them in my hands."

"Tell him I am not Daddy's little girl anymore and it's disgusting to touch a frog!"

Minna took a big bite of her egg sandwich and wrinkled her nose.

"No, Dad, I don't really want to, please."

"How I wish I had a little boy, who would love animals, nature, football."

He looked at me with his deep blue eyes.

"Why won't you agree to adopt a little boy from Africa, Svera. Why"?

Peter let out a deep sigh.

"Why didn't you, bitch?"

I shook Svera violently as she sat on the rug watching Minna eat. I saw fractured pieces of pain in her eyes. I looked at my palms. I stretched my hands to wipe her pain. I scribbled down lines on the back-pad of my mind how I would describe her agony. How I would expose this woman in front of you. She could have saved her marriage, I thought. Her honour. Stupid, ignorant village fool, sticking to her own morals. She could have played games to keep Peter in an illusion that she loved him. She could have kneaded the poison of truth together with the chapatti dough, baked it and stuffed it into Peter's mouth. That could have been the death of Peter in my story. For my own selfish reasons. I didn't have the guts to persuade her. I loved my daughters then. I will always love them. I feel a pain in the chest behind my ribcage to think about their lives as women. I do feel for your pain, Peter, but only as Svera and not as a narrator. How you must have craved for a son. Yet my love for Minna and Nina was deeper than your love for a son, Peter. I would do anything for them. At that point, I swore not to get married again. Peter has made his wish come true. He now had a baby whom he would bring up as he wished.

"I understand you, my brother. You made a mistake marrying this strange, intellectual woman called Svera. She is a handful for you. Find a woman who will do what she is told to. We sympathise with you," one of his family member wrote to him recently.

I remember the night before his arrival. I lay awake in my double bed in a tranquil pose, trying to listen to any sound of love. Jaz my lost love, the man with his pink hat, though he could just be a shadow, an illusion, but his face was so vivid, so soothing, so clear. If I ever meet him, I will be able to recognise him right away. I felt a strange yearning for that stranger. What might he be doing now at this time of the night? Lying beside his lover? Making passionate love to her? I felt a tiny part of my heart feeling jealous, like Radha for her Krishna. Should I, introduce him to you now? The story might turn out to be interesting. Let's keep it a secret, suspense, a thriller. In order to divert your attention, to keep your interest going, I will hide his character away, I will put him in a pocket of memory near my heart, seal him behind pages of another manuscript in a secret cupboard or behinds words in my scrap book. Right now, I want to think of you, mother. What might you be doing at that hour of the night, the midnight hour? I remembered back in the Punjab, after finishing your chore in the house, you would take out a book of Gorky, translated into Punjabi, to sit and read, waiting for Amar to return from his usual nights out. Now, you might be watching one of the soaps on Canadian TV, you call it the 'hospital movie'. My father would be reminding you to go out for a walk with him: feed the ducks, look at flowers, children, people. It must be 5pm there in the dead city of Winnipeg. You didn't like the city. So you didn't like to go for a walk, like you used to back in the Punjab. Every early morning you went for a five miles walk, alone and brought home flowers. It was early next morning. I did not sleep all night and went up to make a cup of tea. I drew the white kitchen curtains with the black zebra and giraffe print to let the light in. There it was again, on the rooftop of the neighbour's house - my favourite black and white bird, the lonely hibernating shining magpie, sitting there teasing me. I always see the single one, flying in any direction she wanted. Maybe she wasn't lonely at all. I wasn't intimidated by her ruthless nature. I wasn't in the mood for grieving the death of my relationship with Peter.

"Remember Svera, one door closes and another one opens. Just try and learn to see through your third eye," Josef had tried to tell me when he knocked at my red door.

When Peter arrived I pretended to manage the game but felt very vulnerable in his presence. I stopped being the poor victim and tried to become the onlooker. That game pleased me so I prevented myself from falling down at his mercy.

I let him sleep in a separate room, upstairs, but he made his presence felt and that was unbearable. It was hard for me to freeze the feeling of love or hate, and try to be neutral. He did not have the need for any compromise. I concentrated all my energy around my daughter's birthday. It was one of the few family events both my daughters valued. We had to gather around that event, in spite of our crisis. For the sake of our children we took our false masks out of the closets. Twentieth century middle class family harmony. In a way it was important, mother, in this part of the world. To keep the tradition alive, I went to do the shopping on the 11th of September.

Peter said he wanted to come along, so we could talk. He was driving. He always did. On the way back he parked the car on the roadside, looking away, he spoke, in a meek voice of a coward criminal. "There is something I want to show you." I looked at him without any feeling. I had no faith in him. I saw him take something out of his pocket and hand it to me. It was a picture of a newborn baby.

"Have mercy on this," he pretended to beg, in a low voice.

I looked at the photograph. I sat motionless for a while. He must have been looking at my reaction but I was totally blank. That was the impression I wanted to give him. I felt no desire to look at him but said, "So this is your illegitimate child from a twenty year old Eritrean girl."

Why was he showing me the photograph? Did he want me to adopt the child? I asked him direct. How stupid I felt. But the words were spoken and couldn't be taken back.

"No, you have no right whatsoever on this child. Do you understand? It is MY child, you understand? You have no biological connection with this child. Give me the photograph."

Once again Dr. Jekyll had turned Mr. Hyde. It was like history repeating itself. He was himself born out of wedlock. His mother was forced to marry the man she didn't love, just to save her honour.

Now he had produced a child outside his own marriage. The fact was that he did not have any dignity, any morals. Had he forgotten his own unhappy childhood? He had told me last year that the affair was just a fling, a short-term pleasure, as a result of his loneliness. The child was then maybe just an accident? My mind flashed back to our visit to Eritrea. A famous old fighter who came to join the party given by Jadee at my departure talked to me. I told him Peter and I had two daughters. "So you only have daughters and no son. You can still do it, comrade," he said and winked at Peter, while I stood there trying to understand what went on between them. Had Peter acted seriously upon that hint? Is that why he tried to get a mistress, a baby? Maybe he did want to produce a son instead of adopting one?

"I did not know that you were so involved with her. You told me it was a fling,.."

I suddenly realised that I was fuming. I reached for the glove compartment, put my sunglasses on to hide my anger and slid the photo in my back pocket.

"Drive home," I commanded.

"Give me my photo back," he demanded.

I said, "No, Sir. This is an evidence. You have cheated me so much lately. This is infidelity, Peter. I have the proof."

"You fucking mean bitch," he spat these words out like a cornered rattle snake. I kept my distance. My dignity formed a dupatta to protect my honour, which I wanted to place around his venomous neck.

"Not more than you, Peter. I have never done any harm to our relationship, never cheated you with another man. I was faithful to you, all these years, while you slept around. Don't you understand what you have done to our children Peter? How dare you have cheated on me," I said in a firm and cold voice.

The calmness of my reply provoked the rattlesnake further. He pulled the car to the pavement, snatched the car keys and strode away.

"Robber. Fanatic. Marxist. Exploiter. Bloodsucker!"

I shouted in the emptiness around me in my car.

"Not only you have taken my pride, my identity, my freedom of choice from me with one blow, you have robbed me of my youth."

I sat in the car for half an hour not knowing what to do, when he returned back to throw the keys in my face, and walk away. It was another defiant spit of his venom.

After sitting for a while, I picked up the keys and switched on the ignition. The car spluttered into life and I could see Peter's petulant backside waddling away further and further, up the road. I was so used to his dramatic actions. He was good at dramatising our fights. I remember an incident in Dar-es-Salaam.

I was making a video film on women and environment which needed editing. I had to ask several people for assistance and equipment. One evening we had an argument about my slow approach. He had wanted me to finish it much sooner.

"You always postpone things, Svera. When you start something, you have to finish it," he would often remind me.

I must admit, I had the tendency to delay things, had other chores to perform - children, food, shopping, poetry, Peter.

That Sunday afternoon, I had failed to drive away to find the guy who owned the editing studio, outside town. Peter started lecturing me. We had an argument and he got so hysterical that he locked himself in the bathroom with a knife, threatening to cut himself. I knew he wouldn't but got such a horrible shock. He had never been that dramatic before. Frightened, I asked for his forgiveness in an attempt to make him open the door. He came out. I apologised, like I always did, to bring back the family harmony.

This time, I looked at him as he walked away after throwing the key in my direction. I picked up the keys, moved the car into the first gear and slowly approached this man-child that I had been married to for so many years. I drove parallel with him for twenty meters or so, but he ignored my presence. I made one last attempt of civility and offered him a lift back to our old marital home. Peter's face was a study. He pretended not to hear my offer. At that same moment the heavens opened. The rain was falling down to show a rage. Peter still pretended not to notice. And he continued to waddle in his boorish and self-conscious way.

"Fa, helvede Peter. Jeg har ikke bruge for dig!" I shouted loudly.

"Go to hell, Peter, I do not need you."

Peter stopped walking and looked at me.

"Need?" he said superciliously, "I never needed you, woman. That was your big mistake. You never realised that."

And with that he produced one of his favourite cookies from his pocket and munched selfishly.

"You know, Peter, I feel pity for the woman you tricked into admiring you. It is clear the woman is looking for a ticket to come to Europe. It's your money and security she wants. Why else would a young woman fall for such a hypocritical old bastard like you," I said.

This made the rattle snake snap like a stick. He turned back, opened the car door and slapped me across the face. I looked at him.

"Try again, Peter. You can't hurt me anymore. You're out of my life for good".

With that I put my foot down on the accelerator and went for a long drive up to Shipley Glen, a well-known beauty spot on the edge of the city. The grey sky shed droplets of rain falling hard on the windscreen like teardrops rolling down the glass reflecting helter-skelter emotions. I let the rain wash my face through the open window, to soothe the hurt, to cleanse me from his dirty hands which hit me, to wake me up and the misty smell of the muddy marsh penetrated into my skin like ghee on parathas forcing me to close my eyes. My mind drifted away from the brown, golden trees towards a distant horizon. In that lurid daze, I saw the trees had suddenly changed. I saw lush green bushes of pink bougainvillaea flowers.

There is large orange sun shining down on flowers. The scene is foreign. A girl of twelve is riding her bike now, stepping down to enter the yard of a big house in the middle of a village. People are gathered in a circle looking at something in the middle of the floor. It's a large black bleeding python, dead. The girl is frightened. She looks at the face of the woman who sits on a chair drinking a cup of hot milk. There's a smile of victory on the woman's face. The girl is relieved to recognise and smiles at the woman, who is her mother. Joshili smiles back at her daughter, Svera.

"Come Svera. Do not fear, my daughter, I will sing you a song my mother sang for me."

"Behold my daughter
Like a flicker from the dawn
Freedom is slithering on the road
Like the energy of a snake
Like the beat of your footsteps
Like the pulse of your heart
The pulse of energy, invites you to trample the snake
Behold my daughter
Like a tiny ray in your tears
Like the anxious breath of a hyena
Do not fear the evil
it penetrates the skin of your fear
Kill the demon, do not cry
Wipe your tears
Like you wipe your muddy toes
Smile and ignite the flicker in your heart.
The dawn of flickers
The flicker is freedom
Keep it burning

Svera feels comfort in Joshili's arms. She feels the burning desire for freedom. She wants to taste it as she had tasted the mango fruit, as she tastes words from her mother's tongue, as she tastes the salty tears running down her cheeks, as she smells Joshili's dupatta, which wipes her tears off. Uncle Karl speaks to her.

"This is a victory over the evil. This snake was a threat to humans as well as this poor cat. As your Mum saw him trying to strangle the cat, she became very furious. You see the cat was chasing all the mice that were eating our corn. We need the cat. So as it happened, everybody was out working in the fields. Your Mum had to fight the python all by herself. She had to kill him. Svera, your Mum Joshili is a fighter." Fighter, fighter, fighter... Jang, jang, jang, Joshili's jang, Svera's Jang, jang, jang...

The last words coming out of Uncle Karl's mouth, with the curled-up moustache on his upper lip, sounded like the beat of a drum. I reeled out of the vision like a rolling stone landing on a leather seat, my eyes still closed. I heard the sound of a running stream of water against a hard surface of my car as I opened up my eyes to watch the scenery of Shipley Glen. My mind slowly drifts back. I looked at the road. This was in the outskirts of the city of Bradford. I suddenly realised it was very late. I had to go back home, to where my children were. Now. Here. I sped towards reality. Peter was going to disappear like a ghost from my past. I had to face the harsh reality, my present.

There it was, my precious Victorian house, twice the size of the house in my vision. It looked even bigger, trying to hold on to its dignity. Despite many, many turmoil's, it was still alive, although a bit worn out in places. It had formed its own identity. I had only tried to decorate it, given it an image, a booster, which lightened its spirit and mine. My husband had turned me into a depressive person. His ideas became mine. I saw everything through his eyes. I saw myself changing according to his needs, then my children's. I had become a slave to their needs. I had stopped being myself, lost my self-respect. Joshili's song and my own fight with the python reminded me that I had let her down. I had let down the notion of freedom. She was trying to revive her spirit in me, reminding me of something I have forgotten. Thinking about the vision that had just passed, I entered the house with a new spirit. I felt I had tackled my own python. I also felt weak after the long struggle. But something within me was beginning to take root. I was never that simple village girl anyway. I had to be different. I had this quest, this thirst for knowledge.

There lay in front of me, a trapdoor. What do I want now? An escape? What should happen next? Firstly, it was the arrival of a puppy.

Morning of the 12th of September. Nothing felt the same from the moment I saw the vision. It constantly reminded me of my search, my struggle, of you, my mother Joshili, of my plight. My daughter Minna was turning sixteen that day. She was not a baby any more. Everything was going to affect her teen years from now on. I had to be a strong mother for both of my daughters. Rubbing my sleepy eyes, I came down from my bedroom to greet Minna with a bouquet of flowers. She was standing beside a cardboard box. I stood half way down the staircase, the cardboard box started to whimper. As I froze in astonishment, I saw two tiny paws crawl up on the edge of the box, two huge black innocent eyes looking out, begging, "I want my Mum, please carry me up."

The little orphan was pleading. In a matter of seconds he was in Minna's arms.

"This is my present to you, Minna, on your birthday. I won't be here for you, darling. Have this little puppy from me," Peter was telling my daughter.

"Oh, thank you Papa, I love him," she said kissing the little sweet devil. I stood there, dumbfounded, watching this motherless creature. They were well aware of the fact that I didn't want a dog in my house. I slowly walked down the stairs and snatched the puppy from Minna. The puppy looked up to me with its huge brown, pitiful eyes that spoke, "I am abandoned. Please take me in, mama."

Tears rolled down my cheeks. I felt as though he was Minna or Nina asking me to protect him from evil. How could I refuse when Minna wanted him so badly? Maybe Peter thought that the little dog would replace the lack of a father in her life, and he knew I would be too vulnerable to throw him out of my house.

So the little dog stayed. I sat together with Minna and the newly bought male member of our small family of three females. I thought about Peter and his newly found family. I thought about his diary that I had secretly glanced at. The entrance from the diary was 18th August, 1995:

"With her African hairstyle, she came down the stairs, helped by the midwife. Her face was pale and tense with pain. I went to support her down to her ward, bed no.6. I knelt by her side and embraced her. "Zainab, we have a daughter, a beautiful girl," I cried out, while tears

ran down my cheeks. I repeated myself and she woke up from her pain.
"Not a boy?" she asked. "No, it is a girl," I said.
I embraced her again and kissed her. "Shall we call her Nadia?" I asked.
"Yes, Nadia," she said.
So, it was decided. I took a small parcel from my pocket, with three golden bracelets, which I had bought the previous day.
"The first one is for you, the second one is for Nadia and the third one for your pains."
She took them on, and I haven't seen her without them the whole first week. (It had been a debt I never redeemed to Svera. I was so young when my children were born that I forgot the birth-present for the mother)."

No, you have never redeemed the many debts that you owed me Peter. Can you call yourself young at 26 in a western country? Justifying your own guilty conscience? If you could initiate anti-American demonstrations, if you could support the Liberation Movements in Africa, you were mature enough to be considerate to your own wife. At least return the gratitude of her many kind gestures. What about that time you lay helpless with a broken arm in the hospital? I was there to support you. What about all that humiliating beating your own woman comrades put you through I was there to nurture your wounds. You even promised to spend our old age together, in India, Peter. A rage of bitterness pressed itself through my heart. I had to block the devious smoke from choking my passion for my children.

Minna's birthday. We had done our best to celebrate the evening. After feeding the puppy, happy and content Minna had gone to her room to sleep. Nina had gone out again to see her boyfriend. After cleaning the kitchen, I went into my favourite sacred place, my exquisite lounge of objects and memories. Peter had gone up stairs to the room I had put him in. I paced up and down the floor reflecting on two days events – the puppy, the diary, the incident on the road when Peter had slapped me after he had shown me the picture of his baby.

"Have mercy on this," his words echoed on my mind. My cheek didn't hurt, it was the heart that felt the ache, the dard.

I should have known, Peter, you have never acted on impulse but taken the decisions that suited you best. You are a robber Peter. The child of a nucleus family in a imperialist country, trying to be a Marxist, out of guilt. I realised that my words had been spoken not thought when I read the diary. I was alone in my lounge. The lights switched off. The tall mute walls fell heavily like the burden of my soul. I was pacing the floor, looking out. The street lamp was shading a drizzling light on the road. Occasional sound of passing cars broke the monotonous atmosphere. Do I feel anything for his child? I had given him 25 fucking years of my youth, nearly destroyed my health, trying to give him the son he wanted. Seven bloody miscarriages in exchange for beatings, grief, neglect!

Strangely enough I felt something soothing within my house. Something, someone, somewhere was reaching out to me, telling me to hold on to my sanity, let go of this double-edged man called Peter. I still try to figure out where I had gained that little insight from, but it was holding my mind from falling apart. It must have been the remnants of my old fighting spirit. The flashing sword of Guru Gobind Singh, the symbol of struggle, was a saviour, a barrier between ending up in a psychiatric ward and withstanding the deadly predicament of my daily life. You should be happy for that, Ma. I did have the little strength you wanted me to have for survival. My brother Jake's face, his broad forehead, wrinkles of worries, appeared in front of me. He tried to warn me once. How can you let him treat you like this, Svera? Peter is a very selfish person who has the ability to destroy your confidence, leave him now, while you can, save yourself from his claws. It will be too late one day. You won't be able to forgive yourself for living this horrible life with him. Now when Mr. Hyde had already performed his devilish experiment, I can't face my brother. How can I. Ma? I had never told you anything.

How will I explain this to you? Will you be able to understand when you read my words? Will it be too late? I imagined how it would be if I had to tell you face to face. It is easier to write. You are a well-read woman, daughter, how could you let a man treat you like this, you will say. I cannot turn the clock back. Forgive me, Ma. Please forgive me.

"You have to explain to me, Peter. Why have you done this? Why Peter?"

I did not know how, without my will, my body dragged me up the stairs to go into his room, to pose this question. He was fast asleep. I suddenly got angry to see him sleeping while I was so restless. He woke up and demanded that I leave him alone and he wrapped himself up into his quilt again.

"I have the right to know, Peter. You have never explained to me why you left me. Why did you do this to us?"

I took his quilt away from his body. I should have known how he hated to be disturbed in his sleep. I must have gone mad with jealousy to see him starting up a new family. He got up, very mad. He started to pull me away and out of his room, but I wouldn't leave. Then he slapped me hard on my head. I fell, banging my head against the door outside his room. He shut the door behind me. There was a deadly silence and darkness, for a long time.

When I woke up, I found myself on the staircase. Nina was standing close to me touching my hair. She had come home late and found me sitting there half faint with a vacant gaze. She needed no explanation. She knew what might have happened. She had witnessed the violence so often before. She knew I must have realised the truth by then. Silently, she gave me a glass of water with two Paracetamol and followed me to bed.

"You have to live your life, Mum. You have to live for us. We need you. You can't destroy yourself. You can't sit and waste your life for that bastard."

I was surprised at the venomous way in which she told me that. The same wounds that scared my body also scared my daughter's. She kissed my cheek, stiff with dried tears.

I finally fell asleep with exhaustion. There were only a few hours left before dawn. Om and Ruby were supposed to be arriving that morning. I got up early, exercised my pranayama pose, drank a glass of distilled water, I took the mask of my trance and went shopping for our guests. Peter announced,

"I am going to fetch them from Leeds. I think they want to talk to me before we all can sit together and figure out what's going to happen."

Yes, what was going to happen?

Ruby stepped from her husband's side in a rehearsed fashion and spoke as if reciting a Marxist text.

"Marriage is a sacred institution. We have to respect it. There can be problems. We should be able to solve them," she declared mechanically. "I have been a social worker. Women came to me for advice," she continued.

I said nothing but I knew very well that she had never done any kind of social work. She was just being boastful and preaching. I felt like revealing my knowledge of her husband's affairs in the seminar in Sweden with wide-eyed female recruits who he inevitably led to Vodka and bed.

"I appreciate the help you are giving me, Ruby, but when you are in prison and someone gives you the keys, you open the door and you escape," I said.

Ruby looked at me nonplussed while Om stepped forward to recite his part of the text.

"Peter has been a tireless worker for the party. The pressure of his commitments makes him behave a little irrationally, at times. That's true Svera. But it is the wife's duty as much as the husbands to save a marriage, don't you think?" Om and Ruby stood there like tennis partners who had delivered the ball into my court. It was an uneven match. I thought of the python, my mother, my brother's warnings. But most of all I thought of my honour.

"Ruby, I don't think you can really understand what has gone on in my marriage. I can no more live my life to please other people," I said looking at the golden coloured basket in the corner filled with newspaper, some of them from Tanzania and Denmark. Oddly, the Danish newspaper, B.T was popping up in front of them all. "Blekingegade Robbery 3rd November 1988", read the headline.

I have to close my eyes to shut out the existence of Ruby, Om and Peter. Once again I have to take you back to Denmark. Don't get confused. While I try to link up the broken chain of thoughts from my past, I need to collect my energy, I need to concentrate. I feel the hurt. I am thinking of the python and I am thinking of cutting Peter's penis. He thought he could stab me, strangle me, but he is just a prick. I need to readjust my thoughts. I need the courage to continue this story. I need to rewrite. I need a drink. Cappuccino would do. What about you, Mum. Can I offer you a heavenly drink, now when you are not a worldly creature anymore? Minna, Nina? Try this. One part Vodka, one part Kahlua on a small heap of ice cubes in your favourite wine glass, add a bit of milk with a little spoonful single cream, having the foam of your own spirit on top, shaking up the memories. Think, listen, drink, drink not much, yet think, do not despair, declare the war against your own weakness. Enjoy both the drink and the robbery which really took place. Of course I have changed the names of the people. But it is no fabrication. Skald. Cheers. Bon nuit.

CHAPTER 22
The Harder They Come

Copenhagen. Patches of snow clung to the concrete pavements as a woman might cling to the solid chest of her lover. The grey wall of snow-laden clouds had slowly dispersed behind the broad shoulders of a blue sky. There's a gentle breeze swirling in the air. Spring is on tiptoes, birch trees rustle with life, people have new hopes. Sun doesn't look the same every year, but in March 1989 it was a half cooked circular pancake pouring down vapours to soothe my hungry soul. I gulp each particle of the mildness in this Nordic country of Denmark; I am trying to pin down peace and tranquillity in the form of a banner. An orange sun dove painted on a dark blue background. Sun dove is a metaphorical image, supposedly emigrating from some exotic lands, just like people who fled their lands in the hope that there will be enough freedom to stop their empty bellies hurting. Like the asylum seekers who escape death from being killed by Military Junta. We are getting ready for International Women's Day celebrations, that evening. It's a huge villa that once belonged to a famous countess and now serves as a shelter for women fleeing domestic violence. I had set up the immigrant women's organisation, SOLDUE, soon after we returned from Dar es Salaam. I am eagerly waiting for the Danish journalist to conduct an exclusive interview for the paper, Det Fri Aktuelt. I think constantly of how we, the immigrant women of Denmark, might be portrayed in the media. I see the urgency of addressing racism, which had sprung to the surface of this social welfare state, like a poisonous mushroom. Fiery wings of the sundove spread in the atmosphere and hover over my thoughts, which get distracted by the receptionist rushing towards me.

"Are you Svera? Your daughter is on the phone. She seems really upset. You'd better hurry up."

I am about to trip down the steel ladder.

"Yes, what's the matter, sweetheart?"

"Mum, seven police officers are demanding to search our house. Please hurry up, I'm so scared," she blurted out.

"Oh, Nina. Don't worry my darling. I am flying home," I assure her and rush outside to jump in a taxi, instructing the driver to drive as fast as he could.

The car speeds off on the tough tarmac road. I am not scared of death. I am scared of danger lurking around my daughter.

I look out of the window and see the horizon suddenly change into a vertical giant. Fumes of the traffic have already glazed the light, like an alum on the fine drizzling skin of the sun. I try to look through the blurred sunlight and beyond. The clear silhouette of Svera on the white sand of Oyster Bay beach in Dar es Salaam, on a yellow khanga, a cup of home-made tea, eating freshly fried mandazi.

"So you are back alive. How was Uganda?" This is an intro of a feature I wrote for Sunday News, October 5th, 1986. Peter has just finished reading the copy and has joined Minna and Nina in the luke-warm water of Indian Ocean. Minna was only six years and Nina eleven when we decided to take a trip to war torn Uganda, from Dar es Salaam via Nairobi. Six months after Yoweri Museveni took over, we saw the destruction, we saw mass graves, we saw hundreds of skulls displayed on stalls like vegetables outside each village together with torture instruments used by the UNLA, Idi Amin's army. The skulls were reminder of war from 1981 to 1985.

With the speed of one hundred miles per hour, I'm thrown out of my six years stay in Dar es Salaam. This is Copenhagen, the capital of a tolerant welfare state, which had changed dramatically in my absence. It had become a troubled hierarchy having to deal with the 'problems' of a two percent immigrant community. I can still taste the salty water of Indian Ocean. I can still feel fumes of bodies decaying in the backyards of houses in each village buried by ruthless UNLA soldiers. Skulls and bones of innocent victims, dug out to display, for the world to see, reminders of Amin's terror. I can hear the danger lurking outside my own house here in Copenhagen, as the vehicle constantly slides head on into an unknown future. The signpost flashing a poster of Malibu drink on a golden sun set beach send strange sensation to my body. My mind is vertiginous, drifting between many layers of past, present, present, past, future, present. The future is blurred as the sun is, right now.

"These bloody Pakis don't want to change. They come here and preach Islam. They live on social help. If they don't want to learn Danish, they should be sent back to where they have come from."

I smell the rotten rat of racism. The shouting taxi driver is an iron fist bringing me back to today's reality. Hatred, conflict, war exist in my present, a solid ground, the road, the track, the fast disappearing present. On the pavement I see the face of a woman with a scarf on her head. Until now I hadn't looked at the face of this white Danish taxi driver, plump, red, frustrated, arrogant, and scared of people who are different from him. He reminds me of Mr. Glostrup, the leader of conservative party who held an extreme right wing attitude against 'foreigners'.

I look at the swiftly disappearing back of the woman with a black scarf. She could be from Yugoslavia, Turkey, Russia, India, anywhere. Even a Dane with her ears wrapped against the cold, maybe even to keep out the shameful sound of racism. My desire to enter into a dialogue with the rude cabby dies within my heart. I check the meter and throw the fare onto the seat as we approach my 'Kolonyhave hus'.

I run inside the gate. I see the broad back of a detective outside the door, while the others had already started searching inside of the house. Some of them are eagerly digging my garden.

"What on earth is going on here? Who the bloody hell has given you the right to force entry into my house, dig my garden, terrorise my daughter. Be assured, we have no gold nuggets or seeds of dissent to plant here." I blast in my perfect Copenhagen slang. Nina looks like a frightened kitten who has just lost her mother cat. I take her into my arms. Another detective produces a search warrant so close to my eyes that they get blurred. I look beyond him, beyond his law. The news flashes like a thundering lightening, even now, when I write this.

I've just read in The Guardian, Idi Amin, one of the most notorious dictators, is in a coma in a hospital in Saudi Arabia. Dictators, terrorists, soldiers, death, destruction. Weapons, oil, wars. Uganda, USA.

The 3rd of November 1988. That calm mid winter day was shattered by the headline of an armed robbery and killing of a policeman in Copenhagen. Peter's old group, KAK and its members had been linked to the crime. According to the story, the group had been sending money and weapons to PFLP, Peoples Front for the Liberation of Palestine, the most fanatic faction in the Palestinian struggle.

Blekingegade is the name of the street in Copenhagen where KAK rented a flat to be used as a depot to collect weapons for PFLP. There were more such depots in other European countries, including France and Turkey. The money was needed constantly either to send weapons, medicine, clothes or for the military training for the cadres of Marxist-Leninist groups. In Copenhagen the most famous robbery of main post office was planned by the five hard-core members of KAK one of whom was a Swiss terrorist Marc Roland Rudin. The robbery took place on the 3rd of November 1988. A 22 year old cop got shot when the group was driving away with their booty.

We had returned home from Tanzania in 1987. Peter no longer belonged to the old KAK. News of the robbery was all over the Danish media on the morning of the 3rd November. We had the biggest shock of our lives. The police had traced Peter's name because of his association with the group in the past. As a result our house had to be searched for eleven hours. Nina and I stand closely watching the seven plain-clothed security policemen. Their hands are moving like slimy crabs, fingers everywhere, eyes like rats and noses sniffing through each article in the house, like dogs sniffing each other's arses. Every single cupboard, all the bookshelves, furniture, suitcases and bags are being scrutinised thoroughly. In the middle of all this turmoil, I hadn't realised whether Peter had been informed of this. Then I saw Nina on the phone, asking him why he was delayed. She had already informed him. After half an hour, he phones back to tell us that he would be coming with a solicitor who would represent us throughout the search. The phone makes a strange clicking sound. It is tapped!

They look through hundreds of books. Old pamphlets, magazines and all the books from the Communist Working Group are packed into a box to be taken away by them, including a copy of my magazine 'Soldue'. I am pacing up and down from one room to another, trying to remain calm. Nina comes close to whisper in my ear. "They even read my secret diary, Mum. They even looked through my under wear. How can they be allowed to do such things. What have I done? Am I a criminal, Mum?" She is trying hard not to cry. Her eyes are red with humiliation and pain. That is what I cannot stand. No body, do you hear me? No one should put my daughter through that pain.

"You have no bloody right. Keep your hands off my daughter's diary. Have you no shame? Where is the so-called privacy you Danes are so boastful about. Bastards?" I snap.

The liberal solicitor is getting uneasy with my blunt anger. She is trying to calm me down explaining we could do nothing about it. It was 10am when the search had begun. Now it is 2pm and the search continues. I asked Nina to fetch Minna from her school and instruct her to go directly to our friends' house and stay until the search was over. I didn't want Minna to witness the drama. It is now 4pm.

"What is this?" one of the officers demanded when he found a foreign address in one of our old books amongst the hundreds on the four wide bookshelves.

"I haven't got a clue," Peter said, annoyed.

Every book was opened. Every title was written down. The names of every video film written down. Pamphlets like 'Working Class in Denmark' were marked as "suspicious" material in their box.

Back in India the police or the military had never frightened me, because of my father. I remember when I was eight, after his lunch, my father often took me with him to his police station to show me around. But the brutal mental torture my family was put under by the Danish police was due to a notorious post office robbery. It forced me to hate the Danish police.

"We are following orders, madam. You see, one of our young colleagues, a cop of merely twenty, was murdered by members of the so-called Marxist-Leninist Communist Working Group. Your husband is a member of KAK.," the cop with a stony expression on his face had told me.

"Not any more. You Harrami! I swear in Hindi. It means Bastard.

"Please restrain yourself, Madam," he snaps firmly.

"Why Mum, why do they have to search my diary? Am I a criminal?" my daughter had questioned.

Years after the episode, I was haunted by Nina's big black eyes full of tears, pleading to know whether she had committed a crime to witness such humiliation. After eleven hours, the search ended at 10pm. Leaving devastation behind, they had all gone.

Yes they are all gone by 10pm. As if stung by the demons, I fly like a hurting bee trying to wipe away all the traces of the debris of destruction. I am like a brooding hen, protecting my daughters. Dark, mysterious, wings spread. They shouldn't have to go through this psychological terror. I cook chilli con carne for the children who eat in front of the TV. I vacuum the rooms as the sound sucks my courage into the black bin of a vague future. My wings get stifled, I lose my appetite. I am scared, my mouth is dry. It's the midnight of March 8th, 1989.

The girls are sleeping peacefully in their room now. Peter is restlessly shuffling on the sofa in front of the T.V. I offer him a cup of coffee. He is now munching his favourite cookies, sipping strong, hot coffee, looking tired and nervous. I am trying to forget the flat faces of muscular C.I.D cops. Time is raging through the night I am unable to sleep. I look out of the dining room window and your face appears like rainbow amongst the dark mushroom clouds. It is drizzling. I do not have the energy to make conversation with Peter. I know we will start arguing about things. So I take out my umbrella and a jacket to leave. I want to find a public telephone to talk to you. I want to phone you Mum, I want to talk to my brother Jake who is in India. My landline is bugged. As I begin to open the front door to step out, Peter shouts out, "Where are you going, Svera.? It's dark out there. Are you crazy, Svera?"

His voice becomes a hollow sound as I have already stepped into the darkness. cloaking the streets of Kalvebod. The echo of his words is a queer-shaped rock hurling through my consciousness, crushing me. I hear voices taking over someone else's.
"Where do you think you are going Svera? Where do you want to go Svera? Where, where, where, where?"
I am frightened in the darkness. Where Mum? Where would I go from here? My thoughts are turning into the wicked ghosts of Halloween. Voices are dancing around me like crazy whirlpool. There isn't another soul about, except perhaps the ones that no one sees.

This housing area called Kalvebod is close to an inter-city railway line but very quiet. We don't even hear any noise in the daytime. I am thinking of Peter. I know exactly what he is worried about. He doesn't like being dragged in to the media. He wants to run away from the forthcoming investigations and the court hearings of his comrades. Where should I run to, mother?

It's cold. The rain has turned into a fine drizzle. The air is misty. Raindrops look like small flickering diamonds falling from the sky under the streetlights. The dawn will break soon. Will it? Might it? I am wandering and wondering. My head is aching with all this thinking. The telephone at the corner of the street doesn't work.
"Foe helvede. Damn it."

I swear in Danish loudly. The black stray lovesick cat sitting on the fence looks at me with her cheeky eyes disapproving my swearing. She jumps behind the bushes chasing another cat. Damn it, I want you mother - now, here, with me. I want you to hold my children in your soothing arms where they can feel safe, the way I used to. I want you to cook Parathas for them. I want to tell you all about my life here in Denmark, my magazine, Peter. I want you to hold me and tell me what I should do, Mama. I am worried about Nina. She has often witnessed the violence of Peter when he beats me, when he throw things around, when he breaks the furniture. And now this. Karen from number 30 has just returned home from her night shift in the old people's home. The night is moistening with humidity and is hanging raggedly over Copenhagen like the watchful eyes of a secret agent, a police cop from Miami. I can see Karen switch on the light in her hallway. I am getting nervous, hungry and desperate for a talk with you. I slowly walk over the gate of number 30, and decide not to enter.

I return back to my house where everything gets smothered under a dark gloom. Peter in the gloom of his sleep, dreaming about Africa, his only safe haven, an escape to run away from the interrogations of the police and the harassment of the media. Reading his thoughts even when he is asleep, I cuddle up on the sofa under the shawl of my own little comfort, pressing my aching bones against the soft leather back, resting my worried head. Soft pillow of colours, images, scenes from Africa try to delude my mind.

I know Peter will persuade me to leave the places where he feels haunted by his actions. Our emotional turmoil would now be wrapped to hide under the table. I finally lay my body to rest, dreaming about you mother.

Oh, how the storm reflected on our relationship, which was already going downhill. The morning and the next and the following many mornings, minutes, hours, days and nights were tense after the police incident. I was tired of being pushed away further as a second or even a third priority. Now it was the police we had to think about. Peter repeatedly uttered his words like a mantra,

"I do not want to stay in this bloody western society. I need a job in Africa. I need to get away. We all need it. I can't survive without you, Svera. My job security is threatened. We need money. I need you Svera. I need you to be there for me. Try and understand, please."

Some of his comrades started putting great pressure on us to come out in the open to support them. I was scared for my children's future. I knew they would be harassed in their schools, in the streets and in the neighbourhood. I did not support their violent methods. I do not approve any violence, terror and mindless rioting either, not in Denmark, not here in Bradford. I did not approve of the killing of the young police cop. I did not find it a rational act to store dangerous weapons in the middle of the city centre and put ordinary Danish people's lives at risk. Some journalists had now started hunting for information from Peter. A splurge of constant phone calls started like nagging channel noise at home. Peter got very upset about it. He had to go underground.

"I do regret sometimes, knowing that you are the graduate among us, with an educational background, Svera. I should have completed my study. Instead I concentrated on Marxist studies. My mother has never forgiven me for that."

I remembered Peter would so often express his frustration. I convinced him it was never too late. He could take up the correspondence course from London. That was partly the reason for him to go in hiding. He was doing his exams in development studies. After reading the news in the media, his mother rang constantly for information about her errant child.

"I was always against his bloody Marxism. I had high hopes of him when he was studying to become a doctor. I had hoped you would turn him into a family man," she said bitterly.

I was to blame for not being able to turn him into a family man. So, when Peter was not available, I answered the calls from various journalists who wanted to interview him. He was becoming a bit of a star. Our Peter. He wasn't exactly Carlos the Jackal but for the first time in his life Peter was in demand. Unfortunately it was the police and gutter journalists who wanted to speak to him.

I had been well settled in my part time job at a centre for immigrant women, which was supported by a church organisation. Once a week I taught Danish as second language to immigrants. In my spare time, after taking care of my children and the house, I had started editing a magazine in Danish. I worked hard, devoting nights to translation, doing layout, writing and waiting for Peter to return home from one of his meetings. I managed with less sleep, less clothes, less luxuries and even less romance. How could I? A woman like Svera? I cannot ask that question to myself, as I am the narrator. I cannot afford to feel guilty, as I have to be objective. I cannot question Peter as it is the past.

Let me rewrite this, not as Svera, but as someone who is writing Svera's story. So, Svera managed with less of everything, including romance. How could she? I am now ruthlessly trying to question, trying to analyse, because I know she thrives well on the illusion of love and romance, so why didn't she demand it?

Rom...man....ance...I am laughing out loud as I remember. I'm in my bed. When I wrote the word romance, I started laughing and couldn't continue the plot further. I had this ticklish feeling on my skin triggered by the word, romance. I can't figure out how Svera could neglect herself so much. Peter's decision to travel back to Africa meant that she had to say good-bye to her association with the magazine, her job, her friends, her security for the future. Peter wanted his family with him. Svera did not want to leave Denmark; she didn't want to leave her husband either. She wanted her children to be with both their parents. That must have been her notion of romance. Bloody hell, I can't do that. I can't and I won't but Svera did that once. Did she really? For love?

Let's go back. Having no choice at all always made me feel restless. I had sleepless nights where I saw visions and ghosts of police pestering my daughter's life. The harsh winter and the pressure of being on constant alert from journalists hunting for news made us all very ill, physically. The whole family went down with influenza. I had high fever for a week, which was unlike me. When I recovered from the illness, my resistance got even weaker. I decided to go to my family doctor.

That was the first time in my life I had asked for tranquillisers. I told him that I could not sleep. There were acute political problems for the family. The doctor was no fool. He had read all about the police chase. He gave me the medication but he implored me not to become addicted to the Valium he had prescribed.

It was already December 1989. Peter had to struggle to get the job in Tanzania, but he succeeded. In fact he manipulated and exploited the situation with the police harassment to get the job. They didn't want to hire him at all. It was June 1990 when Peter finally left alone for Tanzania. I had to stay back to pack up and let Nina and Minna finish their schools. Peter was already in Dar es Salaam in the offices of the Danish Volunteer service taking up his responsibility as the new co-ordinator. It was in that period that I had another miscarriage. That made the situation even worse: work, politics, the police, miscarriage and now uprooting and going back to Africa for the second time - just as my life was stabilising in Denmark, just as my daughters were beginning to feel at home. Nina was not willing to leave.

"Oh, not again, Mum. I don't want to leave my friends," she pleaded. She was going to be fourteen. She had just met this boy Casper who was going to be her friend, yet it was Peter who was making the decisions for us all. It wasn't me, it was Svera who was letting him do it. How could she? Where was Svera, that strong village girl who use to rebel, change and question? Tormented between my blind love for Peter and my children, I finally left Copenhagen with Nina and Minna to join him in Dar es Salaam, the city of tranquillity where I had hoped to patch up my marriage.

Yes the beautiful, blue waters of the Indian Ocean in the city of Dar es Salaam did work as a timely miracle to the wounded family. The gentle breeze on the pure white sands of the Oyster Bay beach was where we spent our time. I would prepare a basket full of afternoon snacks, tea and juice then drive with Minna and Nina to pick up Peter from his office at five. We would all drive down to the beach to spend our entire evening laughing, talking, playing and swimming. Peter had this belief that when he had his wonderful job away from police investigation, our family life will improve. I trusted him. Trust was something people earned. Did Peter earn my trust? Maybe not but there was plenty of peace drizzling down from the soft orange rays of the many sunsets we were going to experience in that Port of Haven. I was where my family was, with Peter. My children had both their parents.

Nina and Minna soon met a group of other local children. Peter got obsessed by his work. I stopped my medication to replace it with my Super VHS video camera I had brought from Denmark.

One day, I walked into the newly acquired offices of my old friends from The Journalists Environmental Association of Tanzania, JET on Uhuru Street. I laid my raw plan in front of the chairwoman's table. It wasn't a professional manuscript, only a sketchy synopsis of a short video film on women and environment. I offered to shoot but it explained what I had in mind.

I had the opportunity to accompany Peter on his long tour around Tanzania where he would be visiting projects during July-August 1991. Initially JET suggested that one of their journalists travel with me, but due to other commitments, he couldn't come. I packed up my SLR camera, film rolls, the Super Eight camcorder and jumped into Peter's Land Rover. Peter was completely engrossed in his work. I think he was rather jealous at my involvement with the local journalists.

In film and video, the images are powerful means of communication. I was good at still photography. I liked to play with shadows and lights. It was the first time I'd tried to create moving images. With my limited vocabulary in Swahili, I knew it would be hard for me to convey in my film, what I wanted. On the other hand I was well aware that the local people had a capacity to communicate if they wanted to tell their story. I decided to initiate a few questions, leaving the rest to those women. As we went along doing the film, talking, singing, laughing, shadows of doubts dispersed to mingle with the light of discoveries. They knew exactly what they wanted to tell.

My journey through Tanzania may not be the one which Mohammed Amin, Duncan Willetts and Peter Marshall depicted in their masterpiece photography books. But I swear to God, I came into extremely close contact with people, especially the women. It was like entering into a whole different world of privacy and personality, where normally no outsider would be invited. Tanzanian women were wonderful and extremely co-operative. They embraced me with their open heart. They made me feel as if we were doing the film together. They posed for me happily singing when they tilled the land with primitive hoes while the sharp sun rays pierced their backs.

They let me into their huts. They offered me food, their joy, their sorrow, their enthusiasm. They offered me hospitality without demanding anything in return. I photographed them planting trees so there would be enough firewood. I interviewed a female potter in Same village who produced pots and ceramics of high quality. I filmed men in West Kilimanjaro with motor chain saws cut down trees in a big forest plantation. I saw Masai women build their huts while the tall handsome Masai men stood chasing flies from their faces. I photographed women carrying water on the shores of Lake Victoria. I remember that on one occasion in a Masai village North of Mount Kilimanjaro, I was filming women collecting firewood from a forest where lions and wild buffaloes sometimes roamed around, I was offered three handsome Masai men escorts. Seeing that Peter remarked,
"I wish it was me doing the filming and there were three beautiful Masai women escorting me."

The result of this fantastic journey was five hours of raw video which I converted into a 25 minutes film on women and firewood. I forgot the time and lived the experience. I had forgotten Denmark, the police, the search, even Peter. Nina and Minna had gone to spend a month of holidays with my brother in Denmark, so I had not had to worry about leaving them alone in Dar es Salaam.

The film 'Kuni', meaning firewood, was finally launched at the Goethe Institute in Dar es Salaam on the 9th of July 1992. I had invited two of the participants of Kuni - Sofia Masanja from Mwanza and Jane Mbagga from Same - to give their comments on the film. When the Deputy Minister for health gave an introduction, I was pleasantly surprised to know that 'Kuni' was the first ever historical film made on women and environment in Tanzania. As Peter had pleaded to use this second term to travel to Tanzania as an escape from his problems, I was now ready to come back to Copenhagen where I would take up my magazine and spend some more years, let children finish their education without having to move again. Peter had other plans on his mind. He started to pester me to move to Bradford in the North of England so that he could follow a course at the University. I was so threatened by his new approach that I argued. He pleaded his love for me.

"I will never leave you again, Svera. I will take up any job, even if I have to drive a cab. Please let me finish my education."

He went down on his knees, offering me a golden necklace with a small diamond he had bought to show his appreciation for my sacrifice. How foolishly I fell for that trap. Diamonds are a girl's best friend. Bullshit. Diamonds, gold, rubies, love, romance are the exploiters of women's faith, gems to be sold and bought in the market for pleasure, sex and need. When I wrote about romance, I was bitter. I am not any more. I am the same romantic, caring, and sensual fool and will continue to be.

Time to wake up from the dreamland of Africa to the present, now, here in this city - Bradford, this lounge, where Svera had spent some of her nights lost in those golden images of the past. Look - that Danish newspaper called B.T in the basket as Om and Ruby sit so still, like ghosts of the present, scrutinising my face. Did they get glimpses of Denmark and Africa or were they lost in their own visions of lights and shadows? Shhhhhh. Listen to what Svera has to say.

"No, Ruby, it's impossible for you to understand. Peter has always dictated my life and this marriage. Now it's time for me to dictate mine."

Ruby and Om looked at each other. I continued.

"Peter has been a problem for years. It is not just a recent thing, Ruby - bank robberies, infidelities, harassment. Yes, Ruby, he beats me. Take a look at this."

I raised my hair and showed her the area above my ear. There was still light bruising from where Peter had lashed out with his arm the previous night.

"He did that to you?"

Ruby appeared shocked. Om shuffled uncomfortably looking at his feet. He remained silent.

"Are you sure it wasn't an accident?" Ruby said.

"You really believe that he could accidentally do this and do you think I will lie about it? What is it Ruby? Whose side are you on?" I said bitterly.

Ruby stood her ground.

"I know Peter. He loves you. He would never hurt you intentionally. I'm sure of that Svera. It must have been an accident. Give him a chance. One year. Think how wonderful it would be. He will come back after one year. It will be like marrying him again. It will be your second honeymoon."

She talked to me as if I was some character in a melodrama and not a real person who'd experienced violence. But then sometimes drama is a part of your reality. I let her. I saw she was struggling to believe her own words. I believe she must have been in her own trance. People did not usually believe that such violence could ever exist between me and Peter. Peter the Marxist. Peter, women's hero. Peter the crusader, out there helping the poor in Africa. There was an uncomfortable pause. Om coughed. His thirty-a-day habit was catching up with him.

"Where did you go for your honeymoon, Svera," Ruby asked weakly.

I could not understand the logic of this conversation and where it was going. Honeymoon, second chance, Peter, love? How could they be so naïve? Om cleared his throat and came forward with a dismissive wave of the hand.

"Pah! Honeymoons. What a bourgeois concept. Whether you spend your first night together or not. What does it matter? Honeymoons, Mother's Day, Christmas - they are all capitalist creations to extract more money from the helpless consumers in our bourgeois society." Clearly Om thought that this political justification would resolve the situation and diminish the embarrassment of discovering that Peter actually beat me. Ruby gave a brief sigh at this intervention. She had heard this script repeated a hundred times before. She looked at her watch.

"Hup! Oh, is that the time? Om has to meet the mechanic for his car. We said we would be back at six. Please, Svera, think it over. Peter is a good man. He fails like all humans. But I know he is very fond of you."

Om made his exit. Ruby delayed for a second in the corridor. She put her hand on my arm and double-checked that Om had left the building. She spoke conspiratorially.

"Whatever you do, don't destroy yourself. Think about your health. That's first. Not politics, not men, not money, your health. Sort out your financial situation. Don't let Peter take everything. You have two girls. He has his mistress. But don't let him beat you, the bastard. Om - he wouldn't understand. He is a man. But he is my husband."

With that she gave me a look I did not understand. I was actually surprised with what she said. I realised she might have had her sympathy with me after all. That she did understand that our relationship was rotten. With that she winked and left.

Puzzled by her changed opinion, I closed the door and looked up the stairs. Peter was standing there in his dishevelled cardigan. He had a biscuit in his mouth.

"Had a good chat with Ruby and Om, did you? Om is a good man but that bitch of a wife - she tells him when he can eat, when he can sleep, when he can go for a shit. Bit like you Svera."

With that he disappeared up the stairs.

I stood there strangely unaffected by his comments. I was detached. I refused to take on board Peter's frustrations. All guilt had gone. I never understood why I felt guilty in the first place anyway. I didn't even want to go up stairs and confront him.

I lay awake in the night thinking this had to be the final farewell. No more of the treacherous games of Dr Jekyll and Mr Hyde in my life. Next morning, the day of 14th, September, 1995, I woke up early. Silently I drove Dr. Jekyll to the train station. The silence interrupted only by the sound of crunching biscuits. How long ago had he last visited the dentist I wondered. He got out of the car and looked at his watch. We exchanged no farewells. A long black coat, suitcase in his hand, taking physical and emotional baggage with him, he dispersed into the night mist like a ghost. He turned the corner onto the platform without looking back. As he boarded the train, Peter was clearly oblivious to the damage he was leaving behind. I turned the key in the ignition and drove away. I looked at the sky, a white lifeless moon, and drove slowly as the fog started to clear. The dawn was soon to break on the horizon.

Back in the house, I stood in the window looking at the rising sun - bleak, psychedelic, vulnerable, strong, transcending energy. Simba the puppy whimpered and made small effort to jump up to the windowsill. He was a bit too small and needed to go through the process of growing. Upstairs, Minna was awake, tumbling around, finding herself, viewing her image in the mirror of illusions, getting ready to face a new day, a new world, without her father. I went into the kitchen to make a cup of tea, preparing the meal for Simba's ever hungry belly, letting my food for thought churn in my mind. He sat by the red door, very attentive, waiting and watching each of my movements until his delicious meat was placed in his bowl. I looked at my Amitriptyline prescription and reminded myself to get some more. I still needed this crutch for my journey. Minna came down for her breakfast. Her watchful eyes, inspected my body posture, but she was unable to penetrate beyond my mood.

"There's only seven minutes before the bus to college arrives and, you know what, you are a damn good woman, Svera Jang – Mum."

CHAPTER 23
The Harder I Try

JULY 96. You *were* a damn good mother. What does being a mother damn you to? Years of jumping, in response to their every whimper, wiping arses, cooking meals, nursing sickness, worrying about teenage daughters each time they are late? Looking at your picture by the bedside, realising, you were a fantastic mother. You hadn't phoned me for weeks. I was yearning for your voice. This morning your letter arrived at my door like a Messiah's blessing. I hold the blue paper in my shivering hands as my whole world brightens up with the thought of your words. I gather pieces of strength from every word. Each pore in my soul is bathing in light.

The only sad news you wrote was about Kuli, my cousin. Her husband, a man of robust health in his late forties, had been struck down unexpectedly by a heart attack. I remember when she used to live with us. She was 38, a teacher and still single. She could have been married years earlier to a man she was in love with. But she was denied the right to do so. He was a friend of her brother's, which was looked down upon in our family. That always struck me as being such a hypocritical cultural norm. Bullshit, Mum. How else were you meant to meet a man? Can you explain it to me? She refused to marry any other man and after years of isolation and loneliness, when her lover got married to another woman, she agreed to abide by traditions. I was twenty then. She asked me to help her find a match. I wrote a matrimonial advertisement in a local paper. There was a huge response. Kuli and I then chose some of the applicants to be invited for the prestigious interviews.

That was great fun. I would interview all those guys, while you sat there as if you were an observer at an important UN interview. If the men expressed a wish to meet Kuli, they would be left alone with her. One of the guys took a fancy to me and he asked you if you would give him your honourable permission to marry me. Before you could utter a word, I interfered.
"No way am I going to get married before my sis," I proudly declared. You asked me if I could come to another room for a word and when you and I were alone you said how foolish it was to reject a handsome guy who also happened to be a solicitor. Chances like that didn't come your way every day, Svera. You might regret it, you said. I was firm and wouldn't listen to any such nonsense. We did find a match for Kuli and she was married to him, a doctor with a huge belly and a heart of gold.

I can never forget the marriage ceremony. She wore dark red silk clothes, make up, golden jewellery and other stuff hanging from her arms, ears and head. She was looking like a Christmas tree in the summer.

"Will you love, comfort, honour and respect him. Will you share all life has to offer with him from this day forward till death do you part?" the priest asked after reading verses from the holy Guru Granth Sahib.

After a couple of years, the husband died of a heart attack leaving Kuli in the wild jungle of norms and restrictions, devastated and a widow. The first time she was denied her right to marry the man of her choice, she felt as if all life had been drawn from her body with the dagger of traditions. Now it was the dagger of Yamraj, the lord of death, who took her lover away from her.

"I don't like this house, Mum. The furniture, the curtains, the colour of the walls, even when I see my reflection in the mirror, the dull light reflects on my face, making it paler. I want to change everything dull in here."

Standing near the kitchen sink, her back against the window from where the late July sun glittered on her charcoal black hair, gave me the illusion of gold. I sat watching Minna, my fifteen year old daughter who was beginning to grow out of the soft bunkers of childhood on to the concrete surface of a young woman. Pieces of sun flickered in her wide eyes through the crystal bowl on the table. A fragment of the blue sky flattened her plump cheeks against shadows. I knew the compulsive hunger twisted her inside out like a violent force to become an independent human being, free of my control, anybody's control. I was not going to stop her, but guide her. Nobody or nothing should stop her. She wasn't my little toddler who couldn't walk on her own free feet. Her eagerness for change forced me to think. Sometimes I would walk around my house speculating on how to replace my old motherly image with the one who understood her yearning for change. I had the same strong urge in my belly. A storm was gathering in my soul to break away from the old images, bits and pieces which constantly cluttered my soul, clinging to the house. The storm in the bathroom had blown everything out of the proportions; not only one but many storms. As I looked through the walls, the aftermath had scattered things everywhere.

Peter once slapped me as I stepped out of my car, outside our flat in Sea View in Dar es Salaam. I had found a packet of condoms in his bag. He had slept with his old flame from Copenhagen who was visiting Tanzania and they had planned a tour in the Serengeti Park. Then there was a seminar he went to attend in Germany. In his hotel he slept with one of the participants from South Africa. I sat sobbing in the dark corner of my lounge because he didn't come home after a party at his work. There were other incidents. My past was like a drug, a puff of marijuana, when I inhaled it, I would hallucinate. Broken chairs, smashed porcelain, ripped clothes, blue eyes, swollen lips, blood clots, dead embryos would fly in the atmosphere, hitting me hard, trying to blow my mind up. I wanted to wipe up the destruction and hold onto something whole and solid. I didn't want to be addicted to my past.

When I saw Minna speaking to me about change, I got drawn into her sparkling world. Her wish for change was like a firecracker. I could feel the energy from the words in your letter and the sound of glow in Minna's determination. Did you receive the aromatherapy kit I sent to you, Mum? I hope you are using it to soothe your aching bones. I had finally joined the long list of other lone parents. I could have done with a kit like that for my aches and pains.

I had just acquired the art of pretending to be self-aware and running my life on a day to day basis. I wanted to convince myself that things were going to be different from then on. I had to make them different. Everything else was changing - the sky, the weather, the cemetery, bushes, flowers, magpies, my house made of stones. They were all adjusting to the change. I should be a part of this process. Minna felt the rhythm. I knew that the doll's house of a girl named Svera had not been completely smashed. The material façade maybe, but the creation she had made with her own flesh and blood, the two little living individuals - Nina and Minna - were still part of her dolls house, this House on the Cliffe with its spirit, this city she had come to love and hate. She will recreate.

"Wake up Svera!"
I almost slapped the sleeping spirit in her.

"You village fool, naïve, blunt, stubborn woman. Wake up."

I drew the heavy drapes from windows, as if they were Svera's eyelids, to let the dawn enter. The sunlight hit the whole room where Svera had been hiding and fumbling into her past. She moaned.

"What the hell are you doing? Stop it. I like my shadows. The light is hurting my eyes. Go away." She flew at me. I didn't move an inch, but resisted her.

"Cut the crap, the bull from your life. I do not want to ditch my story. I need a new bold image of the old Svera. Do you understand that? I am the narrator, for God's sake. I am here to record your life."

"Who am I then? Have you created me or have I created you? I am now very confused,' she said.

I wouldn't know what to answer to that. I didn't want to suggest anything. I knew the change she was going through was sometimes hard, but I knew she would change.

Yes the change always helped me move forward. I started reorganising the interior. Clip, cut, chop, chop. Throwing away the stuff belonging to an era I wanted to leave behind. Most of the signs of Peter's violence were hidden in my soul. Wiping away those signs was a challenge. So there were no limits. No boundaries. No restrictions. I had always wanted the change. Now I felt I was in a head-on collision. Days were short and pregnant with rosy dreams about to give painless birth to new baby hopes. The curled-up sheets wrapped around my uncertainties were left behind like a discarded lover jilted at the altar. Getting up was forgetting my solitude and starting afresh. So it went on. Driving Minna to school, coming back to a changing, breathing house, giving the puppy his meal, wrapping up the emptiness, throwing it away with the rest of the garbage and getting ready mentally to fill the screen with words as a way of coping during this period. My creative spirit blossomed like my pink shalwar kameez - a colour which I started to grow fond of. Puppy Simba cried on the patio for my company. I needed the solitude, time for myself. My socialisation with others once had a purpose. Organising, participating, talking, changing, developing, following, leading, realising, creating.

The crowd of children, youths, the elderly, whites and blacks. They were all around me swarming like locusts on the pavements. I didn't want to get emotionally entangled with them. They would come too close to me. They would want to know the grief of Svera. They would start nibbling the harvest of this process I was going through, my writing. They would take the energy out of me, give me their negative energy back. No, not now. Just now, I loved my isolation. I started thriving on it. The desire for socialisation was sealed in a glacier. Melting it would take a whole hot summer season. I just had to wait.

Peter had said I had become a self-centred person, just another reason for him finding another woman. I knew he always found a justification for his actions. Only a man like him could do that. Do all men find excuses? I did not know any other men than Peter. I used to know my brothers, my father when I lived with them and Jaz. Did all men possess the characters of Jekyll and Hyde?

It didn't bother me not having a group of people around. I knew they were out there, those swarming locusts ready to drag me into their crowd, ready to nibble on my energy, if I let them. I knew how to socialise, but I didn't want to do it. I wanted to be in control now, as a narrator, as a woman who was living the story of Svera. Sitting on the yoga rug in my lounge with your letter in my hand, reminiscing. Words slowly began to grow wings - wings of strength, from one woman to another, changing your energy to mine. Svera, a woman with a weakened spirit needed that, Mum - the wings of strength spreading their light from you to me. I looked at my hands. I looked at your words. I looked back at my hands.

"When you wake up each morning take your palms and touch your face with closed eyes. Then look at your hands. They are the hands of a strong woman. A woman creates so much in her life. She moulds, she shapes, she forges. She is the creator, earth-changing, moving, inspiring, energising."

I looked at my hands again - so many lines, maybe the formation of wrinkles. I have been through so much, seen so much, done so much with these hands. Why now, do I have to be in this semi-hypnotic state?

I looked at my old curtains. They needed to go. Outside the window, the atmosphere, trees, leaves, sky, moved with a rhythm and regularity, interconnecting with each other and with human beings. I was already beginning to sweat, afraid of being without a man when I got old. My mind with its blurred trance would sway from reality to the world of ghosts, phenomena and voices from the past. At the same time I was struggling to form words, to be productive. That's what I wanted to get from my solitude. I have fused my life into this letter to you. It reminded me of my cause and my search. It reminded me of your strength. Ma, your image made waves in my solitude. I wanted to be angry. Only anger against the wrong and the unjust could blow life back into me.

I reasoned with myself. Had I been selfish in my life? Had I not struggled against racism, oppression and injustice? Had I not been faithful to my husband, my children and to my conscience? Yes, yes, I had been. Why should I look down upon myself like this then? I reconciled my contradiction, occasionally at regular intervals. Wanting the solitude, but needing the support, dying to survive. Just a weak super-woman! My mental struggle reminded me of another Asian weak-super woman. She was the partner of a friend from Tanzania, Abdulla. I decided I needed her solidarity, just for momentary relief. I planned to visit Arpana and her partner Abdulla in London.

MONDAY 6 June. Nina arrived to keep Minna company while I was in London for the weekend.
"It will be good for you to come out of this stupid isolation. This town is killing your soul," Nina said to me.
I was strangely excited to travel to London where I had once seen the shadow of the man with pink hat. Maybe I will meet him. Maybe.

FRIDAY 7 JUNE. My bus was leaving at three thirty in the afternoon. My daughter dropped me at the station. I boarded the National Express at Bradford interchange. The bus was not full yet. I made myself comfortable on two seats. I had brought a book with me to read, but there was so much distraction. I just sat, blankly looking out of the window all the way to Leeds, where we stopped for ten minutes to pick up more passengers.

"Can I sit here please?"

I looked up and saw a short young looking guy standing in the aisle. I could smell strong curries, sweat and cigarettes. Oh, my God, what luck. I had to sit with him for the next four and a half hours.

Just as I began to get totally absorbed in my book, another odour of curries entered my nostrils like an unwanted guest. I looked at the young fellow sitting beside me. He was eating his packed lunch, probably prepared by his mother for the trip. I felt hungry seeing the delicious meal. All the other smells had already got accustomed to my system. I ordered a cup of juice. As I tried to open the overfilled plastic mug it spilled on my bag and my jeans. The guy took tissues from his bag and offered them to me.

"Oh, thanks. This cup is really overfilled."

I smiled falsely, a bit embarrassed.

"So are you travelling from Bradford?" he started.

"Yes! And you?"

"Yes. I study at the University. My friend and I are going to London for the weekend to enjoy the night life."

He was a young Pakistani man, 23, maybe 24. Muslim arms stretched large over the city of Bradford. Frivolity, drinking and women could not be safely indulged without somebody's private eye watching.

A Hindu woman with a big round red bindi on her forehead, owner of a corner shop, came to my mind. To some whites all Asians are the same, but we know better. Every time I went into the shop she gossiped about Muslims, things that would make Salman Rushdie sound like a saint.

"They have no morals. They are hypocrites. They commit violence against their women but worse of all," she drew me conspiratorially closer,

"there is girl at the school around the corner. Muslim of course. Not more than 15 years old. I have seen her in the shop. A pretty girl, but her eyes are so sad. Now I know why."

I took the bottle of milk that I had purchased and she looked at me enquiringly. I couldn't resist.

"Why is she so sad?" I demanded.

She drew me closer, looking left and right again.

"I have to be very quiet. These bloody Muslims. They have spies everywhere. It's the father with the daughter. Yes it's true, now she is pregnant."

At this moment an Asian man walked in the shop and she quickly took my change.

"Yes," she said loudly, "Bradford is a funny city."

I didn't want to hear her gossip so put the bottle of milk in my bag and left.

I looked at the young man in the seat next to me. The further we got away from Bradford, the more animated he became.

"We go on pub crawls in London. Very good. No one asks questions," he said mischievously.

"So is there no night life in Bradford then?" I asked.

"Yes there is, but my Mum won't let me go out too often. Even when we do sneak out, there is always an uncle, a cousin or a neighbour around the corner watching you. So we are going to London. Nobody knows us there. Nobody cares. London is where you can be yourself, you know. You can get lost in the crowd of people in the city that never sleeps."

His friend giggled foolishly. He wore two gold earrings and a very peculiar hairstyle. Apparently a back, side and shave. He glanced towards his friend and moved closer to his seat.

"Where are we going to stay then?" He seemed worried.

"I phoned Rasheed last night, so don't worry," his friend assured him.

"But you know what happened last time. We had to wait all evening. Are you sure he will be there waiting for us?"

Half of the people in the bus were dozing while we were busy chatting. But we soon got tired, and sat gazing at the scenery. The noisy engine and the sound of the traffic outside was breaking the silence in the bus. Some people seemed irritated and had faces longer than the journey. My mind was alert with the thought of meeting my friends. How would I make them understand? Ruby and Om hadn't. I felt let down by them. I felt tired. Was it my age? I thought about the Indian shopkeeper in Doris Lessing's book. I thought about the old people back in my country. Even there, nobody really cares for them, not even the state. There is no benefit for them. They merely survive at the mercy of their children or relatives.

What about the old people here - totally ignored by the youngsters, at conflict with society? I don't blame the young people if they reacted to traditions, norms and the religious hierarchy. But then, what about the youths who start misusing the freedom of being British Asians? Why all this hypocrisy of working for their community, multiculturalism, bilingualism, respect for elders? It is all so doubly moralistic - cynicism, chauvinism. A woman sat quietly, resting her face against the window, lost in her own thoughts. The vast grey sky was bending over the earth. The shadows of clouds reflected on her face through the window, as if the sky was stooping over to scoop her up. The woman felt my gaze and looked towards me. Very sad eyes. I thought of a poem I had written when I first caught the plane to Denmark.

The sky is bending
over her
and she is bending, dissolved,
surrendered,
laying down all her weapons.
The stars are
glowing fire flies of the sky
but in her own bewilderment
she can't find any path.
The moon is shining
over the silent valley
unstuck, forlorn
becomes her dream.

The sun still rises
from the womb of the East
piercing, tearing, rectifying
her skin in all directions.

She bends
to gather the pieces

Let us help her
gather those pieces
heavier than her own heart.
She can't lift them.
Her weakness is her strength.
She needs to carry that strength,
she needs our solidarity,
she has to withstand,
she has to resist
the threatening sky, so ruthless.

I could not get back to reading the book. The road under the mighty wheels of the National Express became retrospective throwing me back to the year 1992, when I first arrived in Bradford. It's like working against the tide, the time, the speed.

CHAPTER 24
The Change Was Lurking

SEPTEMBER THE 3rd, 1992. The crescent moon, the pendant branches of trees and the inviting hands of nocturnal sky offered a mystic, soothing glow to my inevitable destiny looming ahead as I sat near the window on a train to Bradford. I had travelled from Copenhagen to be with Nina, Minna and Peter. I had been obliged to stay back in Denmark for a month while the girls started their schooling. I boarded the train from Manchester airport. The train was half empty as we started off from Leeds station. Two young Asian girls sitting on the front seat giggled and made eyes at each other when they saw the handsome ticket collector arriving in our compartment. A woman anxiously looked at her watch every five minutes. Sucking his little pink thumb her baby slept in the pram while she put a jacket on her boy presumably four. She was preparing to get off at Frizinghall. A young man watched her through half closed eyes but got bored after a while. His swollen eyes shifted towards me, carelessly looking at page 83 in my Danish novel, *Sort Te Med Tre Stykker Sukker*, by Renan Demirkan. The train had now caught up to its maximum speed. It was a train going nowhere but moving swiftly. Perhaps, I would soon catch up with myself. My tired pupils tried hard to crawl back to the last page of the story of a Turkish immigrant woman.

"Et par ar efter modtes de ved et tilfaelde igen I spisevognen I inter-city toget fra Frankfurt til Koln. Han havde............"
Coincidentally, they met again in the dining compartment of an inter city train from Frankfurt to Koln. He had gone to attend a seminar with some colleagues. He had lost some weight, his broad forehead had become taller and he had become round shouldered.
"I have a new family now", he said and spread some photos of his wife and children on the table.
His new wife was from his birthplace in Turkey.
"Are you happy now?" she asked him.
He became quiet, put his head in his hands and ran his fingers through his hair.
"What is happiness? I am satisfied, at least for some of the time."
He squeezed the tea bag, added some drops of lemon essence in his cup and smiled.

I took my lavender oil out of my bag to rub a drop on my wrist as new passengers entered the compartment.
I asked the ticket collector if he would kindly inform me when I arrived at my destination.
"Don't worry," he said, "Bradford will be the last stop, on this line."
Will it be my last stop? Wondering, I asked him if he would help me down with my luggage. He shook his little black head from side to side in a peculiar way. I had seen that affirming nod of consent before.

There was still half an hour left. Some people were already getting ready to depart. I had enough of reading and sat looking out of the window. The darkness had robbed the horizon of its orange shades. Finally the train arrived in the city of my fate. There were only a few passengers left at the station. I fixed my luggage on the trolley and walked toward the exit. There was a checkpoint. I wondered why they needed to check the tickets again. A man asked rudely,

"Could I see your ticket please?"

I looked in my big bag, then my purse. I couldn't find it. I must have used it as a bookmark. It was snuggled up between pages 82 and 83.

"A very strange place to put your ticket," he said and looked at my heavy baggage.

His broad pale West Yorkshire face flexed with anxiety.

"Oh, yes indeed."

I smiled. Peter had come down to meet me. He led me to the staircase. I stepped down on the pavement, through the door to a city unknown to the narrator of Svera's story. First chapter was yet to be discovered with all its characters, scenes and psychedelic colours. Nina and Minna threw themselves into my arms as I entered the huge lounge of a house on Pollard Lane. Wrapped between their love and my tiredness, I fell into a deep sleep.

CHAPTER 25
The Traveller Of Shadows

With your permission folks, I, Josef Strauss now make my grand entry. You may or may not recall that I sometimes wander around in my worldly attires in places, like a lost traveller, capsized on the roller coaster of events. Touched by the similarities with other worldly souls, I drag myself out of my past to enter into their present, lost in love, in life, now, a particular street, in a peculiar city, this house facing this wonderful place of rest. Yes the house with its eyes, ears and a benevolent soul that had learnt to communicate with Svera, this house where I now follow her life. I used to live here, a very long time ago.

Before I continue, let me show you around. This is the house with its single glazed windows on Pollard Lane, Peter had rented when he first arrived with Minna and Nina in August 1992. Svera followed a month after. When I set my eyes on her for the first time, I got startled. She looked so much like my sweetheart Anjali. Oh Yes, the same dark innocent eyes able to penetrate your soul deep down. The same aura, style, gesture and even the same oval bone structure of the face. I was wandering in and out of the events, scenes and time, waiting for years, for her arrival, as fate would lead me. I was a visitor, travelling beyond my years. I was moving on the wings of my shadows to emerge into a full scale reality, physically getting ready for a encounter with Svera. On the roadside, I would often stand, looking through her large windows. My dark eyes would bore through the walls like a drill.

Through my piercing eyes, I would watch and analyse what was taking place in Svera's life. I saw everything. She may later describe to you how we met, but, I was the one who had led her to this Victorian house. The house on the hill. Not Everything happens with a reason. She must have come to this city to go through pain. It may well have been a trapdoor of consequence. We shall see.

Do you see phenomena, metros, shadows, aliens, UFOs and even ghosts? Do you sense things? Remember them? We all remember events of the past and drag them into our present thoughts. Sometimes we try to reason things, but fail to do so. Things disappear; get too much entangled in the debris of the past, where we keep on wandering for ages. Lost like ghosts, for too long, like I have been.

Here, Sirs, I will be letting you envisage the Victorian house Peter rented, with two large sitting rooms, a big kitchen with dining area on the ground floor, three bedrooms, a toilet, a bath on the second floor and two bedrooms and a bath on the third. The house was partly occupied by a church organisation and some of the rooms were rented to students before Svera, Peter, Nina and Minna had moved in. My family had once rented a room there before we moved into the house on the hill where Svera and her family also moved to. The huge house on Pollard Lane was in a pretty bad state. I could get lost, wandering around night after night. I like wandering, exploring, realising. I gathered that Peter and Svera liked big stylish houses. The thick, fluffy dark carpets were typically English and very dusty. So were the dark red velvet curtains that matched perfectly with the gaudy sofas - a mix match of odd colours. Real English. Unlike the German or Scandinavian, these English folks don't have the sense, touch and taste for colours and style.

Svera decorated the sofas with light coloured 'khanga' cloth brought from Tanzania. She wanted to change the curtains too, but was afraid to spoil the material in case they had to move again. They did move after six months, into my 'original' vicinity - The House on the Cliffe, facing the cemetery. The baggage Peter and Svera had collected over the years from their travels to India, Africa, Denmark and Canada arrived in containers from Copenhagen. The house swallowed up every item into its huge belly like a hungry python. She couldn't wait. She was so restless. She wanted to settle down. She wanted to turn the house into a cosy place for her kids and her husband who had started to study. She unpacked the whole bloody mess in one go. Soon the house was covered in beautiful exotic objects. Ebony wood carvings, sleek and shining black gold of African wood, basketry, rugs, the sea shells, books. Cities and streets of the world became colourful objects of decoration, intensifying Svera's memories. They reminded her of her past. Sometimes, she sat looking at them.

Once again she ornamented her real living house with those objects she had collected from all the places she had been. Just the way she had her dolls house painted in rainbow colours. Remember? It was the house from her childhood. Now her daughters were the living dolls, of flesh and blood, glowing with energy. Lights and shadows were looming ahead of them. She had no idea, then, that those bouncing colourful energies were going to be trapped in shadows. But at that particular time Minna and Nina were the most energetic living lights, restlessly wanting to change the entire look of their rooms, which were very gloomy. They painted them peach, pink and blue. New furniture was bought to match these shades.

There wasn't enough money left to buy a new double bed for Svera. She could not get used to the thought of sleeping on someone else's bed and tried to bury the ghosts under a thick cotton bed spread. At least she had the luxury of lying under a sparkling new quilt. At least Peter had the decency to buy that for her. He was so generous. It has been some time now since Svera had written to her Mum. Out of laziness? I think it was more to do with her mood. She was becoming moody, depending on those tranquillisers.

The 5th of November is a special event here in England. A figure dressed in old clothes representing Guy Fawkes, burnt, in memory of the foiling of the famous Gunpowder Plot. Fireworks and celebrations followed. The English burnt an effigy of this unfortunate man once a year. He was a catholic. I must admit, the ceremony always struck Svera as strangely bigoted. The golden-yellow heaps of dry leaves on the streets were crushed into an ash like powder under fast moving feet. The fire of passion crumbled but at least there was a stable sky. The nights were more calm yet empty. Days were busy and filled with tasks. After the mid-term holiday week, kids got down to the serious business of studying. The buses were yet to be crammed with humans who would soon be getting ready to celebrate Christmas, busy buying millions of gifts, wrapped in glossy papers. I saw ghosts of Santa Claus with their fluffy West Yorkshire smile pleasing the kids in the many super markets. Nina and Minna had already started humming Boney M versions of the old Christmas songs. It was a time when Svera used to get uneasy, thinking of the stressful rush in the shops. Yet it was that month of the year when she could feel relaxed and enjoy the most beautiful colours of nature. Her Brontë calendar read for November:
O may I never lose the peace
That lulls me gently now,
Though time should change my youthful face,
And years should shade my brow

Yes, the change was lurking like the humid smell of nostalgic memories. Change, the sign of wisdom. Change the harmony of conflicting values. Change, the transition of her endless travels. Should she stop or continue? Where to? The truth was that she was tired of all these travels. Now the change had begun to frighten her. She kept on seeing demon of fear crawl all over the place, behind doors, down in the closed basement, behind the thick red curtains. She was scared to draw them back. Something might jump into the room like a devious monster. Now I wish she had, then she would have seen me standing in the street desperately seeking her attention. I wish we'd met. Instead, she went to see her doctor. The pain in her breast was growing and so was the lump. She had only read about it or heard of it from other women. But having it inside her own body was strange. It felt like a foetus in the womb. Fear was a stubborn poisonous spider that kept on creeping towards Svera's soul, provoking senseless tremors minutes before a break down. The doctor prescribed them as panic attacks. Attacks occurred before the panic. And that was something even a doctor couldn't understand.

The cyst she had developed in her breast was real. It had to be removed sooner rather than later. She always disliked hospitals. The white dressed nurses and grey walls of Danish hospitals were still nightmares in her memories. She could still see the angry, wrinkled face of an old Danish nurse, telling Svera off when she went to have a forced abortion. Svera felt so lonely, depressed and filled with contempt. Lying on the operation table, waiting for someone like her mother to tell her to keep that child. She passed out under the influence of drugs. How she regretted that for years.

Friday the 13th, NOVEMBER 92. It had been a very windy night. Spooky. It sounded like the howls of a hundred hyenas in the Serengeti Park in Tanzania. The stormy winds in India she had experienced were no comparison to these.

The boiler blew out and then the bulb in her bedroom and the one on the landing leading to the attic where I had a room. The house was cold. Svera had to call the landlord to have it fixed. It happened three times that week. Svera had sleepless nights. She left Minna at her school. The fifteen minutes walk through the grassy Golf Course made her energetic. That day she was going to 'sign on' at the Job Centre in town. She hated it. She hated to stand in a queue. But she had to do it. She cleaned up the mess in the house and wanted to light some candles in the kitchen. It was a cold day. The wind was on the rampage with showers marching on the roads like a classless crowd of angry ruffians trampling the city with their vigorous feet. Bravely, she took an umbrella to step outside, feeling the pain in her breast.

Svera was so afraid of the cyst. Her kids had no idea about her pain. She went out during the day, sometimes in order to neglect the pain, but it was very much inside her body. She kept pretending, going to job interviews, to women's groups and to the post office to collect her benefits from Denmark. She was restless and confused about her pain. There was an indescribably strange feeling between Svera and Peter. He took refuge in his study, writing, reading and jogging. He wanted Svera to get a job. There was no compromise.

"Such horrible weather," a woman waiting for the bus remarked.

"The summer is too short in this country."

"Do you live in this neighbourhood?" Svera asked.

"Just across that little lane going between those houses," she replied, pointing towards a path between two tall houses on the road. I happened to stand there too. No one noticed me, not even Svera. I became as dark and gloomy as the clouds in the sky. The bus came and they both got on. I followed silently, sliding on the seat just behind them. Driving down Otley Road, the city looked like a vast bed sprinkled with beads of light in the dusk. My favourite Little Germany, down Church Bank. Opposite Forester Square was the gateway to the city centre. The drive was short but scenic. Svera was so lost in the scenery that she didn't feel my attempt to tap her on the shoulder and try to wake her up from her trance, so she could notice my presence.

A small city with steep roads, beautiful but difficult to penetrate. Every community closely knit within the boundaries of their own little world. Little community, little religion, petty mindedness written over people's faces. Svera was a stranger in that city, just like I always had been. She would be for some time, swallowing its beauty together with its ugliness. The Market Street looked deserted that day because of the rain. On other occasions, it is swarming with the gorgeous outfits of people from various cultural background - tights, skirts, saris, Punjabi shalwar kameez and wavering dupattas, seeming to cover too much from an outsider's eyes. This provincial British city boasted a rainbow collage of different nationalities, cultures, languages and ethnic origins. Thinking about the migration, Svera walked fast on the steep road. I could tell her a lot about migration. But the time was not ripe for me to present myself to her. Her umbrella was uncontrollable and so were my thoughts about her. She trudged through the street as firmly as she could, gasping for breath as the wind tried to steal her strength.

SUNDAY, 15th. The rest of the week had passed. She could now constantly feel the lump. The pain increased unbearably. It felt hard and the pain would come and go. She decided that she would have to see a doctor. Meanwhile her hunt for jobs continued. There were several projects in town but there were many applicants too. She had been called to a few interviews. She waited patiently for their response. Sometimes they phoned and politely told her, "Of course your interview was excellent. You have so much experience, but you lack the local knowledge."

The other day Svera met Ronie from Keighley at the Manningham project. They had both applied for the same job. Ronie told Svera that in most cases employers would already make their minds up when the job was advertised. The interviews were a formality. Svera's experience of working with immigrants in Denmark, East Africa and seemed wasted and lay dormant on her C.V. in the computer. Now the festivities of Diwali arrived in the form of glittering lights. Svera bought little clay lamps and candles from Bombay Stores near Great Horton Road. A cultural evening was organised in Saint George's Hall and Svera, Peter and the girls decided to watch the show. Svera lit candles outside the house to perform the ritual. The whole family was dressed up for the occasion.

The Government's decision to close 31 pits and sack 30,000 miners would turn the Christmas of 1992 into a black cloud of depression. The demand for jobs was steadily increasing, and so was the recession. Strikes and mass demonstrations were the red threads to decorate the Christmas trees that year. As the wound on her breast slowly healed, civil war was spreading in Bosnia. The reports said around 75 people had been killed on average each day there during the war, which had now gone on for months.

MONDAY 16th, 2 am. The night clung softly to the concrete road. The misty sky bathes in an opalescent mist. The house, the walls and every building gleam like shadows and the smell of the trees is wafted in the silence. Svera woke up from a dream. She kept on dreaming while awake. This had been happening to her for some time. One unit of diazepam for sleeplessness didn't seem to work. Often she lay quite and solitary, feeling like a tiny dot in the universe, or a grain in the sandy mountain Himalaya. The night was slowly ticking in her heart. She was afraid to switch the bedside lamp on, which might wake Peter, she left it off. She wanted to write in the silence of the night - a poem, a hope, an urge, a crutch to lean onto. She got up, found her notebook in the dark and sneaked out to the landing to ponder. The dim light created soothing shades on the wall. Minna's chipmunk moved. Even in her cage she could move up and down, climbing on the branches, thinking she was free. She could feel Svera's presence and peeped out to see if she had brought some grapes. Chipmunk loved grapes. Svera opened the small door to put one hand in. She jumped on it to eat the grapes. She did not try to escape from the cage. She was so used to the four caged walls. She had forgotten how freedom tasted.

Svera made herself comfortable on the steps, near the cage, as the chipmunk munched her grapes. From her mind, words of a new poem slowly crept down to wander onto the white paper. They couldn't be held back. They had the freedom to loiter around, if they didn't come out, they would go elsewhere, disappeared into different corners of the house. She had to pin them down. The paper was now half filled. She had so many half written poems. Stretched on the pages of her notebook, they were pulling her arms like spoiled kids, to be taken out for a ride, for an outlet, a completion of their desire.

While we leave Svera, sitting there on the staircase, sleepless in her own house, trying to write, let me peep out from my shadow to admire her face. Let me thank you for listening to me, letting me describe this chapter. You may or may not identify similarities and you may feel a nostalgic recalling of the past. People can relate to things when they read, see or listen to events happening around them. In a case like this one I hope we might form some kind of bond between us. We might even start to think alike. Now I can't think anymore. My energy is exhausted. Things are becoming too complicated here. I might have lost the ability to prevail in the present.

Memories feed my soul with nostalgia. I do have a soul but I can't feel certain things. I have limited thinking. I can't stay too much in my present state. So then, it would be wise of me to take my leave here. Dawn is breaking. I shall retire once again but will be back tonight. Auf wiedersehen!

CHAPTER 26
The City Of Shadows

I was *dying* to get in touch with you. Good evening again. I am Josef, trawling through Svera's life. Svera has been so busy struggling to put her past behind and move on. It wouldn't be far-fetched to call her a restless gypsy or an international nomad. She is classless, colour blind, with no religious convictions. She left them all behind when she took on the journey away from her country. The only thing she brought away with her was her fearless soul. She is one of those individuals who form their own identity. She always adapted well into a new place, new environment, and thrived with new challenges. She would be neither out of place in New York or New Delhi. She was a creature of the city despite her rural upbringing. She had lived in Chandigarh, Copenhagen, and Dar es Salaam, the three totally different capitals of three totally different countries. Now here she was in a city in the heart of the Yorkshire Pennines, the city of the famous Bronte sisters, the melting pot of ethnic minorities who swarmed here to work in the woollen trade. Like the Germans. Like me, Josef Strauss. In the 1830's a small group of Germans immigrated to West Yorkshire and were soon to have a powerful influence on the woollen industry of Bradford. We built the mills that the immigrants worked in. The trade with Europe flourished in the 1860's and 70's and we became enormously wealthy. We did not just accumulate wealth but with the profits we built the splendid warehouse and the wonderful, ornate buildings in the area between Leeds Road and Church Bank. It later became known as 'Little Germany'. We built houses. The House on the Cliffe, Svera had moved into, was our old family house. In its elegant crescent overlooking the celebrated cemetery and my family's tomb, which Svera would examine every morning when she took her dog for a walk. Svera always looked at my family's tomb. There was something about it that drew her in - a magnetic aura. She would often bend over and touch the surname, Strauss, which was etched in the stone. That's where I fell in love with her exotic beauty.

A woman so much younger than her years - a woman who had youthful lovers queuing at her door for favours, but who would soon be rebuffed as she retreated into her splendid isolation. Svera was searching for her lost love, Jaz. Peter came into her life like a transient moon, offering her the two beautiful daughters, Chandnis (moonlights). Then he disappeared. She was doomed to be disappointed. Only compromise on her part would bring emotional salvation.

Our spiritual union transgressed the hundred years which separated her birth with my doomed soul. We were like two spiritual companions two opposites of the same contradiction, lost in love, searching for some banal truths, which already existed within us, reunited in the faded glory of this Victorian cemetery and this hundred and fifty year old glorious house.
I left my secrets in the deep recesses of one of the secret chambers in the basement which she would discover one day, in the full knowledge that she too would fall in love with the young man in front of her. I would monitor her fascination as she would find the painting behind an old bookcase in her basement. I have spent my youth studying art and music in Leeds against the wish of my father, Wilhelm Strauss who wanted me to take over his business. Like my friend, Fritz Theodor who became a musician and moved to Florida, I took up interest in art. My sister Dora had a strong liking for Fritz. The same living room in which Svera so often spends her lonely moments near the fireplace, I had dined and relaxed with my family all those years ago. Time cannot

thwart destiny and it was our destiny, mine and Svera's, for her to be here, now, at this time. She would peer inside of the grandiose façade in which were arranged my family's ashes, as if searching for the reasons why she had come to the city.

This city of immigrants where slogans of racial equality and equal opportunities constantly flashed in the eyes of its inhabitants, blinding their vision, hiding the truth. They walked in a daze through this grey cemented city with those neon signs. Like midnight sleep walkers, with all their differences trying hard to exist side by side. Some people call this place a vivid example of harmony, a unique place in the North of England. We know very well at times this uniqueness, this reality, this jargon turns into nightmares for all the citizens of this city. Some of the sleepwalkers decide to wake up in a frenzy to create havoc. God knows where and how they get hold of the devilish devices to start their petty race warfare. Bang! Bang! Bang. They try and play with their toys to transform harmony into destruction. Haven't we all seen the riots of the 10th of June, 1995? We have seen fighting and killings of one gang against the other. There will be much more destruction, not only in this community, in this city or this country but also in the whole world. I can already see beyond the eyes of my mind, people crazy for power will create wars, destroy and monopolise, if we don't wake up. Wake up!

A shallow cold Monday. The days were becoming shorter. The nights were racing by chasing the sunrise. Svera's lounge was getting colder. The streets in Undercliffe reverberated to the sounds of school children returning home, shouting. Cars sped through the street. Some of them leaving break beat music like fast vanishing smoke signals in the sky. It looked like it was going to rain. In Bradford, it always looks like it's going to rain. Except when the sun is out, then its yellow like the joy of saffron or the cowardice of Paki bashing. The clock ticked 3.00pm. Not mine. I do not wear a watch. They remind you of your life passing. Tick tock, tick tock. Dead. Become a ghost.

But in case you are in the hearse getting carried away with me, let me remind you that we are still wandering in year 1992. December the 18th. Svera looked through a daily paper. A drama and writing workshop for women was to take place at one of the many women's centres in the inner city, starting that day. When Peter left in the morning, he reminded her to call in. He did not like the idea of Svera staying at home while he was at University. Nina and Minna were at school.

"It's such a shame to sit here at home dealing with all the trivial matters of cooking, cleaning washing floors. Do something meaningful, Svera," he would sometimes remind her in Danish. He loved to use the word meaningful.

She sat near the furnace, warming her thoughts. She had drawn a map on a piece of paper to find the place. She was not very good at directions. She hated using road maps. It was always Peter who drove to places, found things, organised trips. She was afraid to venture out on her own. She thought maps would only misguide her in different directions. She got confused. But she did have her own way to find places. The doorbell rang impatiently. Both Nina and Minna ran into Svera's open embrace filling the lounge with their excitement.

"Oh, Mum, how nice it is to be here," said Nina.

Her face shone with red youthful content. Tall, slim, beautiful, she was always very emotional, just like her Mum. She paced up and down in the middle of the room, speaking, each limb of her body vibrating energy. The room glistened with words, gestures and actions. Svera prepared afternoon tea for them.

The real Darjeeling tea she had bought from one of the Asian supermarkets near Bombay Stores down town. Not the Yorkshire or Tetley that the English so loved. Here in West Yorkshire they cook to eat 'tea' the term used for supper. For her, tea was tea as she used to make back home in the Punjab, for her Mum. Tea leaves boiled with water, milk, sugar, cardamom and cinnamon. Have you tasted that real exotic Indian tea folks? One of the few things she had difficulty in changing was her concept of the tea making ritual. Nina had her difficulties too. She never easily adapted to change. Her first reaction to change was always negative. You must see beyond those flowery curtains, beneath the striking wall paper of your lounge in London or your garden with its view of the Juhu beach in the Bollywood city of

Bombay. Maybe you are sitting under a tall coconut palm on the white sugary sands of Oyster Bay beach in Dar es Salaam. What about you, strong beautiful Indian women, in Mauritius, with your rubber boots, toiling in the sugar plantation for that rich India factory owner who speaks French. Do you bathe in the Ocean? Do you read, write? Speak French? Maybe you didn't have the luxury to learn. You who might be having a bubble bath with seashells stuck on the peach coloured tiles in your red thatched straw roofed house in a suburb in Bali, or in a café waiting for something to happen to you right there while you pretend to drink your coffee with loads of cream, looking across the table at two middle aged women having an intimate conversation on dating men. What about you, middle aged man? You walking with a big grin, winking at each young woman passer-by, with ten lottery tickets in your pocket with the money from your state welfare cheque you've just cashed in a post office in the multi cultured area of Paddington. Hey you, Svera, doffing your hat to a magpie? Watch out woman, the wheels of your red bike are turning around faster than your thoughts. I can see you getting entangled with that raggedly handsome guy on the road to Grand Union Canal as a junction of rivers where all the world's trade came together and eventually flowed into an ocean Hey, traveller, are you on a train from Hertfordshire to Loughborough, amusing yourself with these words and the way I describe my story to you? And wow, look at you, woman! I see you are hurt. Now that your husband has cheated on you, you are breaking down, drinking madly, humiliating yourself. Don't do it. How could the bastard leave you? You are beautiful, talented and economically independent. Don't worry, he was not worthy of you. Don't start to chase men. Live your life, sing, enjoy only then your soul mate might bump into you one day. Hey you, Mr.T., you have met so many women that now you don't even feel the hurt, when they leave you. You are enjoying the dating game. Be careful, your heart had been broken many times before. Have you developed a shock absorber in your chest to prevent the hurt? Clever man, sorry I am not available, not to you. I want a strong man. A man who can match me. A man who is not jealous of me. And you, who might be driving in a purple Fiesta on the streets of Johannesburg pondering over this woman Svera's life. Are you sitting on a bench in the famous Tivoli garden of Copenhagen where Peter once told Svera that he was going to leave her on their wedding night? Watch out, the history repeats itself so often, do not make the same mistake like Svera. Can you avoid it? Wherever you might be at this moment, in a house, on the move, in a certain place, in any city of the world, having this story in your hands, try to imagine this scene.

This was the Market Street in the town of Bradford. Peter had led a small expedition, taking his family, shopping in town. The month - September. The year - 1992. Let's recreate the scene together.

He is a five foot, nine inch, dark-haired, blue-eyed, medium-built Scandinavian standing in the middle of the crowded street with his big Viking hands and threatening voice. She is a slim girl of 17, nervously complaining about the clothes she has been forced to buy for her college, anticipating every devious look of the passing, rowdy lads, hating every minute.

Why am I here? What am I doing? She seemed to question in her distressed state. Wouldn't you with all that travelling, all that uprooting, settling in one strange place after another? I have often heard stories from my dad of the immigrants and their children who always had to follow their parents, having no choices of their own. Can you imagine and visualize? It was Peter and Nina. The low whispering voices came from Svera while Minna just stood there holding on to her Mum's hand, very confused.

Let's go back again to the now, this afternoon, where Nina seemed overjoyed to be at college with other kids of her age. On the contrary, Minna was made of a subtle material for me to understand. What went on inside her head was often very complicated, even with Svera and Peter's clever parental eyes. So far she had managed well at her school.

"You know what Mum? Everybody talks to me. And you know the Asian kids? They are very different. They are very open. Boys and girls, they are just like friends," Nina continued like a chatterbox.

Svera smiled at her.

The day was fading under the dull soot-clouded sky. The tall houses on Pollard Lane grew taller when the lemon light arrows from the lamppost on the road pierced through windows of each house. The night is dark now, will be the light tomorrow and so on. Svera left the kids to go upstairs and changed from her jeans to a pink Punjabi silk dress. She was going to catch the City Circular 602 to Manningham Lane, but Peter was late from University. So Svera had to travel by a cab.

"The tea on the table is still hot. I won't be late."
She closed the door behind her.

"Enjoy yourself, don't worry about anything. You look beautiful," he said.
Svera shut the cab door behind her. Peter stood at the door looking in her direction, with a wide grin on his face, waving. Svera understood the meaning of his happiness. At last she was going to use her time constructively. The cab was now somewhere between Oak Lane and Lumb Lane. Svera couldn't understand why the cab driver smiled. The pavements swarmed with people shopping on their way home from work - red, green, yellow, brown masses of fruits, clothes, suitcases, utensils, all colours contrasting. It was Oak Lane. Svera shut her eyes against those strong images.

A shadow emerged from behind the cocoon of Peter's mysterious face. She thought back. It was only a couple of months ago, an evening in Copenhagen. They were staying with a friend of Peter's. The kids had planned to see a movie in town. Svera had to do a lot of washing and packing. The children were leaving to travel to Bradford the next morning. They were going away with Peter, while Svera was staying for a month. Back from Africa after two years, she had to reregister herself under new EEC regulations. The pressure of moving away from Copenhagen, a city she had come to love and cherish. Her dreams of romance, her first love with Peter, it had all started in Copenhagen. And then again, the travel to another unknown destination, the agony of her indecisiveness, the desire of refusing to move. She felt so meek and sad. Peter could simply not understand her. He felt angry. He wanted his family with him. He wanted her to go with them to the movies. There was that usual scene, hostility and so on. Children tormented in between.

Oh, no, Mum, please Pa, don't put us through this mess again, their eyes seemed to be yelling in silence. Peter and Svera argued, shouted at each other, Peter throwing the crockery on the floor in rage. Svera broke down crying. She wept disturbed by the look in Minna and Ninas's pleading eyes.

They had to leave with Peter, leaving Svera behind crying. Slowly a darkness spread in front of her eyes, creating small sharp waves of pain in her mind. Her thoughts were so muddled up that she couldn't form the words to speak or write. Tremors of pain stretched beyond control causing nausea and she began to sweat then vomited. She felt so sick that she thought she was going to pass out. Frightened she phoned a doctor, who came straight away. He was their family doctor. He was very kind. He told Svera that there was no reason to worry, she wasn't going to die. She was just experiencing a panic attack.

I panic at the thought of being found out, to be seen in public.
"Excuse me, mate, you're a ghost, aren't you, we don't want your type around here."
Don't you panic sometimes? Well Svera did not really want to travel again. The doctor advised her to try and calm down, maybe ask someone to come and stay with her. She telephoned her friend Lisa for help, who brought a bottle of brandy. As Lisa poured them both drinks, she started to talk about the evening of 15th of March 1989 when they had met for the first time under peculiar circumstances.

They had lived in the same neighbourhood for years without even knowing each other existed. Each one yearning to meet a kindred spirit, a like-minded person until an interview with Svera appeared in one of those women's weeklies. It was a Danish magazine 'Femina' with pictures and the story of Svera founding the first magazine for immigrant women. Lisa read it and phoned Svera to meet up. Lisa was so thrilled by this woman Svera that they became friends. Lisa loved to remember their first meeting. She was always eager to talk about the wonderful old times, when they used to organise young women in Copenhagen teaching them to edit, to photograph to speak Danish. Now Lisa wanted to know about Africa.

"Ah, yes, Africa! I have been there physically, in the city of Dar es Salaam, the Haven of Peace, that wonderful place of colours. It seems like an illusion, a rainbow. I remember the garden of my friend's house preparing an interview with Jamila, Brenda, Nisha and Sabira at Masasani. It is so vivid," sighed Svera gulping the brandy.

"What is your image of India?" Svera had asked the young woman.

Nisha, the dark one with charcoal black hair, with the longing of Radha in her eyes spoke first.

"Beautiful. Gorgeous. Yes, certain parts of India. I've been there a few times. Rajasthan, for instance. It's so beautiful. But I was born in Tanzania. All my friends, my social life is here. I wouldn't be able to live in India. My cousin came to visit us from India and the first thing he said to me was, "You know you shouldn't be living here. Look at Tanzania, all these African people.""

"What do you mean? I am one of them. This is my homeland. I was born here. I am an African," said Nisha.

"I have never been to India. I consider myself to be Tanzanian. The only connection I have with India is cultural. It's through magazines, clothes, food and films. I feel very strongly about that. But I don't think I'd be comfortable with anybody from an Indian background, anybody who has stayed, been born or brought up in India. They are very different. I can't relate to anyone from India. I don't want to get married to an Indian. I wanna get married to Denzil Washington."

Jamila grinned loudly, winking to other girls.

Brenda said "Well I grew up in India. I was a baby when I was sent to live with my grandma in Goa. I got my education in Bombay. So I grew up between Goa and Bombay, on beaches and sand. It was like heaven. But I feel at home in Tanzania. Here. There's more peace here."

Sabira said "People from all over the World think we live in a jungle here or huts. But they don't know anything about Tanzania. I am Tanzanian. But Tanzania reacts sometimes negatively. I am really curious about India - the food, the ice cream, the mountains, the rivers, the monuments. I would like to go on holiday. A friend of mine thinks he is going to be the president of India one day. He is mad."

Those girls talked for hours, sitting in a garden by the beach at the Indian Ocean, the same ocean that flows along the shores of Bombay in

India, the sunset in the background and an orange flicker of dreams in their youthful eyes.

It was the night of 23rd August when Lisa and Svera talked and talked about their past until the words in the room started to float like stars in a galaxy, making Svera dizzy. She was dreaming of being on a space ship or travelling in a time machine with Lisa who promised to come back the next evening. Svera slept that night with wings of fireflies in her lightened heart. Nina, Minna and Peter were leaving the next morning. This huge continent of Africa was now a concentrated piece of sunshine, trapped in the pages of the many books in Svera's house. Captured images provoked sounds and colours of memories filled with 'Sunshine', 'warmth', 'panoramic landscape', the images well depicted in a photography book, Portraits of Africa by Mohammed Amin. This and many other books on Africa adorned and decorated her bookshelves. But she had been there, she had done all that, seen it through her own curious eyes

She had seen canoes on the Lake Victoria's tranquil waters at a beautiful sunset. Fishing dhows leaving Zanzibar harbour with the house of Dr David Livingstone (1866) in the background. Women dressed in the traditional Buibui, wild dangerous hippos lazily sun bathing in the river Rufiji, the snow-capped Mount Kilimanjaro rising majestically out of the savannah just below the Equator. Ngorongoro Crater at dawn. Masai warriors resting at the backdrop of the Ol Doinyo Orok hills west of Namanga. Women filling gourd containers from the reservoirs hidden beneath the bleached sands of a dried up riverbed. Lions mating in Serengeti Park. Svera had travelled with her camera on her shoulders alone to the many villages in Tanzania capturing images, talking to children, Masai warriors, women. She wrote:

Women

Dust with dust
On the wasteland
Breaking through the hinterland

Like the dawn
Digging, exploring
The land, the market squares
Sweating, wandering
Warriors on the road
Women, treading on
Their subdued anchors
Ujamma, the green dream
An icon like Nyrere, shines
Like a silver snake
On the purple barren land
The hard core guardians
Striving to keep the green dragon

They didn't mean
To subdue their dreams
Dreams of
Warriors of the land
It just happened
The decision
Was already made
When Ujama was born
And the smoky eyes
Were let to shed tears
Under the leaking thatch
The equal rights were
Flung apart
On the alters of
Their village squares

Imprisoned and wrapped
In the cultural taboos
They still perform
The age old traditions
Warriors of the land
Nourishing their offspring
While the tough boys

Sit under the shades
Of their politicised slogans
Eat the sweet dish of
Freedom to shape the history

Tanzania, sizzled in the heat and dust of corruption - Ujama, the so called socialism, the world bank inflated debt, bumpy roads like craters on Mars. The pleasure was melting under her wounded feet. She had lost Peter to Africa. When Peter decided to take yet one more year to finish his study, he chose to come to England instead of going back to Denmark. Maybe it was an escape for Svera too. She cannot blame everything on Peter, the poor bastard, telling her to perform some meaningful errands, like attending a workshop.

The evening of December 18th. Bradford. The taxi queued behind other vehicles at the crossroads of Queens Road. The slow speed made her nervous After a while it pulled up in front of a tall beautiful church. This was Manningham, famous for its own peculiarities. On the left side of the church was the Asian Womens' Centre. Why are all Asian womens' centres flat, grey, square-shaped buildings? Svera wondered. She stepped into the ten square meter hall. A piece of the evening shade fell through the window on the pile of chairs in a corner. There was no other furniture in the room. A mural covered one of the walls.: women shopping, women carrying babies, women giggling, praying, washing, cooking, tending their small vegetable gardens and children playing. Miss Mahmood, the manager, sat drinking her tea in a carefree fashion, waiting for the participants to arrive. After a brief introduction, Svera took her jacket off and pulled a chair from the pile. Posters and leaflets were neatly pinned up for activities on the notice board. Svera wondered if there were centres for other women as well. Miss Mahmood said that she often had to remind everybody to attend sessions. She had to make several phone calls that day. At last women began to arrive, two elderly women with ten young girls in their teens. Lin, the organiser of the workshop, told everybody to try to perform an act through game of cards. Girls started taking part in the game with great zest. Svera was shy. She did not like to act. It was getting late. Lin had to drive all the girls back to their homes. Girls were not allowed to be out alone in the dark evenings even after 5pm.

It was 8.30pm when Lin dropped Svera home. Nina and Minna had already eaten their supper and Peter heated the meal for Svera. They sat by the fire talking about each other's experiences of the day, just like they used to do back home in Denmark. Svera told Peter about the images of women on the wall. She had so often seen them on the street wearing scarves on their heads, some of them covered from top to toe with an Asian bui-bui. Humble, sluggishly dragging their feet across the pavement, with shopping bags and children in their arms. There on the walls they seemed alive, vibrant, so carefree, open, full of fun.

I could see Peter and Svera from behind the thick red curtain. Oh, how jealous I became. But I am Josef Strauss and I am too proud to show myself or my emotions to Svera at that time. I was going to wait for her, even if it would take forever, even if I had to come back again. I would do that for her. But the time was not ripe. Not yet! I was waiting and wandering like a shadow, out of the shadows - a tall, dark growing shadow throwing a little light into Svera's life and then dispersing into them. Again and again and again. Shadows.

CHAPTER 27
Shadows Are Tall

Are you confused? I have no intention of misleading you. If you are wondering, who is talking to you here, I will point it out. In this chapter Svera is the narrator, the one who had started chasing shadows, her own as well. It's me. To escape my fear I had to write poems, a letter, a dialogue or even a description of the shape and colour of this creature called fear. Talking about this devil did me good. Sometimes, words travel on the white foam of memories like sea horses, galloping away in all directions. Poems are born on waves of emotions. They have wings, can fly like fireflies, can shoot like bullets, soothe like a lover's kiss. They are born from an idea or an incident. I wasn't boasting of being a great poet. I couldn't boast of anything at that time. Peter didn't think my poems were good enough to be published - a black poet, a woman. I might get the chance to be published, one day. For the last twenty years, so much had happened around me or because of me, that I found it necessary, to give it a form. There were volumes of written sketches describing the events, but to give them a form was not an easy task. I did not have a space of my own. I always felt the need for it, but it was never available. I did not make it available for myself. I was always surrounded by my responsibilities, as a mother, as a wife, as a woman, trying to liberate other women. What about myself?

My doctor, my psychologist, my counsellor and my friends had so often told me that I was compromising too much. They were right. I did not realise it then. I was blinded by love, which overpowered my logic. Instead of resisting and demanding a space for myself, I would retreat into the corner of depression.

"The way Peter is treating you is not helping you," people would comment.

I believe them now, but what was the escape route from my own indecisiveness? When I couldn't find the escape, I became disheartened, depressed. Peter called them mental problems, in order to escape from his responsibility. In order to escape from the trap that I could see lay outside the emergency exit, I kept on taking medication.

Yes the escape door was there, but I did not reach out to open it. Instead I stayed cluttered. The caged chipmunk looked straight into my direction, with a strange flicker in its eyes. A challenge mixed with inability. And before I could understand his call from the depth of his tiny wild heart, he died of a strange illness. He didn't want to compromise, even if we'd offered him a golden cage. Instead of escaping from myself imposed mental cage, I decided to compromise. I was like the chipmunk. The door to my mental cage was open, but I stayed within the comfort of myself imposed boundaries. I became a prisoner of my own willingness to do nothing. I was afraid of change. Peter was leading a double life. He tried to give me advice and ignored it himself in his own actions. It was June 94, when I found out that he had been cheating on me with another woman, for a whole year.

"Taking care of yourself is good advice, but try to get it right. Your own personal happiness and development is not in itself the aim of life. People can strive for selfish happiness all their life, but never achieve it. The aim is doing something meaningful OUTSIDE yourself," he wrote to me a day before he was to leave.

I was amazed at his double standard. He was the one striving for personal pleasure, taking care of himself by not trying to solve his problems with me. I remembered one of our friends, who had been married for at least twenty years, left his wife, because he had suddenly fallen in love with a younger woman. Peter was even more outraged than I was.

"I simply can't understand how people can fall in love with somebody like that. Love comes when you have stayed with somebody for years and when you begin to know the person well," he had stated.

My father must have loved you so dearly, mother. He had great respect for you. I think he was a very romantic man. I think I am just like him - a romantic fool, caring, down to earth. Seeds fall from my womb on barren ground, on fertile ground and onward into infinity. Some ripen some bleed. I am nurturing, changing and sizzling with the sensuality of an earth.

TUESDAY 22nd. It's still '92. The multitudinous leaves of the autumn were finally crushed down by the winds and a million ruthless footsteps were partly to blame. These were footsteps here and there and everywhere. I could hear them on the foreign lands where the bitter winds of war blew from the North. The British soldiers marching on the soil of Bosnia had all the intentions of bringing peace. Yes, a well planned strategy. A war. Soldiers. Weapons. Kill. Destroy. Justify. Justice and peace. Soldiers sent messages back home to their families who might have to celebrate Christmas without their heroes. Peace or no peace, Christmas was inevitable.

You could never guess if Christmas was going to be white, rainy or foggy, but it now brought tensions that lurked like a hungry cheetah around my house, waiting to enter. I was invited for an interview, to do outreach work, organising youth activities. I placed candles around the house. I hung decorations on the walls, baked cakes and wrapped the presents. And yet there it was, the bloody demon, tension clinging to the walls of my heart like a bat, frightening me. I wanted harmony.

When you phoned me, Ma, I had been crying. After talking to you I caught vibrations through the phone connection of a certain harmony that had existed when you were around. With that strength, I started breathing normally for some days. I also felt as if you, or somebody, were watching over me. You may be my guardian angel. You wanted to know how my dear family was coping in a new country. I couldn't tell you then. I can tell you now that I was so terrified with the disharmony spreading around my family. Peter was studying at the university and he was unhappy with our money situation. Thanks Mum for the money and advice you sent me.

"You've been stupid not to keep any money in your name," you told me.

"Go and put this money into your account."

I looked up at a portrait of Peter hanging on the wall behind the sofa. He was a short, grey-haired man, my husband for the past twenty-five years. His wide, blue eyes were filled with quest and liveliness to fight against all the injustice in the Third World countries. That's what he wanted to do in Africa - meaningful work. He did smile at me. He did support me, if I engaged myself in meaningful (another Nordic expression) work. He smiled when he said, good-bye. I was happy with his smile.

He had started losing his temper quite often. He fought over money. I spent very little money on myself. I tried to buy cheap clothes. I even stitched a few Indian outfits myself. I liked fashionable clothes, but I was afraid to buy them. When I started working, I would buy nice clothes. I went to town with your cheque in my purse. We had a joint account in one of the city's banks. Driven by the desire to have something in my own name, I opened up a separate account. Like a child I felt overjoyed and content. Now I could buy presents. Christmas was approaching. I thought of using the money for gifts. I loved to give presents. I didn't care about getting any. I loved to see the children unwrapping gifts. I gave that gold ring that you gave to me when I left India to Peter's mother when I met her for the first time. She promised to give it to Nina when she got married, but she never did. So I was happy to have some money to spend on gifts. I came home with a smile of confidence, and wanted to talk. The kids were still at school. Peter sat with a newspaper in his hand in the study.

"Aren't you back early from University today?" I asked.

"Yes, I had some writing to do at home. Where have you been?"

I did not want to break the news at once. I was so afraid. I prepared a nice cup of Indian tea for him, standing behind him while he sipped his tea, I gently rubbed his shoulders.

"Today I signed on at the job centre. I also did a little shopping. Then I opened an account in Barclays Bank, in my name, with the cheque from my mother."

I started a long explanation about the importance of having a small account of my own, when I did not own any golden jewellery. It might give me the pinch of self-confidence I needed. I should have seen his outburst as inevitable. He broke into an angry fit, snapping and snarling. Hissing like a python. There was a fierce fight. Frustrated, I wanted to phone you Ma. But he took the phone away from my hand and hit my head with it. I was extremely depressed for days after that, more because of the insult than the hitting.

The kids came home and witnessed the storm. I shivered with cold despair and anxiety. No communication with anyone, I spent my night in the company of my ugly companion, the fear. I was quite disturbed by Peter's violence. A few weeks later, I had finally made up my mind. I wanted to leave him. Peter did not expect that. He got used to his violence and my depressions that followed - my apologies and reconciliation. My children did not expect it. They were used to the patch ups. But they knew this was serious. Peter got so frightened that he begged Nina to plead with me to stay. Otherwise she would not be able to pursue her studies, he told her. He used her to plead with me. I had to give in for the sake of my daughter and so for both my daughters, I stayed. Christmas was then merely a compromise of traditions. We hid the conflicts behind the soft colours of white, pink and blue candles burning on the shelves of our house. We had to pretend that there was a family, at least during this traditional festival. Christmas came and went, but this time the joy was a grey cloud without any silver lining.

This was Bradford. Peter had once again chosen to absorb himself in his studies. The hollow space between Peter and I was wider now than ever before. Strong winds and sleet forced any little sunshine away. I stood helpless, watching the catastrophe. I didn't know how to cross the barrier of my pride, so I was losing out. I was losing him. I didn't like the distance.

Desperate, I went to see my doctor.
"Give me a double dose of Amitriptyline," I demanded.
He advised me not to take them. I didn't want my family to go to pieces, because of me, I argued. With the pills in my pocket, the sky seemed clearer, transparent blue, cold though. I saw the signs of spring, flowers in bloom, everywhere. I was happy. I should be. My family demanded me to be a happy woman, a happy mother, a happy wife.
"Women are the cultural bearer," I had said some years back, when I worked with immigrant women.
Peter agreed with me. Yes, the women out there might be the culture bearers, but I am definitely not. I was not allowed to be.

"A clever decision, Svera. You had to take care of yourself. I was becoming very upset with you. Those pills will help you. I need the peace, the weekends, the evenings, the nights, as much time as I can get for myself."
His voice was as cold as the March day. He then forced his big nose back in the huge economics book. The children were upstairs. I left Peter with his books and went to the kitchen to prepare the evening meal. I saw a shadow through the window - a tall dark and handsome man standing on the other side of the road looking in my direction. Was I hallucinating? Amitriptyline surely did wonders.

The pot with chicken curry (Kuku na nazi - the Tanzanian dish - chicken with coconut) was simmering on low heat. It should not boil over. I have to take care. Looking at the thin wall of vapours, I recalled a letter Peter had written not so long ago. It was 1991 in Tanzania, from one of his usual trips. He had got into an argument with me before he left. I was fed up with his travelling all the time. I wanted him to spend more time with us. Sometimes he would just start up new projects, seminars and meetings. Once we had a huge party, given especially on the occasion of his birthday. One of his colleagues and his wife brought a present for me instead.

"You deserve a small appreciation for all the projects your husband takes on - leaving you alone with the kids."

To Svera- Arusha 17.11.91 (*Arusha is a town in the foot of the Mount Kilimanjaro, the highest mountain in Africa*).

I am sitting here eating breakfast in a small hotel, my first rest after a busy week. I have come to think about you very much. I have been amongst many people for a full week. I have been so busy that I have not even been able to keep my two promises to you: to wash my clothes and not squander money on beers. But what I want to say is that amongst all these people, I am very alone. I think I am a lonely wolf who has his own strange mind- not really fitting to anybody- except you. I miss you, to talk to you and to have our common understanding as a basis for talking. I know I do complain a lot about you. You are also not so easy to tackle. But I must confess that I do not know anybody else with whom I have so much understanding as with you. It is not because we have known each other for so many years - but something deeper, which I think is close to togetherness of minds. We have some invisible bond that ties us together. If you had been with me now, I would not be so restless and hyperactive.

Can you imagine I am MORE busy than when I was with you! You mean a lot to me, and I do not think I could manage without you. Now the children are getting older and we should be able to spend some more time together and do things together. I saw a house being built by an African family, a big two-story house around a yard, a veranda and a flat roof, a real wonderful house for an extended family. Something like this, we should build in India. I hope we will spend some nice holidays in India- this time it should be truly holidays where the four of us are together - not only the shopping, also for talking and having fun. I miss you and the kids. Now we are all trying something new, going to Britain. It is a big country. We will perhaps settle in India. It is even bigger.

I like change and challenges, so for me it is good. I know you would like a more stable life - so would the kids. I don't know if our life will be more stable one day, but I also have this dream inside me, to settle down and stay in one place, which is our own. But - let me confess, I am not ready yet. I wish to gain some more experience and face more struggles before I can settle down. Maybe we could settle down little by little (in India?) whilst still pursuing new goals?

Svera, I think a lot about Nina and Meena, and I know you are doing a great job with them. Maybe you do not know that I appreciate that work: but I do! Very much. They have a wonderful mother, and I am sure they will remember it when they grow older. At their present ages too many things are happening with them to really think about oddities like fathers and mothers. Later on they will realise. Sometimes we quarrel over children, but I must say, that you are doing well - sometimes you do too much for them - and break your own health on them. I love you very much for that. I could not give them half of what you have given! Now I will be coming home after one week. I long for it. I wish you were here with me just now. Svera I love you. I miss you- sorry for spoiling your notebook....Peter

When he came back Nina told him "I don't know you anymore. You are not my father, more like an uncle, who visits me sometimes. I want you to be like an ordinary father, here by my side, always near me, with me." She was fifteen then.

I eventually pulled myself out of my pains, convincing myself that he may have acted the way he did because he felt he could not be the provider. I went to see my doctor for more Amitriptyline. I cancelled the account in my name. We had a strict budgeting system. Every penny that we spent had to be accounted for. I was used to that system from the time I had been a teenage girl in India. You know that, Ma. Don't you? Being the second oldest child, having an older brother busy with university, two younger ones at college, I was the only one who could manage the family economy. You were not bothered with the financial matters. You had too much on your plate.

Now with a family of my own with no job, children schooling and husband studying, I carried on the tradition. But there was a huge difference. You never bothered what I did with the left over money, ma. I was always able to spend it on all those crime novels from a cheap pawnshop, or a few luxuries like the fine hair removing crème – 'Anne French' - or a nice lacy bra or a porcelain bottle of Tibet Snow, an exquisitely perfumed skin cream for you. Peter would not allow such things. He insisted on checking my accounts every week. He was not too happy if I spent a bit of money on clothes, entertainment, or things for the house.

We had our famous family meetings as well, held every Sunday afternoon. Those family meetings at least once a week were useful and contributed to organising our daily routines, an essential link for the gathering of the family. When leading a stressful busy life, it was important to retain the family harmony which could disintegrate into the claws of western individualism, 'I'. School, Peter and I working, having our many activities in the evenings, weekends with no holidays, the family was beginning to disintegrate. I constantly felt this hunger for love and romance to appear from somewhere and come into my life, but it was a thing of the past.

Family meetings were good for everyone including the kids. At least that's what we thought at the time. Now when I come to think of it, my God, what rhetorical intellectual shit it was. Each week ahead was planned in those meetings. Who did the cooking, who did the washing, the clothes, the dishes, the house cleaning. Of course I did most of the chores, having only one part time job at that time. We then hung the plan on our refrigerator. Everybody knew what each person was supposed to do the following week. All families have their own traditions and rituals. We had ours. Back in Tanzania, our children had become dependent on a certain life style, luxurious and lazy. They even neglected simple things like making their own beds. But there was one strict rule they were suppose to obey - to have respect for our house helper. They never broke that rule. We had Lucia from Mbeya to help us with washing and cleaning. She had the authority of any other grown up person in our family. It was not part of African, Danish or Indian culture. It was you, mother, who taught me to treat people equally. When you visited me in Africa, you were so good to Luci. You brought her presents. She was sad when you left. That seems ages ago now.

It is beginning to get dark soon. The shadows are eager to grow taller, just the right time to step aside and face the light of realities. I shall leave to pick up Minna. I cannot continue venturing into the past for too long.

CHAPTER 28
Josef Speaks

Hiya. Where did I get this slang from? Not from Svera. This city. This country, where I arrived when I was a baby. Svera will be gone for a while. It is only appropriate for a personality like me to sneak into this room to flick through pages. I am quite capable of sliding in and out of realities. Holy Ghost, how happy I, Josef Strauss have now become, given the chance to communicate with the reader. Don't worry. No one but you can see me as I make Svera conceive thoughts to form words for you to read. Ok? It's dark in here. This room has no shadows. Shadows are only visible when there is light. Life is made of energy and the light feeds the spark into that energy. Shadows are illusions of light. I could be a shadow, an illusion of Svera's light, life with shadows. We all have illusions in life.

What month, you must be wondering. What year is this? Sometimes, I lose track of time. Don't you? What matters to me now is this story. Svera's story. Well let me remind you. We are still pretty much wandering in the month of Dec 1992. The wintry wind is creaking through the house. The frost permeates through its foundations. I suddenly feel very restless. I want to liven up my poor soul.

You lively up your soul
You rock so you rock so
Like you never did before

You dip so you dip so
And you can dip through my door

Ha, it's the good old Bob Marley - the voice of his ghost, actually. He surely livens up my soul. We are soul mates you know. Ha, ha. Svera listens to this Rastafarian guy with big fluffy hair all the time. She has his poster in her bathroom and in her bedroom. She listens to his music in her kitchen in her lounge, even in her car. Can you keep a secret? Pssst... come here - in your ear! I do not like this guy. Hey! Don't laugh. You think I am jealous even with the cassette... with a dead soul like Bob? You must be kidding.

I was itching to continue this story, so it didn't become static. I think this woman affects everybody's life around her. I heard Ahren saying to her the other day, "Oh, Svera, you give all these vibes to people. There is something mysterious around you. An aura."
He then sighed and sat in front of her like a little schoolboy. She just giggled like a teenage girl in front of him. I was so jealous watching them together. By the way, Ahren hasn't yet entered in her life. Well it isn't going to be that long before I enter into Svera's life. You will then have to say your goodbye to her. She is not going to resist me. Tall, dark, handsome. Sparkling blue eyes. She always fell for deep blue eyes because they reminded her of the water of Sukhna Lake. Even now.

This woman can be hypnotised by deep blue colours. I will be able to draw her into these crystals. Easy, but you, Ahren, she was able to see through you. Your blackberry eyes and your falseness. You just flirted with her innocent soul. You wanted to exploit her for food, for favours, for cheap rent and yet I somehow have this empathy for you, like Svera has. You coconut. Brown outside, white within. Coconut! Handsome, yes, but the biggest flirt of all the men she'd met. Well, I'm going to make sure that Svera will fall for me and you will be out of her life, like a bad wind. Just now I am beginning to grow very restless. Like Svera, I have developed an urge to express myself through this story.

Svera has been travelling a lot in her life. She has become so very - what's the word I am looking for? - I know I have heard it so often from

Svera - yes, so very *cosmopolitan*. Now we are going to talk about culture. I see you raising your eyebrows. Let's get serious. It's again about this unique city where labels of 'tolerance', 'racial equality' and ' culture' are bounced about, like negative energies, in the hands of those who want to use it for their own benefit. Before you start yawning, I will let you dip through my soul's doors (thanks Bob).

There are so many jigsaw streets in Bradford. This one, off the famous Leeds Road. Let's call it Kingston Street. Here you will see people from different cultural backgrounds. Hindu, Sikh, Muslim, Christian, all black and white British. The whole country is turning into a 'melting pot' of ethnicities, a colourful rainbow. Kingston Street is peaceful, quiet but often littered. Here you will see many back to back houses with one tiny kitchen, one small lounge with two bed rooms upstairs for a family as big as three grown up young children and a mother.

Let's call them 'The Bans' family. The mother had come in the early seventies, just like our Svera had left her country around that time (she didn't come here though). She came to Britain to marry a man her family had arranged for her. He is Kulwinder Bans who was living and working in Bradford as a night shift worker in one of the many wool factories. They started this family of 'The Bans' together. The mother had to work in the factory as well until one day the father died of a heart attack. They say he was working too hard collecting money for dowry for those two daughters of his. The mother was left alone with three growing children who considered themselves British. One of the daughters who was twenty seven went out one morning to have her hair cut. She did not work in a factory but had a decent job in an inner city office. She came home with her new hairstyle with a big smile on her face.
"Oh God, what have you done to your hair, bitch. Do you think you will now become a Gori. Do you think I will ever allow you to go out to pubs and smoke and have a boyfriend. Oh Guru Nanak, mere Rab. (my God). Why didn't I die instead of my man?"
"But Mum, please try and understand. I haven't committed any crime. I am working, you know."

Mum would not listen to reason. She was very upset. She sat down crying and wailing hysterically. She was terrified to see her daughter behaving badly, trying to imitate the white culture. Who will ever want to marry her daughter? What would her community say? Now she might start going out to pubs and clubs and have 'boyfriends'. The poor woman could not sleep for days. I have sleepless nights thinking about this. Why are people so afraid of change? Is it easier to hang on to the same old norm? Look at Svera; she has changed so much, she has learnt so much because of all those changes in her life. She even learns from the young, she has learnt to look at youth through her daughters' eyes. This particular young woman of Kingston Street tells Svera so often, "I really wish I had a mother like you. You would be a wonderful mother-in-law as well."

In fact the young woman was allowed to go for a dancing party in town with Svera, because The Bans' mother trusted Svera.

Now I will tell you my secret. I was once madly in love with a Sikh girl, Anjali from Birmingham. Svera looks like her. Anjali's parents and particularly her brothers were so hypocritical. They terrorised the poor girl for falling in love with a Gora like me. I wanted to tell them that I wasn't merely an English Gora but a hot-blooded, tall, dark and handsome German. The oppression of women makes my blood boil. I am Joseph Strauss, the radical, possessed with the idealism of social equality. Even though my father was a merchant, I have seen the grinding poverty of the cotton mill workers. I have seen parts of fingers that have been trapped in machines and woven into the fabric of England. So don't dare to call me Gora. These Asians are bloody racists themselves towards other people's religion, culture, cast, class and colour. I am talking about culture. You may or may not agree with me about culture. I might sound too philosophical here. You might think, bla, bla, bla, Josef Strauss, giving a speech on culture? You don't live in the present, maan. You are damn right to object. But what about all this bull you yourself thrive on. I mean all this junk stuff, the films like *Sleepy Hollow, Blair Witch Project*, your popcorn, hot dog culture, your bizarre horror inventions on video, the bloody internet porn stuff and the chat lines. My God, people have even started textual intercourse on mobile phones. Damn this modern technology. If Uncle Karl saw all this crap, he would close his eyes in horror. Can you imagine? The mad scramble of the lotteries. The constant fear spouted by television. Millennium bug. Meteors from space. Mad cows disease. Flu. God, why don't we all commit collective suicide? It probably wouldn't get more than a ten second clip on the 10 O'clock News, because it's been done before, wouldn't cause an eye brow to be raised. By tomorrow, genocide is forgotten. If we were to listen to the so called experts on T.V we would never bother getting out of bed. Middle class white men moaning to other middle class white men and inflicting their neuroses on the rest of the population. They are all creating jobs for each other. Hell, they have wives and children to feed. There is not enough news to go around. They have to create fears and then jabber on incessantly about them. Do these people ever predict anything correctly? These cosseted Mummy's boys don't have airtime and nobody buys their newspaper. So it might be a good idea at least to listen. You don't have to agree with me. There is this *freedom of speech* - as long as someone's prepared to pay for the commercials between freedom and speech.

Svera who once left her country in the hope of finding more freedom has been constantly fighting, fighting prejudices to be different in this city. Amongst Asians, amongst the well-meaning whites who would purposely support and understand the traditional, subjugated Asian woman - Svera - who doesn't fall into any of the categories. She has been learning and developing herself, trying to avoid getting stuck in a merry-go-round kind of state. That's how her life has been until very recently. I am sure after her fight with the inner demon of fear she is going to manage. Remember she was sitting near the chipmunk on the staircase trying to form words to chase away her fear?

She is now trying to jump out of it, in order to move on. She is breaking out of her trance. She might suffer some injuries like whiplash, backaches, love aches etc. She may even fall apart in a small way. She may get backlashes.

"Why can't you forget the past?" Peter used to say when he was leaving her.

Well, she can forget the past, the rows, the beatings, the miscarriages. She is free from the past. She can get on with the joyous moment of now. Trying to teach others about culture with my philosophies, you would say, raising your eyebrows again. I must admit I have enjoyed your company. Thank you very much for listening to a soul like me. Svera is now back, I can hear her vibrant footsteps drawing closer... closer and closer... I can feel the light, the heat. Oh, it's getting too hot in here. Time .....brrrrrr...I have lost the sense of time, let me just disappear from the scene. I am out of here. Bye. Camera pans off me, Josef. Cut to commercial...one, two, three. That's a wrap. Well done everybody.

CHAPTER 29
The Fear Slides In

Sorry, I am late. I began to lose control of my sensory oars in the river of time while the tide rose high to wash away debris from the troubled, polluted landscape. I was on my way to somewhere, I forgot to turn left at the main junction and turned right, finding myself in trouble. Stuck in the middle of a sea of human faces, immobile behind the wheels of smoke spitting vehicles they waited irresistibly, wriggling their wits to win the game. Time was a monster that chased them to run around its clock day and night, month after month, years, centuries, millennium, eternity. Time was an omnipotent emperor who subjugated his subjects to humility, destruction and defeat. No one but death could see this devil in his eyes, because death is always right on time. The travellers were enwrapped in a purple haze of anxiety when things didn't 'move' according to their wishes. On this particular afternoon, on that broad tarmac road of the city, where I faced a 'traffic jam', people thought they were 'pushed' far enough. Notwithstanding the pressure, they started to behave like an uncontrolled mob of animals. They shouted foul language, they picked their noses, they let their hands and arms fly out in aggressive gestures at each other, until their energy turned into sooty fumes like machines they owned. You could even watch their angry eyeballs running amok on the street, contemptuous of road rage. No one was there to stop or arrest hundreds and thousands of tumbling eyeballs. Only the movement on the road would turn their fury to something positive. This was a situation that was out of my control. Feeling trapped amongst these fellow humans, I tried to manoeuvre my way to Minna's school. It took exactly forty-five minutes for us to drive back from Manchester Road to Otley Street where the house with a spirit waited for our return, a trip I usually manage in seven minutes. Such a waste of time. Wait a second...nothing is static in this universe. Everything changes, everything moves, everything passes, everything born knows the process of ageing, each moment is born anew and dies instantaneously. We live in a world of birth and death, simultaneously...What? Is this Johnny's voice I'm hearing? I can feel his presence, some other 'reality'. In my absence, a form or a spirit had moved into my 'vacuum' space to fill the gap, to continue describing the story of Svera. I could sense someone's presence there. This chair has been moved, touched. It feels warm. Hot, hot, hot. Who sat in my chair in my absence? Hello, who's there? Josef? Ahren? Mum? Uncle Karl? Johnny? Am I imagining that I ever met Johnny? Saw visions, let the spirits out from their closets, shook this woman Svera from her slumber.

Who was Svera? Where was she? Who am I? I am getting used to this stepping on the other side of a world where 'reality' sometimes becomes unreal, where the other 'reality' takes over. Phenomena, forms, other shapes and creatures try to walk all over you. I see them often step into my present incarnation to pay visits. These visitors from my past, whether by accident or by invitation, did keep on bumping into my life. I allowed them to enter into my world. They did take me on trips where I would have never wanted to go. The deep dark crevasses of a world where I met my worst dreaded fears. I had no other choice than to confront myself, my own psyche - me, myself, Svera. I was pushed to the edge, manipulated, disorientated and forced to witness Svera in all her moods - the good, the bad and the dark, her hatred, her anger, her sorrow, her despair, her angst. Svera's unwanted visitors helped her to confront the guilt, the rage, the despair, she had been nurturing in her soul for so many years. They made it possible for Svera to withstand all that lay lurking like a vicious animal under the layers of her self-denial. They taught her to tackle the demon. They insisted on prevailing in her life until the first ray of the dawn hit her. If they wanted, they could have left her alone or they could have evaporated into thin air like aliens from another planet, but they chose to play games with her resistance.

They were testing her will power. Ghosts were the chasing paper dragons in disguise, between the shadows and the light of her life as I chased this woman Svera for my story.

"Give me a break woman," I sometimes tried to shout in the emptiness of her soul. I needed to communicate to her, even when she was entangled in her illusionary world and was stuck somewhere in the past. I also needed the peace, the vision, the logic and an eye of an observer. I didn't want to get drawn in her confusion. I had to keep on skipping back and forth in from past to present to future, to make sense of what was going on and to make her realise exactly that.

Now, One step back, please. Where were we? Yes I was telling you about the night of 16th December 1992. Sitting comfortably on the staircase near the chipmunk in a cage, I tried to express my pain through writing. This was the only way of fighting Svera's fear for survival. It was a psychological warfare against an enemy whose tricks I was beginning to learn, whose strength was being weakened by the weapon of my writing and fighting spirit. I was clearing up the old debris for Svera, for her to give way to light. I had no other choice but to become stronger than Svera. I knew that my enemy was my own weakness - the other Svera who kept on seeing shadows, ghosts, snakes, pythons and turned them into real living creatures. At some point, I had started to resist. Don't get me wrong, it was much later than you'd imagine, much later when I started to realise that the struggle is not merely a physical activity but very much a process within one's mind to free itself from fear. So I had to tell Svera to take a dive into the ocean of herself, to search for that reality. In the deep depth of the sea there was no light but reflection from pearls forming a chain to the surface where it meets the light.

She was just panicking, crying out for help. Help from who? From where? Was it a man, perhaps? Tall, dark handsome, as handsome as Jaz, her lost love, who would come in another form, shape or appearance to save her from all her miseries? Oh no - a woman, a woman like Svera who had touched death.?

Yes sir! She had touched death when someone took a dead embryo from her womb to place on her naked palm for her to say good-bye to. She must have known that depression, medication or killing Peter wasn't the real solution. She must have also known that everyone has to fight against something. We all have to confront our fears, challenge them, shake hand with the devil. Look into their eyes. Let them know that we know their tricks. Trick or treat. Retreat, guys, I am not giving up. Damn you. Come here and face me. I will fight you. Once, twice, as long as it takes me. Many times. Chose to live in mental slavery or be free. We always have to chose. Choices are laid upon the ground before us as soft rugs. As soon as we begin to take that first step, when we start to stand on our own feet, there are choices. Choices are everywhere. Take a pick - to give in to fears or fight them. We all have to wage not only one but many struggles. The struggle keeps us alive.
I wrote:

At times
Fear knocks at my door
Like an agent from hell
Devil's advocate
Under a forged disguise

It comes sliding
Inside my house
Through a tiny crack, sometimes
It's a thought that turns my life upside down
Turns it into shadow
A thief, hiding behind its own deceit.
The trembling hands
Of my uncertainty
Try to chase him away
He creeps behind the long heavy
Drapes of my doubt.

At a time
When I thrive in my own solitude.
He sneaks under my quilt.
As my conscience
Rubs its sleepy eyes
He gets the nerve
To step out into the light.

He jumps all over my body
Performs the sizzling Salsa
Shatters dust on my hopes.
They don't yield to its satanic soul.
They start to fight
Then, he doesn't know
How to resist them.
My hopes and I unite
Struggle against him and resist
Trembling out he goes,
Soaked in humiliation
His tail between his legs
Like a humiliated dog.
Half naked, half alive
Taking a vow
Never to return

Back to 1992, on the staircase of my Victorian house near the cemetery where we had moved from Pollard lane. I sat alone, writing. Watching the chipmunk, being afraid from the shadows of a late silent night and I thought, this cold weather wrapped in its own unique harmony was incomparable to any other place I've been to. This harsh weather was capable of affecting people's moods. It was able to force them into their own secluded isolation. It pushed them into depressions. Unlike in India and Africa, which I knew so well, depression did not exist. There were people everywhere, people with their different faces, millions of them. They were there when you were happy. They were there when you grieved. They were there when you were in pain. They wanted to share everything with you. They wouldn't let you suffer alone. They wouldn't let you feel isolated. But then the sun would almost always shine in Africa, even through the thatched hut of a poor worker or a peasant.

What romantic crap I was spluttering out. Where did it come from? I realised, I was repeating Peter. He used to have such idealistic jabber about Africa verses the West. While I thought about Africa, images came tumbling down, like hot glowing balls from a sun, falling on my open notebook, turning themselves into pieces of a fiery puzzle or building blocks of a Lego game. I gathered them up to find appropriate new spaces to keep up forming the story. To tell you the truth, I didn't instantly do it. While I tried to be the onlooker and not Svera herself, I was vaguely making a rough sketch in my mind without realising or thinking about the plot. I recreated the scenes later on - many many months later, a couple of years later.

I felt a strange relief when I realised, I was observing Svera as well as living her life. There was a gap between Svera the woman and Svera the author. This gap, this emptiness in my soul, formed a craving, the desire to fill up the skeleton of a creation. I felt as if I was a hungry wolf, starting on the hunt, preparing to leap ahead.

Watch Svera, take notes, write diary entries, recall, correct, record each move Svera makes, try to reason with her, tell her off, be irritated, try to fit into her shoes, analyse, understand, structure, plan, make strategies, put order in disorganised words. Like a creator, turn the raw material into something ripe. This was real, this was crazy, but I found myself doing it, amazed at how I was living and recording every event, filling the picture, giving colour, adding fantasy. All this for a good read, to pull your hair, keep you on your toes, interested, glued to the story. However, I did not intend to take responsibility for my actions over whatever had happened while I was there with you mother or you Minna, Nina, or you my lover...s...So, whoever you are, if you try eagerly to turn the reverse side of time, in the hope of finding answers to your own problems, your riddles, your messed up affairs with me, you might be disappointed. I am not part of your game anymore. You can keep on living the way you've always lived your lives. I am moving, my thoughts are moving like a flashing train, faster than time, unpredictable. You'd never know which station they'd arrive at. What plot, what story they'd recreate. In which book you might end up being a character. But you won't know whether it's you or it's a mixture of two characters into one. Some of you wouldn't be worth mentioning. You can't catch up with me. You can't catch me either. I am free from your clutter. If you want, I can tell you how to clean your mess, but it will cost you dear. I know how time is counted in pennies, in pounds, in gold in a capitalist system, so you can't cheat me. I am not sorting out your messy affairs either, but I had warned you!

On the other hand, you might choose to be non-judgmental. You might be wholly swallowed up from head to toe in Svera's story. With your eyes and heart wide open, visualising yourself, your own experience, your own story, your own memory creeping up like monkeys to tap you on the shoulder, revealing the real you. You might say, yes, I have been through this, I was there once in the dark deep tunnel, down in the gutter, deceived, hurt and all that. You will get lost in your own memories, but you will also come out with something solid, of that I am sure. Try and experience. Be bold.

"Now you are going to live with lizards and snakes, Svera. How can you leave a country like Denmark and go to live in a jungle?"

Svera had never been to Africa before. She wanted to explore this magnificent, huge continent. She wanted to know the people out there. This was what I heard from well educated people, my colleagues where I worked as porcelain painter. I just laughed. I knew they were being totally ignorant.

Living in Denmark, then travelling to Africa for the first time, changed Svera's romantic notion of this vast, plundered continent with all its varied forms, political, social and geographical. A couple of years turned into six years in the sunshine jungle of poverty. Africa where Svera did come across snakes and harmless lizards running around in the garden, lions mating in the beautiful Serengeti Park, buffaloes chasing the big four wheel drive vehicles of tourists, hippos peacefully strolling in the grassy planes, monkeys trying to steal food instead of climbing on your shoulders. But Tanzania was not all sunshine, exotic fruits, dangerous animals and beaches. The local people lived and thrived in confusions, under the leaking hut of Ujamaa socialism. Lack of commodities, poverty, corruption and disasters poured like heavy rain-falls, making people toil in all the four seasons. They fought their own battles. They struggled on under the hardship of life managing with the few essential commodities of smiles, mangoes, fish and maize in the market. Everyone had a piece of land, a Shamba to cultivate.

One of the directors at the Danish office in Copenhagen, who interviewed Peter for the Job warned Svera, "Be aware of the fact that Asians are not very popular in Tanzania. They are rich business people, shopkeepers and exploit Africans. They do not mix with blacks."
Svera smiled and said, "I do know that the railway in East Africa was built by the Indian workers. I do know that Indians are not the only shopkeepers in the world. I am not. I have no intention of exploiting anyone. I have nothing to worry about."

Living in Tanzania changed her perspective about Indians, Africans and Western European expatriates. She found out that the so called liberal Danes, Karen Blixon's romantic characters, lived in secluded luxurious houses surrounded by barbed fences. They imported their clothes, cars, furniture, household commodities and even food like sausages, cheese, beer, spirits and bread from Denmark, Sweden and Germany.

She had come across the 'poor' Indians living side by side with the locals, speaking Swahili in the local dialect in the suburbs of Dar es Salaam, wearing Khangas with braided hair. Indian 'Patels' were no more exploiters than the Tanzanian 'Chaggas' or the Scandinavian traders.

As I got caught up in the horizontal wind of reasoning with my past, I realised whose jang I was fighting. I almost felt light touch my soul. I felt someone's presence. You have always been close to me, mother. The cold night had almost vanished from the scene. The sun was vaguely peeping out from the sky making the universe bathe in a mild glow. The air outside smelled of fir trees, candles, puddings and snowberries. The dawn was going to return with a crimson light in my mind. The Svera within me and Svera the narrator were beginning to overcome their fear. I saw a glimpse of light on Svera's brave face when she was finally admitted to have the growth cut out from her breasts. Once more she had a white gown on her body. Once more she was lying in the white-washed room of a hospital where everything smelt of antiseptic. Everyone moved in a clinical fashion. Not in Denmark but here, in this city. Bradford. The young doctor who had just arrived from Karachi drew some lines around her breast with a red marker. He was amazed at how young Svera looked in her late forties. Svera felt embarrassment, but smiled at the young handsome doctor. When she returned home, the streetlights had been switched off. It was December the 21st - the shortest day of the year. Soon January would arrive, followed by February, March and finally April, when things would start to change for the better.

That particular night, I had spent on the staircase, reminiscing on Svera's past. I, the narrator, decided to keep on watching Svera's struggle as I would keep on pursuing mine. The story slowly progressed as I kept on writing. Yes, there was a smell of a certain change in the air. For better or worse, I did not know at that time, but I felt a change within me. Now I knew I could face the world. I was determined to continue Svera's story. I could see she had decided to set the records straight with Peter. So I started to follow her like a ghost, scribbling words of a plot in my mind, as I watched her live her life, as I watched her go downstairs to prepare a nice breakfast for him.

It wasn't me who boiled tea with sugar milk and leaves - the real tasty Hindustani chai Peter always loved to drink. It was Svera who did it. I had no desire to continue to serve this man. I loaned my inhibited physical state to Svera, as I watched the scene unfold in front of my narrator's mind. I jotted down the details of each episode - the way she moved, talked, stopped, froze, panicked and so on. Sometimes, she behaved meekly in front of Peter. He had woken up from his undisturbed sleep. He was talking to the chipmunk. We all talk to animals. Some people even talk to plants. Svera was looking at one placed on the hanging shelf in the large window of the kitchen. The light penetrated as it always did to shine on leaves. She started to clean the large leaves.

"You are a bit dusty. You look beautiful, baby," she whispered to the plant.

In her tender hands, he was thriving. Last year she had a big Philodendron placed on the top of the fridge. She moved it into a half lit corner of the front room. It started to turn yellow, and withered away.

Some people, animals or plants can thrive on their own, while others can't. They are vulnerable. I think it is because they are different. You used to talk to animals. Can you remember, Mother? You gave them names. When I was a child, you named one of our rabbits, Sundari, meaning beauty. You loved animals. You had two grey hounds, when you lived in the village with your brother, the retired military captain, our famous Uncle Karl. You talked to goats and even to buffaloes and calves. One of the calves would come running to you whenever you whispered her name. That was spectacular.

Remember, mother? You had the ability to communicate with animals. I now hear the stories of horse whisperers and recall how good you were with animals.

I must have been fifteen then. You, my brothers, my sister and I, had to move from a small town to a bigger city, a better one. I had to start a new school. It was my first day. The teacher had not yet arrived in the classroom. Everybody was talking, arguing and being loud. I sat silently observing them. Suddenly, the head teacher came into the classroom. She asked everybody to stand up and stretch their hands out. She started beating them one by one with a wooden ruler. I was shocked. When it was my turn, I refused to put my hands out. I said, "I was not talking to anyone. I am a new student." She wouldn't believe me. I got angry. I told her how unfair it was to get punished when you hadn't done anything wrong. She said if I didn't obey her, she would throw me out of school. I said she didn't need to do so, because I was going to leave. I didn't want to be in a school where they beat pupils. I was against violence. All the other students were stunned. You can't disobey a head teacher! I packed up and left.

I came home. One of my other retired military captain uncles was visiting us. He had fought in the second World War, not for the British army but as a soldier in the Azad Hind Sena. He was a freedom fighter. "What is wrong, Guddi?" he enquired as I had come home earlier from my school.
I described the whole episode. He got upset. He said I should leave the matter to him. The same evening he went to pay a visit; to my head teacher in her house. I went to my school the next day. I was never rude to my teachers. I always respected them and envisaged them as people who disseminated knowledge to their pupils. It was the unfairness I was fighting against.

That was far, far back, in the past of Svera. Let's watch her with Peter, now, here. Let's shift our glance from the pages of this book over to those two human beings.

Svera heated the two croissants and put a lot of butter on them. He loved butter. He also liked to eat a lot of meat. I am surprised his heart survived. He was finished in the bathroom and came downstairs.
"You look depressed," he commented as he entered the kitchen. Svera didn't know how to communicate with him anymore.

Three years ago when he wanted to run away she tried to plead with him to listen to the problems they were facing in their relationship. That was when he wanted to go to Africa, for the second time. He told her he wanted to run away from the police enquiries, the newspapers, and journalists. Svera should understand that it was important for him to deal with his own problems. The relationship had to wait. So, Svera felt guilty about her depressions. She was afraid to wake him up, when she couldn't sleep. She didn't dare tell him about her sleeplessness that night. If she did, I knew, he would get very upset. Violence was never a favourite cup of tea for Svera. They both sat down and started to eat in silence. The rustling of the yesterday's newspaper in Peter's hands, Svera's measured glance to his stiff face, the occasional sound of her yawning and the soft sipping of tea make you think their vulnerable relationship was a mirror hit by the fury of discontentment. She had even developed a cold and silent hatred for Peter who used violence on her body.

Her heart had been slowly hardening against this Jekyll and Hyde character whose romantic words once filled her life with delight. In her married life with Peter, there were differences, there were contradictions, there were conflicts, there were also the first ten wonderful years. Peter was crazy about her, because she was his strength.

"There is a strong woman behind every successful man," is no false statement, but Peter had always been afraid of strong women amongst others, his own mother.

"My mother wanted to control me," he would often recall.

"Peter can't accept that you are the strongest in your family," a female friend of Peter told Svera.

"I have known him for many years in the communist party, he has a weak personality."

One of our friends in Tanzania, Alfred Chamma, a singer, a journalist, a poet, was surprised to know we had been married for so many years. "Relationships did not last for longer than two years in the Western culture," he said.

Alfred, you handsome thing, you did fall for me and wrote poems only to be given to me many years later when we met again in London. Yes, you were right, mate. No, not here, I have no intention of disclosing your character further - this place, in the kitchen of my house on the hill, Bradford, where Svera was now. I only intended to expose Svera's animated personality. It bugged me to think hard and analyse her psyche. Where was the bold young, courageous Svera who used to stand up against violence? Just the way she used to do back home in India. Who has she become now? What has become of her? This woman Svera, the one I am describing to you, here, laying her life bare on the stage as you follow one episode after the other.

You might also question Svera as you watch these scenes in the story. But I had to learn to withdraw myself from the person she was, so that I could become the narrator. Sometimes I did mix up those two characters, gave a pinch of my spicy imagination, keeping the track of reality, so the story line could continue... Her bloody honour, her Izzat, the fear to be alone with two growing up daughters, and most of it, her own cowardly weakness became obstacles in her way to achieve freedom.

I watched Svera playing the role of a faithful partner, trying to create harmony in the family. I had a strange feeling about her. Setting the plates on the table for breakfast, she looked like she was lost. She was still waddling in my past, trying to fiddle with my direction as I tried to go ahead with my mission. For a moment, I turned my eyes away from her to look elsewhere. I was searching for a clue to continue. The Brontë calendar on the wall caught my attention. The famous daughters of Yorkshire had enjoyed huge success. They died young and, outlived by their disciplinarian Yorkshire father, have become legendary characters in literary history. I thought of their romantic and tragic nature. I thought of this house. I thought of Josef. Here, I shall describe to you in detail how we had met.

One day as I walked across the cemetery on a short cut to the shops, I noticed a figure out of the corner of my eye. Ghosts always appear in the corner of one's eye, enticing you further into their world. It was in an obscure overgrown part of the cemetery. The type of dark picturesque scenes you only see in films like Buffy the Vampire Slayer or Dracula. As I negotiated my way through the thick undergrowth, I caught sight of it disappearing further into the cacophony of unkempt tombs. I could not help but go further, even though the light was fading and my trip to the shops was urgent. I stood silent, still. There was no sign of the figure and as I was about to return to the path, a strikingly handsome young man appeared before me.

"It's a beautiful cemetery. I have noticed you here many times," he said looking deeply into my eyes.

"Oh," I replied startled, "I thought I saw a fox. I was trying to follow it to its lair."

A cold chill came over me. Was this man a serial murderer? A rapist? A pervert? Was he going to unbutton his cloak and reveal a part of his anatomy to me?

As I stood there frozen, thoughts reverberating around my mind, he slowly walked towards me, as if he was gliding. There was no sound underfoot. And I was immersed in the warmth of his eyes, mesmerised, transfixed. He took my hand. I could only offer it to him helplessly as he examined my palm.

"You are a very wise woman. I can see it in your hand. Many paths have led you to this place. You are not of this city," he questioned, "or this country?"

I felt helpless, my hand limp in his broad but beautifully manicured fingers.

"No." I replied. "I'm...I come from Denmark, but I'm from..." I spluttered.

"Oh. I too am not from this country. I am from Hockenheim, in Germany. My father owned the mill by the cathedral."

There was a pause. Our eyes met.

"Oh. It's getting very dark. Maybe you should go to the shops before they close."

How did he know I was going to the shops? I was about to ask him, but he had gone, as elusive as the fox I had claimed to be chasing. I returned to the footpath perplexed. An old man who I recognised was walking his dog.

"Hopefully, the trustees will clear that path out soon," he said pointing to the undergrowth in which I had been.

"It's a pity, it has grown so much," he continued. "They don't keep up with it. It's a perfect hiding place for those bloody foxes."

"Foxes do no harm," was my riposte, "they never leave the confines of this cemetery."

He grunted and started walking away with his dog, unsatisfied with my response. I looked back at the thick undergrowth about to make my way to the shops. The old man stopped and turned towards me.

"Stay in this cemetery?"

He uttered his words loudly and looked over the walls in no certain direction.

"Tell that to the people who live in that house over there. Their chickens were killed last week by one of your friendly foxes."

The old man hobbled away - a crusty tyke, satisfied that his final reply had reached its resting place.

I looked at the house. It was large, on the corner of a crescent with a perfect view of the cemetery. It seemed to be looking back at me, communicating. It was bizarre. As if the old man had been its agent, pointing me in the right direction. Returning from the shops, I detoured so that I could look closer at the house. The first thing I noticed was the huge For Sale sign standing prominently in the garden. The house looked empty as if the previous owners had left in haste. I climbed the steps and peeped through the window. There was a gap in the net curtains. I was struck by the tasteful elegance of the interior. It was not English, more European, perhaps even Danish or German?

I went around the back and looked through into the kitchen. This was much more modern with central heating and well kept cupboards. There was tiling on the floor. But it still had the unmistakable aura of a well off 18th century dwelling. I noted down the number from the board for the estate agent. Would Peter like this place? My daughters? Would I? All these questions were soon to be answered. Three months later we had paid for the house in cash and the keys were handed over to me. Svera, the narrator, had found Josef.

Back to other Svera, the present, fast becoming her past. Peter came down looking well-rested and asked Svera in the tradition of the Nordic culture if she'd slept well.

"No, I couldn't sleep, but I managed to write a bit," Svera hid the truth in her chest.

"I slept so well," said Peter, "I needed my sleep. I shall be late today. I will go to the library. About your sleeplessness......."

I was standing in front of Peter, confronting Svera, right in the middle of the drama, watching her expression change as she exchanged words with Peter. Her face was totally blank, transparent. She was acting like a puppet on a string, walking in daze, looking down to the floor, trying to explain, making excuses for her depression, her sleeplessness.

"What the hell, woman, why don't you pack up and leave? What are you doing? Who are you?" I screamed at the top of my voice and hoped she might hear or feel me. She took some of my words, wrapped them in a piece of foil and placed them in her basket filled with other objects needed for the decoration of my story. Sadly, I turned away, I tried to fit into her platform shoes. I became angry at myself. I had enough of this weak creature. I wanted to quit.

A pause...

"Why don't you increase your dose?" Peter said. That was his advice. Maybe he wanted to be married to a zombie who asked no questions and created no scenes. He took his coffee and croissant into the lounge. Peter didn't even look at the nicely laid out table. He had to watch the 8 o'clock news. I saw Svera take her tea to sit beside him. She was not however allowed to talk while he watched the news or when he read the newspaper. It would disturb him. He wanted to know what was happening around the world. That was important.

"My God, the British news is so boring. Not very international," he complained.

"Remember to buy the newspaper, Telegraph & Argus. It is Thursday, you know. Good luck with the job hunting," he commanded.

Svera walked him to the door. He hurried into the street to catch Bus 614, which stopped with a screech and so Peter disappeared from the scene for that day. It was quite cold. Out of my pause, out of my thoughts, I made a dash towards my writing pad, stuck a pen on top of it, swung it on my back like a shoulder bag and left. I had to do some thinking. I had to search for my material, set the record straight in the whirlpool of my mind. Svera was left behind to do her own messy thinking.

"Bye, Peter," I heard her say. Svera then locked the door and went back to finish her tea in the lounge. She sat there for some time, relieved but lost. She took out an old photo album from the bookshelf. The woman on the photograph wore a blue dress, standing with Nina at the door to the lounge admiring this spectacular Christmas decorated tree. She had just arrived home from an operation at the hospital in Copenhagen.

It was November 1977 when Peter had another operation to his arm, which was broken during an army exercise. He was in a local hospital. Nina was four and very lively, active and attached to them both. Svera was pregnant. It was a mild Sunday morning when winter aconite still bloomed in Oesterlake Park. She woke up with a mild pain in her stomach. She prepared porridge for Nina. She had never experienced such pain before. Finally it grew so acute that Svera couldn't stand, she had to lie down. She managed to phone the emergency services. Fortunately a female doctor arrived and suspected an ectopic pregnancy and immediately phoned an ambulance. Svera phoned one of Peter's comrades, Lisa, who informed Peter. The ambulance drove Svera away, in the absence of her husband. The walls and clinical hospital bed were white. The sound of life support machine, people in white coats surrounded her bed and the white medicine made her dizzy as her blood pressure fell lower and lower. She could vaguely see a white doctor yawning over her, trying to fix the drip, flirting with the white nurse. She heard white voices, many white people whispering in the distance in Danish. Svera became dizzy and passed out into a blank white space.

"Who is she?"
"Yes, who is this woman?"
"The name is Svera."
"Does she speak Danish?"
"A little...I presume."
"Is it serious?"
"Her blood pressure is alarmingly low."
"Has she got someone - a husband maybe? Is he here?"
"She's very grey. I might have to cut out a square piece from her stomach."
"I think we'd better operate. She may die."
"Help!"

Svera screamed, but no one heard her. She lay there motionless, watching from behind the closed eyelids of her anticipation. Peeping through corridors, doctors, nurses, going in and out, voices, cries, patients, doors opened, shut, clanking of sharp knives, scissors, snap, cut. Suddenly all the voices faded away. Svera remembered partly the reason for her being there, when she woke up in the bed in a ward. Again she was surrounded by the doctors. Between those faces, the smiling face of Peter. She tried to move but couldn't. The doctor asked Peter to have a closer look at her face, as he was unable to detect whether this tanned Indian woman had an ashen grey colour. Peter got worried. The doctor placed his hand on Peter's shoulder and said, "Your wife would have died if I hadn't operated on her within half an hour. Her stomach was filled with blood".

Died! If Svera would have died, there wouldn't be another Svera writing this script. No let downs, no pain, no bleeding, no dead embryo in her palm. No struggle. No going down the memory lane, trying to analyse what had happened, what might have been avoided. Can you predict your future? Do you wish you hadn't done this or that? Can anyone go back and re-live their lives in the hope not to go through same mistakes? What a wonderful world it would be. But we aren't made of bricks, cement, plaster, iron, nails. If we are dead and can't be stitched, we can't rebuild ourselves or recharge our batteries like robots. We live, we die. If Svera had died that day before they'd operated on her, got the dirty blood out, stitched her wound, she would have been a dead thing, not a living Svera, who had to exist in order to live her life, go through a painful struggle, witness all those things. If she had died there wouldn't have been the story of how she had survived, there wouldn't have been the urge to write a story, a script to work upon. I wouldn't exist - I would be a ghost wandering around in a cemetery, waiting for my lover Josef.

Yes, they operated on her, stitched her, and kept watch over her until she was healed, kept her for 15 days in the hospital. When she came home, it was Christmas. She wore the blue dress on that night.

The next photograph is of Peter at a stadium where Bob Marley and the Wailers performed for the April 1980 independence of Zimbabwe. Svera was pregnant with her second child. Peter had left for Harare to attend the celebrations. Nina was four and half. He came back after a month and continued his work with his Marxist group. The group Svera was a member of, 'Clothes To Africa', continued. Weekends, evenings, months, days, hours would be spent on Peter's political involvement. He continued to criticise the ordinary Danes for being self-centred and affluent. Svera turned a blind eye to this reactionary attitude. Like a faithful partner, she continued to support him never opposing his travelling away anytime, anywhere he wanted to.

September 1980, their second daughter Minna was born. As the children grew, demanding more work at home, the distribution of labour became acutely uneven at the same time, Peter slowly drifted away from his political group. Finally in 1981, both Peter and Svera dropped out of their political activities.

Another photograph of Peter when he was seventeen – when he left home. His father came from a middle class intellectual family who married his mother out of shame and pressure from the community. This was back in the forties. His mother had conceived Peter while dating his father. who was a schoolteacher. She was a vulnerable pretty village lass. The marriage was seen as a forced or 'arranged' marriage, thus the father was never happy with this arrangement. The discontent began to show after the birth of their first child Peter who used to witness the violence his father would put Peter's mother through. All she had to hold on to was the little hope that he would change one day, even after the arrival of Peter's twin sisters.

The bastard never stopped. So she had to flee with her small babies to Copenhagen. Then his abuse turned towards Peter and his younger brother. Peter ran away. It was 1967. With only twenty crowns in his pocket he packed up, took the train from Jutland to Copenhagen never to return. First time Peter travelled to Africa at the age of twenty five, as member of the Communist Working Group, he did not have enough money for the trip. His mother did not approve of his travelling to

Africa. She also did not approve of his political life, but he managed to borrow money from her.

He came back empty handed. Out of sympathy, he had given all his clothes to some poor people - the white man's empathy for black people. He came back to Copenhagen. The year was 1973, the year of Svera's arrival. He had to pay back his loan to his mother who was struggling alone. She had managed to study and had acquired a good job. Tired of Peter's laziness, she kicked him out.

"You have to get a job, Peter. You are big enough to manage on your own. You have been so lazy. I can't support you anymore. I have to look after these babies," she told him.

He decided to take up any job he could find in order to pay back the money she had lent him.

As for our heroine Svera, she is slumped over the soft-harsh cushion of memories, in a dizzy, blue confused state, wandering miles and miles in the back allies of her mind. We see her struggling to come out, so she can live in her present. Just now she is gazing in the vacant room as we hear the front door open and close. Svera lifts her head to speculate, who could have entered her house without a key?

CHAPTER 30
Slide Show Of Memories

The key had been stuck to the surface of my backpack for some time. After days and years of good wandering around, I found it. I unlock the house to enter the lounge where I found Svera with a shield of transparent cellophane wrapped around her body. I could see reality through her half-awake state of mind, dozing, switched off from the world, frozen in memories, with an open album of photographs. I take the album away, dust it off and sit beside Svera. I had begun to value my role as narrator more than anything else, so, without disturbing Svera, I turn the pages of the album to peep further into her past.

Before me is a coloured photograph from June 1993, of the shining sun. The girls in the photograph, half my age, dancing, giggling in a puddle of rainwater with red raincoats. The rocky Yorkshire Dales spread like a huge velvet green river under their feet. Dupattas, obedience, norms, restrictions are all forgotten in the back of their minds, back in Bradford. Carefree, they are here to enjoy some innocent freedom like any other girls in the world would like to. They had been dreaming about this weekend for months. They were not so different from the girls I used to know in Africa, Denmark and India - same aspirations, same rebellious hearts - they just didn't have as many opportunities as their peers. A dupatta of traditions and values is always stuck in front of them like a flag, reminding them of honour. They had conflicts with their parents. These young women enjoyed my company. They talked to me about boyfriends, about love, about make-up, about fashion, music, poetry, about everything. They wanted to study and did not want to end up in arranged marriage to somebody from their home as their parent wanted them to. Some of them rebelled against it. I saw a glimpse of young Svera in these girls.

Moving to this House on the Cliffe, had been a long drawn out affair. We had accumulated many possessions. Peter was extremely fastidious. Nothing could be thrown away. His acquisitive nature refused to discard anything. Even the food in the fridge had to be transported in finally manicured cellophane. We hired a van for the move. During the disgorging of our possessions, a small audience developed amongst the mainly Muslim neighbours who lived opposite the house. They were Pakistani immigrants and I, being an Indian woman of Punjabi descent, was always aware of the deep historical wounds that existed. Little did they know that my father had guarded the trains taking Muslim refugees to the safety of the new Pakistani Republic in 1947. Whenever border disputes arose, he ordered his troops to respect the Muslim villagers. Any looting or raping was severely punished by him. My father was a good officer. The Muslim neighbours looked searchingly at me. I sensed they quickly evaluated my position as a middle class Asian woman, my permed hair, tight jeans and high-heeled shoes evinced a look of lust from the older Muslim men. The women looked suspiciously from behind their shrouds, whilst the children hung mischievously around the van. Prodding and poking pieces of furniture, talking loudly in Urdu,

"Hey! She surely is a Gori."

They didn't know that I understood this language. Peter's face remained blank, but I registered the reaction of this welcoming committee. Eventually I broke the ice. I nodded and said hello in Urdu to one of the women who was hanging out clothes in her yard. The woman looked shocked, nodded back and quickly retreated into the house. My use of Urdu changed the behaviour of the reception committee and they suddenly fell silent as they recommenced their daily chores. Two doors down lived Jane with her two adopted children whom I was to meet a week later. She was in her early fifties and a lecturer at the University. I was surprised to find that she was of the same age as I. Years of academic frustration and loveless solitude finely lined her face. She had an aura of disappointment and unfulfilled dreams.

Jane had been to Africa many times and quickly established common ground with Peter. She would often be a dinner guest at my house. She was a pleasant woman who seemed pleased with the arrival of this continental couple and our two daughters. I was later to find the true White liberal woman behind that facade. I do have empathy for her though. Five doors down was the brooding presence of George whom I was immediately sexually attracted to, yet secretly I knew that we would never become lovers. There seemed to exist an intellectual gap that would never be breached. Our brief yet frequent meetings in the street proved to be a stilted affair. How judgmental I was at times. I later found out that in fact George was a nice guy who appreciated my poetry. To the right of us lived two strange looking middle aged White men. Were they friends? Brothers? Lovers? I did not know and I knew I would never find out. Yet I became accustomed to the banging, grating, heavy sighs and even screaming sounds that would permeate through the bedroom walls. I never complained, deciding early on that theirs was a world I did not wish to investigate or be drawn into.

To the left, was a man in his late thirties. He came to the door on numerous occasions demanding to know if I was disturbed by the sound of the radio in his kitchen. Eventually I became tired of his frequent enquiries and boldly demanded to know if he would like to be invited in for a cup of tea, yet at the same time informing this shoddy young man that I was a very busy woman and his visit would have to be quick. He melted from my life, not even to be sighted on my occasional visits to the corner shop.

In the crescent were a number of petty and obstreperous drivers who insisted on parking their cars two feet outside their house. The crescent was far too narrow to negotiate their three litre cars, but these were insistent middle aged men who I imagined drove even to the bathroom when they needed to urinate or they would if they could. These men had teenage children who noisily and aggressively played football against my gate. On one occasion when I had remonstrated with them, one of the car-ridden invalids pulled up, wound down his window and defended the rights of his children to kick the ball around in the crescent. I imagined I would get a petition together, but this never materialised as other priorities took precedence in my life. Despite all this, I grew to appreciate and even love this little crescent. It had been built in another era when the British were still a world power and the confidence and style of its architecture surely reflected that period in stony grey bricks. There was the house itself. I sensed a benign spirit within its confines; protecting, watching and caring over me. Despite its cavernous size I never felt uncomfortable even in the most obscure parts that I was to discover as I explored further. Having the strong urge to throw away the anti-depressants, my mind was semi-detached from the world, in a hypnotic state, just like we found Svera in our last chapter.

The scenario was rapidly changing outside. It was the month of July. There was a chill in the air. Peter had started expressing his wish to leave for Africa again. The reason? He always had one:
"I can't get a job with my qualification," he rasped.
"Africa is where I want to be now. My heart belongs to Africa. It is what I need at this point in my life".
I. Me. Never us. Never we. Never the family. Peter's needs were always paramount, he had the freedom of choice to Africa and in doing so widen physical and emotional distance between us.

Svera submitted easily to his wish, not knowing at that particular time that I, the narrator, was going to witness and describe her story from present to past.

When I returned to my secluded dwelling, I took a ride back to my past, changed the gears and re-wrote some bits, untangled some knots, readjusted to fit in my past, which was going to become my future, like that friend. The bicycle ride took place in my future and not when I was writing this, which was my past, but I was predicting my future, you see. The ride back to my past was to June 1996. I got on a 5 hour bus ride to visit my friends Arpana and Babu, at last arriving at Victoria Coach Station. Travelling on National Express, we raced against time, in between dispersing grey clouds of memories. Together we eloped back to 1992, the year I first arrived in Bradford.

On this bus journey, yin and yang were the light and shadow, playing their tricks or treat while I sat with my closed eyes realising that I was an evergreen traveller, an international nomad, who wasn't bothered about the final destination or to say it in the normal sense, 'settling down'. There wasn't going to be any. I was so used to roads with potholes without signs and little direction in Tanzania. My eyes became blurred and used to the darkness. The distances were longer, they always are in areas with less light, in the lands with less commodities. Some shadows of the past were soothing the journey of my present, like the ones from coconut trees sheltering the sharp sun on the beach of Oyster Bay in Dar es Salaam. Like the ones from the Bougainvillea bush against the hot rays of June in Uncle Karl's house in Punjab. Yours mother, the most soothing of them all, protecting, nurturing, defending me from the vultures of that time. A shadow of Josef who breezed in and out of my life in many forms. I wasn't afraid of these shadows, but at this moment, I felt blinded by the light, struggling to find my way through neon signs, dragon-eyed directions.

The two young guys bade their farewell.
"Have fun and a good weekend, maybe see you in Bradford."
Smiling back, I stepped from the concrete to board the North bound tube to Islington. The time -7.45pm. Negotiating my way amongst the

frenetic crowd with trampling feet, I became part of the relentless bustle and urgency of rush hour London. The traffic hastened by as if it had an aim. It was beginning to be dark as I waddled through the dense polluted air feeling lost and choked. At my friend's house nobody seemed to be home. The little black hole on the grey door stared at me sharply like a raven's eyeball. No message. My throat felt dry urging me to walk down to buy a drink from the corner shop. There was always a corner shop here in England. Unlike Bradford, a white man owned this one.

"Is it possible to pay with card?" I enquired of the owner.

"It's wise not to carry cash in this area."

I heard a deep, soothing male voice over my shoulders. I turned back. A tall, raggedly-dressed guy with handsome face, big shy grey eyes stood close to me. I could feel his hot breath on my neck. I almost swear, I have seen him many times before. He looked youthful, almost as youthful as Jaz or Josef. Our eyes met, lingering for a moment into each other's, then he smiled shyly. I felt speechless. Without saying a word, I paid the shopkeeper and walked slowly out of the shop. I looked back through the window. He had a blue rucksack on his back with a pink hat sticking out from it!

My watch ticked 20.15 and the small street looked deserted. I felt uneasy, tired and cold and a sense of panic seized me. I was sure this man was a phenomenon, a ghost, a form, I have come across many times before, in my dreams like a shadow maybe also in my previous life. Was he really of flesh and blood? How else could I explain that I felt so close to him, although we had never spoken before? I did not dare to look back and rushed inside the entrance of Arpana's house noticing a pile of old newspapers, magazines, dust and the prints of footsteps. I spread a July 1973 copy of the Guardian on the stairs, to sit on and wait. A pretty young man walked past and gave me a surprised smile. A young woman came in.

"You wouldn't happen to know Arpana living upstairs? Have they left any message for me?" I enquired.

"No, I don't know them. Sometimes I see them, but we never talk, Sorry, " she said neutrally.

It was so typically London. All these people crammed into small places yet largely unaware of each other's existence. Lost in the thoughts of this multitude, I sipped my juice slowly. Eventually, I heard the door open and familiar voices chattering outside. My friends had arrived. They looked pleased to see me. To tell you the truth, I was pleased to see them. Even an hour aimlessly spent on the street of this city seemed fruitful. We went upstairs and soon the room was flooded with guests. Amongst the crowd of people I sat in one of the chairs, reflecting on my first meeting with Babu in Dar es Salaam. He was going to give a lecture in the School Of Journalism where I was a student. Babu was born in 1924 in Zanzibar, East Africa, then a British protectorate. During Second World War, many young Zanzibaris were drafted to fight in British armies, mostly in Africa and Asia. Returning home from the war zone, they brought back the reality and the scale of imperialist violence. In 1951, he came to study journalism in London. By then he was already sympathiser of the anti-colonial movement. Up to independence of Zanzibar he was member of the 'left wing' ZNP, Zanzibar Nationalist Party. Because of the conservative elements in ZNP, Babu walked out to create his own 'UMMA' party. However, in the 1963 eve of the independence poll, it was ZNP alliance with a breakaway faction of the Afro Shirazi Party, ASP which formed Zanzibar's new government. But within a month, John Okello, seized the power. He had some link with Babu's UMMa Party. Okello was removed, Karume of the ASP came to power and formed a government in which Babu became Minister for External Affairs and Trade.

In April 1972, when Karume was assassinated while drinking tea outside the party headquarters in Zanzibar, Babu, who had gone fishing that day off Zanzibar's coast was accused by the government of master-minding the assassination plot. He was arrested on his return to the mainland Tanzania and was held in detention until 1978. Once out of jail, he went to America and the made London his base. This time 1995, Babu had gone back to Tanzania when Tanzania held its first multi-party elections to stand as Vice-President for NCCR-Mageuzi with a strong base among urban working class youth and section of the peasantry. He arrived in a heavy rain pour, but was greeted by hundreds of supporters. Babu identified with NCCR, which had a mass popular base, and Babu saw its policies as progressive and democratic. It had the potential to challenge the hegemony of the existing corrupt ruling party the CCM. However, the Tanzanian government quickly enacted court case to disqualify him on the grounds that he had spent more than five years outside Tanzania. Babu remained in the country to help campaigning for the party. NCCR lost after massive rigging by the ruling party.

Friends, writers and poets had gathered to see a video of his welcome to Dar es Salaam. Some of us sat in the kitchen to eat, when Miriam arrived. She had just finished her two years study in London. She was travelling back to her country, Eritrea.
"Let's have a drink." Arpana suggested.
"Yes I would love to," I said instantly, looking at the bottle of Smirnoff greedily. I hadn't touched this triple distilled purity for ages. I thought of my Amitriptyline I had forgotten in Bradford. God had I really become so dependent on those little white obnoxious monsters? The doctor had warned me that I would. I had laughed it off but here I was in this strange city, desperately fumbling for my pharmaceutical reassurance. I interrupted Arpana in mid conversation, "Is there a chemist nearby?" I enquired urgently.

"Why? Have you got a cold? I have some Lemsip in the cupboard," Abdallah joked. I looked around the room and realised the absurdity of my position. I didn't need the bloody pills. I defused the situation,
"No, I forgot to pack my toothpaste," I lied.
"There's a special menthol brand that I've become particularly attached to."
My trip to London proved to be my first test of withdrawal. A test I was destined to pass.
"Arpana had asked me to come along today, especially, so I could be of some help. I know how it is when something as precious as a relationship falls apart. Tell me what has happened," Miriam asked me.
"By the way I was supposed to meet Peter last month when he came to London, but he never left any phone number. I thought it was a bit strange. I phoned his office, but they wouldn't give me his home number," she continued softly in clearly non-enunciated English and

glanced about the room with her sparkling eyes through which she seemed to speak without words. She was thin like all of her other countrywomen, but with a determination and strength reflecting from her soft face. I liked her and did not feel she was a stranger. I could open my heart to this woman, I thought.

"I found it strange they wouldn't give me Peter's home number. What did he have to hide?" she said. The room broke into laughter.

"Apart from his bank robberies?" I piped in cheekily. An icy silence descended across the party of people.

"Peter? Robbing a bank? You'd be so lucky to marry a man that exciting," Miriam laughed.

The room laughed too. I joined in the laughter. Aware, that none of them knew of the police search in Denmark. I observed Miriam. She was an elegant looking black lady.

"Yes, I am very grateful to Arpana. I did not know my husband was in touch with you. I would have liked to speak to you. Maybe he didn't want me to." I said.

A three hour conversation followed with this woman. I poured my heart out to her, revealing everything about my relationship with Peter - the infidelity, the beatings, the early mad passion, my upbringing in the Punjab, the bank robbery in Copenhagen and the police search of the house. She seemed intelligent, non-judgmental and a wonderful shoulder to cry on. She promised that when she returned to Eritrea, she would seek out Peter's lover and warn her about Peter's erratic past. But I never heard from her again. I even sent her a postcard, but never got a reply. I imagined once she returned to her own country, my story would have disappeared from her mind.

After my heart to heart with this woman, Abdullah held up a tape and announced that he was going to show us a video. We sat in anticipation. It was a video of his trip to Tanzania. Dar es Salaam airport. Ndugu Mariama's long and enthusiastic speech. A thousand faces shouting slogans of their support. Tanzanian roads, people, rain, the black faces seemed to have no colour on screen. A night of African dreams with Abdullah - a night of passion with Arpana, Miriam. Africa, India and England blending together. I thought of my time at college in Dar es Salaam, other student colleagues and teachers. Some of them were very young, particularly one - Bob. We always listened to Reggae music. Bob K. was much younger than me. I had developed a feeling of sisterly love for him.

"You are so much unlike other Indians. In fact we don't even feel you are different. You seem like one of us. It's so nice to have you around."
One of my teachers said, "You look European."
I am everything. I can be anything. I have more than one identity. That's why I can cope and thrive anywhere. If only, my husband could respect and not be threatened and push me down, I thought.

The fond memories of Tanzania flooded down from the screen like the Zambezi River. It was 3am, early morning. People still sat watching Ndugu Abdallah on T.V. drinking tea enjoying each other's company. Just like an African night near Oyster Bay beach listening to the splash on the coral reefs. I could hear the sound and the waves of the Indian Ocean when Arpana interrupted my thoughts.

"Let's have a last drink before we go to sleep. A cup of Jasmine tea perhaps?"
Only then I realised how much I needed the nectar for my tiredness. Miriam took her leave with embraces and promises. I made my bed in the corner of the spare room and fell down on the mattress like an over-ripened mango, hit with the dust of memories on my heavy eyelids. I thought about the man with pink hat. Why did he keep on bumping into me? I must be seeing an illusion. It can't be true. No it wasn't real. I kept repeating like a mantra and once again fell in the lap of fantasies, dreams and visions.

India - my town, Chandigarh. Gulu my sister was eighteen. She had gone out and come home very late in the night. She had been to see a movie without informing you, Mum. You were annoyed as you were sometimes. We were often scared of you. When Gulu came, sneaking into the lounge, it was 2.30 in the morning. You stood there with a belt in your hand. I was in the other room, sitting quietly, writing my poetry. I heard your voice and jumped to my feet to see what was going on and was terrified to see you holding tightly to the belt. I thought you were going to hit my sister with it. I stood in front of my sister.
"Don't be so angry, Mum. Leave her alone."

But you wouldn't listen. You were very stubborn. So was I. Frightened, I snatched the belt out of your hand. You were very upset. How could I disobey you? But I had to protect my little sister. Sorry, Mum.

I woke up, remembering the dream. I felt I was still in the Punjab of my youth. How would I protect my children against the damage Peter had caused by the split? Was it right of me to ask another woman for help? I did love him once, but how could I take such humiliation? I got up from the bed and paced up and down the corridor. I looked out of the window, trying to spot the lost Svera in the crowded city of London. I hoped to see the vision of the man with a pink hat.

Upper Street was coming to life. Early morning commuters were kissing their loved ones goodbye and departing for another day's corporate toil. The familiar red London buses trundled on the road. Two police men, a rare sight, walked past on foot patrol. Weren't they all in cars these days? I closed the curtain and continued to think of India. It was all so confusing. India, Denmark, Tanzania, Eritrea, Bradford. Where the hell was I? It was like my life had been one long travelogue, moving from continent to continent. Settling down, uprooting. Black faces, white faces, brown faces. Muslims, Christians, Sikhs, Hindus, bloody Marxists, writers, artists. God, the world was so complicated. I wanted to live on a desert Island with my two daughters, cut off from the amazing diversity of God's earth, but I knew it was not possible. Making a cup of tea in the kitchen wouldn't make much difference but the poem that hung on the wall written by my once favourite poet Pablo Neruda stretched out to lend me inspiration, wakening, strength and perhaps a little comfort.

"Gather me to you like a verse
from the volume of my tragedy
Gather me to you like a plaything
a stone of the house
so our coming generation may know
the way of the water course to the house."

At last, I thought, peace was beginning to spruttle from the cracked patches of this wounded heart. I sat there sipping my tea, suddenly feeling at one. I didn't need the pills. I surrendered to life's amazing beauty. Arpana came to join me in my tranquil state. She looked at the poem too with a kind of telepathic anticipation,

"It's a beautiful poem. Isn't it Svera"?

Tea vapours mixed with the melodious voice of Reshma, vibrating the room of the flat in the city centre where my friends, Arpana and Abdullah found their spiritual union. Shutting out all the noise from outside the window, Arpana and I listened to Reshma.

"It is beautiful," she continued, "you should get published. You're a poet Svera. The way you behave, the way you talk, the way you live your life. I am sure it would come naturally to you. Why don't you write an autobiography? God only knows how much you've been around. It would make a fascinating story."

The seed of suggestion was sown on the raw, barren soil of Svera's mind. The first task was to plough the soil, fill it with nutrients of my strength and start the journey. This journey has taken me through turmoil, winter blizzards, floods and fire disasters for the past 14 years. This is Thursday 25th February 2010 and I haven't been sitting in front of my lighted screen for the past three years. A certain publisher in Leeds got funding to produce this book, but after ten years of vague promises, he withdrew the deal saying that he had used the money elsewhere. Of course it broke my heart. Of course I cried bitterly but now I am thankful, because all these years have taught me a few lessons. The soil of my mind is rich, expectant and very firm. It has a tree with branches and fruits and soon the fruit will ripen to be plucked. And yes I am reading this book, changing a few things, adding a bit more flesh, deleting all that irritates the eye, just like I do in my paintings. This is the beginning of the journey.

Let's go back to Bradford. It is the month of October, 1996. Young people sometimes misinterpret things. My daughters did too. The concept of freedom can be misinterpreted or abused. I wanted my daughters to be 'free', free to learn, to educate themselves. I wanted them to learn how to measure right from wrong by themselves. It would come, slowly. I did believe in them. They had a whole life full of struggle ahead of them. They had to learn to face this male dominated world and its many conflicts. I wished they would acquire strength to withstand most of it.

Looking back, I saw myself digging deep in the routines of chain reactions, chasing illusions in the blind alleys, looking to find something, somebody, thinking I've passed hurdles by running away from restrictions, norms, walls, fences of my land. Once more I am living in the city of dragons smothered with the colours of prejudiced arrogance. Wound around the sea of advancement are their shaky citadels, I wouldn't be able to penetrate each individual, group, community living in isolation, no tradition of integration, pretending to be liberal, not ready to open their doors.

I had been to many other cities and had lost my heart to them - black cities, brown cities and white cities, but this one was a hell of a stranger. Sometimes, I tried to take one step forward to meet people from different communities, but this city did not seem to respond, shawls wrapped against the wind, head down in your beard, walking up and down on the stone pavements. I feel isolated; strangers with sealed lips hiding behind shadows, brick walled buildings with no windows. Lock yourself in. Lock everything else out, cling on to your own in the fear that another culture might contaminate you. Honour and security did not threaten me anymore, those demons lay far behind, it would not be possible to turn back to the previous reality, I had chosen to move, without accepting, without giving in to fear from these. If I wanted to change, I would. I didn't need to be the one who always took the lead either. I had my own isolation to nurture. A fever of appetite propelled me to finish my writing. In that feverish state, I confided myself to my trance, home, my children, my dog, my experience, also with Svera, the other woman. I had set my own norms, my own integrity and then I started to look for something, somebody that I could relate to. Those visions of the past, when I was with Jaz, discussing poetry in India, or in Denmark working with immigrant women, discussing world news, literature, language or poetry in Tanzania. These feelings kept on pestering me. Peter had gone once again. My appetite for food had gone. The hunger to express grew like a wild mushroom in the Kalahari Desert. This city was a barren soil, and not my mind soil. Nothing could grow here. Nothing developed. Yet there were so many resources, so much space. Of course there were contradictions and conflicts. But my generation used to sow productive and progressive ideas cultivating advancement and development.

I had been working in a centre for Asian women as a project worker. When I was interviewed for the job, I was excited. The staff thought I would be an asset to their organisation as I spoke many languages and had a wide range of experience of working in many countries. I wanted to instigate change. I believed that the ideas for workshops should be proposed by the participants. However, the organisation seemed to be setting projects for the women without their consultation. This seemed to me to be fund raising for the perpetuation of the organisation not necessarily meeting the need of the women in the community. These were first generation immigrant women tied to their husband's cultural fascism and they were longing for economic independence and liberation from slavery. Mostly the women wanted income generating or professional development workshops. They struggled against husbands who kept them subservient. One of the women told me that her passport was kept by her husband in a locked box in the fear she might run away. One day a woman in her mid forties rushed in to the centre asking for someone to come and have a look at her cellar. I was asked to investigate. Her house was on the other side of the street from the centre. I was horrified to see her cellar filled with dirty water. She explained that the drainage system had collapsed and she had made several phone calls to the council and to the environment agency, both of whom had sent officers to investigate but neither did anything. It was winter and the stagnant water was stinking causing damp to her lounge. Her children seemed to be regularly getting sick and the woman was at her wits end trying to get the problem sorted. I was baffled. I went back to the centre and told the staff. I was ready to write a report, take photos and sent it to the daily newspaper so it can embarrass the council to do their duty. My manager told me that it was a very bad idea because the council was funding the centre and might withdraw their support. I was amazed and angry at the same time that I left for home early that day with my mouths shut. The irony was that a centre dedicated to the advancement of the Asian women was a means of fundraising for paying wages to the white and Asian middle class project workers without providing for the needs of its clients. Since that day a rift in the attitude of the staff towards me was built so much so that I was moved from the office to the area where there were noisy communal activities making it difficult to do my job properly. I felt humiliated and disheartened and left my job eventually.

One of my other part time jobs was teaching interpreting and translation skills to adults who wanted to use language to get better jobs and help those members in their community who couldn't speak English. One of my students had invited me to a poetry gathering. I hadn't written a poem in Punjabi for years. I had written poetry in English. The poem I went to recite was about a woman who had left her country, afraid of the racial tensions, old feudal values and communalism. The country bled with riots. She had revolted against these values. She ran away without a passport. She wanted to live in a country where there was peace, but where was that? She questioned. She challenged writers, fighters, the old, the young and the good willed people. She asked them to wash her tears away and send her back to a place, a country where there was peace! Where was the peace?

That woman was a symbolic figure. She could be any woman. She could be a refugee from a war torn country. Someone, who had to flee from oppression. You or I, the global travellers, always looking for a better place. But was there a better place? A woman. An ideology. A woman, the creator. A poem about a woman. A revolt in itself. Sometimes a mute revolt, sometimes a volcano with words. A woman, the forgiver. A woman, the fighter. The woman. The peace of this earth. Woman. Earth.

Poetry was one of the few mental strengths that I had during this struggle. Squatting on my Yoga rug in the lounge, I was rocking the boat of these vivid images, memories trying to rest like an infant in the cradle of my years, listening to Bob:

'You rock so you rock so,
like you ain't done before,
you dip so you dip so,
dip right through my door.'

The verminous sea-weed of my relationship with Peter was sinking in the shallow water, while I paddled on ahead, trying not to get caught up in the rotting weeds, to sail on the clear deep water, rowing like mad, my hands blistering, hurting, not able to stop. It went on and on like this for some time. I kept on, rowing, gasping for breath, determined, the more I thought of fulfilling my mission, the more I hasten the speed, rowing ceaselessly, around the clock, on and on, row, quick, slow, pause for a while, panic, move, as I thought of the shore where the shiny grey sky flickered waiting for me to land, to appreciate this majestic neutrality. I looked at the bottle of Amitriptyline and wanted to empty it into the toilet. The night of solitude was returning and it was here that I found my perfect moments of peace, writing, as I did in India. I had to break away from my trance without the pills.

Peter left and I started seeing the shore in the far horizon. I started to prepare for the landing, wrapping myself in a jacket buttonholed with courage ready to meet my companion, the night. Starting to write again I looked back over my shoulders, meeting this shy little peasant girl Svera, catching up with that bold, intense volatile young woman Svera, eye to eye with a grown up middle aged depressed woman having that everlasting trance, walking hand in hand with a romantic fool who chases shadows and illusions, hungry for love. As I sat up in front of this lighted screen, late into the night, with only the lucidity of a trance, which worked like a magic weed, I was to recreate Svera, to relieve her of her miseries - the little girl sitting by her dollhouse, crying for a new doll, the young girl with determination, dancing on the ecstasy of love, flying on the clouds with seven dead embryos in her palm - millions of images in a stream, gleaming with her riotous dreamlike verses, maybe not properly formed or structured yet, like sketches on the canvas of her raw, turmoil. They carved most of the pain out from the infected parts of her soul with the skilled knife of a surgeon. Words were fireflies, injecting life into her.

It's only now when I am writing about this woman, Svera, that I know how she felt - let down, relieved in a strange hypnotic way and strong at the same time. Peter was afraid of this strength. He was unable to give her the same strength back in return. She needed that so much. But then my love began to replenish itself by inner self-belief. I began, for the first time in my life, to like myself. Why not? I had to give this other Svera a chance to be on her own. I had to tell her to let him go. The more she wanted him there, the more he was running away. She had to let him go. Would he never come back? Thus replacing him with my old companion, the night, who was always ready to take me into its arms, waiting for me to embrace it. The grief of parting with Peter was strong, but I like the red hot chilli taste of pain. I loved to digest this pleasure of pain on a passionate, burning tongue of mine. And words were the soothing sweet dish of Rasmalai.

I wrote:
Don't be so sad
for me - Night!
I owe you
too much already!
Remember when
I was a little girl
I shed countless tears
under your silvery robe.
You gave me the courage
in return, to dream,
to hold on
to your gleaming stars.
I was not afraid then
to (cross forbidden taboos).
And my poems nourished
across the forests
of earthly logic,
dipped in contrasts and conflicts,
Not so much
has changed since.
Compassion, warmth

and assets still hang
like worn out curtains.
In the house of caged ghosts
the stage is set
for the audience of
anticipations, perversities
in the volatile theatre.

Like a destitute
I am left
on the escape door
of consequences,
on protuberant limbs,
cracked hands,
with a bleeding heart.

I think I need you
now more than ever before
But don't shed tears
on my failure.
I am not a lone traveller.
There are others like me.

I need you
to look into my eyes
and lead me
through antagonism and logic
in order to accept
that this is not
the end
but a beginning of the end.
My beginning!

CHAPTER 31
The Slide Show Continues

This is...
On the 12th day of Christmas my true love sent to me...
Shadows of speculations
pearls of deprivation
and a bag full of
whispering doldrums.

December1997. Christmas lights flashing overhead, sucking the consumer into spending more money, symbolising victory of capitalism over Christ. It had been one long year since I'd met Arpana and Babu in London. I was still coming to terms with bewilderment, doubt and grief about Jaz and Peter. Some struggles warrant amnesia. Memories are stored in a tunnel in our brain, tumbling back and forth, breaking into pieces, dropping out in unexpected circumstance like photographs drifting past you in the wind. Like in a computer, the mind stacks them on top of each other, in layers, like onions shedding bitter tears. I want to plug a USB lead into the back of my brain and download all my memories onto the computer, before I get old and age has deleted me. If you ponder on memories for too long, they can muddle your mind and distort themselves into something else, ten gigabytes of monkey babble downloaded to the asylum. Did Josef or Johnny really exist? Did Johnny really speak to me? Am I distorting reality into fiction? Would I ever have another encounter with Johnny? Would a hairsbreadth separate us or join us. Would there be a destination to my journey. Would he be a destination for my restless soul and if I wake from that transient dream of love, will this story continue? He might depart, like all the other ghosts. Will he turn out to be a Jekyll and Hyde character? I might become the storm in whose arms he would eventually find compassion for his restless mind. At that time, Svera of this story was confused and she hadn't yet fully discovered the entrance to a mystic kingdom, the harbour of peace, her Sukhna lake, yet she started to long for something.

As a narrator, I had the dilemma of being an observer and having to live her life. This conflict was itself a process of fast change taking place inside me. It was an event. All the other events around Svera occurred even faster. Each time she walked, an avalanche of ice came thundering down, staring eyes followed her in the street. Each time she talked to the squirrel on the tree, faces stuck on the barbed wire fences started to scream, shout. Each time she spoke in metaphors, poets and writers stole her words, bank notes started to grow wings. Each time she moved a finger, voices shot out like pea pods out of nowhere. Each time she blinked, something was taking place in the universe, in her neighbourhood, in this city, in the country, in the world. Everything rotated with an urgency of change. Some change was for the better, some was for the worse.

Hostility was breathing in the air like a virus. Small corner shops had started to close down, the businesses in the city centre stopped flourishing. Health shops, gyms, fashionable stores, like Selfridges, moved away to Leeds. Nightclubs became deserted, property prices fell, segregation of communities became even more visible. Clouds of doubts and fear were in people's minds. There was plenty of talk about moving away to other places. Every evening after 6, the whole city would become lifeless, dead, a ghost town of skeletons. It wasn't safe to walk anywhere, anymore. People got mugged, car robberies increased, racial attacks, abuse, threats, killings.

The Hindu family in the corner shop had sold their business. The Asian youth had already started harassing the new owners by smashing their car or the shop windows until the man of the family decided to take the matter into his hands. He grabbed a big iron rod and challenged the young ruffians. Only then were he and his family left alone to attend the business peacefully. The beautiful, magnificent magpies kept on with their own business of chasing small birds, flying, singing and enjoying their loot and avoiding foxes. Things started to change rapidly in my small family of three female individuals, particularly in Nina's life. From being a girl of fourteen in Copenhagen who was as frightened as a kitten by the police when they searched our house six years ago she had become a young woman of twenty. In

September, she had left her study at Leicester University. After only three months she started to phone constantly.

"Mum, I'm going through a rough time. I do not know what I am doing here. Why am I studying at all"?

She kept on talking about how her best friend with whom she had shared the house had left. How she had been having nightmares about her father and couldn't stop thinking what he had done to us.

I thought about her beautiful face, olive skin and dark piercing eyes while she spoke over the phone. How proud I was of her well maintained slender body when she won the swimming competition in The International School of Tanganyika, Tanzania. I remember her long, slim legs carrying her to win a gold medal in badminton, her bold acting with an English accent in the play 'Charlie and the Chocolate factory'. She easily identified herself with Tanzanian Asians as well as all the other white expatriate kids from the International school. All the handsome boys would queue to date my beautiful Swan, whom I had thought to look like a pink, skinny ugly duckling when she was born to bless my whole world.

She once composed a song:
"Our world is going away,
a little bit every day.
How can we make them try,
to stop letting us die.
Try to save it, by lending hands.
To the people of our world."

She was affected by war, famine and crisis in Africa and elsewhere in the world. She sang with a certain melody in her voice. Now, on the phone, her voice was irritating.

"Mum, you are not listening to me. I know exactly what you are thinking. Be positive, creative, keep on moving, wage your struggle, sing, play your guitar, write. I can't Mummy. I am depressed. Not everybody can cope with their pain, the way you do. I can't cope anymore."

She was crying. I felt bad and wanted to apologise to her and blame myself for letting my marriage fall apart. At least, this miraculous telephone cable was offering a wire of protection to hide my expression, the pain in my eyes. I wouldn't have the courage to face her. If she cried like that in front of me, I would break down.

I was about to play the role of being a mother hen taking her chicks under her warm wings when I recalled her telling me about a guy she had met before she left for Leicester.

"I am really in love with Sam," she had chuckled.

"I met him at Trish's house. He is so handsome, tall, athletic and intelligent. He is so different from all those old-fashioned Asian kids in this city, Mum."

"But Nina, it doesn't change the fact that he has a traditional upbringing, a traditional Indian mother and father, a family and a community full of norms, restrictions and their own culture. Yes, when he is outside or when he is with you, he might behave differently, but I can assure you when he comes home to his family he is very much an obedient Indian boy who would do anything for his mother."

At the back of my mind I was thinking he could be a brother who could kill for saving the honour of his sister. Some of us Asians carry the same old sack of cultural taboos on our shoulders. I felt annoyed. I knew the community so well from all those women for whom I had been interpreting in court cases. Oppressors, killers, fanatics, double-edged male two-faced chauvinistic bastards, our Asian men, they would tell me only to confirm my belief.

"Mum, you sound very judgmental, be careful what you say. Not all Asian are the same. Sam is very different," she kept on arguing.

"Believe me Nina, I work in this community, I know enough to say what I'm saying," I argued back.

"Mum, I need him," she pleaded.

The word 'need' annoyed me and I knew her life was going through a topsy-turvy hiatus in which this man that she 'needed' so much would bring nothing but misery.

It all made sense why Nina was phoning home so often. Of course she was missing that young man who she blindly adored. Security was restored when her adored father was replaced by adored boy friend. She had always wanted her father to stay home with her. When she was fifteen she told her father off for travelling away too much.

"You are like an uncle or a ghost who comes and goes as he pleases. You love your projects outside, what about us, Papa?" she would complain when he returned home from one of his regular safari's in Tanzania. I was scared to hear her distressed voice. I sensed a danger, she might harm herself. She hadn't forgiven Peter for deserting us, but I had to listen to Svera who sat on my shoulders like a monkey, telling me to be stern, instead of feeling pity.

"Listen to me, sweetheart. Try to forget what your father had done. Think about yourself, your study. Enjoy life, your friends. Talk to them, your teacher. Remember, I am always here for you, but you have to make yourself strong. Call me again."

In my heart I knew Nina would not continue her studies in Leicester much longer. There was so little I could have done. Reason, logic, persuasion wouldn't' have worked. It never did. I know, when I left my Masters in Political Science half way, back in India, I had my own reasons. I didn't agree with all the crap of Indian politics, which bored me to death. Their dodgy philosophies did not seem to harmonise with my rebellious soul. You were so furious with me, Mum, when I dropped out of exams. I thoroughly enjoyed the intellectual life, parties, outing with friends and the environment of Punjab University for one full year. How could I persuade Nina? She was my first born, my dream girl, a child Peter never wanted, because of his politics, but when she arrived into our lives we were both filled with joy. She had changed everything in my life. I was fully devoted to her. For years, she picked the thorns from the roses of my life with her lively spirit. She was hyperactive, learnt things quickly and was very demonstrative and emotional. She had picked up some Hindi words from me and tried to 'teach' the other kids in the kindergarten when she was three. One of her favourite words was 'Kabootar' - pigeon. She could say,

"Main tumhen piar karti hoon. I love you Mum."

I used to dress her up, plait her hair in two braids and take her out everywhere in the pram. I used coconut oil for her hair to grow nicely. I massaged her scalp four times a week, gave her fresh vegetables, fruits, cereals and nicely cooked meat. Her body remained slender and graceful as she grew in her teen years.

When she was fourteen, she learned to perform the famous classical dance, 'Bharat Natyam' and was invited to perform in front of an audience of three thousand people in Oslo on International Women's Day. She gave me a card each year on the 8th of March. She consumed books we gave her as greedily as she consumed the chickpea curry with delicious puris I used to cook for her. She read Danish children's books but also Enid Blyton's Famous Fives in English. I thought of her in the crowded city of Leicester with her distressed face, her loneliness, her big emotional eyes full of fear as she spoke over the phone to me.

I kept on waiting, watching over my shoulders, letting seconds, minutes, hours, months slide - to have more light, green trees, sunshine and rainbow. Maybe the glints of fireflies would return to my vision. I kept on moving, towards changes, adapting to new ones, shedding the skin of the old like a cobra. I walked on and on until my knees started hurting from all this walking and digging the past, the present. I climbed the ups and downs of this struggle, the many stairs of my house, the city's steep ambiguous roads with cliffs of difference between its people. I felt the pain when I went out with Minna or Simba or when I entered my car.

You would always worry about aches and pains. I had to go through them. At that moment I did not have the time to reflect. I wanted to walk on, to keep pace with this ruthless creature, time. I had a burning feeling inside me taking roots, like a winter aconite it was shooting through my body, developing towards light, urging me to write. Yes, with light, buds began to grow on plants, on trees, the heavy snow laden nights melted into feather brighter days. I was beginning to shed the weight of responsibilities that I had carried all those years as a woman, mother, wife. Ounce by ounce to shed the memories of Peter, ghost of my past.

Spring was in the air, baring its honest and simple entity. Nina was nearly 21 and in those young blossoming years of her life, she had to withstand so much pressure of growing up into being a woman, having a family that was breaking apart, but I knew she was going to survive. She had her own strength plus mine, the way I had yours Mum. Nina eventually decided to come home. Minna and I were startled by her arrival. She just walked in through the door one evening. Simba jumped to lick her face. She sat down on the floor to bury her face into his thick coat. She was hiding her emotional state, hiding her tears and sobs. Minna was excited to have her big sister home again.

What was my part in all this fuss of Nina moving back, leaving her study half way? What else was my purpose other than to offer the comfort of a mother, the hospitality of this house and a listening ear to her grief? For some days there was peace, happiness and togetherness - three struggling women. We had each other, but the peace did not last for long, as nothing else does, these days. Nina had a purpose in coming back home, to be with her lover. She was now on the roller coaster of emotions. She was clinging on to Sam as if he was a life raft in a sea full of stormy waves.

"You shouldn't phone me in Eritrea, let my children keep contact with me," Peter roared down the telephone in between munching, I presume, his favourite biscuits. Despite his laudable principals, there were certain bourgeois comforts that he insisted on having, even in a war torn country like Eritrea. I knew he would have them especially shipped out from Denmark. I had phoned him to talk about our daughter. He constantly munched and continued his diatribe down the phone, "Tell my daughters to ring me. That's OK, but not you. Send me a postcard if you must every six months or so," he arrogantly uttered.

I heard his young naive bride in the kitchen in the background. No doubt Peter had decided which was his favourite dish. She now dutifully ensured it was on the table at the same time every night. She called out in the background in broken English and Peter left me hanging on the phone for ten seconds, while I could hear him barking orders to her. Yes she was where Peter wanted her to be, the way I had been for more than twenty two years. Bastard. I felt like shouting and screaming down the phone at him. The arrogance of his biscuit-munching voice made my blood boil. The breathtaking contemptuousness of his dismissive invitation to send him a 'postcard every six months' made me want to take the first flight to Eritrea and storm into his house to beat him senseless with a chapatti roller that he had watched me toil over for all those years. Of course I said nothing of the sort except to remind him that it was soon Nina's birthday and he shouldn't forget to send her a birthday card.

"I'll wire her some money," he said clinically.

"Make sure she spends it wisely. I don't want her to spend it on drinking and worthless men. What does she do in Bradford anyway? Does she go to night-clubs?" He enquired.

I told him of the new man that had entered Nina's life and I also told him of my doubts. Of course Peter took a contrary position.

"I like the sound of him. At least he has a good job."

I heard more clattering in the background. His young bride sounded restless all those thousands of miles and oceans away.

"Look, I am going to have to hang up now," Peter said with finality. "Make sure my daughters get my number."

With that the crackling line terminated and I imagined him rushing to the table for his well-prepared meal. The rest of the cookies in his pocket would have to wait another hour before he would start consuming them in his ever-hungry stomach, I thought with amusement. Good job he was no longer eating away at my heart.

My amusement did not last long as I now had to think of how to tackle the situation of having a young woman of 21, living at home having left her studies. That young woman living with her mother Svera and her sister Minna was a changed person. She would rise at mid day, make her breakfast, leave a mess in the kitchen, do her scarlet nails, paint her eye brows, and toenails, go into the lounge filling her ever hungry tummy with at least three hours of afternoon soaps, spend a further two hours in her untidy attic room to come down looking like a European version of Madhuri Dixit, to go out. Once a week she would buy a copy of the local newspaper and flick through jobs. Having six A's in her Alevels, being multi lingual, with creative fingers, she wasn't ready to get herself consumed by the exploitative job market.

"I would rather do some meaningful volunteer work with OXFAM. I hate working in a small grey cemented office building from nine to five for such low wages", she would argue. In my heart I agreed with her. Compared to other Western European countries the wages here were outrageously small, but I wanted her to become emotionally and financially independent and maybe contribute to our household expenditures. Her tense face glowed like a woman in love as she talked about Sam. She had become very restless and was always on her guard when I asked her where she would be going each evening.

One Friday afternoon, she put her bag down on the chair and went over to stand by the window where I had so often stood to watch the sky and reflect, remembering my past.

"Tonight I am telling you the truth, mother. I am going to see Sam. Please don't worry, I shall return by midnight."

A wasp flew through the open bathroom window and landed on the glass jar I used to place my toothbrush in. I couldn't find any killer spray in the house for the poisonous creature. Rotating only its round eyes, it sat dead still. Reluctant to kill this beautiful insect I tried to chase it away with a rolled up newspaper. It flew stubbornly away to roam about in the house. As the evening slowly closed in, I grew anxious. I went downstairs to look out of the patio window. The waspish clouds were drifting away in the sky over Otley Road. The yearning to communicate with you by words through this mechanism of telephone line, Mum, stung me like territorial hunger. While Meena slept peacefully in her bedroom, I decided to retire into mine. In the middle of writing, I fell asleep. At 3.30am I woke up with a terrible pain in my tummy. Instantly, I thought of Nina and rushed up to her room.

The flickering grey light was forcing its way through the net curtain of her attic room. I switched on the bed lamp to find her. Her bed was not slept into and the digger wasp rested on her blue satin pillow flashing his yellow, black skin, warning of its hunger to sting. I panicked and killed him with a copy of 'She'.

A photo of you, Svera in your thirties, and Nina, six, hung on the wall beside her bed. The Svera of thirty stared directly at me. Those eyes with a cheeky flicker seemed watchful, the eyes of a woman, mother, deathless goddess, witch, lover, sinner, saint.

"Why can't you ever relax, Svera Jang?" she spoke to me, smiling.

My pulse stopped for a second. I forced myself to sit down on Nina's bed and shut out my senses.

For some time, I had been writing about this woman, Svera. Everything she had done or was doing now, went down, recorded on paper in the form of words. I tried to keep a sharp eye on her activities, at the same time reminding myself to be objective about her. I had taken the approach of a staunch onlooker to this woman's life. She always seemed to be in a strange trance. She was very stubborn - a simple, village woman, emotional, vulnerable, naive, fighting her own battle, not listening to reason, Peter's logic.

"You are a peasant girl, I wish you could use more logic," made sense to her now.

Did she become more logical? Maybe not. She kept on being emotional. Sometimes the light of inner strength flickered through her eyes. When it was there, others could see it. Ahren thought he knew her well.

"I think you are stubborn and tough. You look great."

"I will break your trance Svera," said Johnny.

Was she the deathless goddess after all? Are you wondering who Johnny is? Don't. I will tell you in a minute, hour, day, month, year. One day I will, in another book, but then I won't be the old Svera. I will have changed so much that you wouldn't recognise me at all. .

A long time ago, I had stopped feeling any empathy with Svera. Analysing her story and living it at the same time, was tough, but I was determined to be ruthless. That particular night, I was restless. It was as if I was standing on a balcony, looking down at my own life. While writing about her I was living her life. I had this tool for changing her as I wrote. I could live her life as I wrote or write about her as she lived. On the other hand, she was mastering the skill of infiltrating my activities like a spy, a secret agent playing double. At the same time she was a spiritual witch who could predict, feel and see through dirty water. She always questioned, prodding, nagging, making me feel guilty. The bitch. Just the way you did mother. Please take no offence. The Svera in the story and the Svera, I, were beginning to irritate each other. Get on each other's nerves. I thought about going on strike and telling Svera to write her own bloody story, but blood is thicker than water, I am her. Sometimes we had a connection. We were learning from each other. Eventually we had to merge into one, the old Svera would leave the Svera, I, in peace, after, snip, snip, snip, shredding her life into pieces, with her productive critical scissors. Bullshit, crap. I didn't like it a bit. Sometimes I didn't like her existence at all, as if she was demanding me to undo the mistakes the old Svera had made in the past. Was it possible? Is it possible?

I can clearly remember one incident where I wish I had been stronger. Copenhagen 1988. Nina was starting to readjust herself into Danish society. We had come back from Africa, after spending five years. Nina was invited to a typical Danish birthday party. She was not allowed to drink, smoke or have boyfriends at that age, thirteen.
"Mum, can you please come and get me out of here," she pleaded, crying on the phone in the middle of that party. She was terrified to witness kids of her age smoking dope, drinking, snogging. She was not exposed to those freedoms in Tanzania. Svera did not like the freedom Danish kids had. Drugs sex, drinking. Svera didn't make her daughter strong and streetwise, teach her to cope with the pressures of life.

Staring at Svera's photograph, the wasp of memories started to encircle me. I felt the itch, before I was bitten.
"Your daughter is soon 21. Have you changed, woman?"
Svera in the picture spoke again, pointed fingers, questioning me mockingly.
"Fuck off, woman!" I muttered angrily and turned away to avoid this shadow. I had her on my back like a monkey all this time, didn't want to hear or feel her. It was 5am and Nina had not yet come home. My tummy ached again. I went down to my bedroom to write.

8.30am. No sign of Nina. I phoned Sam's mother.

"Could you please tell me whether Nina is with Sam? She didn't come home last night. I hope they haven't had an accident."

I tried to stay calm.

"Oh. So you are implying that my son has spent the night with your daughter? He would do no such thing. His car is parked outside. He must be asleep in his room. He has football to go to."

She was annoyed.

"Kids don't listen to us these days. I warned him not to mess up his life. This boy won't ever listen," she said.

"Please phone me as soon as you hear from Sam," I insisted.

The woman was clearly more concerned about Nina and Sam spending the night together than for their safety. Time was running out. It was midday, I phoned Nina's friend Trish who promised to look for Nina and assured me not to worry because she knew where Nina might be. I was worried and thought of ringing the police when suddenly I heard the front door open and Nina appeared in the hallway. Looking down at the floor, she murmured words that no one could understand. Simba tried to jump up to approach her, she pushed him away. As Minna and I watched silently waiting for her to speak, she looked at us with her dark eyes and pale skin telling us that she had a lot of Vodka to drink and was vomiting all night. I knew she might be telling the truth, but couldn't hold back my anger.

"You could at least have phoned me Nina. I was so worried. I was just about to inform the police."

"Why didn't you?" she snapped.

"Yes, I feel stupid having contacted Sam's mother and your friend Trish. I trusted you Nina," I said in an attempt to mortify her.

Oh, how stupid I felt in front of this young woman who wasn't the child of six from the photograph. I was forgetting the other Svera, who was then in her thirties. Looking at her photo reminded me of the way I had been - young and rebellious. We best recognise in others, what we recognise in ourselves. How could I forget about being logical and all the trouble I had caused you, mother. Once I got so fed up with your restrictions and nagging that I went off to live with my cousin who lived in a huge bungalow with dogs, buffalos, land and his own jeep. I had the nerve to buy a new outfit and went to spend the night with my friend Sushma so I could take the next early morning bus to Nangal, a town sitting at the foot of the Shiwalik Hills and three hours drive from Chandigarh. You were so terrified. My best friend Sushma deceived me. She sneaked out to inform you. Amar came to fetch me without even exchanging a glance. I had stepped upon his honour. I wanted him to talk to me, to understand me, respect me as a growing up woman in her twenties. I wanted him to include me in his group, in his nightly plunders, politics. He didn't want me to.

"Girls are not supposed to."

He didn't know how to approach me. He didn't even have the guts to go against norms and marry the woman he was in love with. How could he understand a woman like Svera, who was his own sister? He was good at leading the Naxalbari movement. You felt hurt by my thoughtless action. You tried to talk to me about your so-called norms and honour, which I had rejected time after time. At least you communicated.

"Have I not given you the choice to study, to go out, to have friends? I give you more freedom than any other mother could to her daughter of your age. What do you want Svera?"

Now I realised the pain, the anxiety of a mother. Here I was, fuming inside, feeling justified with my anger, not even trying to defuse the situation. I could at least try to understand. I could have chosen words wisely and play the game to fit into her thinking. I couldn't. A few words formed themselves into an apology, but crumbled down half way. Helpless, I looked at Minna who touched my hand gently to remind me that time was running and we should leave her sister alone who now stood half way up the staircase, looking at us like a innocent victim who demanded justice. Then suddenly Nina burst out crying loudly, of maybe guilt, shame or perhaps self-pity and with the intention of giving me a bad feeling. Once again words in my mind began to stumble, in an apologetic gesture but before I could utter anything from my stubborn lips, she left to sulk further in her room upstairs. It was certainly a nightmare she had put me through. Do I always have to forgive her, because she was hurt? I wanted to communicate with her, but couldn't. I had to keep my promise to take Minna to the preview of the film 'Babe'.

I couldn't forget the encounter with Svera in her thirties as I went around doing my daily routines in my huge house, cooking, shopping, tending the dog and writing to you in the night, while waiting for Nina to come home every night. So this was it, Svera was urging me to write to soothe my grief, managing this struggle. I wanted to re-ignite the flicker I saw in her eyes, as I sat there, in my bedroom, in front of the lighted screen, writing each word, learning to be more and more objective and not bite my lips in my pain. I became the narrator. Svera was a woman I wrote about. She was me and not me at all. She was an extension of me. I was the light, she was the shadow. She was the light, I was the shadow. We would have to cross the boundaries, soon. Maybe.

As I sat there, being pinned down by that woman who made me reason, question and realise. I was a wrestler in a bout with herself, three falls or a submission. I became uneasy. I felt the urge to calm myself with this little meditation trick, to balance my mind and body in one. Only then could I energise my soul, which needed that shakedown. I had learnt to watch Nina and Meena closely as they went through their own struggle to grow up as women. I was there for them and at times, I was there for myself. I couldn't boast about giving them all the attention they needed, but I tried to listen and support them through their pain, as my mother had supported me and her mother had supported her. Like a link through the ages, generations changing, rejecting, learning, making the same mistakes, discovering themselves.

CHAPTER 32
Josef Moves In

"ROOM TO LET. Spacious Victorian house, centrally heated £55 per week, would suit professional person."
I had placed this ad in the window of a local post office two months after Ahren had left. I interviewed two or three inappropriate people until one day there was a knock at my door. On opening it I was startled by the man who stood in front of me.

"So you haven't had any trouble with the foxes Svera," he said with a smile.

"Remember me? We met in the cemetery. I've come about the room. Is it still for rent?"

I had a number of initial reactions, but the first was suspicion. I had only put my phone number on the advertisement. How did he know that the room was available without phoning first? And how did he know my name?

"Before you ask," he said, "I've known you since you first arrived in this city, I've been watching you. In fact I've been watching over you, Svera Jang. I recognised the phone number in the advertisement. I had a friend who lived here. A spiritual friend. A young man who just left." My suspicion melted away.

"You know Ahren? You are a friend of Ahren?" I said with a relief.

"Yes. He told me that the room was available." I felt enormously attracted to this young man, as I had when I met him in the cemetery. My next reaction was delightful anxiety. Would I fall in love with my tenant?

"Come in," I said hesitantly.

"Would you like a cup of tea?"

There followed a conversation that seemed to last for hours. The depth of the young man's knowledge and his psychic ability to delve deep into the recesses of my mind both amazed and frightened me. But ultimately I felt drawn to him. At the end of our conversation, money was given to me, the key to the house had been handed over and he departed leaving behind a beautiful leather case in which he told me were some of his rudimentary possessions. The next day he returned with two suitcases. He didn't have a car. His parents I deduced were no longer alive. He seemed old beyond his years. Although only 34, he spoke with great wisdom on many subjects. His measured tones soothed my mind. His obscure presence did not disturb me while I worked in my bedroom. He had no T.V., never received telephone calls or mail, never had visitors. He disappeared for days on end. When he returned, he would explain that he had been visiting friends in Scotland or Wales and although I longed for him to describe his journey in greater detail, he never seemed to volunteer the information and I felt strangely reluctant to press him further. One day during one of his prolonged absences, I noticed that his door was slightly ajar. It was against my nature to prowl in another person's room. However I couldn't resist further investigating the secret world of my mysterious tenant. The room was sparse and perfectly arranged. Nothing was out of place. The first thing that struck me was a book in German on 'The historien om De Dr. Jekyll ond Heir Hyde'. I picked it up. It was an old edition printed in Hamburg in 1896. Why did this book keep on returning to my life? Wait a minute, he did tell me he was German when I first met him in the cemetery. Perhaps it was there that he went on his prolonged absences. Germany or the cemetery I wondered oddly. As I flicked through this curious book dissecting occasional words, I sensed cold air pervade the room, a presence behind me. A hand quietly touched my shoulder. I dropped the book. It was Josef.

I spluttered my apology, "I was cleaning the hallway...I noticed your door was ajar...I saw the book on the table. I..."

I stopped myself and looked guiltily down at my feet.

"I'm sorry. I've no excuse. I shouldn't have been in your room."

At this moment he did a remarkable thing. With the expertise of an experienced gigolo, he gently cradled my chin, looked deeply and hypnotically into my eyes and kissed me gently on my lips. He uttered a reassuring word of forgiveness, leaving me standing helpless, a quivering emotional jelly, in front of this handsome mysterious man. He then proceeded to undress me in a skilled manner. I offered no resistance as he peeled off each article of clothing with the assurance of an aristocratic artist. I had become a mere canvas in his hands, as he gently moved his slender fingers like a delicate paintbrush across my aroused and excited skin.

"You have a soft walnut skin," he cooed into my ear, as I stood naked in front of him. He walked to the window and in a disciplined and efficient manner closed the curtains and he ran his fingers down my spine like a pianist preparing to open me up to perform his concerto. He took my shivering hand in his and led me like a lamb to the large bed. I lay down in full nakedness and watched him as he slowly undressed. Methodically, efficiently, he removed his clothing in an unhurried fashion. He showed no signs of nerves even though I was a woman experienced beyond his years, lying naked waiting for him. He was the master of all he surveyed as he removed the last piece of clothing. It was now an opportunity for me to observe his body. Tall, muscular, finally tuned. His stomach was flat. His upper thighs thick and smooth, flickering with a slight muscular strain. His eyes filled with lust, yet with a feminine vulnerability, watched me intensely. I was aroused. I wanted him urgently. I spread my arms, inviting him to enter the cathedral of my existence. He approached and whispered my name, "Svera," and laid beside me, close. The invisible air between us seduced my name. His lips were luminous butterflies, entering obscure places on my body, spreading a shroud to conceal me from the world. His skin was fresh, sweet and young and there followed a night of love making, the like of which I had never experienced before. His muscular body was hovering over me, tightening the grip he held me close. I shut my eyes and like a floundering fish in the net of his splendiferous desires, I felt breathlessly satisfied.

The clock on the wall stood on its one-legged pine crutch leaning to rest for a while from its fleeting urgency. I sensed the rays of light flitter through the window. We must have been lying there for hours. Time didn't matter, but the presence of Josef did. In the arms of his light I was a shadow, filling myself with so much energy that I realised I had a slight pain in my chest. I opened my eyes and found myself alone in the room. I had known he would soon disappear on one of his many mysterious visits to unknown destinations, but I didn't realise it would be that soon. I did not want to wait for him. I felt a chill around the bed and heard the echo of his words.
"I have to travel away, Svera. I'm a merchant. I deal in things from the other worlds. You are so deep, caring and genuine. I enjoyed your company and you will always carry me with you, even though I may come and go. I am a free spirit. Please don't stay in the darkness. All these years ghosts have been chasing you. First there was Jaz, then Peter, and oh, I almost forgot Johnny. I am neither Peter, Jaz or the man with a pink hat in your dreams. Love, have faith, hope. You will always be the giver, learn to take as well. Enjoy life..."

The room was scented with a peculiar air. I remembered the same strong smell of Jaz and Ahren. Words were floating in the air like particles of light, sometimes transparent as if they were meaningless, they still filled my inside and yet there was a strange emptiness around me. My clothes were scattered on the floor. The bed sheet was wet, untidy and there were a few hairs on the pillow beside me. What was this? Was I struggling with something? Was there a man called Josef? Why had he chased me throughout these years, when I was going through the pain? Why had he entered into my life, now? What did he want from me? What did I want from him?

"Enjoy your life. Live dangerously. I am a free spirit. I once loved life in all its magical rainbow colours. One thing I can assure you is that there is nobody else but your own higher consciousness that will guide your way. I always exist in your thoughts, you in mine. I want your body, mind and soul to step out from my shadow, seek light, Svera Jang. Seek light..."

Words he spoke went around in my head again and again
for a long time as I ruminated on them.
I looked for something, a shape, a worldly thing, anything.
Thoughts were sheathed in the armour of words
to teach me to step out of the shadow of illusion.
I am talking to you mother, and to myself
and to you, the universal person that embodies us all.
So you dress yourself in words, just the way you want to,
in your style, in colours of your choice.
You step outside of the boundaries of your domain,
parade around on the catwalk of this worldly stage
like an actor
constantly surrounded by an audience.
There are thunderbolts, flashlights, rules, directions and crossroads,
the hidden eyes of sophisticated electronic devices,
scrutinising each word, each step, each move you make,
skin colour, fingerprints, colour of your eyes, ID cars,
trying to mess up your life, with pictures, sounds,
words and other commodities.
You are being watched, being judged, labelled for your actions,

baddies' from a gangster film, 'stalkers' aiming to hunt you,
pointing fingers at you, by those who rule or govern you -
your parents, your children, your teachers, your bosses,
your friends, your neighbours, your partners -
they are all victims of the same game,
actors in the same play -
they are your strengths and your weaknesses,
the hangman's rope by which we haul ourselves from the storm.

You forget to see through things as you try hard to join in the game
imitating others, like monkeys becoming more and more fake,
unreal, take orders from higher bosses, unable to decide for yourself
even when you have more knowledge, ability, you become robots
forgetting the basic values of humanity, you try to fit in,
tell lies, striving for your own selfish goals,
become self indulgent, self centred, self important, self defeating.
Then, when any small crisis suddenly strikes your life,
you do not know how to react.
You either start to pray in temples, mosques, cathedrals
to be forgiven for your sins or take the 'wrong' side,
join forces with the wrong powers to destroy others.
You are the self-defeated, brainwashed by the system you live in.
You have no urge to rebel against any norm, any static reality.
You have learned the skill of selling yourself so well
you've become just like any other commodity in the supermarket
wrapped in glossy jargon to be hired on your face value
and if you are paid what you're worth, then life is cheap,
but you'll be charged a lot for what you want.
We're Consumers, buying, selling, trading, bargaining
with our feelings, even love, passion, and sacrifice
has become just another commodity, factory fodder,
cheap thrills and disposable emotions.
You phrase words to climb the ladder, using and abusing each other.
You've forgotten the good old concept of love
like the one between Romeo and Juliet, Heer and Ranjha.
For you nothing comes for free -
the whole place is a big fucking market

competition, power, control of the raw soul,
disasters, war, torture, killing of the innocent,
political makeover for the catwalk, a fashion show.
Camera rolls...Action...Take one -
more lights please, everything is blinding.
Can you see? Can I? Maybe you can.
Can you compete? I can't.
Did you feel let down? I did.
Do you see? I tried.
Not everyone can...

The words he spoke, I recorded for us all to interpret. The words you are reading will create a picture of me in your mind and you are going to judge me. From being a consumer, you will become the judge as well. I wonder whether it would be your thoughts which turn you in that direction. My words don't. Thinking and writing words, I think of language. In my head there is more than one language. Some words in Hindi are both male and female. You project your thoughts and they become words. Words are just an extension of yourself - they aren't the real you, they are of course your own thoughts first of all, but the language gives you the weapon to form them into words. You adopt words, as if they were orphan babies. You mould them into any shape, colour, image - however, there are some words you can't translate into another language. They change meaning, shape, tone and message. If words are extension of thoughts, this strange tenant of mine, is he just an extension of me? How else can he know so much about me and the thoughts within me? I had never told him about Peter. Following me for years? What did he mean? I did see him. He was there with me physically, although he looked pale, almost like a phantom, a shadow. Was it Jaz? Maybe it was the man with a pink hat haunting me. I had seen his shadow three years ago on my visit to London. I will let you ponder over that one.

But this was the dawn of November 28, 1999. I spread my arms to touch the emptiness around me and ran my fingers through the light coming from the window. A shadow followed my movement across the wall as the sun reappeared. I might have to take a step back sometimes, to reflect, but what good was sight in the pitch black, at last I was able to step out of shadows whenever I wanted to and whenever it was necessary, but I was going to take control of the events around me. There was a mysterious tranquillity in the room. I could still hear an echo in the hallway. Josef with his words had travelled away from the room, down stairs, to go outside this house, into another world, which I had slowly become a part of. I heard the door creak open and close after he had left. I knew I'd see him again, in another form, somewhere else, in another city. Out of nowhere, when I least thought of him, he will appear before me. I realised I had been sitting on my bed, reflecting for hours. I wanted to lie down again, stay in the bed and analyse my dreams, see through the walls of this house, beyond the broad window, beyond the narrow boundaries of this city and watch exotic lands where Josef's sea of words would be lapping the shore of my illusions.

I watched pieces of sunlight giggling like small babies in the room, staring with their innocent eyes towards me. This was my own room, my own space where I could be in the centre of my own universe and the world could be as I would chose it to be. Free from battering, free from mental torture. Free from the process of aging body that is trampled on by those forceful oxen allies called Time and an abusive husband Peter!

Watching the babies of awakening penetrate into my safe haven where thoughts were my sacred solitude, I yawned and stretched my arms in acknowledgment. My words would soon enough become a commodity arranged in phrases, sentences, lines, pages, chapters, books stacked on shelves waiting to be consumed by someone else's solitude wanting to fill itself with words.

I dragged myself away from dreams and lifted myself from the bed where the night had seen mysterious events. The moon was a wolf howling. It was Simba starting to whimper, reminding me of his existence, waking me up from my stupor. The little lion was howling with hunger. As I stepped down from the stairs, he jumped up my legs and sought my utmost attention. He was so cute and innocent, had no idea what his owner, Svera Jang, had experienced last night. I picked him up, put my cheek against his fur. He at once responded with affection by licking my face. He was shivering with excitement knowing he was soon to be fed. That was his way of communicating with me, without words. Bought for my daughter Meena on her 14th birthday, he was a bundle of joy in her life. At such a time of change, he arrived in our house like an orphan, deserted by his mother, ready to be looked after by some kindred spirits. He was black, had brown patches and the face of a little devil angel. Simba never wanted to be left alone on the landing and always craved after human warmth.

"You can't replace yourself with an animal. I don't need a puppy or another baby in my life. You realise that, don't you," I had reasoned with Peter when I had found him conspiring with Nina to buy a dog for Meena against my wish. Bastard. I kicked the cupboard with my foot and took a packet of dried fish out for Simba. The best dog food, a lead, grooming gear, rubber toys, a mat, bowls, dog shampoo, dog biscuit and a tiny brush for his teeth were bought from a newly opened pet shop in Idle village. It was like looking after a helpless baby, a new member of our family.

I sat on the chair watching Simba chomping his food greedily, thinking about Josef the way he quivered over me last night. His words went around in my head like the wheel of a bicycle turning on its axis, moving forward, moving, moving. I imagined him to be somewhere out there, a walking phantom, a burning candle, a moth circling around the flame of life, burning at both ends, disintegrating, trying to come to life, again and again and again.

"Sau baar janam lenge, sau baar fanaa honge
Ae jane wafaa phir bhi ham tum naa juda honge..."

Where would Jaz be now? Still in India, maybe writing revolutionary poetry, getting high on the bliss of that smoky sweetheart, who once was his illusionary addiction? Maybe dead, reborn in the form of Josef, to be with me. I wished that I had Josef's ability to see beyond everything. I wished I was a ghost and could travel in time, or a magpie with fluttering wings to fly ahead of my thoughts, before shaping them into words. Or I could travel behind my shadow, so I could see into the future and step out into the moment, now, at just the right time so that it could be as it was always meant to be.

I found myself battling to chase away the painful memories of the past twenty five years of abuse. I was doing a lot of spading, digging, making the soil ready to sow the seeds of my search, writing a lot of poetry, trying my hand at sketches for short stories. I was recording events in Svera's life and I desperately needed some feedback. By chance, I met Andrew Doady in a poetry event. I knew his first novel, 'Flyer', was coming out. He agreed to read some of the earlier chapters of this book. "It's powerful, there's so much you haven't told the reader yet. You have kept your pain secretly locked in one corner of your heart. Are you scared to reveal all of it? Keep on writing, rewriting, edit, be ruthless. Let's meet again," he said.

A year later when his book came out, he wanted to give me a copy. He ordered a beer for himself and a brandy and Coke for me. As he read through my writing, gulping the words with his beer, I saw the amazement on his long thin face with finally trimmed beard.
"You have certainly made a tremendous leap in your work. Keep it up. Be ruthless with your editing."
He smiled. I had also brought my poetry book. We happily exchanged our commodities. I listened to his advice, listened to the wise words of the man with a pink hat.

I had assumed that with a dog she loved, a Mum who loved and supported her and a sister who at least came home at night to sleep, she was managing fine. I swore to myself when I sometimes watched her shower her attention on Simba. She was burying the hurt of her broken family behind Simba's thick fur, but I knew each nerve on her neck as she tensed, each reflex passing over her face, each glint of pain in her eyes. My little girl of two who felt secure when her trembling hands clutched her mama's breast, as we sailed in a small boat crossing the Indian Ocean - same feeling of security seeing a python crossing the road when we drove through Serengeti Park. Now in her teen years, the dinosaurs of adolescence had spit foam of insecurity over her personality and she was fragile as a china doll.

Whenever I went to pick up Minna from her school, there would be a wry smile on her face, a vague posture and short answers to all my queries. I was unable to see through that wall she had created between us. I was looking for an opening. There must be somewhere I could enter and see what was going on inside her.

"Mum, I have a headache today, I can't go to school," she would say - sometimes, a sore throat or a stomach ache. I often wondered if she was feigning. I knew at that stage of our lives, she was not good at expressing her thoughts to me and neither was I able to communicate to her. One day when she had gone to town with her friends, I went up into her room to clean up, or perhaps to look for some clues. Behind books, under her pillows, her bed, the curtains. In the wardrobe, on the table, I found it. 'It' was everywhere - a complete disorder, signs of degeneration, reflecting the state she was in. It was so unlike Minna. There were clothes all over her bed. Dust, pieces of papers, dirty socks, books on the floor. I started collecting the pieces, the rubbish and the dust that had taken over her everything, deviously. As I started sorting out objects, her clothes, putting up the clean ones on the shelves in her wardrobe, I found some empty beer cans.

"Oh, my God?"

A loud cry blew out of me. An independent Asian woman who lives alone, owns a beautiful house, works, has a posh car, dates, has male lodgers, organises events, goes out in the night, drinks. An Asian woman confronting cultural norms at each step, suspicions from the community, self doubts, whether or not she had been a good mother to her children, rejected by her husband, left alone to take care of her daughters, looked down upon by other Asians because she couldn't produce a son, because she married an outsider. Maybe my daughter looked down upon me as well. She blamed me for not keeping her father with us. Both my daughters were hurt. Like her white peers at school, Minna was taking to drink, maybe smoking, drugs. I knew her father would have said, "This is not a problem. In Denmark children start drinking at that age."

I tried to reason with myself thinking that maybe she was using the empty cans in her artwork. No, they were well hidden under layers of her clothes. I carried on with the rest of the cleaning, thinking.

"Oh, Guru Nanak, no. Please don't do it to me. Have I deserved this?"

"I don't believe it, my little sister growing up and starting to booze," Nina said anxiously.

"Let's ask her first, before you draw any conclusions," I warned.

It was one of the first Thursdays with late opening hours for Christmas shopping. Minna came home, had her dinner and comfortably settled herself down beside Nina on the sofa.

"We have found some empty cans in your room, Meena. You know you are too young for drinking."

"I had them last week," she answered, looking at the floor.

I looked at the dark night looming outside the house, encircling the city like a black python. In the well-lit lounge of ours, there were shadows of exposure on Mina's silent face. Shame or guilt? Hurt or vulnerability? She wouldn't speak up either.

"If you don't answer, I am going to be very angry. You'd better speak up," said Nina.

"It was in school," she admitted, "Lisa told me to bring them, so we could all drink in the toilet. She told me to put them in my locker."

"What if the teachers had found out?" Nina said.

"Do you want to talk, Meena?"

I interrupted Nina's sharp accusations.

"Why do I need to explain it to Nina?" shouted Meena.

"She doesn't give a shit about me. She is always out with her boyfriend. My father has left me. You don't understand me, Mum. What am I suppose to do? Tell me!"

"What will Papa say? How can you be so stupid?" Nina kept on.

Simba slept on the rug by Minna's feet unaware of the small crisis his three female owners were going through, making whimpering sounds, dreaming in his small little world of peace and harmony. Minna bent down uttering words of affection to pick the puppy up as I watched her. The pink top with a low-neck line revealed her full breasts. She was a woman - long black silk hair gliding over her shoulders, bathed, smelling of Jean Paul Gaultier perfume. She ran her slender fingers through puppy's fur. Studded with anxiety, her tense face began to reflex self-indulgence and a peculiar vulnerability, yet she looked mature. For some time, she sat silently stroking Simba, studying my face. She had a fighting spirit, even when hitting Nina in the pretext of a sisterly game she was struggling to express herself. But this had never happened before. Suddenly, she got up, looked at us and burst out.

"You think he cares? If he did, he wouldn't have left us. You think he is some kind of a hero. He is not. I hate you for still loving him Nina. I hate everything. Leave me alone."

Her eyes were very red now. She stormed out of the room. The woman became child. I gently put my hand on Nina to stop her rushing after her sister.

"She'll calm down," I reassured.

"You shouldn't have gone on at her like that, Nina. I should have followed her more closely."

But I should have known better.

"You can't blame yourself for everything, Mum," Nina said, pacing up and down the room, listening to Meena sob in the kitchen until she reappeared in the room and crumbled into my arms, begging forgiveness and promising to write down why she had been drinking. This was what Meena wrote:

"I feel grown up in relation to other kids in my school. I am not myself, I laugh strangely. I try to look like others. Try to fit in. Don't feel like doing anything. Don't even feel like killing myself. Don't like my life. I feel bored and lonely. Every time I go out I am nervous. I can't speak English in front of my family. Every morning when I go to school, my heart palpitates until I reach my locker. I have invisible friends. I hate to be with my boring classmates. They only go to town for shopping or watch T.V. It's not like Denmark, my home. I don't like being here. I easily become stressed, tired. Mama doesn't allow me to use makeup. I don't care much about Mama and Papa, but would like to have a normal family life."

The nihilistic content frightened me. It went on in this bitter depressed vein for four pages of blue touch paper, ready to ignite and fire my indignation. Fists of rage hit the bones on my back. I sensed a distant memory so fresh and vivid that a searing pain ran through my whole body.

Seven months after the police raid into the Kalvebod house, Copenhagen city, October 1989. It was the community fair. Music, fireworks, children's face-painting, food. Minna and Nina had already gone to the festival with their friends. Peter had got a letter from Danish Volunteer Service. Rejection of a job he had applied for in Tanzania. He wanted to run away from the police investigations. He was very upset and was writing a letter in response. I was finishing cleaning the kitchen and had backache due to my periods. We were getting a bit late. He stormed into the kitchen demanding to know why I wasn't ready. I had a glass of water in my one hand and Paracetamol in another. I swallowed the pill, walked towards the bedroom and was about to put the glass on the table, so I could get ready. He pulled me onto the bed and started to hit my body with his clenched fists. I was laying helplessly on the bed, trying to protect myself, trying to suppress my crying, in the fear that the neighbours might hear me. He continuously hit me. I started to scream and cry desperately. I tried to push him away from me. In the process he hit the wall while I cried with pain. I didn't care. I was very angry and wanted to run out. Looking in the mirror I couldn't find any traces of his violence as they were hidden under my clothes, carved on my soul like nails, infecting my skin, I was bleeding with shame, pain and humiliation. Eventually, I gathered my strength, thinking of Minna and Nina and slowly got ready to go.

I smiled at my beautiful daughters who were busy with face painting. A friend offered me a glass of Liebfraumilch, the same wine I drank when Peter was leaving me for a trip to Sweden to study Marxism on my wedding night.

"This wine is a life saver!" I sarcastically laughed.

My friend Karen didn't understand, but said, "Are you OK, Svera?"

"Are you OK, Mum?" Nina, put her hand on my shoulder.

"Are you hurt, my daughter?" I heard your voice, mother. Gulping the white, terrible, cheap stuff, I pinched myself. Karen filled up my glass again. The more I drank, the more thirsty I became, thirsty for answers, drenched in pain that began to sink down in the goblet. I was drenched in anticipation, watching Peter sitting on the other table talking to

Thomas about Africa. People were dancing to the tunes of 'Flyv min Fugl'.

"Fly my bird, over the quiet roofs of the city
Carry the dreams of the children on your back
Quietly the day travels with the moon's white sickle
Cuts through the night a foreign beach
Aia, aia, with the forbidden thoughts

I looked at Annisette on the stage. She was the 'Savage Rose', a Danish jazz/pop singer. 'Flyv min Fugl', fly my bird.... My head painfully swayed to the rhythms, my mind flew across the oceans, to the distant land, Punjab...to come and put my hurting body in your arms mother...I stayed on through the night, the moon's white sickle was turning into glorious dawn...I stayed on in my relationship for the sake of my children...carrying their dreams in my motherly lap...I would ride the punches and find a new meaning for hammer and sickle.

Feeling the pangs of anger, I started to cry...a wail let out of my throat. Both Nina and Minna were gone to sleep. Everything was silent. The rhythmical dense night stepped down from the sky to offer me a soft rug full of stars, as it had done before, in times of crisis. In its clear light I saw the python loom outside the house, hissing, trying to revive the feeling of fear in my mind, but in my solitude, I felt a strong urge to fight and kill the snake. Each limb of my body got stiffened. I went up to lie in my bed, slowing down, breathing steadily, concentrating in a hypnotic state to focus on one spot, in the middle of my forehead. Slowly I noticed the periphery of the flicker turn into the shape of a woman. Svera the mother, the woman took a long glance at the youthful Svera in the photo on the shelf. She was forgetting her own youthful rebellion and experimentation. I saw her rising, from my own body, then standing up, ready to leave. I am left behind on the bed, watching. I see her shutting all the windows and stepping outside. The snake is waiting for her, coiled like a spring for a chance to enter the house. Without blinking, she stares deep into his round eyes. He is baffled and starts to run away. She chases him, running in the darkness, following his grey shining skin. There is not a soul on the streets, just the sound of her running feet and her strong urge. Suddenly, there is a strong flash. Everything is exposed. The python is blinded by the light. She jumps on his body, trampling with her vigorous movement, tearing the layers of misconceptions until she is bare. The snake is choking, bleeding, slowly dying. A silvery vehicle appears. Its doors fly open to reveal another woman, an old wise fairy with a huge piece of silvery cloth in her hands who turns Svera gently away from the dead body of the snake and covers her with the robe, then cradles her in her arms. Svera is exhausted lying in her gentle embrace, softly crying with tiredness, hearing voices.

Your children are alone. Go back home to them, they need you. You have been fighting for too many years - the battle of a woman, the battle against the evil. Every woman has to fight that battle. You have survived. You have my blessings. You will win in the end. I am with you. I am within you. I am your strength. I am your mother. I am your friend. I am your soul mate. I am. . . I am. . . Svera can hear her no more. She is sleeping in her arms now. A deep sleep.

I woke up in this city of ghosts and memories. In my bedroom, the screen was lit and the window of my room was open. The black and white reasoning, the love and the hate, seemed to be fading down the path left behind, their ghostly, paranormal limbs jerking, making crackling sounds, I could almost hear them.
"Bye Madame. We'll think of you sometime."
My God. I gasped to see the neutral grey sky spreading like wings over the city and closed the window. I stood in front of the glass, which was flashing my image. I saw myself gazing with wide-open eyes.
"You have killed one python. There will be others."
"Why do you destroy yourself like this, Svera? You are so beautiful and intelligent. Why grieve so much? Leave the ghosts of Jaz, Peter, Josef behind. I'm here with you. Come to me."
I was hearing voices. Who were these people? My father. Uncle Karl. Amar. Jaz. Ahren. Josef. You, mother? Someone was there in the room. It seemed very much of flesh and blood. Two strong arms stretched towards me. I turned around facing the huge mirror on the wall. Oh,

no, it was a tall woman, with a mysterious smile. Her eyes were flashing like Shiva. Her usual trance was back. Again! Oh, no!

"Come to me Svera," the voice whispered again. I turned around once more and looked across my bed.

"I am here as well as within you. You have been thriving in my company. I am your father, your Uncle Karl, Amar, Jaz, Peter, Ahren, Johnny, Josef. I'm what you make of me. Is it true Svera? Is that what you have been searching for? Do you think I may be your strength, your weakness, your soul mate? I have survived on my own. Do you think you will? Svera Jang. I do exist, but I also exist in your dreams. Look at me, I'm as naked as truth, face me, touch me, feel me, recognised me, Svera Jang. Haven't you? I'm not the Lucifer of your dawn. I am that dream we all chase in the blind alleys of our desire. I am. . am your. .."

This was Josef. My God, what is happening? I saw the woman in the mirror stepped outside to approach him and gently placed her hand over his mouth. He was suddenly helpless as she slowly lowered her arm and kissed him gently on his now vulnerable lips. It was her turn to take control. She beckoned him towards the bed and they both silently undressed. She knew they were going to be together. She knew he was going to go away on one of his mysterious journeys. She also knew she had him within herself and that wouldn't leave her ever again. She held him there where she wanted him. She finally had this power over him. Then I heard her plead, "Don't leave me yet Josef, I need a bit more strength. My daughter is going to wed a man who I see is going to hurt her badly. She won't listen to any reasoning. Peter is not a ghost. He still affects my life by affecting my daughter's. He is supporting her decision against mine..."

I couldn't believe what she was saying. How could she be so weak after all that, she'd been through? No, no, no. Not now Svera. Wake up, I shouted. You have worked so hard to break this illusion. She didn't even notice my existence. I rubbed my eyes and watched them, helplessly. I had no choice.

"Hush, Babe."

He was reassuring, kissing her tears away.

"This is not a power game between you and Peter. Your daughter is not going to listen to you. It is her fate. She has to go through her own struggle, just like you did. Let her. Go and support her, Svera. You have always been good at that. You have touched many people's lives. You give courage, sincerity, compassion, love, to many people. Why stop now? No, Svera, you have been fighting this struggle, this Jang. It is your fight. You do that girl, with dignity. I'll be proud of you. I shall be there to support you," he said.

He gently cradled her arched body into his encompassing lap and rocked her to sleep, the way Svera's Mum did all those years ago in the Punjab. Minutes, hours, months passed. The physical and spiritual union between them was so strong. He reminded her somehow of Ahren, yet he had a maturity that Ahren lacked. His depth of knowledge on so many subjects astounded her for one so young. Politics, art, love - he could talk for hours on these subjects. He listened attentively to what Svera would say. That was the most beautiful aspect of his character. He cared for her, for the world, for this house. It was strange how he knew about the annex in the cellar. It had been walled up for so many years. Yet Josef causally observed its presence. Josef did not have the key for the cellar. Only one existed that was permanently attached to the house and car keys. Yes, he inspired fear, apprehension and danger. Yes, hours, months passed.

Whether or not he had ever existed as a man in flesh and blood like Ahren had, they both reminded Svera of something. Was it her search she had made love to? He, it, left her fulfilled.

Something snapped in the atmosphere. Thundering sounds came from outside. It was the rain. If it didn't rain, the illusion would have lasted, if the illusion lasted, the woman of the mirror could have got lost in her trance, forever, so the nature helped her, something always stepped in to protect her. This time it was the rain that did it. The woman went back inside the mirror like a ghost and disappeared.

CHAPTER 33
Who Is Svera?

This bedroom faces the famous Undercliffe Cemetery in Bradford, West Yorkshire, December 1999. This was Svera's bedroom. I am the creator of her story. I exist in between the fine lines of reality and fiction. The voice of Jimi Hendrix's 'Voodoo Child' is playing in the background. It takes me back to my adolescence, where my soul would rise high on the bliss of love and romance, listening to Hindi film songs. Music still uplifts my soul. It takes me high on its magically tuned sea waves. Drowned in the heavy dose of Jimi's voice, mixed with dewberry smoke from the essential oil burner, I am daydreaming. I don't need marijuana or brandy or Amitriptyline. I am trying to get rid of my tranquillisers. A half burnt cigarette in the ashtray seems like a dead bullet shell. Two black beads stuck to the picture frame remind me of a drunk whose eyes pop out with a hangover. I do not want to be addicted to smoking, but holding a sleek Silk Cut, exuding fire watching the ash burn down, like time passing, gives me the illusion that I can pin down my place in time and space. The trouble about time is that as soon as you arrive, it's gone. We get addicted to the illusion that we hold about ourselves. I am this I am that. Then when I die, I won't be this or that, not I, me, ego, Svera, just a jumble of memories, desires, potentials and dreams. I am addicted to dreams as well as to books, periodicals and pamphlets, videos, photographs and paintings: India, Denmark, Africa, Canada, USA, France, Portugal and Mauritius. Memories, memories and more memories. Where do memories exist? On a gravestone? In a jam jar at the back of my head? So where could they exist? - fading in the space, bending with time, moulded in words, affecting our actions, reminding us to continue. Do you realise how much Svera had gone through by being in this house? Memories poured like pink haze from eucalyptus tree, down into the screen to become words with fiery tails. She took you flying like a magpie, travelling through time and spaces. Walking like a yogi on the thorns of life. There is never enough time to count the clock ticking through the minutes, hours, days, months, years and still she has so far to go. This is a journey of smooth highways, stumbling in the back alleys of dreams, making mistakes, learning, chasing fantasies, hanging onto memories, ticktock time passing, thriving on the struggle because its conclusion is contentment.

Sound of beautiful rain slap against the windowpane, creating an illusion of fog and breaking the dream spell, returning it into new reality. Johnny comes into the picture. Tall, raggedly handsome, maybe but an ageing hippy who has created a stubborn shell around him like the skin of a tortoise - thinning, soft grey hair, blue eyes. Bastard. He has stolen my heart, against my will. "I have always been searching for you. You are my Radha, my soul mate, my lover, my friend". He coaxed Svera into the world of his illusions. Svera was always attracted to blue eyes. They were a reminder of her past, of Naxalbari fighter Deep, Sukhna Lake. How many men did she not meet? How many of them fitted the bill or even offered to pay it, like she would?

This is Svera's bedroom - lost in time and space. There is only one eternal moment and that's now. I am writing this letter to you mother. I am describing Svera's story here, for Minna for Nina and for anybody else. I am stepping back from this window, watching my shadow walk into a dream, back to Svera's past. This one is not from long ago. Remember her fight with the python, making love to Josef? Nina had left and made up her mind to get married to Sam.

"His Mum is pressurising him. She doesn't want us living together out of wedlock. What will their community say?" she said.

"Don't you see that it's the wrong reason to get married, Nina? There's always going to be an emotional blackmail like this one pressing you to marriage. There will always be this taboo, a norm that binds you, this barrier to cross, that honour to be stepped upon. Do you want that?" Svera had made her last effort, but was resigned to accept that the marriage of her daughter was inevitable. Nina her first-born was high on love and the ideal of romance.

"But I love him Mum, I can't stay without him. My father will pay for our expenses. He will even give us a honeymoon in the Caribbean." Nina's wedding date was set and Svera's heart was in pieces, breaking with the thought that her own marriage to Peter, her own ideal of romance, were shattered, breaking with the vision that her daughter's marriage may already be doomed by impassable cultural barriers.

A July afternoon. Seconds, minutes, hours, months, years have gone by. The Manningham riots seemed a thing of the past. A gentle sunshine touched Svera's feet as would a daughter's blessing. She walked on the pavement, greedily gulping the mild air, joining the other consumers who were happy addicts to the cheap bargain hunting in the shopping malls of love. They indulged themselves in a 'drink, dance, eat and be merry attitude'. The tables in Love Apple Cafe were always laid to attract these hungry sleepwalkers. A flux of travellers, students from Spain, China, and the Middle East had come to Bradford. They consumed words like hungry wolves, arming themselves with the weapons of knowledge, language, and business. Svera flicked through the menu and ordered her favourite Latte and a Mocha coffee for her friend Sharon, followed by Greek salad and a bowl of olives with creamy mushrooms. Their drinks were served in two large porcelain tumblers, each burning with frothy cream that rolled around the shiny metal spoon stirring up a spiral of memories.

"They can try. I shall fight them. The harder they come, the harder they fall. I shall not be subdued, ever!"

Sharon smiled apprehensively. She seemed a completely different person from the time Svera had first met her at Leeds Metropolitan a year ago during a meeting against fundamentalism. At that time Sharon had been wearing a traditional Shalwar and Kameez with a black scarf on her head - a picture of obedience, living at home, working hard.

After the meeting they had exchanged phone numbers and later Sharon came to discuss the discrimination against her progressive way of teaching at the University. It was a way of seeking Svera's support, but Svera had her own problems and did not feel able to help much. Sharon took this hurtfully and was so upset that the communication between them had broken down. Then, one day, when Svera had almost forgotten about her existence, as she often did with angry ghosts from the past, Sharon phoned. She wanted to apologise and they agreed to meet. So here they were, sipping coffee and Svera observed the transformation in Sharon. It was dramatic, like a butterfly emerging from a cocoon. Svera realised that under Sharon's mask was a radical woman determined to liberate herself from oppression. Black tights replaced the shalwar, the kameez by a loose top and the headscarf by a black beret that seemed to symbolise a letting go of the chains that bind you. Maybe Svera was now wearing the chains. Tied up by her own thoughts and worries, she was confused about the wedding, her relationships or lack of them. She was confused about confusions, confused whether she ever existed, except in a memory of the other Svera, or in between the fine lines of those words. Sharon had come out of her confusions and shed her chains. Svera had inherited them, albeit temporarily. From confusion comes clarity.

"I am so confused Sharon. My daughter is getting married. I am terrified. Peter has agreed to finance her wedding. What shall I do?"

"How much does this estranged husband of yours know about the Asian community here? Does he care at all?" Sharon said, as Svera lit her fifth Silk Cut within the twenty minutes that they had been sitting there.

"When did you start smoking?" Sharon asked.

"Oh I can't sleep night after night thinking about Nina. I do not approve of any of this."

"There's nothing you can do, Svera Jang. Nothing. Try and listen to me. Nothing on this earth can stop your daughter from marrying Sam. Think about yourself. You once left your mother. Did you listen to her?"

"And are you still on Amitriptyline?"

"Of course. I have to be. It's part of the plot, he, he he!"

Svera laughed hysterically.

"I can't cope with the pressure of living and describing Svera's life. Peter is trying to break me and my daughters apart. He is playing the game of divide and rule by supporting Nina financially, against my advice."

"You know very well you don't have to take any bloody pills - a woman like you."

"For God's sake don't say that, Sharon. You are not my psychologist or my doctor."

"But I'm your friend, Svera."

Svera looked out through the large glass window, sipping her coffee in silence. A police car had just arrived to park on the cafe' pavement and three Asian police officers came out with pistols hanging from their belts and truncheons in their hands. They walked towards the nightclub on the corner.

"A lot of police have started to patrol our streets after the bloody riots and I do feel safer," remarked an elderly woman at the table looking across the street.

Svera gazed at a black and white photograph of Audrey Hepburn. Across their table, a white English male sat with his partner, while a curly haired girl of four, burger in hand, stood by her side. Sharon suddenly stood up as if she had seen a ghost. Maybe it was the police, the white diners, unease about her new clothes, maybe she saw someone she knew and didn't want to see or didn't want them to know she was there. Asian women are always on their guard, but she wanted to leave. Without saying a word she walked in a huff towards the toilets. When she came out she glanced around and the smile returned to her face, perhaps demons of fear had disappeared.

"I had almost forgot about this, I had prepared it for you last night." She took a cassette from her bag to place on the table.

'Spiritual Ecstasy', a remix of the old Asha Bhosle's 'Chura Liya', a song from the film Yaadon ki Baraat: Procession of Memories. The little girl with curly hair had finished her burger. She looked at her Mum who was hypnotically staring into her partner's hungry eyes forgetting the steaming quiche on the table. I could see that the little girl found it rather unappetising and she ran off to chatter to other customers to kill her boredom. Even boredom dies. The thought of children brutally slaughtering boredom, invaded Svera's mind like an army of disturbance and left just as suddenly as an unfinished poem.....

"......I was brutally slaughtering boredom,
circumcising arguements
mangling laziness,
bobbitting Peter's penis............"

The two friends left the cafe to shop at the famous Bombay Stores. Svera had to buy a dress to wear at Nina's wedding. They chose a long white chiffon skirt and a pretty little top with crimson embroidery, plus a long waistcoat probably hand stitched by a poor worker trying to bind together her fragile economical existence in one of the many slums in Bombay, the city of joy. Svera chose a silver hand bracelet, matching earrings and silver sandals to go with it. Dying with anxiety to try her new outfit, Svera bade farewell to Sharon and rushed home.

"Men are not worth falling in love with, Svera. I know I am not supposed to give you this advice, but go with your heart, fall in love again, find a lover who can appreciate and admire you. Have fun, Svera Jang. Live your life to the full."

Svera looked in the mirror - a beautiful single mother dressed, ready to give her daughter away in marriage. The long white skirt, red top and silver earrings seemed to speak back to her reflection. She longed for Johnny to sneak out of the mirror or slip in from a crack under the door to make love to her. He was not a ghost. Was he? With his blue rucksack, pink hat, soft voice, big blue eyes. How could he be a ghost? He had spoken to her in London.

She looked in the mirror again. How young and desirable the woman in red silk sari seemed. A man enters the room, takes her by the hand to lead her towards the bed that is covered with rose petals. She is shy as he lifts her chin up to look into her big smiling eyes. It's her wedding night.

"I will make this trip a heaven for both of us, Svera," he moans.

"Svera?"

"Svera, are you looking for yourself in the mirror? Svera, it's easier to come to terms with memories when I write about them through your eyes."

There are ghosts in memories. Who else can hear the mind talking to itself?

Svera heard the noises like the noises coming from downstairs that needed investigating. She could stumble across the truth, like she stumbled on the hole in the carpet in her high-heeled silver sandals. Svera could read her own mind, like she could read the old newspaper popping out from under the hole in the carpet. It was dated 1892 and a face with big eyes stared out at her. Shocked, she almost fell down, but gathered the frills of her skirt in her right hand and straightened herself up. She was about to pick up the newspaper when she heard Minna's scream.

"Mum, Mum, I am so scared hurry up, there's something behind the bookcase, in the basement. Hurry, please, Mum..."

The House on the Cliffe was at least one hundred and fifty years old and had a very peculiar basement with large stone tables in the middle and three old wooden carved bookcases, which were kept in the same place as Svera's family had found them when they first moved in. The bookcases stood against a wall partly illuminated by a dim bulb under a lampshade. Minna was looking for a lost book and when she went down to check the old bookcases she had discovered a small chamber behind one of the layers of books. Normally, she was scared to go downstairs in the basement.

"Look, look, Mum, this is not very clear, but it looks like a book, or a diary. It's old and very dusty. I can see. Yes, it's Ange...le..ra. ANJELERA! Anjelera J. Dang's Diary. Year 1892? This is strange. Who was Anjelera? J. Dang. Mum, I am scared."

Minna's pale face and big brown eyes looked huge with the dim light. Her shadow fell on the wall behind them.

"Maybe there are other clues. Let's see," Svera whispered in a low voice.

There was no light in the small chamber with an ebony wood door and an iron handle and when Svera Jang put her hand inside she felt a small picture frame. She pulled it out.

"It's damn dark here. I will go upstairs and get a big candle, Mum," Minna said.

Svera didn't answer and started to touch the dusty glass surface with her hand. There was a cold draft, she felt the chill. The picture was filled with stains. Svera continued to clean the glass with her fingers as if it was Aladdin's lamp. She felt that if she continued to rub and rub a Genie, or Johnny would appear in front of her eyes. Then she saw something in the picture was glowing in the dark, staring at her - a pair of dark eyes. She felt hypnotized and closed her eyes.

"Anjelera? It's you, isn't it? I can't see you in the dark," he spoke.

"Sorry, my name is Svera."

"Oh, I'm sorry, but your face, your hair, the flicker in your eyes - you look like Anjelera. My name is Johnny," and he held out his hand.

He was dressed in his shining black trousers, white silk coat and black shoes to match, looking dashingly handsome smiling. Svera was wearing a white chiffon skirt and a red top, red lipstick, white sandals.

"Come, Josef, please stand by my side in front of this mirror," she pleaded. "I'm nervous."

"Josef? Who is he? I am Johnny. Svera wake up. I told you a mirror in bedroom is a bad omen. I don't want anything bad to happen to you. Mirrors sometimes bring bad luck. You might not be able to see anything in the mirror. No Anjelera, I want to keep you in here, in my heart. I must admit, I'm jealous of your beauty."

He looked at me avoiding the mirror. His appearance was pale and sad. Perhaps it was because he wore that flashy white coat.

"Why do you look so discontented, Johnny?"

"Just an old memory flashed by, seeing you dressed like that. I once attended my friend's wedding with Anjelera. With this dress, you look so much like her."

"Who is Anjelera?"

"I met her... er...in 1886 when I was 35. She was a Sikh girl from the Punjab."

"What are you saying Johnny? 1886? Are you kidding me? You never really told me about Anjelera."

He quickly corrected himself.

"1996, I'm sorry. Listen, Svera. I met her in Birmingham on one of my trips, a business trip my father had sent me on. She was 25, so beautiful, so elegant, so genuine, honest, bold and sizzling with passion. She struck my life like lightening. I fell in love with her. Every week I went to see her. She would come to see me in my hotel room, secretly, of course. In those days, it was nearly impossible to meet openly. We were both mad. Her family, her dad and brothers found out and oh, my God, what havoc they brought. I was ready to marry her. No, they wouldn't allow it. They sent her away to the Punjab. I was heartbroken, Svera. I think I died with grief in 1892. I was only 35."

"You are not dead Johnny, I have seen you. I have met you. I can even touch you. You are here with me."

"Sorry, I am lingering into the shadow of my past. Please forgive me, Svera Jang."

He was whispering now covering his grief stricken face with his hands. I could not hold back. I went over to him, to take him in my arms. It was now my turn to comfort him. Our eyes met and there was a flicker, we felt connected. His blue grey eyes bore deep into mine. But then he lowered them. The connection was gone again. A cold draft swept into the room mysteriously. The flicker extinguished. But the light had penetrated deep into my soul. I knew from then on I would never demand a physical connection from him. Again, Jaz came into my vision, then Ahren. I was puzzled. I looked in the mirror and then at Johnny whose shadow was sliding towards the mirror entering it, just like Svera did. Who was left behind? The room in this city? A shadow of Johnny who wasn't Jaz, nor was he Josef? The real Svera, the narrator with an old photograph?

People come and go, like brief companions who walk a while beside you on your path. I have walked a long way with Jaz, Peter and Ahren. They seem to slide into the mirror of the past. Now I walk alone and wonder where I am, wondering who I am. I do know I am the narrator, but you see, even for me, it's difficult to separate myself from myself.

Someone is shouting, "Mum, Mum, where are you? The lights have gone out. I have found candles. Oh there you are, Mum," Minna was saying.

Who is Anjelera? Who is Anjelera? Who is Anjeleraaaaa - an echo kept on buzzing in my ears from the depth of walls onto the air like a firefly, repeatedly:

Lights are gone out again. Total darkness.
Lights come back. I sit in front of my computer, writing.

A few months have passed since the incident in the cellars. You phoned me last Saturday, Ma. Your voice glistened on the air like charcoal embers in a tandoori oven. I felt the warmth for hours as you spoke, you sounded like a clarion call, trying to tell me something, you insisted that I come to see you. You were a bit uneasy about things. You said you felt pain in your chest. Haven't we all? - from mothers to daughters, to grandchild. Everything is passed through the generations.

I, Svera, talking to Johnny about his life, about Anjelera, about culture, religion and politics. I told him I hated both when they exploit people, especially women and children. He said no one understood him. His colleagues at the college thought he was weird. To him they were the ones that were fucked up. So he left his job. It's easier to be with yourself when the whole world is mad.

The telephone rang. It was my brother, Amar, from Canada. His voice was flat and lifeless like the punctured tyre of a car. He was not the same Amar I used to know from the Punjab - the vagrant force. Now I wish I had accepted your perseverance. It's too late Mother. How can I ever ask for forgiveness? I had this dream last night. You were sitting on this majestic wicker chair in my bedroom. You seemed so serene. I had a dead embryo in my hands like the piece of a misconceived dream. Dreams die young in their sleep. You spoke:
"This is the inevitable death of your past. Travel towards your future, maybe with or without Johnny. You have just begun the process. I'm peaceful now. I take my leave from you. Don't be afraid of death. I'll always be in your dreams, to give you comfort and courage and my good wishes. Have peace daughter."
You closed your eyes.

I regret not coming to see you. Now I can't. You have always been there for me, with me, showing me the way. You are gone. I wish I had attended your funeral yet I will continue this letter as if you have never left. The flicker of your strength is alive in my soul, mother.

After talking to Amar, I started crying. I kept thinking about you, the Punjab, my father, Uncle Karl, Amar, Deep, Jaz, Ahren. I sat there for a long time, tried to communicate my thoughts to you. I felt the energy penetrate from you to me. The day departed from me like you did, bowing towards the horizon, respectfully, leaving the fragments of light behind. The ebony shadows, reminded me of my past and my tasks. I went upstairs, to my bedroom. The screen of my computer was lit. The chair was snug. Jaz? No, not again, I thought silently. No Jaz, you disappeared in your own smoke a long time ago. You are travelling on a journey of your own. You had me but lost me. Peter, huh poor you, I wish you well in your endeavour to revive your history. Losers always beat themselves. Johnny? Where are you Johnny? Johnny? Oh, Johnny.

You think you can undo the past mistakes. Johnny, you are still alive, not in this house though, not in this city, maybe you are learning the game of lights and shadows. Is this Svera? Svera...Svera...Svera...I need you. Oh yes Svera, it's you girl, my dawn, my own shadow, which was becoming the light, the dawn, stretching her arms, inviting me to sit and write and write and write. All night long until the shadows dispersed into the light, the Dawn. I had learnt to play the game of shadows and lights. I could now step out of the shadows and into the light, without the mirror. I would have to do it without the mirror, I will remove this mirror, energising myself, repairing, learning, making mistakes, living, loving, sinning – whatever - learning and moving forward. Shadows are part of the light, not a place to dwell for too long. It's the light we seek. The flicker, when I close my eyes to meditate. Light and shadow don't have any rules. There are no rules, nor logic, everything keeps on changing, why can't we?

"Mum, are you asleep? Why do you keep on rubbing the picture? Look I can see a man. He is tall, has blue eyes, a big nose and...look he has a blue strap on his chest. It could be some type of a bag, a rucksack. Mum, look!"

Minna was speaking constantly. Svera could not hear her. Her eyes were fixed on the face of the man on the picture. It was Johnny's face. She could swear. He stood beside Weilham, Alma, Helger, Dora, Heidi, Edith. Josef Strauss (1856-1892). He was 36 when he died. Svera had come to Britain in 1992, exactly a hundred years after.

CHAPTER 34
A Soul Shakes Down

December. On this particular night, instead sitting in front of the lighted screen, I am walking on tiptoes along the exquisite corridor watching firecrackers shooting into the night sky...nights...years, in transition from the years...err...to 2000...I begin to count, one, two, 10, hundreds of firecrackers. There could be millions of them. The years of my life, almost like another whole century stretching itself like Palladium in front of me. I can now begin to live, love, give, take, hate, sin, spiritualise, like a super white witch, of course with the unusual flicker in my eyes. I have in my golden goblet the thick Kahlua from the past, the clear bubbling Vodka of the present mixed with a colourless cream of the future. I sip the liquid, walking softly, peeping through the windows of the past, bringing light to this moment, the present which instantly becomes the past, each step I take, each breath I inhale, each staircase I climb, the next moment will be the future, but I can never get there. The future is not for me to predict.

"We're gonna have a soul shake down for it, tonight," Bob sings.
His sexy voice stirs me up like a cocktail of love and sex. Can you really mix the two? You can, you can't. You can, you can't. Yes you can. Ha, ha, ha! I am drunk. Why did he die so young? Bastard. Why did Jaz, Uncle Karl, Dad, Mum. Why did Peter, Ahren, and Josef leave? Actually he was Jaz, because Jaz never disappeared from my life totally. Or was he Ahren, he looked like him. Some of our dreams don't die young, they keep on growing, stubbornly staying by our side, but do our dreams come true? Some of them do. Josef could be the wishful thinking who would emerge into all those men that Svera kept on meeting and rejecting, because she was so obsessed by his vision - tall, dark and handsome. I did try to warn Svera that whether it was Jaz or Josef, she shouldn't wish to meet the image in another man but she didn't care.

Johnny was quite screwed up right from the head to his burning bottoms. He was really of flesh and bones, but half dead anyway. Not a ghost, but so much lost in his past, buried alive in there. He did die once, well almost. A fantastic sculptor. He fell in love with me. No, not here. I will describe him to you another day, in another story, in another city with a totally different setting. Watch where you are stepping. One day it may pass you in the street, pull your arm, lead you to the bookstore and show you the face staring out from the cover, maybe that face will be yours. I am hungry for more stories, but I will stop wandering for a moment and yet I know my search is not over.

Now I slice the quarter of a succulent piece from this ripened mango of memories with my razor blade fingers tapping onto chapter 34. It is the 31st December 2000. Microsoft Word is getting dimmer on screen, disappearing, just like my past. I have to replace it with a new fantastic version, maybe an Apple Mac where I could have final cut pro, photo shop, Quark Express. I will rewrite, weave dreams, illustrate them, put sound and photos. The sound of the firecrackers is getting dimmer, disappearing like a shadow, the light will appear from the death of shadows. The Big Ben on the TV screen ticks, sliding to get to midnight where it will turn into the beginning of another era. Before the old disappears, the new one will have already arrived. This is life. Everything feeds itself on the old, renewing itself - death, birth, life. For a moment everything lightens up, the firecrackers in the sky, the bubbling champagne until all sounds, all colours, will stop, just for a moment, then vibrating the new energy reappear again and again and again. The wheel of life!

Everything floats in this universe in the form of energy - the sweet and sour juices of the past, the present float in this room like the moon walker making ghostly shadows on the painting on the wall. My daughter discovered the painting yesterday together with the diary of Anjelera Young in a hidden chamber beside one hundred year old carved pine bookshelf in the basement of this house with a spirit. The picture now hangs on one of the walls in my bedroom. The memory hangs by a nail on the walls of my mind. My mind hangs by a thread suspended from reality. Spirits, ghosts, memories, they are reappearing again. Another Kahlua. Would you like to taste this cocktail? And you Mum? When you are a ghost, you could take up this offer. No norms and restrictions for the ghosts. Maybe you did drink, without me knowing it. You Indian women, you know how to solve all those crisis, you'd been through. Actually, you could have tasted the fine Scotch, dad always brought home with him on his leave from the forces. I remember you must have, sometimes I saw you in a jolly good mood.

I can feel the cold draft. The candlelight flickers momentarily, illuminating the eyes of a handsome, tall man in the painting, forcing me to look at him. Josef Strauss. Am I drunk? You bet I am, a little bit. Love, sex, spirituality - what a cocktail to stir. Why did Jaz die so young? Did he really die or just disappear to become a ghost? It's still a mystery. Oh well, he wasn't meant to be with me, but Anna will be arriving with the tale of her ageing wish to be with a man who can give her love, happiness, dreams, everything. Just like any woman would wish. I look out of the stained glass door. There she is, wearing the golden curls of Tarot cards and Runes on her wise head, a bottle of champagne in her slender fingers, painted nails with golden colour. Gold is in this year - golden memories of the golden past. Anna and I light the pink candles on the windowsill near the statue of Buddha. We sit comfortably on the blue cushioned chairs. The purple Rune cards are mapped out on the beige table in front of us. They throw the golden glow all over the place. "You know the guy from Doncaster I met through Ashville, he has met someone local. I really liked him, you know," sighs Anna.
Glints of sadness illuminate her oval eyes.
"Johnny phoned," I answer in my own dreamlike state.
"Who is Johnny? The cheeky bugger with a pink hat? You really should screw him," Anna said.
"I think I did. Or was it Josef?"
We belly laugh.

Tormented between hope and despair, I had started to believe in Kismet, Runes, cards and clairvoyants. I turn the Rune card in my hand. It's a card called the Hagalaz.

The moon is hidden,
thunder strikes.
How can you sleep
when your very own bed

calls in the lightening?
Look around you.
Nothing is the same.

The Rune of elemental disruption of events that seem to be totally beyond your control. Hagalaz has only one upright position. It operates through reversal. When you draw this Rune, you may expect disruption, which in other words is the Great Awakening. The form of the awakening may vary. You might experience a gradual feeling of coming to your senses, as if you were emerging from a deep slumber. You have to strip away the layers of misconception.
"What happen to Josef?"
Anna mixes the cards again.
"Only time will tell."
"So ask it. Hey you, time! Tell or else."
"What about Johnny?"
"Who knows, maybe, sometimes I may, if I want to. He will become a character in my story, not this one. He will be part of a plot."
"Huh, you are clever. Another love story? A thriller?"
Anna laughed.
"Maybe, who knows."
I moan and feel the yearning for Johnny.

This was another decisive turn in the life of Svera Jang. The woman, the creator, the narrator - the rhythms of the search beating in its battle. One and two and three and four and five and six. There could be another century full of events. If not mine, then my daughters, or yours and yours.
Saa baar jannam lenge
Saa baar judaa honge

As I predicted, I will have to return on another day, with another story and in another time - maybe in Johnny's voice. Ha! Don't be scared. You think I am soon going to turn into a ghost. Not yet. I have too much to account for. It all adds up. Live, write, sing, love, spiritualise. Well this is the tale of a night when I was sitting in the wicker chair watching Svera in front of her beloved screen, writing, writing about writing, quite intense, smoking, even swearing. I was not used to her smoking or swearing. The smoke gets abusive, but I am so used to the sound of the silence of the night - a silence you could bag in a vacuum, a silence you could gather in your palm, roll it around like a chapatti, give it a shape. This was a soundless night. The house did not creak. The street was empty. The sky and the stars hung pendulum, crisp like a freshly ironed cloud without a ruffle. Then, *bang, bang!* There were two shots in the air as if coming from another planet, another time. I thought Johnny was playing games with me. I was startled. The blanket on my lap slid and an urge forced me to get up from my chair. Then I saw Svera walk towards the window and tip something over, the infamous wicker chair where I so often confronted Peter, Jaz, Mum and now Johnny. I felt a hand touch my shoulder. I stopped to look back. Svera had gone back to her writing. There was no one else in the room, but something whispered a warning to me, not to look out of the window. I wasn't supposed to turn into a ghost yet. Then everything became silent again and I went to my bed, fell asleep peacefully.

Arif was a writer, an acquaintance of mine and lived on Leeds Road. He experienced harassment by young Asian boys because he was different. He was categorised Afro-Muslim by the Abdullah gang in his neighbourhood.

"I yearn for vigilantes. I yearn for the common people - black, white, Sikh, Hindu and Irish - to join together like a multicoloured rainbow and expel the ruffians from our streets. They speak of hispanophobia, but it is we the humble citizens who have to endure their naked aggression and blinkered intolerance. Who are the fascists now in this city? The National Front was expelled twenty years ago to be replaced by an equally insidious form of dangerous intolerant tyrants. How these new gangsters flew out of their cars when they won the local election in this satanic town. They became councillors to represent who - the abandoned working classes of the inner city areas? The pensioners and unfortunates who didn't get out before the Liberal establishment, abandoned their homes to the great multicultural experiment whose virtues they extol from the safety of their white, middle-class havens where they never see a black man, an Asian, a Chinese, an Irish. How dare they? These cringing goal ridden Liberals," he had fumed.

The next morning arrived like a teenage boy with a sack on his shoulders filled with news to deliver. Boys get bored and run away to play football or turn into men like Johnny who I might already have met by the time you read my story. He still enjoys watching the game on the screen and plays games with my mind. He doesn't know that I do the same, that I know what he does. Let's place Johnny in the hard drive of my memory for the moment. When he is not around, life is enjoyable and serene.

The morning turned into a beautiful sunny day and then beautiful sunset and the night entered the gates of this city on the wings of delusion, where cultural extremes collided into each other. Words and actions flew like bullets, touching people, brushing dwellings, sweeping streets, making new barriers. The rule of the mob persisted, carrying lethal weapons to shoot in every direction. Blacks, whites, Asians trying to invade each other's territories, enabling each other with thoughtless actions. For me it was time to kill the hatred towards yesterday and build new safety in respect for each other. I felt a sense of belonging even amongst the ricochet. It was here that I faced and collided with the ghosts from my past. It was here I confronted my fears and embraced the ghosts with good vibes. It was the ghosts of the present that pestered the lives of girls like Svera, Sita, Najma, Sara, and Julie, those living demons with rough heavy voices, sharp threatening fingers, trampling feet. They gave orders, declared wars, stuck thorns of norms, taboos, their barbarian lust, slitting their throats, fires of repression burning their innocent victims alive, girls like Svera, girls who wanted their freedom. Freedom from what. for what purpose? Would they find it, the way I did or would they find it in Marijuana, the way Jaz did? Priests, Mullahs, Bhaijis are people with good faith who dress up with decent words, wearing turbans but flashing swords - swords of judgement, declarations of war, fires of repression.

CHAPTER 35
The Sound Vibrates

Everything passes.
Everything changes.
Everything born knows the process of ageing.
Each moment is born anew and dies, instantaneously.
We live in a world of birth and death simultaneously.

I'm on the road, M1 North, coming in from the South. The longing to keep on this journey is driving me crazy. Everything is in constant change, inevitably, everything passes, to become the past. I bless myself with this moment. Future is what we thought yesterday of today. This moment was the future of yesterday, and will become the present of the next and will vanish to become the past, making us rotate on the axis of time. I see a dot of a rainbow in the universe, just like I am a tiny dot, a part of every other dot, sending my energy to another dot, negative or positive. I breathe the energy of other dots, giving them mine. The air is shining with colours like a pixilated pointillist painting. I move on, reorienting myself, all the time. Am I crazy or is the whole world dotty? I'm listening to the whispering wind, which brings me the energy from outer space. I spread the seeds of change. Change represents speed, movement. Thought-provoking ideas in my mind have words, pictures, images. The mind conceives thoughts then words are formed to express, to communicate, to inform. Then actions follow, sometimes a beautiful creation, but sometimes destruction.

I'm driving at 90 mph, enjoying the speed. Even the slight rustling of the breeze stirs me. I can't stay still, passively consuming words and pictures. I have to do the skipping, like my childhood, in Uncle Karl's courtyard - one step forward, one step backward, children's game. Later in life, as my interest in photography increased, I found that to be an interesting game of light and shadow, positive and negative, the yin and yang of life. I learnt to step out of the negatives, to cancel them and to create positives to step into the light.

Sometimes we touch the truth, taste it, not able to swallow the bitter taste of change. Truth waits to be ambushed around the corner. The road reminds me to be alert for signs of danger. My mind works fast. I think and form words from my experiences, spicing them with imagination. Thoughts can only come out into the light if you project them to the world screen otherwise they creep in your mind like ivy, strangling, smothering, leading you to question what you gained and what you lost.

Looking through the screen of my memories, I'm trying to hold the wheel of time. Steady, Svera. I watch the flashing light signals ahead, beyond this road. I have driven along it so many times. My thoughts travel east, west, north, south, here, there and everywhere, beyond boundaries, cities, across the seven seas, this universe.

I had this peculiar phone call last week in the middle of the night, just as I was about to sleep:
"Hello, is this you, Jang?"
"Svera, yes I am Svera Jang. Who's this?"
"You always ask questions. Let me ask you some. Where do you want to be, Svera? What do you want, what do you want to know, Svera? I can easily detect but can't experience your pain. I can only see you through your poetry. I live here, there and everywhere. Let's say I live in a big city, like London. I am as tall as your wishes. My eyes are as deep as the blue water of your Sukhna Lake. My hair is as grey as the depth of your years. A musician, sculptor. I am the one who forms words, shapes colours, tells tales. I step in and out of words. I can make a rainbow, have no ties with anything, anyone, anywhere. I am myself. Shall we meet?"

I had heard this sound before, the note of a symphony, words of a poem. I picked my thoughts to receive the call - a line of connection, a meeting of minds, whatever you want to call it, I felt excited like a teenage schoolgirl. How would I react when I met this stranger? What am I doing? Who is this? Should I try a new venture, a new journey, make another error, be abused by another man, a Jekyll and Hyde frustrated male? Just now, what would I tell Svera, my consciousness, myself, my daughters? What am I doing? I have to finish my writing. I am picking up thoughts, transforming them into words, these words, as I look beyond Svera's life, living it, arriving at the doorstep of Svera' house, after a long journey.

Hey, my bed has been touched. There's a strong odour in the room, the cushion on the wicker chair crinkled, with Dr Jekyll and Mr. Hyde open on page 65.

"....and in a moment, like a schoolboy, strip off these lendings and spring headlong into the sea of liberty. But for me, in my impenetrable mantle, the safety was complete. Think of it - I did not even exist! Let me but escape into my laboratory door, give me but a second or two to mix and swallow the draught that I had always standing ready; and whatever he had done, Edward Hyde would pass away like the stain of breath upon a mirror; and there in his stead, quietly at home, trimming the midnight lamp in his study, a man who could afford to laugh at suspicion, would be Henry Jekyll."

I think of my father who had given me this book in India. He is no more a light in my life but a shadow, like my past. The man who brought me into this world died on November 20th, 1996. November is an important month in my life now. I met the man with a pink hat in November. His story will be a totally different one. I might have to live a tall tale with him, experience him, write, whilst I live in his story with Svera, the other woman. Then there will be three Svera's. This book of Dr Jekyll and Mr Hyde keeps coming into my mind, reminding me of something - a time in my life when I was in a constant struggle, on the crossroads of illusions. I could either keep on this journey or succumb to the desire of finding myself an ideal man. Even if I did, I might have made the same mistakes. I will be aware of the mistakes, live them, watch them, create another plot to occupy my creative mind and then another story will be born.

I looked at the old curtains in the window, stiff, frozen in an era, heavy with dust, incubating mites, ghosts and nightmares. They hung stubbornly, constantly reminding me of the past. They had to go. I went down town and bought 15 metres of soft cream flowered silk cloth to make new ones. I changed my drenched bed sheets, pillow covers, lit the pink scented candles in the room and slept peacefully.

I was woken in the night by a soft rustling sound outside my window. The warm rays of the big orange moon trickled down, touching the earth. Rooftops, jostling with wrinkled dreams, bathed themselves in the glow. It was a spectacular moment that sent shivers running from my feet upwards to my legs, knees, belly, racing towards my heart, turning into a stirring soft storm. The winter always seemed colder with each year. We forget that it is always so. The calm, multi-coloured spring pushes herself through the air and so my good old golden romantic urge, like a little girl, pulls my hand, my arm, my heart in all directions. I wanted to do something totally crazy, exciting. A connection had taken roots in my mind with someone.

"What am I doing?" This and other questions make my heart go dizzy. Who is this man? I even start to imagine what he will look like, until the day finally arrives when we are supposed to meet.

I was not able to sleep the whole night. It has been a long time since I had enjoyed such an encounter. I felt vulnerable. I took a long warm bath with lavender drops in the steaming water. I dressed in my favourite black trousers, pink lipstick, the cat ring on my index finger.

Battling with my thoughts at the breakfast table, I eat my favourite yoghurt with cherries, a cup of tea steaming with vapours. Light drizzles through the window, bringing life to the white and black Zebra curtains. I think of Johnny. Where would he be now? Cradling the babies of his own illusion? Maybe playing with his newborn or trying to come to term with his lost youth. Perhaps. Why am I talking about him? I know nothing about this person I am going to meet and that's exciting. I smile in the mirror, adjusting my pink lipstick, ready to drive down town. I park my car and step out in the wintery rain. A cold shower falls on my face, the fine fog mingles with my hot desires, my cheeks are warm, I feel a coldness in my feet. Nervous, I look towards a glittering city. Amidst flashes of thunders, cold rain and heavy grey clouds, there's a fine thin silver lining, a shimmering ray. Many years of storm seem like a passing thing. This is the beginning of a new era.

I walk alongside the glass building of Waterstones bookstore. What a day for shopping. People are rushing around the shops, walking swiftly towards Forester Square, where I am supposed to meet the one I spoke to. With eyes fixed in my direction, I see someone dashing towards me.

"Is this you, Svera? Where are you heading to? Meeting a man again? Oh, Svera what are you doing, woman? How can you?"

"Who are you? How did you recognise me? Why are you speaking in metaphors?"

"You are the lonely one looking like yourself, Svera, always searching for something. I speak in metaphors just the way you do. The language binds us."

Laughter spreads like a soft rug of introduction between us. It takes me into its strong arms like a hug, a kiss softly on the right cheek, the on the left. We look deep into each other's eyes. I close my eyes. I try to keep my wobbling steps straight and look up. First it's a shape like a man - Josef. Then it looks like an old fairy, my mother. Then it turns into Ahren, then my father, my daughter, Johnny with his favourite pink hat. What is happening? I am dizzy. I am daydreaming. I look up towards the sky and see something, slithering in the air, a shining object, a rainbow. There is no body, no form, to be touched or seen, just laughter, a voice in the air. Where is it coming from? I touch my heart, my soul, my mind, my body and then suddenly, something strikes like lightening. Now it is my turn to laugh. I laugh out loud. I suddenly realise what I am up against. I feel relieved.

"Let's go, I will take you to a small cafe that I go to when I come here - your favourite: Love Apple. I hope you don't mind sitting with me, trying to reason with me, as if you are me. I have been helping you to write this story. I pushed you to your limits. This is only the beginning. Your story will continue. Your book is finished. You have arrived, Svera. You, the dawn. You are at my doorstep. Do you realise who I am?"

"I...I... Oh...thank you for teaching me."

"Oh, please, let me thank you, for giving me the honour, but don't forget your mother, your father, Jaz, Ahren, Josef, your daughters, Johnny, they have all been with you. They all encouraged you, Svera."
She pointed her fingers at me, breezily.

We had both been very curious and were delighted to see each other. We sat silently, throwing shy glances at each other, not knowing how to continue with our conversation. I was drinking cappuccino. She was drinking Indian tea with hot milk, sugar, cardamom, talking about each other frankly. She seemed nervous at times and very frank at others. I had known her since the day I was born. I had become more confident and determined. She had helped me become the person I now was. I owed it to her. It must have been a struggle for her to create me. It was as if she had been sculpting me for all those years. I responded to her skill, to the change. Now, finally, we met, face to face, drinking tea and coffee asking each other questions, communicating. Our eyes stared at each other saying, "This is the way. To wage a struggle, to continue, to make mistakes, to learn."

We talked and talked and laughed simultaneously. It was soon time to leave. She had to go. She promised to leave part of herself behind, together, with all those people from the past and the present. She looked at me with passion, stretching her hands across the table to hold mine. They were warm, moving, healing.
"I have been waiting for this meeting for a long time. It all started when I saw you struggling. My instinct pushed me to make this connection."
"I was not sure of anything. My wounds were raw. I did not want to reflect my pain in your story. I wanted you to draw away from your pain and be more objective. My pain would have destroyed our relationship. It would have destroyed your search, had I met you earlier.
"Are you sure you want to leave?" I asked.
I tried to look deep into her eyes, probing. There was no regret for my past. She wanted to look forward. There was a connection, a flicker. I wanted to thank her, my mother, Joshili, my father, Jaz, Ahren, Josef, Minna and Nina, and of course Johnny - everyone who had touched my life. Would my search continue forever? I knew the search was forever. If it wasn't, there was no point in living. Was there?

"Yes, the time has come for me to take leave. There is no doubt about it. When I leave, well, let's leave it for you to find out. You are warm, passionate, honest. You stir things within me, shake my soul. I just wanted to be with you, for this last time, to take some of your energy." She paused for a moment.

"Well, goodbye, Svera. Keep it up. You are being watched by your own spirit, your guardian angels. I will keep an eye on you, as I have been doing. I change forms. I am sometimes Josef or who's that man with a pink hat – Johnny?"

When she spoke his name she winked at me. *The bitch*, I thought as she looked at herself in a small mirror, readjusting the pink lipstick on her lips, smiling.

I was thrilled with this short but delightful encounter. I looked at her for the last time. There was an empty look in her eyes - a void. I walked out of the cafe, sad, not daring to look at what I had left behind. The rain had stopped and pieces of dim sunlight fell at my feet like jasmine buds. I could feel the fragrance around me. A gentle breeze touched my clothes, stirred my heart. I felt a hand touch my shoulder. I looked up at the sky and saw not one but two rainbows. The city was oozing with colours, sounds and images - beautiful vibrations. I had now begun to see through them. Returning home I started another letter:

Dear Mum ...

The sound vibrates.........

Indigo Dreams Publishing
132, Hinckley Road
Stoney Stanton
Leicestershire
LE9 4LN
www.indigodreams.co.uk